Focus

Book 1 in the Vision Time Travel Series

Kendra Rumbaugh

PEREGRINUS
BOOKS

Peregrinus Books

PEREGRINUS
BOOKS

Published by Peregrinus Books. Book Cover by Kendra Rumbaugh.

ISBN:
Paperback: 979-8-9891519-1-2
eBook: 979-8-9891519-0-5

Interior formatting by KJ Waters Consultancy

CONTENTS

This book is dedicated to my boys. Always remember that wonderful stories can have bad chapters, wrong paths can lead to great destinations, and failures create resilience.

ALSO BY KENDRA RUMBAUGH

Double Vision – Book 2 in the Vision Time Travel Series- Available now

Foresight – Book 3 in the Vision Time Travel Series

Chapter 1

THE FIRST TIME

First times in general are rarely graceful or life-altering, we stumble through them just hoping to retain some dignity. My first time was simply a clumsy accident. It lasted only a moment really and didn't provide me with even the slightest hint at how earth-shatteringly momentous this event would be to the course of not just my life, but for the lives of everyone who has ever and will ever exist.

I focused completely, trying to remember what he had said. I hadn't written it down in my notes...thought it was just an extraneous detail. I could practically see Dr. Marshall, standing at the podium in the loud blue tie he had worn that day. The details of the scene were etched almost perfectly in my mind. All I had to do was just focus on the damn word he had written on the slide right next to the picture of the T-cell.

I blocked out everything else around me, every single sight and sound, and focused on Dr. Marshall's lecture that day...the cadence of his voice, the slate gray color of his slides. I had always had a talent for recall. Not quite a photographic memory, but if I concentrated hard enough, I could usually conjure the images I sought.

I closed my eyes and reached back into my memory, straining to see what he had written. And then, after a few moments, I began to see it! It was as if the word was materializing through a fog. The first letter of the answer was an 's', I was sure of it! But just as I was tantalizingly close to plucking

1

it out of the abyss, a nauseous feeling took me by surprise. The stabbing pain in my gut was so severe I almost buckled over.

OK, I am *not* going to get sick right here in class, I tried to convince myself. I swallowed hard, pushing down the nausea, and tried to visualize the answer again. However, as queasiness washed over me, I realized that the situation was bad...really bad. I knew I should hurry to the restroom, but I almost had the answer! My stomach lurched and I knew with certainty that I was going to be sick right there on my desk in front of the whole class! Even worse was the realization that if I did not finish my final exam, I would jeopardize my chance of a 4.0 for the semester. I closed my eyes tight and let the nausea wash over my body, sweeping me towards the deep end.

I pressed my forehead against the cool wood of the desk and swam in black sickness. I could feel the minutes ticking by and knew that I did not have long to pull it together. I told myself that I couldn't just lie there and let my 'A' slip away. I had worked way too hard all semester.

Taking a deep, steadying breath, I sat up straight and tried to open my eyes when a new, stronger swell hit me. It felt like a tidal wave crashed against my entire body, slamming it against the back of the chair. Simultaneously, I felt a pressure building in my ears. I cupped my hands to them, but the pressure continued to increase until I thought my eardrums would burst! I was on the verge of crying out as the pain crested, but suddenly there was a loud 'whooshing' sound and mercifully the pressure eased as my head felt like a deflating balloon.

I sat with my eyes clenched shut and my hands cupped over my ears, waiting for the next onslaught, but it never came. In fact, I was beginning to think that I would actually be able to keep my breakfast down. Slowly, I opened my eyes and quickly scanned the room. I braced for another round of nausea or perhaps a few odd looks from a classmate or two but was completely unprepared for what I saw.

Sure, the scene was all familiar, but the whole atmosphere of the lecture hall had changed. This was not the quiet, mass concentration of a final exam. People were shifting in their seats, there were murmurs of conversations and Dr. Marshall was...lecturing? And this was not just any lecture, he was talking about the one thing I had tried so hard to remember a few minutes ago, "The T-cells cross-link upon encountering a *superantigen*..."

What the hell? How sick was I? But the thing was... I didn't feel all that sick anymore. I wondered if I had lost consciousness, and was having an incredibly vivid dream. I had been up most of the night before studying for this last and most difficult final, but all-nighters weren't that unusual for me. I was determined to make all A's in my first semester of college, and I had spent many late nights glued to my desk, studying my meticulous notes and I had never reacted like this.

I pinched myself like people always do when they think they're dreaming, but the pain assured me that my nerves were intact and reactive. I took another look around. Everything looked pretty normal...if it were three weeks ago, the day Dr. Marshall lectured about T-cells. I pressed down on my temples and tried to figure out how the hell I was going to explain to Dr. Marshall that my final exam was incomplete because I was having visions.

A girl sitting in the next aisle glanced in my direction, looked away, and then quickly did a double-take. There was a vague look of confusion on her face, and I thought she was about to say something, but before she got the chance, everything started to vibrate, then shake, and that invisible tidal wave hit me again. The jolt took me by surprise and I was knocked off balance. I felt like I had fallen right out of my chair, except I never hit the floor. I just kept on falling. I closed my eyes tight not knowing what to expect next on this roller coaster from hell.

After another loud *whoosh*, all motion stopped. My head throbbed unmercifully and I was completely disoriented. I sat perfectly still. The room was quiet. I could hear pencils madly scrawling on paper, low coughs, and papers shuffling. When I finally dared to open my eyes again, I saw my exam sitting in front of me. Another quick look around the room assured

3

me that I was indeed taking my Immunology final, just as I was moments before.

This was *not* OK! I struggled to maintain my composure. The voice of reason in my head kept reassuring me that I was just overly tired and stressed about finals because frankly, it was either that or I was going insane. My first impulse was to bolt, and just get out of there, but I had to finish my exam. No matter what, I had worked too hard to blow my 4.0!

I looked down at my paper. It was only half finished and I started to panic, assuming the hour must be almost up! But when I looked up at the clock, I was amazed to see that I still had twenty minutes left! It was incredible. It was like no time had passed since I was struggling to find the answer to question number twelve. The answer...the answer was...*superantigen*!

I easily finished the rest of my test, snatched my backpack, and bolted over to Dr. Marshall's desk.

"Finished Evan?" He asked, cheerily.

"Um, yes here you go." The shakiness in my voice almost scared me.

"How did you find it? Too easy?" He asked, trying to make conversation.

"Um, yes...I mean no... it was fine, thanks." Professors were always asking the good students about the rigor of their tests. Sometimes I thought they were just as insecure about their ability to write tests as we were about our ability to take them.

"Evan, are you OK? You looked flushed." He looked genuinely concerned.

No, basically I'm losing it, I thought. "Yes, I'm fine, I just have a headache." I had to get out of there, pronto.

"Well, I should have the grades posted online by tomorrow. Not that you need to worry about your grade, I'm sure. So, what are taking next semester?"

Why had Dr. Marshall picked now to get chatty? I agonized. "I haven't quite decided yet," I lied. "Dr. Marshall, I really need to get going...have to pack the car and get on the road, you know." I lied again.

"Of course. Well, have a wonderful holiday, and don't be a stranger. You should definitely consider registering for my advanced Immunology seminar next semester. It will be mostly grad students, but I have no doubt you'll be able to keep up."

I was already halfway out the door before I mumbled something like "I'll think about it." I had to get back to my dorm room and try to make sense of what happened. I practically ran out of the Biology building and headed towards the quad. The sun was bright as usual and it was warm for December, yet I felt so chilled that I had to wrap my arms around my body to keep from trembling.

The campus was relatively deserted. It was the last day of finals and half the students had already headed home for the holiday break. As I neared Holden Hall, I prayed Taylor would be gone already. Although I had spent four months sharing a room with Taylor Dorsett, I hardly knew her at all. What I did know was that she was the epitome of the girls I had avoided in high school...beautiful, blonde, and perky. Everyone loved her and everything had been handed to her on a silver platter. It's not that she was a terrible person or anything, but the problem with girls like her was that there was no depth. True character and personal depth only came from a struggle to overcome....something. When everything comes easy how can you have any true appreciation for anything?

Taylor had spent her first four months at college consumed by finding the 'right' sorority, surfing the 'rate-your-professor' websites, and planning her curriculum based on the 'hotness' scores of the professors. She was at Harper College for only two reasons- 1. Because her parents were alumni and wanted to keep her in Texas and 2. To get her 'M.r.S. degree.' Taylor's four years of higher education would be spent maintaining a minimal GPA, partying, participating in sorority functions, and identifying the perfect young Republican that would keep her in the manner to which she had grown accustomed.

My motives were completely different. Ever since I could remember, I had been acutely focused on my future. As an only child, I had always felt more comfortable around adults than playing with other kids. In fact, I never really 'played'. I much preferred reading books to the incredible effort of making friends. I was an Army brat, which meant we had moved every few years from one base to the next; Fort Sill OK, Fort Bragg NC, Fort Bliss TX, and Hamburg Germany, to name a few. I learned not to get attached to people or places because they were bound to change. Books were my constant, my escape.

It wasn't that my life was so horrible I needed to escape. In fact, despite the different locales and people, my life had been pretty boring. School was never a challenge, and most of the time I just resented being stuck in that microcosm of melodrama and runaway hormones called high school. I could not wait to be an adult, live by myself, and have my own career and money. We never had much money, and I knew that it was something I needed if I was going to have real independence. So, I dug in, studied hard, ignored all the distractions, and focused on my future.

After watching a PBS documentary on 'virus hunters' when I was twelve, I decided that one day I would be a scientist. I wanted to make a real contribution to society, lecture all over the world...be revered. I wanted people to read about my incredible discoveries in history books and I wanted these incredible discoveries to save lives.

Although the army schools I attended weren't great, living overseas opened my eyes to different languages, cultures, and religions. I filled my brain with everything I could. Back in the States, I finished high school as a national merit scholar. I was accepted to colleges far better than Harper, one even Ivy League, but they were too expensive. Harper offered me a full ride, and I was too practical to pass it up. I rationalized that I could save prestige for graduate school.

The only real problem with Harper was that I had to live in Blythe, Texas. I suppose it was as good as anywhere was, but there was just an eerie flatness I couldn't quite get used to. It was also in the middle of nowhere with two hundred miles of nothing but arid plains in every direction. Despite the isolation, I loved college. It was so different from high school. Everyone had their own life, and except for the sorority/fraternity crowd, no one cared what you wore, how your hair looked, or even if you bothered to show up for class. As long as your checks cleared, no one even cared if you existed, and that was just fine with me.

I quickly learned that there were two types of college kids. Those who *wanted* to be at college, and those whose parents wanted them to be there. I competed with the first type for the highest grades in my classes, and the second type kept the curve intact. I wondered though, as I reached Holden Hall and headed up to my room, how well my grades would hold up now that I was going insane.

I unlocked my room and found it in its usual state of disarray. Taylor was gone, thank God, but it looked like a tornado had blown through. I waded through the discarded handbags and dirty laundry, and just as I was about to collapse on my bed, I noticed a small package wrapped with Christmas paper sitting next to my pillow. The tag read "To: Evan, From: Taylor, Have a great holiday and try not to study too hard." Inside there were a dozen chocolate chip cookies. I was flabbergasted and briefly considered that maybe I had been too hard on Taylor.

For the next hour, I lay in my bed eating cookies and analyzing what happened in class. I could think of three possibilities: 1. I was indeed going crazy, and this could range from simple mental exhaustion following a challenging semester, to a full-blown mental breakdown, maybe schizophrenia; 2. I was ill- again the possibilities ranged from a common virus to a brain tumor; or 3. I had just time-traveled three weeks into the past to retrieve a test answer. After considering the formal possibilities, I realized that number three actually should have been combined with number one. I then did what any normal person searching for a diagnosis does, I Googled my symptoms- nausea, disorientation, chills...I left out time travel. Again, the result was an overly comprehensive list of diseases ranging from the flu to brain aneurysms.

After ruling out at least one hundred different diseases and disorders, I decided that there was nothing I could do about what happened during my final unless I wanted to go visit the campus health clinic and tell them the whole story. I decided that the incident was probably caused by an overly tired brain straining too hard to focus on one answer and vowed to get plenty of R&R during Christmas break.

I always had a tremendous ability to focus. My mom said that even when I was very little, while most babies lost interest in a task after a few minutes, I would look at a book, play with a puzzle, or color a picture for hours, blocking out all other stimuli around me. Before I could communicate, she worried that this was some form of autism or even perception problems, but I developed fine. Apparently, I would simply lock myself into my own world of concentration.

Even now, I can recall memories from my early childhood in vivid detail. Typically, I could pull up a memory like a photograph and scan through it looking for some small detail. I often used this ability to picture a textbook page and scan for an answer, similar to the way I had envisioned Dr. Marshall's T-cell lecture. However, it had never been accompanied by nausea or invisible waves that jolted my body around before. But despite all the weirdness, I had still just finished my last final, and was pretty sure I'd aced it. That meant I had just completed the first step to graduating at the top of my class. Between advanced placement credits and summer school, it was totally doable in just another two and a half years.

My plan was to earn my Ph.D., maybe from Stanford or Berkeley, by the time I was twenty-four. That would mean I could spend a few years doing post-doctoral work, maybe in Europe, and then be running my own research lab well before I turned thirty. The most eminent scientists...Einstein, Pasteur, Hawking...had all made major discoveries before they turned thirty. So, I had no time to waste.

Lost in my plans and schemes, I barely heard the knock at the door. I hadn't heard a sound over the last few hours and had assumed that most people had already cleared out. So, I was surprised when I opened the door to find Taylor's friend McKenna standing in the hallway, looking fairly annoyed.

"Hey, is Taylor around?" she asked, not even meeting my eyes while her fingers quickly typed a text on her phone.

"No, she left early this morning, I guess she wanted to beat the traffic into Houston."

Her head shot up and she looked at me contemptuously, as if I had Taylor locked in the closet. "Hmm...no wonder, she didn't answer any of my texts." McKenna sighed deeply, clearly disappointed with the situation. She shoved her phone into her purse and then eyed me critically as if she was carefully debating what to do next. Then she said, "Weeeell, a bunch of us are going down to the Depot tonight...since *you're* still in town, I suppose you could come." McKenna reluctantly made the offer almost as if it was painful to do so. I had the distinct impression that she considered it Christmas charity, like donating to the Salvation Army.

"Thanks for the invite but I have a date tonight," I lied. My usual excuse was that I had to study for a test, but since finals were over, even McKenna wouldn't buy that one. A sarcastic smirk spread across her face, and it was clear she didn't believe my excuse.

"Alright then, well have a Merry Christmas, Lane," she said fumbling in her purse, trying to locate her vibrating phone.

"Yeah, you too," I said, not waiting until she walked away to shut the door.

Lane? It didn't even sound like Evan for Christ's sake! Although they did have the same number of letters and she got three out of four correct...I supposed that was close enough in McKenna's world.

McKenna was a sorority sister of Taylor's. They were the same breed, and after their freshman year, they would be able to live in the same house and discuss the intricacies of whatever twenty-something reality TV circus was on, ad nauseam. According to the rules at Harper, all students had to live in the dorms their first year. After that, most people moved off campus, especially the frat boys and sorority sisters, and of course, the rich kids whose parents either rented or bought them their own house.

My scholarship paid for the dorms, so I was pretty much stuck. Sure, I could find a job and a roommate to share the cost of an apartment, but what was the point? I spent most of my time in class or at the library. Plus, there was no way I would sacrifice the time I could be volunteering in a research lab to bus tables at some restaurant, just to pay rent.

With no plans to go out and no tests to study for, I resigned myself to a dinner of cup 'o' noodles, and a long boring evening. It just seemed like too much effort to go out for a real meal. It wasn't like I didn't like to eat, quite the contrary, I loved a good steak, barbeque ribs, enchiladas, but I found eating to be a social event and it seemed kind of pointless to go through the effort just for myself. Then there was the fact that most of the time I was just too busy to eat or too broke to afford a good meal.

Since I had moved out of my parent's home, where full-balanced meals simply appeared on the table at six o'clock every night, eating had become just a necessity to stop the annoying growling in my stomach and keep my head clear. The unintentional, but not unpleasant, side effect was my resulting slim figure that even gorgeous Taylor found enviable. She was always dieting, exercising, and trying to banish the 'freshman fifteen'.

I finished my noodle feast while flipping aimlessly through the four TV channels we had. I was quickly becoming unnerved by the thought of the two long, boring weeks that stretched out in front of me before classes resumed. Being stuck in Blythe by myself, with nothing to do really sucked. However, going home for the holidays was not really an option. First of all, home was whatever Army base my parents happened to be stationed at, and as of two months ago, that base was in Guam. Spending hundreds of dollars on airfare to Guam wasn't practical at the moment.

My mom hated that I was spending the holidays alone and urged me to find a friend "to go home with at Christmas." The thought of following someone I barely knew home to a family of complete strangers was laughable. I wasn't even very close to my own family, and she thought I should spend the holidays with someone else's? Crazy woman. Anyway, I hadn't met anyone at Harper to whom I was even remotely close. I had a couple of regular study partners, and oh, my organic chemistry teaching assistant, Yun Zhang, was nice, but we didn't hang out or anything.

The boy situation was even worse. I had never actually had a *real* boyfriend. The idea of putting my feelings on the line like that scared the hell out of me. Trusting someone with my innermost thoughts and desires was just too risky. There had been boys I had casually dated, I wasn't completely innocent or untouched, but none to whom I had any kind of emotional attachment. Except one... There was the one time I had let my guard down, and boy had that been a mistake. I shuddered at the painful memories associated with him.

Anyway, boys were just a distraction from my goals. I had to keep focused on the prize, and it wasn't like I ever wanted to get married anyway. Too many bright, driven women ditched their aspirations for some guy. Then they ended up divorced, bitter that they let all their dreams slip away and wondering what they could have been. I had watched my own mother, dragged around the world following her man, never leading her own life or having her own goals. She existed entirely for my father and me, and she had grown into a very sad woman. She was completely dependent on my dad to make money and decisions for her. Nope, that was not for me. My life would amount to more than that cliché.

Chapter 2

UNDER WATER

I n the days leading up to Christmas, I tried not to think about the bizarre episode in Immunology class. I distracted myself by spending long hours surfing the web pages of Harper's faculty, trying to find potential research opportunities. I found some interesting projects and narrowed them down to three possibilities. Dr. Shaw, an environmental toxicology professor, was studying the effects of one type of pollution, called environmental estrogens, on the reproductive patterns of frogs. I wasn't so interested in frogs, but I saw how her research could potentially impact human fertilization.

Dr. Patel's research was focused on cloning genes from the arid-tolerant manzanita shrub into commercial cotton plants, to make them more drought-resistant. An agricultural project didn't excite me very much either, but I knew that experience in purifying DNA and cloning genes could be very useful. And lastly, there was Dr. Lanzarra's infectious disease project. She was a microbiologist researching why common, innocuous bacteria that are found everywhere in nature, could turn deadly and cause life-threatening diseases in hospitalized patients. She compared the effects of these bacteria in normal versus genetically diseased mice. Hers was by far my favorite project, and also the least likely to get.

Essentially the more interesting the research, the more students there would be vying to get a spot in the lab. Junior researchers who already had

Ph.D.s and were willing to put in long hours of post-graduate work for very little pay were given priority, then graduate students, and lastly undergrads. Freshmen, like me, with no research experience were almost always ignored by the top professors, even though we were free labor.

The reality was that getting a spot in a good lab and then gaining some real experience performing experiments would be no easy chore. My primary competition was the 'pre-meders', the cult of students who had dedicated their entire existence to getting into medical school. They all had the same checklist of 'life experiences' they needed to complete for their medical school applications: maintain a high GPA, score well on their medical school entrance exam, volunteer at a hospital or nursing home, spend a semester abroad, and gain research experience. The icing on their cake was to get a good recommendation letter from a respected research professor. They didn't really care about research, scientific inquiry, or making a significant discovery, but they were voracious in their quests to complete their checklist.

The problem was, once their research box was checked off, usually after one semester, they were on to the next item on their list, leaving their research professors with incomplete data sets and no real progress to show for the time the professor, or the professor's graduate students, had spent training the eager pre-meder. Since most professors had been burnt by these students several times, they were very reluctant to take on under-grads, which made my chances that much slimmer. I learned all this from my O-Chem TA Yun Zhang who had traversed all these hurdles herself and was now 3 years into a Ph.D. program.

My strategy would be to use the holiday break to learn as much about the research of my top picks as possible. Read all their published studies, and then dazzle them with my in-depth knowledge and passion for their field of research. If I could come up with some particularly tantalizing line of inquiry then maybe I could even peak their curiosity enough that they would eventually let me try my own experiments. The hard part was just getting my foot in the door. I would have to convince them of my dedication and commitment to a career in scientific research and assure them I would not be requesting a recommendation for medical school.

—ele—

I spent a few days after finals submerged in research papers and scouring the library for background reading to help me understand them. I felt like I was beginning to get a grasp on the material and was anxious to start contacting professors, but of course, none of them were around. Offices were locked and the campus was deserted. I could have started sending some inquiry emails, but I didn't want to start off as the obnoxious student who bothered them while they were trying to spend a quiet Christmas with their families. Damn the holidays! Sitting in my room, alone on Christmas Eve, all I could do was wish for the holidays to be over and classes to start again. I had already registered for Spring classes, purchased my textbooks, and bought a fresh supply of multi-colored highlighters. I was ready!

Although it was my first Christmas away from my parents, I was used to quiet holidays. We didn't have many extended family members, at least not many who we were close to, so holidays were usually just the three of us. Sometimes my dad would bring home soldiers from his unit who were alone for Christmas. Sometimes we would even eat Christmas dinner in the mess hall. This year I would eat in the dorm cafeteria and speak to Mom and Dad on the phone.

Mom had sent me a large package of wrapped presents that I had opened on the first day of the break because I was so bored. There had been a series of paperback novels about fungus-infected zombies that were particularly popular, a couple of movies I had already seen, and a gray turtleneck sweater. Mom was not the best gift giver, but I supposed it was my fault for never giving her any clues about my likes or dislikes. She still bought me tons of novels, even though I hadn't read for pleasure in years. There just wasn't time after all the required reading I had to do for classes. Still, I would act delighted on Christmas, when I pretended to open the gifts over the phone with her. To be honest, I wasn't much better though. I usually just bought my parents a gift certificate to a restaurant they liked. However, since I wasn't familiar with the fare in Guam, this year I had just sent them an email gift card for Amazon, pretty unimaginative.

Texas was fifteen hours behind Guam, so I calculated that it was already noon on Christmas day for my parents. I thought I should just go ahead and call them, but Mom insisted that I call on Christmas day, my time. At least it would give me *something* to do on Christmas day, I reasoned. I knew it was bound to be an extremely long day with nearly everything closed. Exhausting all other options, I decided to do something I had not done in years, take a long hot bath.

The bathroom was Taylor's domain, I was just a tourist. Since I took so many more classes than Taylor did, my days started much earlier. I could usually shower, dress, and eat in under twenty minutes. I didn't linger to do my hair or face or put together outfits (not that I had any to put together). Typically, I was on my way to my first class, hair still wet, coffee mug in hand, hours before Taylor was up. I usually didn't return to our room until after dinner, and then it was straight to the books. Taylor was out most nights, either on dates or with her sorority sisters. So thankfully, we didn't have to see each other much.

Even though Taylor had left, there was still not an inch of countertop to be seen amongst the array of sprays, spritzes, gels, lotions, creams, and sundry other cosmetics. As long as I had a small corner for my tiny collection of toiletries, I was content. Honestly, it was perfect for Taylor to have a roommate who required so little bathroom or closet space, and I never had to jockey for study time at our only desk...a perfect arrangement.

I ran the bath and even threw in a few of the 'milk and honey' hot oil bath beads that were in a pretty glass jar on top of the toilet. I just hoped that they were meant for the bath and not the toilet. I pulled my hair out of its default ponytail and shook out the auburn waves. I hadn't had a haircut since I moved to Blythe and as I turned sideways, I could see it was well past my bra strap. I thought that I should leave it down sometimes, but it was so thick that it took forever to blow dry. It was so much easier just to leave it wet and throw it up in a ponytail.

I wiped the steam from the mirror and took a long look at myself. The usual dark circles under my eyes were nearly gone. It seemed that a few days with no tests to study for, and undisturbed sleep, really did help. My eyes were the only feature with which I was completely happy. They were large and almond-shaped, and a very unusual shade of bright green with brown and orange specks. At least one of them was. The other was hazel. I had a condition called heterochromia, where one eye was one color and the other another color. Apparently, it only happened in like one out of every million people or something. I just knew that *I'd* never seen another person with it.

All my life people had commented on my eyes. When I was younger, they had made me feel self-conscious, as all things do that make you stand out in any way. All the kids had called me 'cat' because they said I had cat's eyes. It upset me so much that when I was twelve, I begged my mom to buy me contacts so I could make both my eyes the same color, but that frivolous and expensive request was promptly dismissed.

I sucked in my cheeks and noticed for the first time that my face had changed. I had always had a 'baby face' that lacked definition, but now I could see cheekbones and some structure to my jawline. I guessed that the subtle transformation was due to the few pounds I had lost during the semester. I looked older, more mature. It was weird, the longer I stared at my reflection, the more I felt like I was seeing myself for the first time.

Stripping off my sweatpants and t-shirt, I saw that the change wasn't just in my face. My whole frame was much thinner. I had always been tall, and weight had never been an issue, but as I ran my hands over hipbones that were starting to protrude, it occurred to me that I certainly shouldn't lose anymore and should probably start paying more attention to balancing my diet. I found it strange that I hadn't noticed my clothes fitting any looser. Although considering that my standard uniform of sweatpants and t-shirts was not exactly form-fitting, it was hardly surprising.

I sunk into the hot water and immediately felt light. It was nice to have the place to myself with no need to worry about monopolizing the bathroom. I wondered what Taylor was doing. The Dorsetts were oil people who had lived in Houston for several generations. I guessed that they were probably spending Christmas Eve at their Country Club with all the other oil tycoons. I bet Taylor would come back after the break with a whole new wardrobe and maybe even a new car, even though the BMW she currently owned wasn't even five years old. It was a hand-me-down from her older brother who was given a new Audi convertible when he was accepted into Yale Law. I juxtaposed these images with memories of my family's Christmases. Although I was an only child, I knew it had still been hard for my parents to afford presents some years. Still, Christmas was always my favorite holiday. Mom always put a lot of effort into decorating, baking, and making whatever housing area in which we happened to be living feel like home.

My favorite Christmas was when we were stationed in Hamburg, Germany. I must have been about five years old. That Christmas was one of my first memories and the only real memory I have about living in Hamburg. Mom said that it had snowed for days, and the base was completely shut down due to the weather. I just remember the feeling of utter delirium and anticipation knowing Santa was on his way. I woke up very early that Christmas morning. It was still dark, and I snuck downstairs to see if he had come. I remember the momentary shock of my bare feet, warm from bed, hitting the cold hardwood floor.

I stood in front of the Christmas tree in absolute awe. The lights on the tree were lit and in their soft multi-colored glow, I could see the most beautiful object I had ever seen in my life...a Victorian-style dollhouse wrapped with a big red ribbon. It was the best present I had ever, and would ever receive, and at that moment, I was the luckiest girl in the world.

I vividly remembered that odd combination of shivering cold and sheer euphoria. I could practically smell the pine of the Christmas tree and see the details of the tiny wooden shutters that partially covered the real glass-pane windows of my dollhouse. I wished I could live forever in that moment, anticipating the endless hours of fantasy that would be played out within the walls of that exquisite miniature backdrop.

I closed my eyes and strained to remember the details of the dollhouse's interior. Beyond the shutters and glass-paned windows covering the front room, I could almost make out a piece of miniature furniture. What was in that front room? Was it a tiny armoire or a piano? I tried to focus on that one detail as if using a magnifying glass on a photo. Something shiny and black...it was almost clear...when...it happened again.

The whoosh sound was loud, and the nausea hit me suddenly like a hammer. I felt my body being pulled under the water, causing ripples so violent that water slushed over the rim of the tub. The sickness was so intense that if it weren't for the pressure pushing my whole body down, I would have thrown up. Then suddenly my head submerged! I opened my eyes underwater and saw the blurry light of the bathroom growing dimmer and dimmer as I sunk deeper.

I could not breathe. My body flailed, but I couldn't get to the surface. I felt like I was losing consciousness. I knew I was drowning, but I was powerless to pull myself up. I sank until the light from the bathroom was almost completely extinguished. It was like looking up at the moon from the bottom of a swimming pool. Then everything turned black. I closed my eyes, and my body went limp as the darkness swallowed me. Finally, I couldn't continue to fight my body's powerful urge to breathe, and I prayed I wouldn't die as I surrendered and opened my mouth in a gasp.

To my complete shock and utter relief, I did not suck in a lungful of water, but instead, pure heavenly air. I gasped, filling my lungs more than they had ever been filled. Pain shot through my chest as my body violently rejected the air streaming into my lungs. My body lurched and I doubled over into a fetal position, collapsing into a fit of coughing. My heart was racing, and my head was pounding. It took several minutes to restore my breathing to its normal rhythm and during this time, I couldn't think about anything but the primal desire to live, to breathe.

Finally, I felt like I could stand up. I rose to all fours, and my wet hair fell around my face like a curtain. I breathed deeply, steadying myself. I willed myself to stand up even though my legs were trembling terribly. My head swam and I saw bright white dots dancing all around me. I concentrated on remaining conscious. Then slowly, the dots disappeared and the dizziness subsided. Slowly, I became aware of more sensations and sounds. It was freezing and water was dripping from my body. I was alive!

I parted the curtain of hair that blocked my view and looked around. I could not believe my eyes! The tub was gone. My entire bathroom was gone! I was standing in a dark room lit only by the dim glow of a hundred little multi-colored lights. Directly in front of me was a beautiful, antique-lace-colored, handcrafted, Victorian-style dollhouse, wrapped with a red ribbon.

The room was freezing and I was naked, standing in a puddle of water. As if on cue, I started to shiver violently. I grabbed a brown afghan that was draped on the nearby couch and wrapped it around my naked torso. I listened carefully but could hear only my breathing and pounding heart. I could smell pine and something else, something that made me feel calm amid utter insanity. The smell, in fact, the whole atmosphere, was familiar. It smelled like my mother. It smelled like my home, my childhood. I was standing in the middle of our living room in Hamburg, Germany on Christmas morning!

It was a place I barely remembered, but somehow it felt incredibly familiar. I suddenly felt a strong desire, no need, to find my mother. I turned too quickly and slipped in the puddle that had formed around my feet. I lost balance, stumbled and almost fell. I righted myself and headed towards the stairs, trying to remain calm and fighting the urge to scream for her at the top of my lungs. It was darker away from the glow of the tree, but the sun was just starting to rise, and the faint light of dawn seeped in through a window somewhere beyond the top of the stairs.

I was still freezing, but the adrenaline coursing through my body warmed me. When I got to the top of the landing, I listened again. It was still quiet. I could see there was a bathroom directly ahead and that the light was coming from a room to my right. I walked slowly down the hall, feeling the wood floor creak under my weight. I stood in the threshold of a small bedroom. Below the window was a twin-sized bed with what looked to be a yellow comforter. The bed was disheveled as if someone had just woken up. Beside the pillow was a small object I recognized immediately. It was the Raggedy Ann doll that had been my favorite toy, best friend, and loyal confidant for many years until I lost her one day at the mall. I had cried for weeks after her loss.

This was my room! My room in a home I could scarcely remember. Fear almost paralyzed me as I struggled to understand what was happening. In a panic, I backed out of the room and quickly made my way back down the hall. My feet were still damp, and I tried not to slip again. I had to find my mother. I knew that if anyone could help me it was her.

I turned a sharp corner and immediately jumped back when I saw her standing directly in front of me! I almost screamed at her startling sudden appearance, and it was not until I was inches from her face that I realized I wasn't looking at my mother at all, but myself in the hallway mirror. My hair was soaking wet and plastered down my neck and back. My face was stark white. Even in the dim light, I could see that my eyes were wild and terrified. I turned away from my reflection, took a deep breath, and walked towards the open bedroom door just beyond.

The smell of my mother was strong, and as soon as I stepped into the room, I immediately knew she was there. I could hear the soft steady breathing of slumbering bodies. The room was dark, but I could see figures lying in the bed, warm and cozy under the covers. I suddenly worried whether my mother would know me. Would she think I was some crazy person who had just broken into her house on Christmas morning? No, of course, she would know me, I reasoned. She would hold me and help me.

I walked quietly around the foot of the bed. It was best not to startle them. After all, my father was a soldier with guns in the house. I decided I would wake my mother quietly and we would go downstairs together, make tea, and figure everything out. As I rounded the bed, I could just make out her face. Her hands were folded under her cheek as if she were praying. She looked so peaceful and young and content. There was a glow about her that I could not place. Her face was smooth, free from the lines of age, worry, and stress. I always thought of my mother as a sad woman. She was reserved and somber, but here in the dim light of this cold Christmas morning, she looked... happy.

That's when I heard something very unfamiliar in the space to my right. It startled me so much that I jumped at least an inch off the floor. I spun around and madly scanned the room for the source of the noise. I strained to see into the dark space. I could see a small shape in what little light entered the room. I tried to process what my eyes were seeing. At first, I thought it was another of my presents...a bassinet, another doll. But then I heard a small cry and the tiny being lying just beyond my reach stretched out its little arms. I took a step closer and peered into the bassinet. The baby was swaddled in a light blue blanket and as it turned its head, I could see its eyes flutter open. The baby stared straight at me, and I was dumbstruck.

Before I could process any of the million questions swimming in my mind, the baby opened its mouth and began to cry. My mother stirred and I suddenly doubted myself. I thought I should just get out, hide, and wait until later. The baby cried louder; its eyes still fixed on me. I was frozen in place, my mind racing. Mom mumbled and reached out towards the bassinet. I jumped back just as her arm grazed my leg. I tried to make a break for the door before she saw me and lost my footing again.

Falling, I reached out and grabbed the first thing I found, and the cradle lurched forward hard. The baby slid and hit the side of the bassinet. It let out a louder more urgent cry. I was about to take the cradle down with me, spilling the baby out onto the floor, when I instinctively gave it a sharp push back up. The bassinet righted, but with nothing to hold on to, I continued to fall. As I fell I could hear the baby's cries becoming frantic and indistinct words in my mother's voice.

I braced myself for a hard fall but did not hit the floor. It had disappeared, yet gravity was still pulling me down. The cries became fainter, and the whooshing sound filled my ears. The falling began to feel more like a pulling that originated in my stomach and pulled me down, down, down. Then there was a loud splash. All motion stopped and my head was pounding. Opening my eyes, I saw that I was again lying in my bathtub. Water surrounded me like a warm cocoon. No, there was something else cocooned around me...a brown afghan blanket.

I couldn't get out of the tub fast enough. I floundered onto the floor like a fish and scrambled to my feet. I knocked the jar of bath oil beads off the toilet and blue glass shattered across the floor, while beads spilled in every direction. I ran out of the room trying to avoid the broken glass, but I felt sharp pain as some of the shards punctured my feet. Clutching the afghan to my chest, I ran out of my room and down the hall to the stairwell. I took the stairs three at a time, slipping and sliding as my feet were now damp with blood instead of water. Somehow, I managed to make it to the first floor without tumbling down the stairs.

When I reached the nurse's office I was completely out of breath. I tried the door, but it was locked. As I began pounding something snapped inside of me and I lost it. I couldn't remember the last time I'd cried. I prided myself on never showing emotion, but something ripped inside me, and all the fear and confusion poured out in the form of hysterical weeping. I had been pounding on the door for several minutes when Nurse Thorn ran up behind me, still carrying her take-out dinner.

"Honey! What's wrong? What's happened?"

I could tell from the look on her face that she was almost as frantic as I was. Lord knows what I looked like standing there...soaking wet, basically naked, feet bleeding, sobbing inconsolably. She must have thought I was crazy, or that I had been attacked. Nurse Thorn ushered me into the small exam room and covered me with a dry blanket. She knew there was no point questioning me until I calmed down, and I'm not sure how long we sat there... me crying and her patiently silent.

Eventually, my sobs began to subside, and my head began to clear. Sensing this, Nurse Thorn delicately began to ask me questions.

"Honey, what's your name?" she asked in her West Texas drawl.

"Evan, Evan Wright," I stammered.

Nurse Thorn was a short, slightly plump woman in her fifties, I guessed. She wore a polyester pantsuit that was about two sizes too small for her and it made her look like she was bulging around the bodice. She was a typical West Texas woman, big hair with a lot of hairspray, and tons of make-up. Her hair was sculpted into an organized pile on top of her head, not quite a beehive, but similar. She had a kind face, and an easy way about her, that immediately put you at ease. I had seen her before for a sore throat about a month after I arrived at Harper, but I didn't think she remembered me. I guessed she probably saw hundreds of students in a month.

"Evan, hun, can you tell me what happened to you?"

I had absolutely no idea what to say to this woman because I had no idea what the answer was. I simply stared at her as if she was speaking some unintelligible language.

"Evan, did someone do something to you? Were you in your room? Were you by yourself?" she asked, looking at me expectantly.

Then I realized where her questions were going. She thought I was a date rape victim, maybe even still high from the roofies.

"No, no one else...yes by myself," I managed to say.

"Did you break something, a glass or something?" she asked, looking down at my feet.

"Yes, I was in the bath, and then a glass broke." I didn't even want to think about the rest.

"OK, now we're getting somewhere. What else happened? Why were you so upset?"

Again, I didn't know what to say. I just knew I couldn't tell her the truth. I just looked down, avoiding her probing stare.

"Well, why don't you let me check you out? Would that be OK?" she asked.

I agreed. Maybe it was a good idea to make sure I was OK, at least physically, I rationalized. Nurse Thorn retrieved her instruments from the other side of the room and gently guided me to the exam table. She measured my blood pressure, and temperature and checked the reactivity of my pupils. I suspected that she was looking for signs of intoxication. She finished the exam by cleaning my cuts and probing my feet for any remaining shards of glass.

"Well hun, other than some pretty superficial cuts on your feet, you seem fine."

Physically, I thought, but mentally I'm screwed.

"So, Evan, how are you feeling now?" Her eyes were wary.

I thought carefully about how I should answer. If I told her what actually happened, she would call my parents and then...what? It wasn't like they could just drive down and pick me up. My mother would be frantic. My story would sound so crazy that maybe Nurse Thorn would even have me committed! No, I knew that I absolutely could not tell her the truth. I was going to have to extract myself from this situation. Nurse Thorn was not going to be able to fix whatever was wrong with me and her calling my parents would not help either. I was going to have to figure this out on my own.

"I think...that I was taking a bath and um...just relaxed too much. I must have fallen asleep and slipped under the water." I shuddered at the thought of being pulled under. "Maybe I inhaled a bit of water and panicked a bit. The shock of it must have spooked me and then after I knocked the jar off the counter, I accidentally stepped on some glass." It sounded lame and I knew it.

"So, you got spooked and panicked a bit?" she repeated.

"Yes, I think that's what happened." Minus the almost drowning, Victorian dollhouses and phantom babies, I thought.

"Do you want to call your parents?" she asked.

There it is, I thought. I tried to sound upbeat, "Actually I really think I'm fine now. I think all I need is a good night's sleep."

Nurse Thorn took a deep breath, opened her mouth to speak, and then sighed. She wasn't buying it. "Evan, please understand my position. I come back from the cafeteria to find a frantic, wet, half-nude, bleeding young lady pounding on my office door, so scared she can't even speak for thirty minutes."

Was it really thirty minutes? I wondered.

"Now, many kids get depressed this time of year. It's lonely to be away from family during the holidays, especially for the first time. You are a freshman right?"

I nodded.

"Many kids get involved in things that aren't good for them as a way to escape the loneliness or to fit in with a new crowd of friends."

Jesus, it was like a bad after-school special. I wondered if she thought I was trying to kill myself, free-base meth, or both. Suddenly, the reality of my nakedness underneath the blanket was humiliating! I could not believe I had gotten myself into the situation I was in. I felt like an idiot.

"It wouldn't hurt you to talk to someone. I think it would be a good idea if we gave your parents a call tonight, and then made an appointment for you with one of the counselors after the holidays." Her voice was patient and calm and I could see that there was sincere worry in her eyes. I realized that I was not only going to have to lie convincingly but also make some concessions if I was going to satisfy her.

"Yes, I think you're right. I *have* been stressed this semester and come to think of it, panic attacks *do* run in my family. From the descriptions my mom has given me about what they feel like, I'm pretty sure that's what happened. I think I fell asleep in the bath, choked on some water, then became disoriented and had a panic attack. Since this was the first one I ever had, I didn't understand what was happening to me. Then, I cut my feet on the broken glass and became even more panicked," I lied. "I will definitely ask my mom about her panic attacks tomorrow when I talk to her. You see my parents live overseas and it's the middle of the night for them."

"Oh, where do they live?" she asked.

"My dad's in the Army, stationed in Guam." I knew she could easily check this out, and hoped she didn't know much about geography or time zones. It was the middle of the afternoon on Christmas day there, a perfect time to call. I tried to distract her from considering this fact, "I also think talking to a counselor is a great idea and I will make an appointment after the holidays."

Nurse Thorn eyed me skeptically and I thought I was done for, but then her face softened.

"Well, I guess if you promise to follow up on this...panic attacks can become crippling," she acquiesced. "If you're sure you're fine, why don't you get a good night's sleep, and I will check on you in the morning."

"Thank you, that's very kind." I was sure that she was not expected to work on Christmas day. Although she could just be protecting her ass, I considered. It certainly wouldn't reflect very well on her if a student committed suicide right after she had released them from her care. I got up to leave before she could change her mind.

"I will get that back when I see you tomorrow." Nurse Thorn gestured to the blanket wrapped around me. "But here, don't forget this." She said, holding out the wet afghan. My breath caught as I reached out to take the unworldly relic.

Chapter 3

REVELATIONS

olden Hall shared a ground level, which included the cafeteria and administrative offices, with Murdoch Hall, the boy's dorm. I reasoned there would be less chance of being seen if I took the stairs again. I couldn't risk getting on to the elevator with someone in my naked state. So without hesitation, I headed full speed down the main hallway towards the stairwell. I had just made it through the door, into the stairwell, when I saw a man walking down the hallway in my peripheral vision. I did not take the time to get a better look before darting up the stairs, taking them three at a time as I had done on my way down. Every here and there I noticed a partial bloody footprint.

I made it to my room without seeing anyone else and locked the door tightly behind me. I dressed in my pajamas, poured myself a glass of water, and lay down on my bed. I couldn't deal with cleaning the bathroom or even thinking about what had happened. In fact, I was more exhausted than I remembered ever being! I closed my eyes, blocked out every thought, and immediately fell fast asleep.

It seemed like I had just closed my eyes when I was startled awake by a loud pounding on my door. True to her word, Nurse Thorn had appeared bright and early on Christmas morning to check on me. I greeted her, working hard to convey confidence and sanity, and after I had relieved all of her concerns and assured her that I had a full day of Christmas activities planned, she went on her merry way. As I watched her walk down the hallway, I suddenly had the urge to run after her. Normally I treasured solitude, but right then I did not want to be alone with nothing to do but think about my 'condition'.

I made a pot of coffee. Strictly speaking, we weren't supposed to have appliances like coffee makers or toasters in our rooms, but everyone did. The one thing Taylor and I had in common was our love of java, and she bought the good stuff. She had even outfitted us with a grinder, so we could use fresh whole beans. Having a rich roommate did sometimes have its advantages. I lamented how I would miss the good coffee after Taylor moved out next year. Just the wonderful aroma of the brew made me feel more alert. I knew I had to keep busy, or I would go crazy. I decided it was time to face the music. I put on my slippers to avoid getting any more cuts and stepped gingerly into the bathroom.

The whole of the previous night's events came rushing back to me, in one horrible vivid stream. I had never felt that scared in my life...that feeling of drowning...lungs burning for air. I shut my eyes tight and tried to push the memory away. But the problem was, if I didn't allow myself to think about it, I would never figure out what was happening to me. I had to be analytical...think like a scientist...try to remember any detail that could give me some insight into what had happened. I drained the bath and started sweeping up the glass and bath beads that littered the floor.

Whatever was going on with me had happened twice, within a few days. I thought about the similarities...headaches, nausea, dizziness, and the feeling of falling. I tried to remember if I had ever experienced these symptoms before. The closest incidents I could think of were bouts of the flu and the time I had mono, but those weren't even close to what I had experienced in the bathtub. No, whatever was happening was something entirely different.

Since I had been so focused on trying to remember something both times 'it' happened, I wondered if 'it' was just my mind's way of recalling deeply buried events, like when people are hypnotized to recall the details of a crime scene or repressed memories from their childhood. Those people report being able to recall a memory as if watching a scene in a movie. They can fast-forward, rewind, and zoom in on details. So, maybe I had put myself into some kind of hypnotic state, I reasoned. I mean, maybe I was just seeing things I had seen before but forgotten.

It wasn't like I was really there...in the past. It wasn't like I was physically interacting with my history. Then I remembered it! I ran out of the bathroom and frantically searched for it. I spotted the blanket I had forgotten to return to Nurse Thorn lying in the middle of the floor. I yanked it up, and sure enough, underneath, there it was in a heap...still damp...the brown afghan. I clutched it close to my chest and started to cry because that ugly brown afghan was proof that I wasn't going crazy. Whatever was happening to me was not a figment of my imagination. It was certainly bizarre and very scary, but losing my mind would have been even more terrifying.

Coffee in hand, I sat down at my desk and opened my laptop. I searched phrases like "hypnotic visions" and "unveiling repressed memories." Most of the legitimate, medically sound information I found was based on Freud's theory of "repression," where the mind automatically banishes traumatic events from a person's memory in order to prevent paralyzing anxiety from taking over. Overwhelmingly, these repressed memories involved some kind of sexual abuse experienced in childhood.

There were several types of repressed memory therapies, including journal writing, visualization, and hypnotherapy. I read about regression therapy, which is based on the idea that everything a person has ever experienced is recorded and retained in their mind. I read that these memories are stored in different levels of the consciousness and that only very focused therapy could bring certain, deeply buried, memories to the surface.

The more hokey information on regression therapy dealt with "past life regression" where people uncovered memories from their past lives under hypnosis. Of course, to buy into any of this you first had to make the jump into believing in reincarnation. Although I found the notion utterly ridiculous, I had to admit that some of the accounts were fascinating.

One famous case occurred in 1953 and involved a homemaker named Betsy White from Wisconsin. Betsy, who had been plagued by severe anxiety around water, sought the help of a psychologist who specialized in regression therapy. During several years of hypnotherapy, she revealed that she had previously lived during the mid-1800s as a Ukrainian fisherman. Betsy provided numerous specific names, dates, places, and events about her previous life, many of which were corroborated. However, the most interesting part of the story was that when she was in a hypnotic state, not only did her voice deepen and sound distinctly male, but she would lapse into broken English peppered with Russian. Supposedly, neither Betsy White nor her husband knew Russian.

Eventually, Betsy spoke exclusively in Russian, when under hypnosis, and conversed fluently with a Russian language professor. The professor revealed that she was speaking a regional dialect that would have been spoken during the 1800s in the specific area of Ukraine where Betsy claimed to have lived. Once Betsy uncovered that her previous male self had drowned during a terrible storm, on an ill-fated fishing expedition, her anxiety ceased.

Of course, the most logical explanation for these accounts was simply that the patients and/or their therapists were being deceitful and making up an elaborate hoax to fool the public. All of these 'recollections' could have been manufactured after minimal research. Dates, places, and events could have been determined, and languages could have been learned. However, despite my natural skepticism, and considering my own recent unexplained events, my mind was open to alternative possibilities.

I spent the rest of the morning and afternoon researching memory regression, hypnosis, transcendentalism, out-of-body experiences, reincarnation, and karma. These ideas, in one form or another, have been embraced throughout history by every culture in the world. It was clear that human beings were desperate to believe in something beyond what they could physically touch, hear, taste, see, and smell.

The problem with all of these concepts, and the reason they went against every fiber of my being, was that they were scientifically unproven. I wanted to dedicate my life to the doctrine of scientific inquiry. This meant only accepting carefully recorded data that had been acquired in a controlled experimental study. None of these new-age theories had been even remotely studied in a scientific manner, and very few of the 'experts' attached to these fields were credible scientists.

The other major difference in all the phenomena I read about, and my own experiences, was that I could not find a single account of someone producing a tangible object from their projections. The fact that something material had emanated from my 'vision' suggested that I was dealing with something new, something that had never been described before. The very existence of the brown afghan, which sat cradled in my lap, suggested that my situation could be studied in a logical, controlled manner.

Even though I didn't have any real answers, my research had provided me some comfort. I always felt more confident when I was armed with knowledge. I closed my computer and focused on my more immediate needs. If I wanted to avoid people, even the few that remained in the dorms, I thought I should head down to the cafeteria for my Christmas feast early. It was only 4:00 pm but I was famished. As often happened when I was engrossed in study, I realized I had not eaten all day.

I took a quick shower and threw on some sweatpants and a T-shirt. I grabbed a few of my research papers and headed downstairs. I always armed myself with reading material when dining alone. I found that reading, or even pretending to read, was an effective way to discourage people from talking to me. It was like an invisible shield, no one wanted to disturb a person engrossed in their reading.

The offerings in the hot line were slightly less disgusting than usual. My scholarship paid for room and board and that meant free meals, as long as I used my meal card in the cafeteria. I had to admit that cafeteria food was one thing that had not improved since high school. After the obligatory exchange of salutations and wishes for a Merry Christmas with the minimal staff that was working, I found the most remote corner of the room and sat down to eat.

It looked like I wasn't even going to have to pretend to read, the place was deserted. But then I spotted someone sitting alone at a table way at the other end of the dining hall. I jerked my head down a second too late. Eye contact had been made! Don't look up, don't look up, I thought, but my eyes betrayed me, and as soon as they did the figure gave me a little wave and started to rise. Crap! I thought. He was coming over. I grabbed one of my papers and stared intently at it, pretending it was the most fascinating piece of printed material I had ever seen.

"Hey, do you mind if I sit with you," he said.

My ruse had not dissuaded him, and it wasn't like I could say "no."

"Yeah sure," I said in a flat voice.

"You stuck here for Christmas too, huh?"

Brilliant observation, this one must be a genius, I thought.

"Yeah, it appears so." I was tempted to continue reading my paper and just pretend he wasn't there, but that just seemed too rude, especially on Christmas. I put the paper down beside my tray and looked up at him properly.

He offered his hand and said confidently "I'm Aaron James, Christmas outlander. Nice to meet you."

Despite myself, I smiled and introduced myself, "Evan Wright, nice to meet you too." Something about his face was warm and disarming.

"So do you live in Holden?" he asked.

Another brilliant question... Of course, I did, or I wouldn't be eating here, would I? I thought. Aaron was obviously not the sharpest tool in the shed. Either that or he was just as bad at making small talk as I was.

"Yep, third floor," I answered.

"Oh, wait a minute, aren't you Taylor's roommate?"

I was taken aback, everyone knew Taylor. She stuck out like a beautiful sore thumb, but I was genuinely surprised he recognized that I was her roommate. I tried to remember if I had ever seen Aaron before. He certainly was not in any of my classes. He must be one of the frat boys who hovered constantly in the space around Taylor. He probably saw me one night while picking her up for a date. He certainly was her type, tall, dark, and handsome, probably with a major void between his ears.

"Yes, I am. Do you know Taylor?" I feigned interest.

"Oh yeah, I've known her since we were kids. We spent many long summers playing tennis at the club together," he reminisced.

Terrific, another oil heir, even worse than a frat boy, I thought. I really did not care to hear all about the leisurely summers he and Taylor had spent sipping Shirley Temples at the country club. Now that he knew I was her roommate, I assumed he would probably spend the rest of the meal trying to divulge inside information from me about Taylor's likes and dislikes as a way to gain an advantage over the numerous others vying for her affection.

"Taylor went home for the holidays" was all I could manage.

"Oh, I'll have to tell my dad to keep an eye out for her around the club," he said.

I began to eat faster, willing the meal to be over. We sat, without speaking, eating our food until the silence became uncomfortable. I looked up at Aaron and he was staring at me as if he was waiting for me to say something. I guessed it was my turn to speak.

"So, why didn't you go home for Christmas?" I hated to encourage him, but etiquette overrode my desire to be left alone.

Aaron's eyes lit up like I had just given him a present. "Too broke. My car crapped out, and after shelling out to fix it, I only had enough money left to pay for a flight home or buy books for next semester. I thought buying books was probably more sensible. I suppose I could have risked driving home, but even on a good day I honestly don't trust my car to make it any further than Abilene," he laughed. "My mom's used to it though, I didn't make it home last year either, but being one of five boys, well six if you count my dad, she probably doesn't even miss me. One less mouth to feed," he laughed again.

"You're not a freshman?" I asked, a little confused.

"Oh, you mean why am I still living in Murdoch if I'm not a freshman, huh? Well, my tennis scholarship pays for the dorm, so if I lived off campus, I would have to get another job. As it is, I'm busy enough with tennis practice, out-of-town matches, and my work-study job at the library. So, I just stay here. It's not so bad really, the good thing is that there are usually plenty of people around to keep me company. Growing up in a house with four brothers and people always coming and going, I would probably go crazy kicking around by myself in my own place. But listen to me going on and on about myself. How about you? Why didn't you go home?" he asked.

I really didn't want to talk about myself, and I was admittedly a little bit intrigued by Aaron. So far, his story wasn't at all what I had expected, so I ignored his question and asked him another, "So you don't live in River Oaks, like Taylor?" I probed. River Oaks was the most affluent district in Houston, in fact, it was one of the wealthiest zip codes in America, just after Beverly Hills.

"Oh, Lord no. We live in Pearland. My dad is a pro at the Dorsett's tennis club. Mom is an elementary school coach, so we all grew up playing lots of sports. I was practically born with a racket in my hands. I spent summers helping my dad teach lessons at the club. I always stood in as an opponent for the kids he was giving lessons to so he could stand on their side of the court and analyze their swings. Taylor took lessons every summer and she got to be pretty good. I see her around campus sometimes but haven't been able to convince her to play a match."

Interesting, not at all what I expected, I thought. I wanted to keep him talking and keep the focus off me.

"So what's your major?" I asked. I was betting on Kinesiology, thinking maybe he wanted to be a coach like his parents.

"Poli Sci" he answered.

Most political science majors were law school bound, although I thought that with Aaron's congenial personality, good looks, and warm smile he may be aiming for politics. "What do you want to do?" I probed further.

"Community organizing. I'd like to start an after-school program for at-risk kids. Teach them tennis and stuff. I think it would be fun. There's plenty of neighborhoods in Houston that could use something like that" he said, face aglow.

Was this guy for real? I wondered. I looked into his eyes and going against my pessimistic nature, I thought that he could be the real thing…naïve and idealistic, but real. The next hour passed quickly. Talking with Aaron was easy. I didn't have to work to make conversation like I did with most people. His whole demeanor was warm and inviting. I thought that he should definitely go into politics. He was just the kind of guy you couldn't help but trust. As the conversation gently flowed, I kept it directed toward him. I felt my guard loosening, but I still didn't want to talk about myself. He told me all about his four brothers. He was smack in the middle.

Although his life was pretty average, his stories kept me interested. Actually, way more than interested, I was enthralled really. His stories were so detailed, his imagery so vivid. I could practically see the cul-de-sac of the Houston suburb where he grew up, he and his four brothers causing havoc throughout the neighborhood. Something about the warm tone of his voice and the slow, steady cadence of his speech soothed me.

As an only child, I had always been fascinated by sibling dynamics, and Aaron's stories about growing up in such a full house fascinated me. However, as he spoke about his brothers, my thoughts couldn't help but wander to the baby I'd seen in my childhood home.

As Aaron spoke, I gazed at his face. His dark eyes were so expressive and they lit up when he talked about his family. His whole face became animated and I noticed that when he smiled one side of his mouth was higher than the other, forming an Elvis-esque smirk. He gestured with his hands a lot, acting out certain parts of his stories. I watched his hands. They were strong and athletic. The muscles in his hands and forearms were so defined from playing tennis that the long sinewy tendons of his forearms bulged and flexed as he gestured. I followed the line of muscles up his arms and could just make out the bulge of his biceps under the sleeves of his t-shirt. His shirt fit snuggly and accentuated the definition of his chest.

He was tan for December, and as he turned his head, I noticed there were random golden highlights throughout his otherwise sandy brown hair. It almost looked like they were professionally done, but Aaron did not strike me as the type of guy who would spend an afternoon getting his hair colored in a salon. No, I suspected that the long hours spent practicing in the West Texas sun were the cause.

His hair wasn't messy, but stylishly unkempt. His long bangs just grazed the tips of his eyelashes, and he had a habit of running his fingers through his hair to push it back, and when he did, I could see a small, jagged scar just above his right eyebrow. I inexplicably found myself wondering how he got that scar and wanting to reach out and run my fingers across it.

It had been so long since I looked at a boy this way. For the first time I could remember, I wasn't thinking of excuses to end the conversation. In fact, I probably could have sat there well into the evening, but soon after finishing a story about an elementary school bike accident involving four of the five brothers all piled on one bike, Aaron started gathering his things to leave. I had been so comfortable sitting there listening, his movements startled me.

"Well, I guess it's time for me to be on my way," he said extending his hand again.

"Oh, OK." I tried to mask my disappointment, lifting my hand like a robot, to meet his.

"I signed on to work at the library tonight."

"On Christmas?" I asked skeptically, trying to sound nonchalant.

"Yeah, some of the cataloging has to be done when the library's closed, and that's not often. I just figured there would be nothing else to do anyway and I could save myself from boredom while making a few extra bucks."

I realized we were still holding hands. Awkwardly, I gave his a little shake and then pulled mine away.

"Well, it was very nice to meet you, Evan Wright," he said.

"Likewise, Aaron James," I returned.

He rose and for the first time, I realized how tall he was. He had to be at least six foot three. He started to walk away then turned around and said, "You know it's another long week until classes start, we should do this again. I still don't know anything about you."

I smiled despite myself, quickly looked down, and mumbled, "That would be nice."

I halfheartedly started gathering my tray and papers to leave when I realized that he was still standing there looking at me. The surprise must have shown on my face because he said, "Oh, sorry. I'm not trying to freak you out or anything, but I feel like we're friends now. So, can I ask you a question?"

Despite myself, I liked the thought of being friends with Aaron, and happily answered, "Sure."

"Were you running around the halls last night wrapped in a towel?"

This question should have mortified me, but in the lightness of my mood, it unexpectedly made me laugh. "Actually, it was an afghan" I answered.

～ℓℓ～

The phone rang only once before she picked up the receiver, "Merry Christmas sweetie!" she boomed into the phone.

"Merry Christmas, Mom!" I tried to sound excited.

"How is everything in Blythe? Is it cold?"

"No Mom, it almost never gets cold here," I bit my lip suddenly remembering the turtleneck she had sent me.

"Oh, well it's not very Christmasy here either. It's a balmy 80 degrees today" she lamented.

"Wow, and I thought it was warm here." Ugh, I hated making small talk. I just wanted to tell her what I was going through. Instead, Mom told me all about their Christmas day on the island. Dinner was in the mess hall as usual. We compared the awful details of each other's cafeteria Christmas dinner. I thanked her for the presents, and she told me about the things she planned to buy on Amazon with her gift certificate. She asked about school, and I filled her in on my week of finals and about how I was sure I would get straight A's this semester. Her voice beamed when she said how proud she and Dad were of me.

After all the usual topics had been covered, she asked if I wanted to talk to my father. This was a rhetorical question, but an exercise we always had to go through. My father hated to talk on the phone. It was not that he wasn't interested in what I had to say. He would often sit in close vicinity to my mom as she spoke with me, occasionally interjecting a few "don't forget to tell her..." or "make sure to mention that..." He just hated the phone, and when we did speak, the conversation was very to the point, quickly covering a few key topics. So, our relationship mainly existed via email, and that was fine with me. We had never been very close, which was funny because in many ways we were so similar. He was a guy's guy, a career Army man, and I often wondered if he couldn't relate to me because I was a girl. Maybe it would have been different if he had a son...

My voice broke when I told Mom I should "probably get going," and she picked up on it right away.

"Evy, what's wrong? Are you feeling lonely? I realize it must be hard for you this year, it's your first Christmas alone." Her voice was full of worry.

I made an impulsive decision to just put it out there. There was no point beating around the bush and if I was wrong, she would just think I was losing it in my loneliness.

"Mom...did I have a baby brother?" As soon as it came out, I regretted it.

There was an audible gasp and then a long silence. I held my breath, afraid to make the slightest sound. As the seconds ticked by, I knew I was right. After a moment, I heard shuffling sounds on the other end of the phone that sounded like she was moving to another room. I guessed my father had been close, listening in. I heard a door close and what sounded like stifled sniffles. I suspected she was crying and felt cruel.

"I didn't think you remembered anything about him," she whispered.

"I don't, not really, just flashes of a memory. I was thinking about that Christmas in Hamburg. The one when we had that big snowstorm. I thought I remembered something...about...him."

"He was only...with us for a few months. He...went to sleep one night and never woke up." I could hear the depths of her sadness and finally understood why she was the way she was. I always thought she was unhappy with her life, or lack thereof...just a bitter woman who had sacrificed any career or life of her own to follow my father around the globe and take care of me. There was so much more.

I didn't know what to say to her. I regretted even bringing it up. I felt like I was torturing her. The odd thing was that I also felt the dull pain of sadness for the brother I never knew. It was buried deep down but rising to the surface. I just needed to know one more detail.

"Mom, what was his name?" I asked.

She hesitated, then took a deep breath and said, "Aaron...Aaron James Wright."

Chapter 4

EXPERIMENTING

I couldn't sleep. My thoughts scattered in fifty different directions trying to understand what this new revelation meant. I had a brother, and he died. Even if he would have lived, he would be only thirteen now. Was this some kind of crazy cosmic joke? Was it just an incredible coincidence? No, I was sure that my new friend Aaron had something to do with what was happening to me and I was going to have to find out how we were linked.

Even though a thousand questions swam through my mind, one was particularly compelling. I couldn't stop wondering if I was just an idle observer in all of this or an active participant. During both of my 'episodes,' I had been concentrating hard, trying to remember something. I wondered if that absolute concentration somehow set whatever happened into motion, and if so, could I control it?

I thought of the Native American shaman I had read about online. Supposedly, they could leave their bodies and enter some spiritual dimension after days of intense meditation. I speculated that this was due more to peyote than something supernatural, but still, I wondered if I just had to sit around waiting for the nausea to pull me down or if could I intentionally project myself into a memory.

I decided to perform a sort of...experiment. I tried to think of a harmless, average memory from my recent past. If I really could project myself into a memory, I wanted it to be in a familiar controlled environment, where few people would be around. I settled on the evening before my Immunology final. I had been sitting at my desk studying my notes. I thought of the material I had been studying early in the evening before Taylor had arrived home.

The room was dark, but I still closed my eyes as I tried to focus on the notes I had been studying. That evening I had been trying to memorize the 'alternative complement pathway' that immune cells used to destroy bacteria and viruses. I pictured the pathway, the exact way it was laid out on the pages of my notebook. I could see my sketch of the antigen/antibody complex, and next to it there was an arrow labeled "C1-complex." A flow chart, illustrating the rest of the pathway's components, followed below.

I selected one specific detail, a picture I had drawn with multi-colored pens, depicting a cell swelling and bursting due to the 'membrane attack complex'. I remembered that the cell was light blue and burrowed into the side of it was a big red and yellow hollow tube, which was causing the cell to burst. Small, light blue fragments were breaking off in all directions. I was not a very good artist, but I focused all of my attention on envisioning the imperfect details of the picture.

It didn't take long before I began to feel something. The air in the room seemed heavy around me. Fighting the urge to look up, I kept my eyes closed tight, concentrating on the picture of the cell. Gradually, I felt a faint tugging that started from inside my stomach and pulled me flat against the bed. I was nauseous again, but not nearly as queasy as the times before. My vision remained steadfast on the image of the bursting cell. The tugging in my stomach became stronger, pulling me tight against the mattress.

The pulling continued, building into a tremendous pressure. I felt stuck, like an object being pulled through an opening that was way too small. It felt like there was a rope tied around my waist and chest, and it was pulling me down so hard that it felt like the rope would snap. Suddenly, I heard the now familiar loud "whoosh" and simultaneously felt my body abruptly slip, like I had finally been pulled through the too-small-hole.

Like Alice, I began to fall down, down, down into the rabbit hole again. Then, as suddenly as it had begun the falling stopped and my eyes snapped open. I was lying on the floor right next to my desk, only a few feet away from my bed. I lay still for a moment collecting my thoughts and waiting for my stomach to settle. I listened carefully. I could hear music and voices coming from the next room. As opposed to the quiet of the last few days, the dorm was now alive with the bustle of a normal Thursday night. Composing myself, I stood up and looked around the room. My books and papers were scattered all over the desk and my notebook was open to the page illustrating the alternative complement pathway! I could clearly see the colorful picture of the bursting cell. I walked to the bathroom and peered into the mirror. I touched my reflection. I was standing there in my pajamas. I was really there!

Just then, I heard a key jostling the door open in the other room! I spun around and ran to my desk. My mind reeled as I tried to decide what to do. So much for avoiding people, I thought. My timing had been completely off, and now Taylor was home. I had to act normal and avoid interacting with her. I wasn't sure what would happen if I spoke to her. As she walked into the room I stared at the pages of my notes, pretending to study.

"Hey Evan," Taylor's cheerful voice sang. "Still studying for finals?"

"Uh, yeah..." I had to kill the conversation before it started.

"Wow, you look comfy, already in your pj's huh?" she observed.

"Uh, yeah. It'll be late when I'm done...I don't want to have to worry about changing later" I lamely explained.

She did not respond right away, and I really wanted to look at her face and try to gauge her reaction, but I didn't dare look at her. I kept my head down, staring at the pages in front of me. I was on pins and needles waiting for her to speak again.

Finally, she sighed and said, "Evan, you know I've been thinking. It sucks that you are going to spend Christmas here all by yourself. It's just so sad!" She paused as if waiting for a response. I remained silent. "Well anyway, I would love it if you came home with me and spent Christmas at our house. I've told Mom and Dad all about you, and they would love to meet you! Even my brother Simon will be home from Yale for the holidays. It will be fun!"

I swallowed hard and almost choked. Taylor had invited me home for Christmas? How could I not have remembered *that*? I had no recollection of the conversation at all. I must have been so deeply immersed in my studies that I completely ignored her. She had been worried about *me*, and I had completely blown her off. I felt horrible.

"So...what do you think?" she asked hopefully.

I hated ignoring her again. It was almost painful, but I reasoned that if this was the way it had gone the first time around, I couldn't possibly change it now. I mean if I turned around and congenially agreed to go home with her for the holidays what then? Obviously, if I were in Houston with Taylor then I wouldn't be sitting here having the dilemma I was having!

I despised that I had to do it, but I decided to play it safe and continue to ignore Taylor. So, I didn't answer her, but instead just made an "Uh huh" noise, in a tone that clearly meant "leave me the hell alone." I was such a bitch.

She sat down on her bed behind me and was quiet for some time. The atmosphere was tense and I found pretending to study torturous. The music and laughing from next door was a welcome distraction. Finally, after several minutes, Taylor walked over to the coffee maker and began grinding beans.

"Well, I suppose if you're going to be up late studying, a fresh pot of coffee couldn't hurt," she said softly, not really speaking to me anymore.

I supposed she had grown accustomed to the uselessness of trying to converse with her unreceptive roommate.

I sat, stealthily watching her. She truly was beautiful. She was wearing a loose camel-colored cashmere sweater, slim-fitting dark jeans, and two-inch high-heeled chocolate-colored suede boots. Her perfectly highlighted blonde hair hung in flawlessly flat-ironed layers around her face. She was thin and my height, looked taller because she only ever wore impossibly high heels. This always struck me as silly because, with heels on, she was well over six feet tall, and most of the guys she dated were much shorter. I always wondered if her height intimidated them. Maybe that was the point.

After Taylor started the brew, she turned towards me. I quickly averted my eyes, pretending to ignore her again. She went to our closet and retrieved her suitcase, heaving it onto her bed. She was puttering around the room now, fiddling with dresser drawers, pulling garments out then putting them back in. Eventually, she headed to the bathroom and shut the door.

I wanted to get out of there. I felt so awful about my behavior, that if I stayed, I was not going to be able to continue the façade. The problem was, I didn't know *how* to get back. It had just happened before. I tried to will myself out. I visualized lying in my bed. It was dark and quiet. Nothing happened. I put my head down on the desk and closed my eyes, thinking "out, out, out." Still nothing.

I could hear sounds in the bathroom, and I knew Taylor was going to come back out any second. What did I have to do? I was beginning to panic. My heart was racing, and I worried that I would be stuck, doomed to repeat the last few days in some kind of alternative reality.

I stared at the picture of the bursting cell again. I tried to think about how I got here. The pulling, the sensation of falling, I tried to access all that sensory information. I gave into that feeling of helplessness and plummeting out of control. I even tried to embrace the nausea. Then, my head spun, and it wasn't just the memory of feeling dizzy and out of control, I really did feel lightheaded. I fought against my human nature to suppress these feelings and instead gave in to them. My whole body thrust forward and I fell, well actually plunged, out of the chair. I was falling again and this time I wasn't as scared. My body was compliant, and I just let go. Instead of a terrifying free fall, I was gliding through space. I pictured myself as a giant winged dove sailing through time and space.

After what felt like half a minute or so, I landed ever so gently on my bed. My head hit the pillow and it felt like I was lying on a cloud. I did have a dull headache, but it was so completely opposite from my experience in the bath. I wasn't panicked or terrified. I almost felt content. My eyes fluttered open long enough to scan the dark room and assure myself that I was in fact in my room. Then I closed my eyes and immediately fell fast asleep.

<hr />

The next morning, I awoke full of energy and excitement. I had done it! I had willed myself into a memory. My head was filled with every detail of the previous night. I quickly grabbed my journal from the desk and began writing everything I could remember, recounting the entire event. I tried to write down every sensation and thought I had experienced. I paid great attention to recording the process of both entering the memory and extracting myself. I also wrote down every word I could remember Taylor saying to me.

I felt a little sad writing those words, but I was resolved to make amends, to be a friend to her. Surprising myself, I also felt a serene happiness that Taylor had invited me home for Christmas. She viewed me as more than just a roommate. After documenting my experience as completely as possible, I made a pot of coffee. We were running out of beans, and I realized that I needed to do some shopping and stock up on supplies.

Coffee in hand, I felt even more rejuvenated. I was so proud of myself that I was bursting. However, I rationalized that if I was going to experiment with this power, or whatever it was, there had to be rules. I began to list them:

1. Always be alone and in a safe place when focusing on the past. Never again in a crowded classroom, and certainly not in a tub of water.

2. Dress in appropriate attire. No more running around naked, or even in pajamas.

3. Never tell anyone what I am doing, lest I spend the rest of my college years in a straitjacket.

4. Record everything in my journal. Once I figured out the secrets of traversing space and time, I would need detailed notes for the dozens of scientific papers I intended to publish.

5. Treat this like a scientific experiment at all times. See above.

I left space to add additional rules later if need be. Then I turned to a fresh page of my journal and began writing again. First, these were the things I knew:

1. I could project myself into a memory if I concentrated very hard and focused on every tiny detail of the scene.

2. When I arrived in the past, my current body occupied the space of my past self, dressed in whatever I had been wearing at the time.

3. I could interact with people in the past, and lastly,

4. It was possible that when I returned to the present, I came back with whatever I was holding at the time.

There were so many more unknowns, which I also began to list. First of all, why was this happening to me, and why only now? What happened to my past self when my eighteen-year-old body was in its space? What would happen if I changed something in the past? Would there be some kind of space/time continuum catastrophe and the whole universe would implode?

I thought about every sci-fi movie I had seen about time travel. I just knew that for time travelers in the movies, it was always extremely dangerous to change any little thing. And then a bizarre notion popped into my head...is that what I was, a time traveler? The thought made me laugh out loud. I could not believe how preposterous it all was. Still, another question seeped its way into my mind. Was this ability limited to my own memories, or could I travel into someone else's?

—ele—

The cool air was a welcome change after being cooped up in the dorm for days. I walked briskly across the quad towards the engineering complex. Harper was founded in 1925 so it was not a very old school, not compared to the East Coast Ivy Leagues, with their rich history, lush green landscaped panoramas, and ivy-covered buildings. Still, Harper was pretty in its own way. The architecture was Spanish Renaissance-inspired, and even the parking garages were ornate. However, without exception, the most elaborate building on campus was the football stadium.

Football was a huge deal in West Texas, starting from elementary school. Harper was no exception. The 'Harper Warriors' were the main source of pride and income for this small college town and a major part of Harper's culture and tradition was centered around football rivalries. There was even a huge statue of an Indian chief riding a horse smack in the middle of the quad. Legend was that the horses' rear pointed directly to Junction City, TX, home of Harper's biggest football rival.

The shopping district was just east of campus, opposite the dorms. I didn't own a car and hadn't really found a need for one. Blythe was small, and everything I needed was right around the university anyway. Things were still dead around campus, which made shopping easy. My first mission was a gift for Taylor. I felt like I owed her that...and more. I had never been into the quaint little boutiques that lined University Avenue, because my shopping had been limited to the essentials... groceries and textbooks.

The smell of patchouli stung my nostrils and almost made me gag, as I walked into a small, cute-looking store called "Needful Things." The shop was way too stuffy and warm, and I would have turned right around and walked out had the clerk not been so excited to see a customer on this slow shopping day. She jumped out from behind the register and hurried over to greet me.

"Hi, can I help you find something" she said, too cheerfully.

Wow, no sales pressure here, I thought realizing that I was going to have to buy *something*. Begrudgingly, I told her I was looking for a gift for my roommate. The saleswoman looked to be in her sixties, very thin, and wearing a bohemian-styled, flowing, flower-print dress, synched with a macramé belt. I suspected that both the belt and her sandals were made of hemp. This one was obviously stuck in the 'age of Aquarius', I mused and imagined her rolling around in the mud at Woodstock.

She asked me a few questions about Taylor's personality and then led me through the store. There were loads of candles, tie-dyes, and tapestries lining the walls. I even saw an organic foods section in the back. Faint music was playing in the back room. It sounded like a 'Grateful Dead' tune my mom used to play. When we made our way back to the front of the store, she leaned over a glass showcase that contained jewelry and retrieved a pretty, elaborately etched, sterling silver compact case.

"It's antique," she explained, turning it over in her hands. "You can place your favorite compact powder in it." She pressed a clasp, and it popped open to reveal a hollow big enough for a powder cartridge opposite a tiny aged mirror. She clicked it closed and handed it to me. It was heavier than it looked. I examined the etchings more closely and noticed they were rose vines wrapped around the edges of the compact. The metal oval felt warm in my hand, comforting, almost familiar. I flipped it over and noticed something else. There was an inscription that read, *'Love, E. L.'* I could not believe it! My middle name was Lynn. I took it as a sign.

"It's perfect" I gushed, and it really was. I thought Taylor would love it. It wasn't cheap, but I felt so badly about the way I had treated Taylor that I would've paid double. I also spotted some bath oil beads in a pretty jar and bought them to replace the ones I had broken. The jar wasn't labeled, and I just hoped they weren't patchouli-scented.

Purchases in hand, I left the shop and deeply inhaled the fresh air as soon as I hit the sidewalk. Next, I picked up the essentials, cereal, fresh fruit, juice, and several new notebooks. My last stop was the coffee shop. I decided that instead of buying the cheap stuff at the grocery store I would stop in and get a bag of the good whole-bean stuff that Taylor always bought. I was waiting in line at the counter when I heard my name being called from across the room.

"Evan! Hey, Evan!"

Aaron sat in one of the nooks at the far side of the coffee shop reading a book. Aaron...Aaron James, my mind flashed to the baby looking up at me from the crib.

"Can I help you?" the barista asked.

"Uh, yes. Can I get two pounds of breakfast blend... and a large vanilla café au lait?" I quickly decided I could stay for a bit. Juggling my shopping bags in one hand and coffee in the other, I headed over to sit with Aaron. He jumped up as I neared, helping me with my load.

"I was hoping to run into you," he said, and my heart skipped a beat.

"Oh, really?" I asked, trying my hardest to sound casual.

"I realized that I didn't get your phone number yesterday, and they won't give out dorm room numbers...I tried."

I hated that this pleased me so much, I did not want any more *complications* in my life. However, I *did* need to find out more about him. I had to know if there was a link between him and my brother. I assured myself that was all there was to it.

"Well, here I am." I teased, and then silently chided myself for sounding too flirtatious.

51

"Yes, here you are."

The way he looked at me made me blush. His eyes were a deep, rich brown and I found it difficult to tear my gaze away from them. There was a brief, but uncomfortable silence, and then Aaron ran his hand through his sun-kissed hair exposing the scar above his eyebrow. Before I could even think, I blurted out "So you never told me how you got that scar. Was it the bike accident with your brothers?"

"Well, yes actually. The Great James Gang bike disaster...I had no idea you were paying such close attention" he mused.

Jeez, I'm lame, I thought. I was sure that he was going to think I was obsessed or something, spending all my time thinking about him and his stories... Then it occurred to me. Aaron's stories, the memories of his childhood... The way he had told them had been so vivid that I could picture every little detail as he spoke. As soon as I made the decision, I was on a mission. I had to know every facet of that bike accident. If I was going to have any chance of making my plan work, I had to be able to picture the scene completely.

I began inundating Aaron with a million detailed questions: Was it warm that day? How were each of the boys positioned on the bike? What did the houses in the neighborhood look like? On and on I asked, and surprisingly Aaron never ceased to answer each question in amazing detail. He motioned with his hands, emphasizing the exciting parts, and never seemed suspicious of my penetrating questions.

He was completely happy to talk about his childhood and acted like we were talking about the weather. Now and then he volleyed a question at me, which I answered as briefly as possible, and then focused the conversation back on him. I quizzed him until I could picture the scene in my mind.

"So how exactly did you cut your eye?" I still wondered.

"I don't really know." He stroked the scar. "I just remember the blood running into my eyes. I couldn't see a thing."

Finally, my questions and coffee were exhausted. Sensing my impending departure Aaron asked, "Can I walk you back to campus?"

"Sure, you headed home?" I asked, happy that my time with him was not over.

"No, gotta get to work. I'm trying to get as much overtime as possible. I'm working the evening shift at the library for the rest of the break."

I felt like a slacker and suddenly remembered the tall pile of research papers I still had to read. I knew that if I was going to be knowledgeable enough to start contacting the professors on my list, I had to start studying, but I was too preoccupied with my own little research project.

The walk back was over way too quickly. Aaron carried my shopping bags, and we chatted casually about the courses we planned to take and our plans for the future. He insisted on carrying my bags all the way up to my room.

"Hey, you should come by the library" he suggested, handing over the shopping bags. "I'm on checkout duty so it's going to be pretty boring, but we could hang out." Aaron leaned against one side of the doorframe, gripping the opposite side, as if he was holding it up. Again, the sinewy muscles danced up and down his long arm. I forced myself not to stare, but we were only inches apart and the air suddenly felt electrified.

"Uh...yes, actually I have to uh...find some..." Pull it together Evan! I thought. I sounded like a twelve-year-old with a crush "...some background information on the research papers I'm reading." His tall, broad stature consumed the space between us, and his proximity was unnerving. I quickly stepped back and crossed the room, placing the bags on the counter.

"Great! I'll see you tonight then." Aaron said with a little wave and turned to leave.

I felt a surprising pang when I realized that he hadn't followed me into the room. "Sure!" I called after him.

I was screwed.

I wrote down the time in my notebook "7:05 pm." I turned out the lights, lay down on my bed, and tried to relax. I emptied my mind of everything except the picture of a crisp, clear Fall day in Pearland, Texas. Most of the leaves were still on the trees but their vibrant color signaled their imminent descent. The sun was warm, but the intermittent breeze chilled any exposed skin and blew the loose leaves down the deserted road.

Aaron's house was a cream-colored, ranch-style spread with blue trim. The subdivision was track-style, so all the houses looked alike but were painted slightly different colors. Dozens of tall, mature oak trees lined the road and blocked out the late afternoon sun, casting long shadows in random shapes down the asphalt.

I tried to envision every detail Aaron had described, but nothing happened. I closed my eyes tight and willed myself there. I pictured myself standing on the road in front of Aaron's house. There was a small flower garden surrounded by a tiny wooden fence, shielding it from the discarded baseballs, Frisbees, and bicycles that littered the front lawn. There was a tacky garden gnome standing proudly in the middle of it like a sentinel. I tried to smell the fresh air and scent of the flowers growing in the garden that I knew was Aaron's mother's refuge from the stress of five active boys.

I felt nothing. I ran the details in my mind, over and over again. I tried to hear the whoops and hollers of the boys flying down the road out of control on Aaron's oldest brother Joe's bike. I could almost see them... Joe on the seat with Will standing on the bike frame behind him. Jack was scrunched on the bar in front of Joe, and Aaron was perched precariously on the handlebars. Something was not right though. No matter how hard I focused nothing happened. Maybe it just isn't possible, I thought. Maybe they had to be *my* memories. Maybe it just was not possible to glean enough detail from someone else's descriptions.

Finally, I gave up. Sitting up, I turned on the lights and looked at the clock. I had been at it for over an hour! I felt silly and disappointed. Well, the evening wasn't going to be a total bust, I told myself. I grabbed my pile of research papers and headed over to the library.

Aaron was sitting behind the check-out desk staring into space. As soon as he saw me walk in his eyes lit up and he ran over to greet me.

"Evan, thank God. I was about to slip into a coma! I've seen a total of two people all evening." I liked that someone was so happy to see me.

We spent the next several hours talking about Aaron as usual. In addition to all the other facts I already knew about him, I found out that he played the drums and had spent most summers working at his father's tennis club. He was allergic to shellfish, just like his mother, but besides that, he ate almost everything, except peanut butter. He absolutely hated peanut butter or anything peanut butter-flavored.

His favorite childhood experience was when he and his granddad went to a Houston Astros game, without any of his brothers. This was soon followed by his worst childhood memory, his granddad's funeral. He told me about his brothers. He was closest in age to Will, who was only a year older, but Jack was his confidant. Jack was seventeen and a senior in high school. He beamed as he spoke about him, and it was clear he was very proud. He told me all about Jack's girlfriend and their plans for prom. I desperately wanted to ask Aaron about his romantic past, but that was going way beyond casual conversation.

Finally, the conversation came full circle to the fateful bike accident. I tried to glean any additional details from Aaron. Maybe there was something I was missing. I asked him to physically describe his brothers again. I knew their ages and could even picture their faces at this point! Eventually, it seemed there was just no more to learn, and I suspected that if I kept asking about that one event, he was going to think I was seriously crazy. So, I let it go...almost.

"Well, I can only imagine how worried your mother must have been," I commented, as Aaron told me again how he had to get seven stitches in his head.

"Worried, ha! She was furious at Joe. He always got the blame for everything we did because he was the oldest" he laughed.

"Still, she must have been frantic. I can just see you with blood gushing down your face." The thought of it made me feel a little queasy.

"Well, imagine seeing it through my eyes!" he laughed.

I just stared at him for a moment, and then it was as if a light bulb literally went on inside my head! I was on my feet in an instant.

"Aaron you're brilliant!" Did I actually say that aloud, I wondered. I could tell that I had just by looking at his face. He was totally confused, but I didn't care. I had to get back to my room. I quickly gathered up my things and mumbled something about having to call my mom.

"Will I see you tomorrow?" He called after me.

I was out the door before I could answer and bounding across the quad. I had been so stupid. I had been trying to picture *myself* in Aaron's memory, standing in the street in front of his house, watching the bike accident. The problem with that was, I had never been there! I had to picture the scene through Aaron's eyes. It all made perfect sense!

I threw open my door and tossed my pile of papers on the floor. I scribbled the time, 11:15 p.m., in my notebook. Turning off the lights, I sat on my bed, back hunched and knees up. Resting my forehead on my knees, I tried to envision sailing through the crisp cool air on the handlebars of a red Huffy bike. All the details were the same, the track houses, flower garden, and shadows on the concrete, but this time I was seeing things from Aaron's perspective.

Everything was in motion. The houses and trees flew by. The wind was cold on my face. The sound of boys laughing and shouting behind me was loud in my ears. I imagined struggling to keep my balance while precariously perched on the speeding, teetering bike, hands tightly gripping the handlebars. I struggled to experience the exhilaration of it all. Then, after several minutes, I started to feel something! It was faint, but it was building.

The tugging started at a point in the pit of my stomach. I tried to give in, not resist it. I focused harder, projecting my whole being into the scene.

I was falling. The feeling was almost familiar now, I anticipated the nausea before it took hold and was able to keep it at bay. This time it was more like leaping than falling. I felt the air moving past and heard the whoosh. My eyes were still closed tight as I flew through space, faster and faster, beginning to *really* feel the cold wind on my face.

Then a thought occurred to me. What if I, Evan, suddenly appeared riding on the handlebars of that bike? I was willing myself to be there, trying to become Aaron in the memory. What if it really happened? Where would the eight-year-old Aaron go if I was in his space? Would I go flying off the bike, when it inevitably hit the stone? Would I bust my head open and need seven stitches? Why hadn't I considered this before? I suddenly realized that what I was doing was a *very* bad idea, but it was too late. I was propelling through time and space and couldn't stop myself.

The wind rushed faster and faster past my face, as we accelerated. My whole body tensed as I braced myself, waiting for the impending disaster, but suddenly all motion stopped and I was sitting...still. I kept my eyes clenched shut and wondered if I was back on my bed...if it hadn't worked after all. I thought maybe my last-minute doubts and panic had reversed the process. I started to open my eyes, expecting to see my dark room, but before I could even get them open, I realized I wasn't in my room at all. I could feel the breeze...hear birds.

When I opened my eyes, I saw Aaron's childhood home all around me, just as I had imagined it. I *had* done it! I was in Aaron's memory. I looked down at my body. I was sitting on the curb opposite the cream-colored house with blue trim. I was wearing my sweats and clogs and it was me! I wasn't sitting on the handlebars of a bike speeding out of control...thank God! I could not believe I was actually there. It was absolutely and utterly amazing! I laughed out loud.

My mind buzzed with a billion questions and even more possibilities, but at that moment I was too excited to waste time pondering them. Aaron was somewhere close, and as soon as I looked up the road, I heard them. They were at least a block away, but they sounded like a herd of wildebeest. The noise made me wonder how his mother had put up with them for all of those years.

They were getting closer by the second. I wasn't sure what to do. Should I hide? Would he see me? Did it matter if he did? Aaron was a little boy in the middle of an adventure, why would he even notice a stranger sitting on the curb? I decided I would stay put, plus there was no time to do otherwise. I could see the bike rounding the corner, making its way onto the cul-de-sac. The sight of four boys on one bike was comical and I would have burst out laughing if I hadn't known what the outcome would be. I realized that I was worried for him!

They were yelling, I think out of excitement *and* fear. I could tell that there was no way that Joe could see where he was going. They were going way too fast. I looked into the road and saw it, just a few feet from where I was sitting...a big stone right in the middle of their path. I knew this was the cause of their crash, Aaron had told me. They were going to hit that stone and crash right in front of where I sat.

They were approaching fast, but a thought crept into my mind and I realized that I still had time to dart out and kick the stone away. I could prevent it all from happening, the crash, the stitches, Aaron's scar. All I had to do was move that stone, but doubts weakened my resolve. What would the repercussions be? I didn't have time to think it through and I was too scared to tempt fate, so instead, I prepared myself for the carnage.

The noise was deafening. The boys were only feet away. I stared at Aaron. Ridiculous Aaron was brazenly looking straight ahead, laughing his head off. He was barely even holding on! When the front tire hit the rock, it was like everything happened in slow motion. Aaron instantly became detached from the bike and was sailing through the air, and I swear that he was still laughing! The other boys were also hitting the ground, except for Joe who somehow managed to stay on the bike, which skidded sideways across the ground. I heard metal scraping against asphalt and Jack was crying loudly.

Aaron hit the pavement, face-first. I couldn't look. I closed my eyes and waited for it to be over. Amazingly, he never cried. I heard all the other boys, yelling while clambering to their feet, trying to get to Aaron. When I finally worked up the courage to look at him I saw blood gushing from his forehead. It covered his whole face and dripped onto his clothes and the ground. Then I saw the front door of the cream-colored house fly open. Aaron's mom was running out, yelling "What the hell, Joe!"

Luckily, I was partially hidden by a bush and I tried to maneuver so that I was even more obstructed. Surely, it would look strange to see someone just sitting there, doing nothing, while a little boy was bleeding. But no one was looking at me. They were all focused on Aaron and stopping the bleeding. I could have been wearing a clown suit and they wouldn't have noticed.

I sat there through it all. Joe was running back and forth from the house, bringing wet towels, bandages, and whatever else his mom demanded. When they finally decided that Aaron should go to the emergency room, Aaron's dad went to bring the van around. I watched Aaron's parents and all five brothers, including the youngest Sammy, who wasn't involved in the crash, pile in and drive off.

It was over and I had witnessed the whole thing! I had seen it happen with my own eyes. I stood up and walked over to the spot where Aaron had been lying. There was a small pool of mostly dried blood. Then I noticed something else lying in the road a few yards away. I walked over and picked it up. It was a white rabbit's foot. There were spots of dried blood on the fur, and hanging off the foot was a small star-shaped charm that read 'Houston Astros'.

It was Aaron's! It had to be, I thought, remembering the story he'd told me about his granddad taking him to the game. He must have lost it during the crash. I squeezed the foot in my hand and thought of Aaron on his way to the hospital. It had been shocking to see him hurt like that, harder than I would have thought. Suddenly I had the overwhelming desire to go back. I wanted to be back to a time when Aaron was safe, but I had one more experiment to try.

I went back to the curb and sat down. I wanted to see if I could bring it back with me, like the brown afghan. I put the rabbit's foot in my pocket and shut my eyes. I began thinking of my room, my bed...concentrating on the return. It didn't take long to feel the pull. As I felt myself slipping into the void, I opened my eyes to take one more look at Aaron's home.

The sun was setting; it was dusk. The figure was faint but I could see her clearly enough. A little red-headed girl was standing across the street staring at me. The sight of her startled me, quickening my fall. As I fell, I watched her shrink until she was just a small spot at the end of a tunnel. Then she disappeared entirely and there was nothing but dark and gravity, pulling me down.

⸎

I jumped out of bed and looked at the time- 11:26. Impossible, I thought. Only minutes had passed since I had noted the time in my notebook! This meant that except for the ten minutes or so it took to get into the memory, virtually no time had passed. Yet, I know I had been at the accident scene for at least 15 minutes. How could it be possible? How could any of this be possible for that matter? Then, I remembered, tentatively reached into my pocket and pulled out the rabbit's foot.

I was ecstatic! A million plans raced through my head. Aaron would be my experimental subject. It all made perfect sense. I needed to find out as much about him as possible anyway. I had to figure out the link between him and my brother. Plus, he was such a good storyteller, obviously capable of providing me with an unlimited supply of vivid memories that I could visit. I pulled out a new notebook from the pile and titled it "Aaron's Memories."

I held the rabbit's foot tight in my hand as I wrote. It was a touchstone to my sanity, proof that I was not just imagining the whole thing. I transcribed every detail of what I had just experienced, every sensation. There was no possible way that *this* was memory regression. It hadn't even been *my* memory! I also started another list of questions: What happened to my body while I was in the past? Did I disappear? I rationalized that, since no time passed while I was away, my body probably just stayed put, but I noted that I should film myself to see if that was really the case. What about when I returned? Had that little redheaded girl witnessed a woman suddenly disappear?

I had to make sure no one was around when I was entering or exiting the past. I stroked the rabbit's foot and wondered about it and the afghan. Apart from the sheer impossibility of the physics involved, had I interfered in some way with the course of history by taking these objects? The universe was still intact obviously, but had I changed something even subtly? I had to be cognizant of the potential repercussions of my actions. I added a new 'rule' to my list: 6. *Never take things from the past.*

I thought about how I had to envision everything through Aaron's eyes to get into his memory. It had not been that hard because he was such a good storyteller. However, how much detail did I need to know? While it was true that the memory was just how Aaron had described it, there were plenty of details he hadn't told me about. Yet, I was still there. So, I wondered...could I visit other people's memories? I couldn't see why not. I mean if I could learn enough detail to create vivid imagery on which to focus, it seemed to me that I could visit anyone's past.

I tried to think of everyone I knew and consider all the possibilities. I glanced at the abandoned research papers sitting on the floor by my desk and felt a pang of guilt. How would I ever get a position in a good research lab at the rate I was going? Then it hit me like a ton of bricks! I had been so naïve, my vision so limited. *This* would be my research project, my grand endeavor. I was so focused on thinking about individual memories that I hadn't even considered the possibility that I could go way beyond. Anywhere actually, I just had to envision it.

I was *already* a scientist and I would answer some of the most important questions that had plagued humanity, the ones that even the most brilliant scholars in the world had never come close to answering! What constituted time and space and to what extent could the mind manipulate their continuity? With this ability, I believed I could answer these cosmic questions and many more. Where to start though? I knew I had so much to learn. I had already registered for my next semester, but I realized I was going to have to amend my schedule.

In hindsight, I realize that the hubris of a teenager in possession of massive power, but little life experience or wisdom, is an epically dangerous thing.

Chapter 5

RESEARCH SUBJECT

I opened my computer and began scanning through the course offerings from the History department. Most of the course titles sounded so dry, "Western Civilization I and II," "United States Diplomatic History to 1913," "British Politics, Society, and Culture Since 1688" blah! I didn't think I would even be able to stay awake through the lectures. Then I skipped down to the upper-level courses and saw some that looked promising:

'3305. History of Modern Medicine'. *A chronological study of the treatment of diseases and medicine as a social institution in different societies.*

Now that was more like it! Right up my alley. However, I didn't think it would help me much with my grand endeavor. I continued to scan down the page.

'3301. The Age of Chivalry'. *A study of Medieval Europe that considers the customs of knighthood through chivalric ideals, feudal monarchies, and the rise of a powerful bourgeoisie.*

'4320. A History of Sexuality in the United States'. *Discussions on topics including gender and sexual identities, courtship, marriage, reproduction, and prostitution in the context of Western society.*

There was such an extensive list of varied topics. I had not realized the History Department had so much to offer. I had simply viewed History as a boring freshman-level course that I had been lucky enough to place out of. I continued down the list and found exactly what I was looking for '4301. History's Greatest Mysteries'.

OK, the title was a little corny but the course description certainly sounded intriguing. It was a senior-level course, but I didn't notice any specific prerequisites listed. It was a must!

Next, I clicked on the link to the Philosophy department. Again, I saw many exciting potentials:

'3304. Existentialism and Phenomenology'. *Consideration of the meaning of human existence through the study of thinkers such as Nietzsche, Heidegger, Husserl, Merleau-Ponty, Sartre, and others.*

'3330. Philosophy of Science'. *Inquiry into the nature of science including the examination of basic scientific concepts and the forms of scientific reasoning.*

I thought they all sounded compelling and decided that I would just have to wait to see which were being offered in the Spring semester. I next scanned through Physics courses:

'3302. Cosmophysics: The Universe as a Physics Lab'. *Deals with topics from astrophysics, cosmology, and cosmic ray physics. For majors, prerequisites: PHYS 2402, MATH 3350 and 3351.*

'4340. Metaphysics'. *Consideration of the nature of what there is (ontology) or of the nature of the universe as a whole (cosmology). For Majors, prerequisite: PHYS 2601 and 2205 and MATH 3206.*

All the courses that sounded promising were reserved for Physics majors and had a heavy list of prerequisites. That was no help. I switched over to Psychology.

'4320. Psychoanalytic Theory and Research'. *From readings in psychoanalytic theory, a hypothesis will be chosen and tested by the group. The results will be discussed with psychoanalysts. Topics will vary.*

'4323. Perception: Theories and Applications'. *A survey of the methods and findings in perception. Emphasis on demonstrations of perceptual phe-*

*nomena; theories of visual perception (cognitive and ecological); and appli-
cations. Topics include illusions, depth, and motion.*

'4324. Cognition'. *Introduction to cognitive psychology, including perception, attention, memory, language, problem-solving, decision-making, and
the development of expertise.*

Although I was satisfied that I had compiled a list of good candidates,
I performed one more search. This time I selected the keyword option to
search through all the course descriptions in every department. I first typed
in "time travel" and got no results. Next, I tried "memory and time," but
still no results.

Typing in "science and time" yielded a long list of courses ranging from
'5388. Neural Networks' to '5422. Sedimentary Geology of Carbonates'.
I tried one more permutation, "science fiction and time." There were only
two results this time, a literature class on writing science fiction and fantasy
and a course offered by the Film Department called '2301. Impact of Sci-Fi
visions on the 21st Century'. OK, I knew I was going to divert significantly
from my planned curriculum, but this was a little too much.

I logged in and accessed the class schedule for which I had already
registered. My schedule popped up on the screen and I selected 'edit'. I
searched for my first choice, 'HIST 4301. History's Greatest Mysteries',
crossing my fingers that it was offered in the Spring. I scanned down the
page and spotted it:

Course: 4601. History's Greatest Mysteries (M, W, F; 1-2 pm)
Instructor: BrowningStatus:FULL

No! I could not believe that the class was already full. I didn't get it, most
students didn't bother to register until one or two days before classes started. This was unacceptable. I HAD to get into that class, it was imperative.
I decided I would have to make an appointment to meet with my advisor
Dr. Chaney and see if he could pull some strings.

After an hour of juggling my schedule around, I was satisfied. All the
rest of my top picks were still open, although there were a few with over-

lapping times, so I had to make some tough choices. I ended up dropping 'Virology' and 'Invertebrate Physiology' in lieu of "Existentialism and Phenomenology" and "Cognition." That still left me with the second semester of "Immunology," "General Microbiology" and "Advanced Calculus II" from my original schedule. I left the 1-2:00 p.m. Monday, Wednesday Friday slot open for "History's Greatest Mysteries," and planned to go see Dr. Chaney first thing the next morning.

—*ell*—

The days leading up to New Year's were amazing. My visit with Dr. Chaney was successful and I was able to charm him into approving an override for 'History's Mysteries'. He was a little resistant because it was a senior-level class that had already been expanded. However, I think he was so happy that I was diversifying my curriculum that he would have put me in any class I asked for.

Dr. Chaney was a big fan of the 'well-rounded' student and had always thought my plans were too narrowly focused on Science. He was curious about my course choices though, and wondered what these changes would do to my 3-year plan. I explained that the new courses had to do with a research project I had started working on, and that they may add on another semester, at most.

So, I was all set for an interesting semester, to say the least. I had purchased all my books, although there wasn't a book listed for the History course, which probably meant there would be a lot of outside reading. I had hoped to start reading about all of the great mysteries we would be discussing in class, but it would have to wait until the semester began. Until then, I decided to focus on Aaron. I wanted to visit more of his memories, hone my skills, and learn as much about him as possible. We had seen each other every evening that week, spending hours talking in the library, and I had settled on two more of his memories to visit.

The first was when Aaron was playing capture the flag at summer camp. He had been the one to capture the other team's flag. It was one of the happiest and proudest moments of his adolescence. I liked this memory because it occurred at night and I reasoned that it would be easier for me to stay undetected. The second was his grandfather's funeral. This one would be trickier as there would be so many people around, but Aaron had provided such a great description of the areas surrounding the church that I thought I could arrive somewhere outside, and then blend in with the crowd.

I had been focused on garnering as many details as I could about these two events and directed the conversation to them whenever I could. Of course, I couldn't take notes on what Aaron told me, but as soon as our conversations were over and I was back in my room, I transcribed all the details I could remember into my notebook.

I felt bad asking so many questions about his granddad's funeral, but it seemed like something he wanted to talk about. His grandfather had been very special to Aaron and he loved talking about him. He had been in the Army and fought in World War II, even storming the beach at Normandy. He was captured in France and held as a P.O.W. in a concentration camp for six months. So, Aaron and I had a history of family military service in common and he loved asking me about all the Army bases on which I had lived.

Aaron had traveled very little outside Texas and was anxious to hear about all the places I had been. He was especially intrigued when I told him that I had been to Omaha Beach and even toured Colleville-sur-Mer, the nearby cemetery devoted to Americans who had died at Normandy. Aaron asked me about every detail and vowed he too would visit one day.

I found myself sharing more and more with Aaron. I still tried to focus our conversations on him, but sometimes I would suddenly realize that I had been talking about myself for half an hour. I told him about our travels and all the different schools I had attended. I told him about my parents and their new home in Guam.

I liked the way Aaron watched me as I spoke. He stared at me with complete attentiveness. So many people never actually listen; they just wait for their turn to talk. However, Aaron never grew distracted or seemed bored. In fact, it was the complete opposite. His face was animated as I spoke, smiling when I described something happy, frowning when it was sad. He was not only the quintessential storyteller, but an excellent listener as well.

I found myself not only sharing more details of my life with him but also trying to make them sound more interesting and entertaining. I was just disappointed that I didn't have as many exciting stories as Aaron. With no siblings and very little extended family, I felt like my stories palled in comparison. Aaron didn't seem to think so though. He always asked lots of questions and drew out details that I hadn't thought about in years.

One evening I was telling Aaron about how when I was ten years old I made the mistake of watching a movie about possessed marionettes. He was staring at me, rapt in the story when he suddenly blurted out, "Evan, your eyes are amazing. I mean truly spectacular, I don't think I've ever seen anything like them before."

I completely froze. My face was hot and I suddenly could not look at him.

I could tell he was embarrassed too, and you could cut the tension with a knife.

"I'm sorry. Did I say that out loud?" he nervously laughed. "Never mind me, making awkward declarations runs in my family. Please continue your story."

I tried to continue describing how I became convinced there were demonic puppets living under my bed, but I had lost my train of thought and found it difficult to make eye contact with him. I felt completely self-conscious and exposed. Finally, I mentioned that it was probably time I headed home.

"Please don't. I'm sorry...I just lost my...Well, I was out of line."

Lost my...what??? I wondered what he was about to say. I didn't know how to answer him. My stomach was fluttering and I had goosebumps. I had turned into that nervous schoolgirl again.

After a few moments of uncomfortable silence, he spoke again, "Evan, I've really enjoyed spending time with you. I feel like we've become really good friends and I don't want to lose that." His eyes were imploring. I felt my whole body drawn to him like a magnet. "I didn't mean to embarrass you. It will never happen again."

What?! I felt deflated because the problem was, I *wanted* it to happen again. Yes, his compliment had caught me off guard and even embarrassed me a bit, but despite the tension and awkwardness, I felt alive. I hadn't felt that way in so long, not since... Well, that time was different and I didn't want to think about *him* in the same league as Aaron.

I was conflicted because, while I was driven to concentrate on school and my new 'research' project, my whole being wanted to be near Aaron. I didn't see him as a distraction like I saw other boys. He was a vital part of my work, and in many ways, he had become my obsession. I didn't dare communicate any of this to him though. I still wasn't ready to put my feelings out there. However, I did not want to dissuade him either. I thought of the most neutral response possible.

"I don't mind," I answered, finally meeting his eyes and managing a sincere smile.

The rest of the evening was uneventful, although the energy between us had definitely changed. There was clearly a mutual attraction. Despite Aaron's protests, I left before his shift was over, so he couldn't walk me home. I needed time to think and the night's cool breeze was a welcome relief to the charged air and nervous excitement I felt around Aaron. However, by the time I was safely back in my room, I wanted to be with him again. I decided it was time to visit another memory.

—— *ell* ——

I dressed in dark jeans, a black T-shirt and sneakers. I secured my hair back in a ponytail. I wrote the time in my notebook, turned out the lights, and sat in bed. I visualized a warm summer's night at Camp Alpine, nestled in the mountains of Big Bend National Park. I could see the log cabins, and the small stream dividing the girls' camp from the boys'. I knew that later that night there would be a thunderstorm and the rain would swell that stream, causing one of the girls' cabins to flood.

Aaron was the captain of the 'Pirate' team who were trying to capture the 'Buccaneers'' flag. The flags were located in two adjacent fields and heavily guarded by team members. Aaron had hidden in the hayloft of a barn that was close to the fields. From his vantage point, he could see both flags in the moonlight. He had waited half the night until the Buccaneer guards became distracted, then crawled over one hundred yards through the tall grass on his belly. He had captured their flag, winning the Alpine trophy and bragging rights for years.

I pictured the dark red barn. I tried to smell the hay and cattle. It was dark except for the moonlight seeping in through the small window and the gaps in the wooden beams. I tried to see things through Aaron's eyes. Looking out from the loft, I could see the expanse of the fields, twin flagpoles jutting up from their centers. I could make out dark figures circling the flagpoles, protecting their charge. I could hear the faraway shouts and laughter of kids in the distance. I focused completely on each detail until I felt the pull. I fell fast then, feeling the waves of nausea simply bounce off me. I was almost beginning to enjoy the feeling of falling, which was amazing considering how terrified I had been of it only a week ago.

When I stopped falling, I was sitting on a pile of hay in the middle of the dark barn. I let out a sigh of relief that I had not materialized right on top of Aaron. I looked around and could see the loft high up the far wall. There was a steep ladder leaning against it. I wondered what time it was. Was Aaron still crouched up there, planning his attack? There was no way I could simply climb up the ladder to see. No, if I was going to get a look at him, I would just have to hope he was still waiting in the loft. I would hide in the shadows and wait until he came down on his way to capture the flag. Once he was gone, I could climb up and watch the whole scenario play out!

I had to move though. I was sitting right in the brightest part of the barn, where the moonlight from the loft shone down, casting a soft glow right on top of me. I surveyed the barn and spotted the darkest corner right underneath the loft. Quickly, and as quietly as possible, I made my way across the length of the barn, sticking to the shadows along the walls. Even though my steps were light on the sawdust-covered floor, I heard the animals stir in their stalls. They sensed my presence, and I hoped Aaron didn't as well.

Finally, I made it to the dark corner and sat down trying to make myself as comfortable as possible. I guessed that I could be in for a long night. Thank goodness, the hay was soft. The loft was directly above me now and I was on alert for the slightest sound. My ears pricked every time one of the animals shifted in their stalls. I pictured Aaron above me, lying in the hay, waiting for the perfect opportunity to strike. He would climb down the ladder, only feet from where I waited.

The base of the ladder was illuminated in the moonlight, so I anticipated being able to get a good look at him. I leaned back, resting on my elbows. I felt exhilarated. Even though I was stuck in a dark barn, the large door at the far end was open and I could see that it was a beautiful evening. Despite the dark clouds that were starting to gather, I could see a million stars in the sky. Although the air was thick with the stench of livestock, the fresh smell of hay and the imminent thunderstorm permeated the barn. I felt so vibrant, all my senses were alive!

Minutes ticked by. I had no idea how much time had passed. I made a mental note to wear a watch on my future 'trips'. Every now and then I heard someone yell relatively close, but nothing from the barn...not even the faintest sound from the loft. From the shouts, I knew the game was still going, but as time passed, I began to seriously doubt that Aaron was in the barn at all. Maybe I had gotten some part of the story confused, out of sequence.

I still wasn't willing to climb up to the loft and check, but I thought maybe I should leave the barn. I could go wander around the camp a bit. Everyone would just think I was another camper, and maybe I would even spot Aaron running around somewhere out there. I could hear thunder in the distance and see intermittent flashes of faraway lightning. I knew I did not have long until the deluge. I needed to get moving.

As soon as I stood up, a pair of strong hands clapped around my mouth. I would have screamed if I could. I tried to bite the fingers, but their grip was too tight. Frantically I struggled, trying to break loose. I began trying to will myself out of the memory. Then, I felt hot breath whispering in my ear, "Is it you?"

Recognizing his voice, I immediately stopped struggling and my captor released his hands. I managed to whisper "yes," but didn't turn around.

Suddenly he had swiped my legs out from under me and I was falling back onto the hay, with Aaron landing right on top of me. It was so dark in this corner of the barn that I could barely make out his silhouette even though our faces were inches apart.

"I thought you were going to stay by the flag. Someone could have seen you come in here." His voice was light and playful. His body was pressed against mine and I felt like I was on fire. I didn't want to talk, didn't want him to move. I managed a soft "Uh huh."

"OK, I'm gonna go for it. There's no one around their flag. It's now or never!" he declared. No! Don't leave, I screamed in my head.

He started to lift off me, and then suddenly lowered himself back down. His hands stroked the sides of my face, and then his lips were instantly on mine. His kiss was forceful, but still tender and soft. I returned it passionately, confused by what was happening but completely willing to just go with it. The heat welled in my chest and I clasped the back of his head, pulling him into a deeper kiss, which was over way too fast.

Aaron jumped up and made his way to the foot of the ladder. He stood in the moonlight facing me. I shrank in the darkness, trying to remain as concealed as possible. He was magnificent standing there. The sixteen-year-old Aaron was shorter and thinner, but it was unmistakably him. His hair was different, much longer, but in so many ways, he looked exactly the same as the Aaron I knew. His shoulders were already very broad and his body was toned from tennis. Even in the dim light, I could see the familiar warm friendly glow of his smile. A sly grin spread across his face and he abruptly turned and ran out of the barn.

I contemplated climbing the ladder to watch Aaron in his moment of triumph, but I was delirious, and I collapsed back on the hay. I fell back, and the ground disappeared. I was falling back into the present, still feverish from my experience.

Back in my bed, I laid still, replaying the kiss in my mind. I licked my tingling lips and could still taste him. I crossed my arms across my chest as if I was still embracing Aaron. As I relived every delicious detail, anxiety slowly began to surface from the back of my mind and I wondered, while I was kissing Aaron, who had *he* been kissing? It certainly wasn't me. He wouldn't even meet me for another three years.

My pulse quickened and I felt my face getting hot again. This time it wasn't because I was embarrassed or yearning, it was something else...I was *jealous*. I was jealous of the girl that Aaron thought he was kissing in the barn all those years ago.

I wondered though, why hadn't he known the difference? If she was someone he knew intimately then surely he would have realized that the body pressed against him, the hands that pulled him close, and the lips that had surrendered so easily were unfamiliar. No, he must not have known her well, I rationalized. She was probably just a summer fling, a camp romance.

I wanted to get up, sit at my desk, and write all the details of my journey in my journal. However, I was just too tired to move and too content to do anything but savor the moment. The last thing I managed to do before sleep took over my body, was glance at my bedside clock. As I drifted off to sleep, I noted that, as before, only a few minutes had passed.

—ℓℓ—

I vowed not to let what happened with Aaron in the barn permeate into the present. I convinced myself that I would go to the library and everything would be normal. However, despite how hard I tried, I couldn't stop staring at his lips while he spoke. I had never noticed how full they were, even when they spread into his Elvis smirk, which they seemed to be doing *a lot*.

It was almost like he was trying to draw my attention to his mouth, and the thought of our kiss kept flashing in my mind. I tried to keep focused on the conversation, but all I could think about was what it would be like to kiss him again. I desperately wanted to ask him about that night at summer camp, just to see if he would offer any new details. I doubted it though, he had never once told me about past romances, and I had never asked.

"Did that ever happen to you?" I heard Aaron ask, but I had no idea what he was talking about. I realized that I had not been listening for some time.

"Aaron, I think I need to start reading up for Microbiology class," I said, totally blowing off his question.

"Oh, OK...really?"

"Yeah, I've heard it's a tough class and I want to get a jump on it before the semester starts." I opened the textbook that I had only really brought for a prop because I never actually ended up studying during our evenings together.

"Well, OK, that's probably a good idea then," he sounded disappointed.

I plugged in my earphones and turned up the music, but I realized pretty quickly that I wasn't going to be able to study either. Oh well, I thought, at least I wasn't obsessing about his lips anymore.

I was finally starting to make some sense out of the page I had been staring at for half an hour when I heard a faint ringing over the steady rhythm of the music blaring in my ears. I looked up to see Aaron answer his cell phone. He glanced at me, then stood up and crossed the room. He kept glancing in my direction, and I tried to pretend I wasn't paying attention. He was animated and clearly arguing with someone. Stealthily, I turned my music off and strained to listen in. I would have been able to hear a lot better without the earphones, but removing them would have been too obvious.

After a few moments, he returned to our table. He was definitely upset and I wondered if I should pry. Well, we were friends, weren't we?

"Everything OK?" I asked nonchalantly, pulling out my earbuds.

He hesitated and then looked up at me. His eyes were sad. He started to speak then stopped as if he was conflicted about answering me. It was so strange. Aaron was normally so happy-go-lucky. I didn't like seeing him disturbed like this and I was desperate to know what was wrong, but I didn't want to push him. So I just sat quietly, waiting for him to come around. Finally, he looked up and forced a smile.

"Sorry to be such a buzz kill," he said, trying to sound upbeat.

"It's no problem. I just hope it's nothing serious."

"No, just a little trouble at home...nothing major. So, how's the Microbiology?" he said making it clear that the subject was dropped.

I was annoyed that he hadn't confided in me, but I had no right to be. Wasn't I keeping all kinds of secrets from him? Plus, it wasn't like we were anything but casual friends anyway.

The rest of the evening dragged on uncomfortably. Although Aaron put on a happy face and tried to be congenial, I could tell he was worried about something. As for me, I had put an honest effort into trying to study, but my heart wasn't in it.

We walked home together after his shift was over, both of us distracted by very different things. We separated at the division between Holden and Murdoch. Usually, Aaron ended the evening by asking if we would get together the next day, but this time he only said "Good night."

I moped in my room. I was dying to know what that phone call had been about. I considered trying to go back to that moment in the library. I thought maybe I could think of a better way to handle the situation. Maybe there was something different I could have said that would have made him open up to me. I pondered the possibilities but decided against it. For one, I couldn't think of what else I would say to him, without feeling that I was pressuring him.

I rationalized that since I was already depressed, now was the time to visit the memory of Aaron's grandfather's funeral. I had seriously debated whether I really wanted to see it. I didn't want to do it out of morbid curiosity. It's just that Franklin James had been so important to Aaron that I felt that I could learn so much about Aaron and his family by experiencing the event for myself.

This trip provided a bit of a wardrobe concern though. I didn't own any clothes that were appropriate for a memorial service. I perused Taylor's section of the closet and found something that would pass. It was more of a cocktail dress, but at least it was the right color and it fit me perfectly. My real dilemma was the shoes. I doubted that I would be able to walk in any of Taylor's ridiculously high heels, which were at least one size larger than my feet. So, that left my limited selection of flip-flops or clogs. I settled on my least shabby pair of black clogs. My plan was to just get into the church, make it to a pew, and sit down in the back as quickly as possible.

— ℓℓ —

As soon as I arrived, I knew I had forgotten one very important thing... a coat. I was freezing! I didn't remember Aaron mentioning that it had been so cold. Although it was May, it was ridiculously chilly. I was alone in a wooded area just by the church. I could see people funneling in and I made my way over to the crowd. By the time I reached the church, I was shivering and I noticed that a few people were giving me funny looks. I could not get inside fast enough.

The warmth of the vestibule was a comforting relief. Several easels holding photos of Frank lined the foyer and people were milling around, chatting about him in hushed tones. I could see grainy barely distinguishable photos of him as a boy, formal photos of him in uniform, wedding pictures, and many pictures of him with his grandchildren. His whole life was on display. I wondered if that was all a life amounted to in the end, just a collection of random snapshots.

I went from easel to easel studying the photos, trying to imagine all the things this man had experienced in his eighty years. There were so many pictures of him surrounded by family. I could easily pick out Aaron in the photos, and he was in many. There was Frank pushing Aaron on a tricycle, Aaron sitting on Frank's lap reading a story, the two of them playing catch... so many happy memories. I had never known my mother's parents and there was only a grandfather that I barely knew on my dad's side. Looking at the photos of Frank's big happy family made me feel very alone in the world.

I made my way through the crowd and into the chapel. It was crowded, but I found a seat in a relatively empty pew in the back. This was the first time I had been around so many people during one of my 'trips'. I felt like such a trespasser and kept worrying that somehow I would be found out. However, I took in everything, and although I felt the exhilaration of accomplishment that I always felt after successfully traveling back, it was dampened by the somberness of the occasion.

I strained my neck to look for Aaron and his family. I guessed they would be seated near the front, but the room was so crowded it was hard to see. There were easily a hundred people in the small chapel and there was still a steady stream coming in. The church was beautiful. While it was true that I had not spent much time in churches, I had toured many cathedrals throughout Europe. This wasn't anything like those. Cathedrals had their own grand, gothic beauty, but this church was warm and homey.

Ornate stained-glass windows lined the walls. Similar to the cathedrals I had seen, these windows depicted different scenes from the bible, although it seemed there were many more from the New Testament here. The pinnacle was a large window at the far end of the church beyond the pulpit, just above the choir loft. The scene was of Jesus sitting on a rock in a garden, surrounded by children and sheep. I was glad it was a nice, pleasant picture. So often, the depictions were of unpleasant scenes that I found more scary than spiritually comforting.

Lining the front of the pulpit were more flower arrangements than I had ever seen in my life, from wreaths on easels with sashes that said, "Anchors away!" to more somber-looking bouquets in beautiful vases. There were so many flowers their aroma made it all the way to the back where I sat.

Looking through the crowd, I noticed several older men in military uniforms, which made me very curious as to why Frank had not had a military funeral. As a former soldier, especially one who had been a war hero and a P.O.W., Franklin James would have been entitled to the full military honors, including a canon salute, a bugler playing taps, and burial in a military cemetery.

He had also been cremated, which was surprising to me. I could see that instead of a coffin, there was a beautiful urn set atop a podium at the front of the church. There was a large picture of a younger Frank beside it, and something else. I strained to see what it was. It looked like a small box, but I couldn't make it out. My best guess was that it was a box containing Frank's military medals.

As the last people found seats, the organist started to play louder. The tune was a requiem that I recognized. The hushed conversations faded to silence as the doors at the back of the church opened and in walked Aaron's family. His father was first, followed by Aaron's mother holding Aaron by the hand. The rest of his brothers followed with a few other family members I did not recognize. They walked down the long aisle slowly as if on a death march.

I found the scene utterly disturbing. Why should a grieving family be made to walk in like this under the full inspection of so many onlookers? It seemed voyeuristic and distasteful. It was the stark opposite of the wedding parties that invariably marched down this same aisle all the time. People full of happiness headed toward their future, and people full of grief headed to mourn their past.

After an agonizing eternity, the family made it to the front pew. Now I could only see the backs of their heads, but it was obvious why Aaron had been the one holding his mother's hand. He was upset and crying. I could see his head bobbing up and down and his mother dabbing him with tissue.

My heart broke for him. He loved his grandfather so much, and it couldn't be easy for a ten-year-old boy to display his emotions in front of so many people. The requiem finished and the pastor rose to the pulpit. He said a few words of welcome, then delivered a brief sermon on the frailty of life and reassured us that Frank was in a better place. I hoped he was right.

Next to speak was Aaron's father. He was reverent but not sorrowful. He shared joyful memories of his childhood and said that he could not have had a better father. Aaron's grandmother had died a decade before and since then Frank had lived at Aaron's house. So ten-year-old Aaron had lived with his granddad his whole life. Frank had been like a second father to all the boys, and Aaron's father thanked him for helping to raise his sons. The deep love and regard he held for his father was so apparent.

I thought of what I might say at my father's funeral one day. It was sad to think about him dying, but it was even sadder to realize that I would not have these kinds of things to say. To be quite honest I felt like I hardly knew the man. I silently promised myself I would try harder to forge a real relationship with him before it was too late.

The stories continued, told by the people who knew Frank best. I had already heard many of these stories from Aaron, like how Frank had led a failed escape from the prison camp in which he had been held. This attempt had nearly cost him his life, but his spirit was never crushed. In fact, he kept up the morale in the camp by always managing a smile whenever he saw another prisoner, even when he was in severe distress. This story was told by a fellow P.O.W. who had traveled all the way from Maine to attend Frank's memorial service.

It was amazing to hear the story told by someone who was actually there. There were other stories I hadn't heard, like how Frank volunteered every Saturday at the homeless shelter in downtown Houston, which could be a rough place, but he never missed a day. He had made a special effort to spend time with the veterans who had found themselves homeless, and it was one of them who shared this story with us, during which there was not a dry eye in the house.

Frank's was the first funeral to which I had ever been. I had never actually experienced this kind of loss in my own life, but as I listened to the eulogies, I couldn't help but think about the brother I'd never known. He must have had a funeral. Could I have been there and not remember it? It struck me that I didn't even know where he was buried. These thoughts consumed me and I found myself truly mourning. I wasn't mourning for Frank, but for my brother and the life he never got to live, for the pain my parents must have suffered, and even for myself... so alone in the world.

"Hun, it's going to be all right," I heard someone whisper.

An old woman sitting in the pew in front of me had turned around to offer a tissue, which I gladly accepted. There were so many things I needed to know about my brother. I had to find some way to talk to my mother about him. I sat through the rest of the ceremony reflecting on the divergent paths a life can take and the impact we can make on others. Frank had never made an amazing scientific discovery, but he had touched so many people's lives and his contributions had been truly significant.

After all the speakers were finished, the pastor led a prayer, and then the organist began playing again. The tune was different this time, more hopeful. As if on cue, the family rose and began their slow ascent back up the aisle. As they got closer, I could see that Aaron's face was red, puffy, and streaked with tears. He clung to his mother and looked down.

As soon as the family had exited the chapel, the extended family made their way into the aisle, and then others followed in a well-choreographed order, emptying from the pews at the front of the church first. Since I was in the very back, I would be one of the last out. I didn't mind though, it was interesting to watch the parade of diverse people walking past me.

Suddenly, I spotted a flash of red hair entering the aisle. It disappeared momentarily, but then she was in full view and I immediately knew it was the little red-haired girl I had seen after the bike accident. Of course, she was older, but there was no mistaking her. It was as if she sensed my realization because, at that exact moment, she looked up and locked eyes with me. She was quite striking. She had these large unusual gray eyes. Her face was dotted with freckles and her long curls were the most intense shade of blazing red I had ever seen.

The girl was walking with a woman that I took to be her mother, but as soon as she saw me, she stopped dead. It was so sudden that the person walking behind almost fell over her. Her mother, who was now several steps ahead, stopped and went back. The girl was staring at me with the strangest expression, and I couldn't tear my eyes away from hers. The line of people was now completely stopped behind the girl and those who had been in front of her were exiting the church, leaving a large gap halfway down the aisle. Everyone else still seated was trying to figure out what the holdup was all about. The girl's mother crouched down imploring her to move. She kept asking her what was wrong. Then the girl began to raise her arm, very slowly as if in a trance. She raised it level with her shoulder and outstretched her pointer figure directly at me!

I didn't know what to do! There were still a lot of people in the rows in front of me and I ducked my head behind them. Everyone was starting to turn around, trying to figure out to what or who she was pointing. The girl just stood there silently and perfectly still, pointing at me.

Her mother was becoming very agitated and demanded to know what the problem was. I quickly weighed my options. I could either wait for her to call me out, or I could make a run for it. Either option was going to call attention, but I thought that if I could just get to the woods quickly, perhaps I could get back without causing too much of a stir.

I stood up, preparing to run, and heard several loud gasps. Fear and adrenaline surged through me and my eyes darted back to the girl. She was on the ground! People were rushing over, surrounding her. There were shouts and confusion, people who had exited the chapel were now running back in.

I moved to get a less obstructed view and saw the girl jerking on the ground in convulsions! Her gray eyes had rolled back and all you could see was white where her irises should be. Her hair was wild and her dress was completely disheveled. Her mother was frantic and people were running back and forth from the chapel. Someone was yelling to call an ambulance.

I had to get out! I ran up the aisle to the chapel door. I flung it open and crashed full force into a man wearing Navy blues who was rushing in. I murmured an apology and shoved past him. I kept my head down, not even trying to find Aaron.

As soon as I made it out of the vestibule, I sprinted towards the woods without looking back. It was drizzling and even colder than before. I made it to the tree line and crouched behind a large oak. I was out of breath and felt like I was hyperventilating.

This was all wrong! Aaron certainly had never mentioned *that* happening, I thought frantically. If it had happened before wouldn't he have mentioned it?! I held my head in my hands and tried to collect myself. I needed to focus to get back, but all I could think about was that girl convulsing on the floor, eyes rolling back.

Was she dying? I wondered, looking quickly back towards the church. Why was she pointing at me like that? Had *I* somehow done that to her? I had to focus! I pictured my room, eyes closed tight. I blocked out every other thought. The last thing I heard before falling through the tunnel was the ambulance siren.

Chapter 6

DECEIT AND RETRIBUTION

I was wet and shivering uncontrollably. I hugged my knees to warm myself and stop the tremors, but after fifteen minutes, I realized that I wasn't shaking from the cold anymore...it was the horrid image of the young girl's convulsing body. I tried to clear her face from my mind, but I could not stop thinking that *I* caused it to happen.

She had pointed at me, right at me. Then those terrible convulsions ... I was so tired, but I managed to stand up and take off Taylor's dress. It was dripping wet, and I hoped it wasn't ruined. I carefully hung it on the shower rail and stumbled into bed. I was suddenly thankful for the fact that my trips into the past were so exhausting because even though I was consumed with guilt and worry, I could not keep my eyes open. I quickly melted into a blissfully dreamless sleep.

I woke up the next morning full of anxiety. I spent the better part of the day trying to think through what had happened. I transcribed all the details I could remember. I tried to understand how I could have possibly caused the girl's attack. Nothing like that had ever happened before during my 'travels'.

One thing was for sure though...the same girl had seen me twice, in two different memories. I wondered if the shock of seeing me again had sent her into some kind of fit. I had to talk to Aaron and find out what happened to her after I left. I needed to know if she was all right. I wasn't sure how I would bring it up, but I had to find out.

Although I didn't have any answers about the girl yet, writing in my notebook forced me to do some serious soul-searching. It was New Year's Eve and I decided to make two resolutions. First, I was going to give people more of a chance. If there was one thing I had learned from my journeys, it was that people weren't the open book I had always assumed them to be. I had been surprised to learn the depths of Frank's, Taylor's, and even my own mother's character and experiences. Frank had changed people's lives, not by closing himself off, but by reaching out and getting to know people, and allowing them to know him.

My second resolution was to stop visiting Aaron's memories. I didn't understand what had happened to the little red-headed girl, but I knew that I didn't want to risk interfering with Aaron's past, present, or future any more than I already had. I was only beginning to learn what I could do with my ability and I had no idea what repercussions any of my actions might have. I didn't want to use Aaron's life as an experiment anymore.

I was just going to have to get to know him the old-fashioned way. The thought of it was exciting and I felt a little melancholy that my alone time with Aaron was coming to an end. The holiday break was almost over. That meant no more long evenings alone, talking in the library. Taylor would be back soon, and it would be back to the grind of classes and studying. Although...who was to say that I couldn't study with Aaron? He would probably be a little busier once there were people in the library again, but I was sure we could still manage some time together. Of course, he would have tennis practices and tournaments away, but I was convinced that we both wanted our relationship to continue.

I decided I would take Aaron some dinner. The library was closing early, and we had discussed walking over to the observatory where we could see the fireworks display happening out at the lake. The evening couldn't come fast enough. By 5:00 pm I was already headed over to the library, take-out

Thai food in hand. I was desperate to talk to Aaron and find out what happened to the little girl. I just had to figure out a way to bring up Frank's funeral without putting a damper on the whole evening.

I walked through the big double doors and straight over to the check-out desk. I didn't see a soul and assumed Aaron must be somewhere in the stacks. I started unpacking the food and heard an unfamiliar voice behind me.

"Hey! Miss! You can't have food in here."

I turned to see an older man wearing glasses that were perched on the tip of his nose. He looked very stern and was shaking his bony finger at me. I scanned the lobby desperately for Aaron.

"Uh...I know. I was just bringing dinner to a friend who works here." I tentatively admitted, not wanting to get Aaron in trouble.

"Oh really? Who's your friend?" he demanded.

Well, there's no way out of it, I thought. Seriously though, how much trouble could we get into for having food in the library? We had only done it every single night of break!

"Aaron James." I gave him my saddest 'pity me' eyes, throwing in a little pout for effect.

"Well, Aaron's not on tonight. He had some family business to take care of, and now *I'm* here." He was clearly not happy about this latter fact.

Suddenly I remembered the odd phone call Aaron had received. I had completely forgotten about it until that moment.

"Do you want some Thai food?" I asked the man, smiling sweetly.

As I headed back to the dorm, I tried Aaron on his cell but he didn't pick up. I hoped it was nothing serious. Just as the fact that I would have to spend New Year's Eve alone was beginning to sink in, I got back to my room and saw that the door was cracked open. I was debating whether to call security when I heard Taylor's voice! She wasn't supposed to be back for another two days. I scrambled to remember if I had left any incriminating evidence lying around. I was fairly sure I had locked my journals up in the desk drawer, as I did every time I left the room, and I knew I had put her dress back in the closet.

Peeking through the crack, I could see her unpacking her suitcase. She was talking to someone on the phone. Trying not to disturb her conversation, I edged in and quietly started unpacking the now-cold food.

"I told you I would!" she said before hanging up the phone and tossing it on the bed. She still had not seen me and I didn't want her to think I was eavesdropping, so I softly cleared my throat.

"Evan, oh...hi," she said sitting up. She seemed upset and I felt bad for disturbing her.

"Hi Taylor, you're home early. Um...how was your holiday?" I mentally scolded myself for being so bad in uncomfortable situations.

"Not the best," she said.

OK Evan, remember your resolution...be more understanding and open up to people, especially Taylor, I thought.

"Oh, I'm sorry. Is that why you're back?" It was a good start.

"Yeah, I had to get out of Houston. My parents were driving me absolutely crazy!"

"That's why I sent mine to Guam," I said and smiled warmly at her. She managed to return a faint smile. "Are you hungry? I have tons of Thai here."

"Actually, I'm starving. I drove all the way home without stopping to eat unless you count the entire bag of beef jerky I wolfed down between Odessa and here. Well, the diet resolution doesn't start until tomorrow." She shrugged. Same old Taylor I thought.

"Wow, Evan! You got all this food for yourself? How much can you eat?" She asked, loading a plate.

"I knew places would be closed tomorrow so I got extra," I lied.

We ate and casually chatted about inconsequential things like the weather and her drive. It was easily the most time Taylor and I had ever spent talking. Then I remembered her gift. I jumped up and retrieved the compact case from my dresser drawer.

"I didn't have time to wrap it, because you came home so early, but I saw it and thought of you. You can put your favorite powder in it, see." I pressed the clasp and opened the case for her.

I did not expect her reaction. She held the case cradled in her cupped hands, just staring at it. I wasn't sure what to think. Maybe she hated it or thought it was silly. It looked like she might cry. I didn't know what to do or say. I was no good with emotion.

"Evan, I love it. It is one of the nicest things anyone has ever given me." It was a little melodramatic, but the sentiment was genuine.

"Taylor, if there's something wrong, you can tell me you know." I really did want to help her.

"Thanks, Evan. That's so...unlike you." I winced at her blunt honesty.

"Well, you're not the only one with a New Year's resolution," I said quietly, my face heating up. "Mine is to be nicer to people." I thought of how rude I had been to her that night before finals. "I know I can be a real bitch." I stared down at my food. Emotional declarations were not my forte, and I guessed this little scene was just as awkward for her as it was for me. "I just want you to know that I don't mean to be, I just get so wrapped up in myself sometimes."

I glanced up just long enough to see that her mouth was actually agape. Just then, Taylor's phone rang, thankfully rescuing us from any further discomfort.

I went into the bathroom to give her some privacy and when I came out, she was all bubbly and smiles.

"I think we both need some fun tonight. That was McKenna. There's a big New Year's Eve party tonight at the sorority house and we're *both* going."

It sounded like something I definitely did not want to do. "I don't think so. Actually, I have plans..." Well, I *did* have plans, and Taylor didn't need to know they fell through.

"What plans?" she demanded. "To watch the ball drop in Times Square on a 'Rockin' New Year's Eve'? No Evan, you spent Christmas alone and I'm not going to let you spend New Year's alone too!" She was definite. Then she added the guilt. "Plus if you're not going, I'm not. And since you're trying to be nicer to people..." A wry smile crossed her face and I instantly regretted my declaration.

"Well, I can't go, I have nothing to wear." I made a feeble last attempt.

"We're about the same size, you can wear something of mine!" I knew that was coming.

"I'm going to give you a whole makeover...clothes, hair and makeup! This is going to be sooo much fun!" She was almost giddy.

"Sounds more like torture than fun to me," I snapped. She rolled her eyes and headed to her closet.

"So let's see... something fun and flirty..." she was fingering some bright pink abomination. I could not let her get too carried away.

"What about that black dress? It looks like it would fit." I pointed to the dress I had placed back in the closet just a few hours ago. I prayed it was completely dry, and hadn't shrunk.

"What this?" She pulled out the dress and examined it. "Well, it doesn't really scream wild and crazy, but I guess it could do. We'll just have to dress it up with the right accessories."

Accessories? This was turning into a nightmare!

Taylor chose a slinky, spaghetti-strap mini-dress for herself. It was covered in silver sequins and was gorgeous, what little there was of it anyway. Once she was ready, she turned her attention to me. She looked me up and down, critically inspecting every inch.

"So...uh did you want to shower then?"

"I *had* a shower today, thank you." I was feeling extremely self-conscious under her gaze.

"Well, those sweats look like they haven't seen a wash in days."

"I would appreciate it if you didn't insult my hygiene habits. Both my clothes and body are perfectly clean."

She snorted and went into the bathroom. I could hear her rummaging through drawers and cabinets and she finally emerged with an arm full of beauty products. "OK, at least go wash your hair," she demanded.

I marched off to the bathroom like a child being sent to timeout. When I returned with a towel wrapped around my head, the place had been transformed into a salon! The dress was hanging on the doorframe, with jewelry, belts, and shoes laid out on the floor beneath it. She had various small appliances plugged in and heating up where the coffee maker normally sat. Make-up and hair products were spread all over the desk.

"What on earth?" I was in awe.

"Sit down" she demanded pulling out the desk chair.

"I can't believe I'm going to let you do this," I said.

"Just shut up and sit back. Let me work my magic. You won't even recognize yourself when I'm done."

"That's what I'm afraid of." I squeezed my eyes shut as she came at me with a pair of tweezers.

Taylor plucked, pinched, and prodded my face using instruments I had never even seen before. She applied makeup to places I didn't even realize it was supposed to go. All the while, she jabbered on about skin tones, definition, and color palettes. She said I was a Fall and spent a long time considering the perfect shades to accentuate my eyes, which she observed were my best feature. She scolded me for not having a better skin-care regime and I promised to do better.

Once the makeup was applied, she made me put on the dress before starting on my hair, so it wouldn't get messed up. I stripped off my clothes and she helped me get into the dress without letting it rub against my face. It was all way too complicated, I thought.

"Evan, what I could do if I had your body...and those amazing eyes..." Taylor lamented.

"What are talking about? You're beautiful!"

"Not like you are."

I was shocked! Taylor was the envy of every girl and the fantasy of every guy who laid eyes on her, and she was jealous of me? "You're crazy, or blind," I said.

She just sighed and turned her attention to my hair. She unwrapped it from the towel and combed it out. It reminded me of grade school. I always had long hair and during carpet time, the other girls would sit behind me and play with it. I had always found that relaxing. This wasn't all bad I thought as Taylor dried my hair. It was like having the most popular girl in school suddenly become your best friend.

"You know your hair is so beautiful. It really is a perfect shade of auburn and even has natural waves. It's a sin to wear it up in a ponytail every day."

"It takes too long to blow dry," I explained.

"Evan, there are girls who would kill to have half of your natural beauty and you just waste it. You're so weird."

In the end, she didn't end up using much product at all on my hair. I thought she might straighten it with a flat iron like she did her own, but she said the soft waves were prettier. She stood me up and walked me over to the mirror. She was right, I hardly recognized myself! Standing there next to Taylor I didn't look like the ugly stepsister I had always imagined myself to be, I glowed.

"I look...." I couldn't find the words.

"Amazing" she finished.

I had to admit that although I had always found all the primping Taylor went through a silly waste of time, the results were amazing!

"It's just because of you...the make-up and dress." I couldn't help but turn this way and that, looking at myself from every angle.

"I only brought out what was already there, buried under dirty sweats."

"They weren't dirty!"

As Taylor finished getting ready, I phoned Aaron again. There was still no answer and the phone went straight to his voicemail. This time I decided to leave a message.

"Hey, it's Evan." My voice was all high and girly, I hated leaving messages. I dropped it an octave and continued. "I couldn't find you in the library tonight. I hope everything is OK. So, Taylor's back and she's forcing me to go to a party at the Sorority house with her. Not really my thing, but she won't take no for an answer. Anyway, give me a call when you can."

Taylor emerged from the bathroom looking radiant and announced that it was time to go. I slipped on the black clogs that I had worn with her dress before and she nearly bit my head off.

"What do you think you are doing? Are you intentionally trying to sabotage all my hard work? Please put on some shoes that aren't completely ridiculous."

"These shoes aren't ridiculous, they're comfortable and they're the best I have."

"Comfort has no place in beauty or fashion. I can't be seen with you in those shoes, so you're just going to have to wear some of mine." She strode over to the closet again and started pulling out boxes.

"We *have* to take you shopping," she said, then lined up several pairs of potentials. I chose the least intimidating, a plain pair of black boots with small silver buckles. I put on my thickest pair of socks to help them stay on.

"Taylor, I'm going to fall and break my neck in these heels," I warned.

"You'll be fine, but if you do fall, try not to mess up my dress," she said sarcastically.

After I was properly accessorized, we took off. We took Taylor's car, thank God because I couldn't have made it a block in those boots. Within ten minutes, they were already killing my feet.

I checked my phone and saw Taylor doing the same. I still wasn't sure why she'd been so upset before, but she was obviously just as disappointed by the lack of new messages as I was.

"So, you never told me what you did over Christmas break. Did you spend the whole time studying?" Taylor asked, making conversation as she drove.

I debated my answer for a few moments, and then said, "Actually, I spent a lot of time with Aaron James." For some reason, I felt almost scared to say the words, and my eyes were glued to Taylor's face nervously awaiting her reaction.

"Oh, you know Aaron?" Her interest was piqued, but she kept her eyes on the road. I tried to judge the tone of her voice. Was it indifference, curiosity...jealousy?

"Well, just... we were both stuck here over break... and we kind of hung out."

"Isn't he a sweetie?" Her tone seemed innocuous enough.

"Uh, yeah... he's very nice, I guess." I needed more information! "So, he tells me you two have known each other for years. Do you ever hang out anymore?" I casually inquired.

She sighed and said, "Yeah, I've known him since we were kids. Aaron and his dad taught me how to play tennis. After lessons, we used to have a blast sneaking around the club. We would play 'undercover agents' and pretend we were solving heinous crimes that had been committed by the members." She giggled thinking about it. "I haven't seen him much since I've been at Harper, seems like we just don't travel in the same circles anymore. He has asked me to play tennis with him though, I should make some time for that..." her voice drifted off.

I wasn't ready to drop the subject. "So, um you guys never..." I wasn't sure how to put it so I just let the words hang there. I willed her mouth to say "no."

Taylor's head spun around and she looked at me incredulously. "Me and Aaron? No!" she gasped.

I had not expected *that* kind of response. "Well, why not? He seems nice enough." I pried.

"Yeah, he's awesome *and* hot, but completely attached. He's been hopelessly devoted to Becky Hammond ever since we were little." She shook her head slowly. "What a waste."

I felt like Taylor had just punched me in the gut. It was impossible! I *knew* him. In some ways, I knew more about him than anyone. There was no way he could be 'hopelessly devoted' to someone. Who the hell was Becky Hammond?

Then, for some unknown reason, I realized that I had known the answer before the question had even formed in my mind. I swallowed hard. "Striking red hair and freckles...?" I murmured aloud, afraid of the answer.

"Oh, you've met her, then?" Taylor was puzzled. "I didn't know she made it to Blythe very often. Was she here for the holidays?"

There were a million more questions I wanted to ask Taylor, but we had just pulled up to the sorority house and besides, part of me didn't want to know any more anyway. I was dazed as we walked in and made our way through the crowd. I was so angry. He hadn't lied or anything, but an omission like that was just as bad. He had totally misrepresented himself. He had led me on. I knew I had been stupid to let my guard down...to care about him. It was just like before... I felt like I would cry, which made me even madder. I hated feeling weak and pitiful.

—ℓℓ—

Taylor was leading me around the room, introducing me to all her friends. Although I recognized most of them I had hardly spoken to any of them, and I didn't want to now...not in the mood I was in. Then Taylor spotted McKenna. The two of them screamed and hugged like it had been years since they last saw each other.

"Oh hi Lane," McKenna said. Then she did a double take, looking me up and down, and said, "Wow you look...different. Did you do this, Taylor?"

"Guilty," Taylor said, grinning from ear to ear. She was thrilled to have her work appreciated.

McKenna didn't linger, she grabbed Taylor's arm and dragged her away to fill her in on some urgent piece of gossip. Taylor glanced back at me and mouthed "Sorry." I didn't care though, I wanted to be alone. I wanted to go home and curl up in bed. I wanted to throw a glass against the wall. I wanted to slap Aaron James in the face. I wanted to do many things, none of which included partying. I didn't have a car and the sorority house was miles away from campus. So, I did the only thing I could think of to get rid of the horrible acidic feeling in my gut. I drank.

I was not a drinker and had a very low tolerance, but I didn't care about anything right then. I just wanted to escape. I went straight over to the bar being manned by some goofy-looking frat boy in a lei and grass hula skirt.

"What'll ya have?" he ogled me, making me feel very uncomfortable.

"Whatever's the strongest," I said.

He started pouring several different liquors into a blender, then added some fruit for good measure.

"Try this. It's called a zombie maker. After a couple of these, you'll be toast."

"Toast sounds good," I said as I took the glass.

"Wait a minute. You are twenty-one, right?" His hand was still firmly around the glass. I rolled my eyes, and he just laughed, stroking my fingers before finally releasing the drink.

I scanned the large 'great' room but didn't see Taylor. I wondered how long she would want to stay. I found a window seat in the most inconspicuous corner of the room, but the place was packed and I soon realized that Taylor's makeover had been a little too good. I was being assailed by frat boys. I tried to be polite at first, but as I consumed more and more alcohol, my tone grew ruder. I was in no mood for flirting.

The one good thing about all the attention was that I didn't have to go to the bar to replace my drink. Guys were offering beverages left and right. I knew it was a bad idea to keep drinking, but I was beyond logic or reason. The closer it got to midnight, the more people poured in. The house was crowded and stuffy, and Taylor was still nowhere to be found. I hadn't seen her since we first arrived and I was *so* ready to go.

Finally, I could not bear the inane prattle of the guy sitting next to me any longer. Without a word, I got up and walked out to the patio. I walked past the gazebo on the veranda, which had become the makeshift smoking section, and out into the yard. I stumbled twice and almost fell before steadying myself against a lattice. Between the alcohol and the high heels, I knew there was no way I was going to be able to stay vertical for very long.

I gazed up at the house. It was a big white Victorian, complete with columns and ivy growing up the sides. It reminded me of my dollhouse, and just like my dollhouse this one was full of fake plastic people, I mused.

Alone in the cool air, I tried to clear my mind, but it was lost in a drunken fog. I had only been drunk one other time, and that had resulted in disastrous consequences. I had hoped that the alcohol would deaden my senses enough that I didn't have to feel the pain of Aaron's betrayal, but it hadn't. The pain was dull but throbbed and taunted me. Well, at least I knew the little redheaded girl was OK, I laughed aloud to myself.

Suddenly, someone came up from behind and grabbed me around the waist. I spun around, my hand raised ready to slap them. At the same time, I heard Aaron's voice.

"Wow, you look amazing!"

It took my alcohol-soaked brain a few moments to process everything. Then I *did* slap him... hard.

"What was *that* for?" his eyes were wide and he was holding his cheek.

"That's for Becky Hammond! I thought she might want me to do it" I spit the words at him.

"Taylor."

"Yes, Taylor did happen to mention how you had been *devoted* to her your whole life." I tried to stand straight, but I could feel my body sway and hear my words slur.

"I was afraid this would happen. I wanted to tell you before Taylor got back. I thought I had a few days left, but I *was* going to tell you."

"Look, it doesn't matter anyway. We only met a week ago. We're barely even friends." I couldn't look him in the eyes.

"I think we both know that's not true," he said in a soft, breathy tone.

Then I did look up into his eyes and they were inches from my face. He leaned in to kiss me and I felt the familiar electric charge run through my whole body. I was so angry with him but the pull towards him was out of my control, a force of nature I could not stop. I thought of the barn and ached to feel his lips on mine again. I closed my eyes and felt his lips touch mine ever so gently, barely grazing the tips. His mouth was open slightly and his breath was warm and urgent. The kiss started soft, hesitant, and exploring, but the heat was quickly building. Then the fire was consuming both of us and the kiss could not be hard or deep enough.

It was as if the whole world had imploded until there was nothing left but he and I locked together. But there *was* something else, someone else, and I began to see her face through the haze of lust and alcohol. I saw her on the ground, helpless. It took all my strength to break away from his kiss, but I pushed his chest as hard as I could.

"Evan, I'm sorry," he said.

"I just want to find Taylor and go home," I said. I started to walk and stumbled again. This time Aaron reached out and steadied me.

"Look, just sit here and I'll go find her. You're in no condition to be wandering around." He tried to take my hand, but I yanked it away. Instead, he motioned to a low wall that bordered the veranda. I sat and he bounded off into the house. I had so many thoughts and feelings running through my mind, but I was too drunk to fully comprehend any of them. I was also starting to feel sick and thought I might throw up.

I heard the crowd in the house now counting down in unison and I knew it must be midnight. I wondered if I could see the fireworks and leaned back too fast. I fell backward onto the ground with my legs still up on the wall. Aaron reappeared then, looking down at me.

"Problem?" he mused.

I was furious at him and this did not help. I struggled to get to my feet, ripping both the dress and my skin on the concrete wall.

"Whoa...let me help you." Aaron attempted to lift me, but I fought him, trying to keep my balance at the same time.

"Where's Taylor?" I demanded.

"I couldn't find her. I looked everywhere. McKenna said she disappeared with some guy right before midnight. So I'm taking you home, come on."

"No, absolutely not!" I refused.

"So what, you're going to walk? You can barely stand up."

"I'm sure I can find a helpful guy inside willing to take me home." I wanted the words to sting.

He glared at me and I could tell I had gotten to him. Then without saying a word, he walked over and picked me up, like a groom carrying his bride over the threshold. I struggled, kicking my legs and trying to slap him again.

"Stop it, Evan! Be reasonable, you know you need to get home and you can't trust some drunken frat boy to do it."

"Oh, and I can trust *you*?" I snapped. I stopped struggling though. I was furious at Aaron, but I knew he was right. I let him carry me through the house and out the front door to his car. People cheered as we walked through the crowded house, thinking they were witnessing some incredibly romantic gesture. I crossed my arms and locked my jaw, trying to convey my misery.

It was the first time I had ridden in Aaron's car, and he was right, it was pretty much a piece of crap, especially in comparison to Taylor's Beamer. Still, I didn't want to throw up in it so I stared at the streetlights trying to slow the spinning in my head.

"Evan, I really need to talk to you about...Becky." There was something about the tone of his voice when he said her name. There was a familiarity, a tenderness, that I hated.

"Not now." I squeaked out. I couldn't concentrate on not throwing up *and* pay attention to what he was saying. We drove the rest of the way in silence and luckily, I was able to keep down the contents of my stomach. When we got to the dorms, Aaron agonized about how to get me to my room. I slurred something about doing it on my own, which clearly was not realistic. The problem was that it was well after hours and technically, he was not allowed to be on the Holden side. Moreover, there was the fact that I was smashed, which was also against the rules.

Aaron left me outside while he went to check out the situation. Within a few minutes, he was back, sweeping me up into his arms again. He had sweet-talked the RA into letting him take me to my room and into overlooking 'my condition'. He carried me to the elevator and up to my room. He had to fish the keys out of my purse and get the door open, all while trying not to drop me. I was only half-conscious by this time.

Aaron put me into bed and started pulling off my boots. The only thing that made me madder than his betrayal was that I was now depending on him to take care of me. I did not want to owe him anything. As these thoughts entered my drunken mind, I started kicking my feet. He tried to hold them steady and unzip the boots, but I was kicking hard and the heels were making contact, clearly inflicting the pain I intended. Finally, one boot went flying off, across the room.

"Just leave me alone!" I yelled at him. He gave up on the other boot and stood to leave.

"Are you sure you're going to be OK?" he asked hesitantly.

"Get out!" I was relentless.

He pulled a trashcan over to the side of my bed. "Just in case," he said. "Evan, once you're sober we need to talk. I hope you can at least give me that."

I rolled over and grunted. I just wanted him to leave so I could pass out.

He turned off the light and closed the door behind him.

— *ele* —

I was so tired, but every time I closed my eyes, the room spun. I had to open my eyes and fix them on the glowing digits of my alarm clock just to stop the spinning. I was miserable. I just wanted to sleep, but every time I closed my eyes, I felt like I was going to puke.

I tried not to think about it, but my mind drifted to the only other time I had been drunk. It was the summer before my junior year in high school. We were stationed in North Carolina, having moved there early in the summer. I had spent my days at the swimming pool on the base reading all day and getting a tan, and one of the lifeguards started paying me a lot of attention. He would sit chatting with me instead of sitting up on his perch where he was supposed to be. He was gorgeous! He was tan and built and I was the mysterious new girl in town.

It turned out that Bret was captain of the swim team and one of the most popular boys in school. I was the envy of all the high school girls at the pool that summer and I could see them shooting me dirty looks. Despite their scrutiny, Bret and I had a wonderful summer, and I fell fast and hard.

The week before school started, Bret had a big back-to-school bash at his house. I was apprehensive about the party all along. I wanted to keep Bret to myself and wasn't ready to meet all the kids I would be going to school with. I already felt a foreboding about school starting.

Bret's parents were out of town and the party got pretty wild. I was nervous around all the other kids. I could feel the eyes of the girls who were part of the 'in' crowd, scrutinizing every inch of me. I knew they were trying to find my faults and come up with reasons why I wasn't good enough for Bret. I was trying too hard to act the way I thought would make me look cool in their eyes, and stupidly I got drunk.

I didn't want to think about it...how I had let him...it had almost destroyed me. Why couldn't I just sleep? I agonized. I closed my eyes tight and tried to stop the spinning. I willed my body to sober up, but it was no good. I felt like I was on a tilt-a-whirl. The bed was spinning so fast.

Then I was sure I would be sick. There was no time to make it to the bathroom, I threw my head over the side of the bed, hoping I was in the vicinity of the trashcan, and let go. I hated throwing up! It felt like I was dying. When nothing was left to throw up, I collapsed back on the bed and vowed I would never touch alcohol again.

I actually felt a little better though. My head was clearer and the spinning had stopped. I rolled over and closed my eyes...finally succumbing to the sweetness of sleep. However, just as I was sinking into oblivion, I heard the door open. I closed my eyes tighter to block out the light that the open door cast across the room. I hoped Taylor wouldn't make too much noise or turn on the lights. I prayed she would just go to bed and not notice the state of her dress. She closed the door, and I heard her stumbling around. She sounded just as inebriated as I was. Lord, had she driven home? I shuddered. I knew I should check that she was OK, but I was just *so* tired.

I let myself sink into sleep, but just as I was drifting off, I felt Taylor climbing into bed with me! My god, she's so drunk that she doesn't even realize she's getting into my bed! I realized with a shock. I didn't even have time to react when I suddenly felt her touching me. My mind scrambled to make sense of the hands that were sensually rubbing all over my body!

What on earth is she doing!? My mind reeled. Does she think I'm someone else....or...no she couldn't possibly be...? The touching became more forceful in places that made me *extremely* uncomfortable! Then I heard something that confused me even more and sent shock waves through my mind!

"Damn Ev, you feel so good. Your body is smokin' hot."

The sound of his voice disgusted me and I could taste bile in my mouth. It wasn't Taylor, and it wasn't even my room or my bed. I was back...on that horrible summer night. What I thought were only bed spins were in reality the sensations of falling into a memory, and of all the memories, why did it have to be this one? I cringed. It was the worst night of my life and now I was reliving it!

He was pulling at my dress, caressing my thigh. He was lying behind me, spooning my body. I felt like that insecure, helpless girl again. His face was close, his hot breath in my ear. I could smell the beer on his breath, and it made me sick. He ruined my life and I had been too stupid and complacent to fight for my reputation, but I would now. The anger welled up inside me.

I brought my knee up as far as I could then swung my bent leg back, smashing the heel of the one boot I still had on right into his crotch as hard as I could. He wailed and fell back, off the bed. I sat up quickly, preparing myself for a fight. The room was dimly lit and I could see him lying in a fetal position on the floor beside the bed, moaning. It made me happy to see him in pain. He stayed like that for quite a while, trying to recover. He tried to speak, but all that came out were strained coughs. Finally, after several long minutes, he composed himself enough to speak.

"What...the hell...are you doing? Trying to emasculate me?"

"Yes, actually" I answered.

"What did I do? I thought you wanted to..." he lapsed into another coughing spell.

His innocent tone infuriated me. How could he possibly think he was the victim here? I lit into him, unleashing two years' worth of pent-up rage.

"Do you think it's OK to take advantage of a girl that has passed out? Don't you realize that is considered rape? Do you want to be a rapist? Is that what you are?" I was yelling at him with all the venom I could muster.

"Take advantage... what are you talking about? No! I wouldn't have..." he was stuttering and clearly shocked by my accusations.

However, I knew quite well that he would have. "And what will you do now that I've refused you? Are you so insulted that you will just tell all the kids at school that your conquest was successful anyway? Maybe even make up a few disgustingly vulgar details to make it sound more interesting? Will you even think for one second about what those lies will do to me, as you are trying to be the big stud for your friends? Do you have one iota of understanding how devastating stories like that can be to a sixteen-year-old girl, with no friends, already insecure about her new home and school? Can you even comprehend how that could damage her psyche forever and cause her to never want to trust anyone again?" I couldn't see the details of his face in the dim light, couldn't judge his reaction, but he was completely still and silent, taking it all in.

"And what about next time this happens? Maybe the next girl won't get off so easily. Maybe next time you won't take no for an answer or be satisfied to simply ruin her reputation and self-image with lies. Maybe next time you'll just force yourself on her. Do you know what happens to rapists in jail?"

"I would never force anyone...." he mumbled, trying to sit up. "I'm sorry I scared you like that, but you're blowing this out of proportion. You're drunk, talking crazy!"

"Maybe I am, but if you say a single word about me to your friends, I swear to God I will cut your balls off! Now get the hell out of here!"

Without a word, he rose and limped slowly out of the room, hands cupped to his crotch. I collapsed back on the bed. I didn't even concentrate on getting back. I simply closed my eyes and fell into the soundest, most peaceful sleep of my life.

Chapter 7

METAMORPHOSIS

I woke up with the most excruciating, skull-splitting headache I had ever had. My mouth felt like it was full of cotton, all my muscles ached and my stomach was still nauseous. I saw that Taylor's bed was empty. She hadn't come home and the sight of her empty bed filled me with worry. It was so ridiculous that I didn't even have her cell number! I supposed I could call Aaron to see if he had it, but despite my worry, that was out of the question.

My mind flashed to the previous night's events...to Aaron and Bret. Although I was still pissed at Aaron, my thoughts kept returning to our kiss. I realized now that he had been kissing Becky in the barn, it hadn't been my kiss but one that I had stolen from her. But last night, that was different. That was all about him and me. I debated whether I should give in and listen to his side of the story, but the pain was too raw and I was still too angry.

Then I thought of Bret. I felt vindicated. It was as if this huge weight I had been carrying around for years had been lifted. I felt tough, independent, badass. In fact, I didn't really even feel angry with him anymore. I had been consumed with hating him for so long, and now it was like it had all dissolved away. I had regarded him as this despicable monster who had ruined my life, but now I was having trouble even remembering exactly why.

It was an odd sensation. I had all these memories of high school, of how awful I had been treated after that night...the horrible stories and rumors. They had been so vivid and stabbing before, but now they were vague and muted. I was having trouble even recollecting a single clear memory of that year. The images were cloudy and disjointed. It felt almost like the scenes were rearranging. And then I wondered...had I changed my past by confronting Bret?

I certainly had changed the way things had played out between us, but had that affected everything else that transpired after that night? In my gut, I knew it had. My bad memories of high school in North Carolina were disappearing, and it wasn't just the memories. I could feel a change in myself. The weight was gone and I was a different person.

I should have felt scared by the effects my retaliation on Bret was having on me, but it felt too good. Even though I was incredibly hungover, I felt a confidence I had never known before. I had to write it all down and record every single detail before they faded.

I tried to sit up and felt a wave of nausea. I felt like I was going to puke...*again*. Remembering that particularly disgusting detail from the previous night, I peered over the side of my bed into the trashcan. It was empty and the floor around it was clean. For a second I wondered if I had imagined that part of the evening. Then I realized what had happened and laughed out loud. I hadn't puked on *my* floor at all. I had puked on Bret's floor, right next to the bed...right where he had fallen! Excellent!

Once I drank a few glasses of water and took some Tylenol, I set to writing down everything that happened with Bret. I also added another rule to my list: *7. Always travel sober!* I strained to remember all the reasons I had hated Bret before. He had lied, and told terrible stories about me and him that night. I couldn't remember specifics, but I knew they had hurt me, ruined my reputation and my chances of ever fitting in at that high school.

I wondered what had ever happened to Bret. I had a vague recollection that things had turned out bad for him. It seemed there had been an incident, maybe he was drunk? I had a vague recollection of a car or swimming accident, but it was almost like a dream now, hazy, undefined. I couldn't remember specifics, but I knew things had not turned out well for him, or had they? It was so bizarre. These things happened only a few years ago but I could hardly remember... One thing was for sure. My trip into the past definitely changed things, put events in motion...rearranged them somehow.

I opened up my favorite networking site and searched for Bret Anderson. I clicked through the pictures until I spotted him. Wow, there he was! I thought, gazing at his still handsome face. Bret's profile picture was a headshot of him emerging from a pool. He was wearing a swimming cap and had one arm in the air, as if in triumph. It was clearly taken after a race. I looked at his profile narrative, and the thing that immediately jumped out was that he was a freshman at Dartmouth! He was even on their swim team.

Bret Andersen was attending an Ivy League school? I could not believe it. It seemed like he had been such a screw-up our senior year. Dartmouth had been one of the schools to which I had been accepted, but clearly athletic scholarships paid more than academic scholarships. I should have been furious, jealous, or at least begrudged, but the truth was, I didn't feel any of those things. I was almost...happy for him? It was crazy...like I didn't know myself anymore.

It was the strangest feeling. I could vaguely remember two divergent pasts. Both were fuzzy, but one was coming into focus by the minute. As I made these realizations, I quickly recorded them in my journal. I tried to capture every thought and feeling. I tried to record every memory, even as they transformed and shifted. I wrote in my journal how I suspected that by confronting and challenging Bret I had changed both of us, the extent to which I didn't yet know.

As I wrote, I felt myself coming to terms with what I had done, and amazingly, nothing about it felt wrong. Everything seemed to have worked out for Bret and me too. Of course, there was no way I could be absolutely sure that I hadn't screwed up something or someone else. The only thing that I could be sure of was that I had changed the past and myself in doing so. I had *changed* myself!

I wondered what would have happened if things had turned out differently. I mean I was completely smashed, I could have said or done anything! What if I had changed myself for the worse? What if I had ended up pregnant at sixteen?! The sheer thought of it sent chills down my spine. I knew I was playing with fire, and I had to be smarter...more careful. I added another rule to my list: *8. Never, ever change the past!* Every time travel book and movie could not have been wrong about it being a really terrible idea.

—⁓⁓—

Taylor finally made it home mid-morning looking as puny as I felt. I was so relieved to see that she was OK and even happier to see she brought breakfast burritos. After some good hangover food and coffee, we both felt better. It turned out she had hooked up with one of the football players and they had spent the evening 'dancing'. She had the common sense to know that she was in no shape to drive home and ended up crashing at the sorority house. McKenna told her that Aaron had taken me home and she apologized profusely for leaving me on my own.

"So classes start tomorrow, and I still need to buy books and supplies. Let's go shopping today! Want to Evan?" She was way too excited about textbook shopping.

"You think the stores will actually be open?" It was New Year's Day after all.

"There's only one way to find out right?"

"Sure, I guess I can go with you for a bit." The truth was that I was having fun with Taylor and I certainly did not want to sit around thinking about Aaron all day.

"By the way Taylor, your dress took on some collateral damage last night." I felt terrible, that poor dress had certainly seen some action! "I promise I'll pay to have it fixed though."

"Don't sweat it! I never liked that dress much anyway. It's too plain, looks like something you would wear to a funeral."

I smiled to myself as Taylor shrugged and finished her burrito.

We got ready, both of us moving a lot slower than usual, and headed out to the shops. My 'new attitude' and the fact that I was going out with Taylor inspired me to put a little more effort into my appearance. I didn't go as far as applying makeup, but I did leave my hair down and put on my best pair of jeans. I even wore the turtleneck sweater my mom had given me, even though it was seventy degrees outside. The campus was alive with activity. Even our floor in Holden was busy with kids returning from their vacations.

We headed off campus, Taylor driving a little faster than I would have preferred. Her driving made me nervous. First off, her BMW was a stick shift, which she attempted to drive while checking her cell phone, searching for songs, and holding a coffee cup! Secondly, she liked to drive fast. It was unnerving. We headed down University Avenue, straight past the textbook stores. I swung my head around, watching them fly by.

"Um...I think you just passed the bookstores."

"Oh, I already have my books. I just said that to get you out," she said nonchalantly. "We're *really* going to buy you some new clothes. If we're going to be hanging out together the sweats and clogs have got to go!" she said giving me an appraising look over her sunglasses.

"Taylor, thanks for the kind sentiment," I said sarcastically, "but I really can't afford to buy a new wardrobe. In case you haven't noticed my parents don't own Exxon Mobil."

"Well, mine do. Partially at least, so don't worry about money, OK?"

"I can't let you do that. I already feel bad enough about ripping your dress. Please don't make me feel like your charity case."

"Look Evan, I don't see you as a charity case. We are friends now and it's honestly not a big deal to buy you a few things. The money is nothing, really."

"I don't know..." I just didn't feel right about it.

"OK, how about this? I really need to get my grades up this semester. You let me have my fun by continuing your makeover and you can have your fun by giving my brain a makeover...teach me some good study habits and whatnot."

It didn't sound so bad when she said it like that.

"Plus, even if you say no, I'm still going to buy new clothes for you, but you just won't have any say about what I pick. Then I'll relentlessly guilt you into wearing them."

"Fine! You've worn me down." I huffed.

Taylor drove us to the upscale shops across town that I never would have dared to walk into before. The next several hours were an endless blur of dresses, sweaters, blouses, jackets, jeans, and shoes. After I looked at the price tag of the first dress I tried on, and realized that it was almost the same amount as a semester's tuition, I stopped looking. I could hardly fathom it, much less allow myself to think about what else I could use the money for. However, I did convince Taylor that I was not going to need any dresses. I was insistent about it, and she finally acquiesced with the exception that I at least buy a skirt or two.

I had to give Taylor credit though. She never imposed her style on me; instead, she let me decide on my own. Taylor's style was a cross between preppie debutant and party girl. I didn't know if it was the 'change' I was going through or what, but my style seemed to be intellectual scholar meets biker chick, and I had to admit that I loved the fitted brown leather jacket and riding boots that Taylor found for me. They both had a kind of distressed, rugged look to them and the tawny brown color of the jacket looked perfect with my hair.

The boots did have a heel on them, but it was wide and nothing close to the height Taylor wore. I knew that the weather in Blythe was not going to give me much occasion to use them, but wearing those boots and jacket made me feel even more badass than I already felt. I wanted to take on the world.

We made our way to the food court both carrying more bags than we could handle. I bought us some frozen yogurt, which was the least I could do, and we sat in an exhausted stupor. We had been at it for hours, and lord knows how much money Taylor had spent.

"How can you spend this much money without thinking twice about it?" I wondered aloud.

"It's just money," she said shrugging her shoulders. Noticing the look of consternation on my face she continued. "I know that sounds shocking and indulgent, but that's just how it's always been for me. It's just what I'm used to."

"Do you realize what the money we just spent on clothes could do for a poor family?"

"My family gives tons of money to charity. It's not like we're heartless, money-grubbing tyrants. My dad has his own foundation that funds several philanthropic causes. So if you're feeling *that* guilty why don't you just take that beautiful leather jacket and donate it to the homeless."

I gasped. I loved that jacket! That was below the belt and she knew it.

"Point taken" I conceded.

"OK Evan, time to spill the beans about our mutual friend. What went on between you and Aaron over break?" Her eyes were all sparkly and I could tell she had been dying to ask.

Crap! I knew it was coming, but now she was looking expectantly at me and I was going to have to say something about Aaron and our... relationship. "Nothing *went on*, well not really, plus we're not even talking anymore anyway." She was hanging on my every word, waiting to hear something juicy. "I mean we kind of hung out during the break, but then I found out about Becky and..." I trailed off. Taylor must have realized that *she* was the reason I found out about Becky because she made an 'oooh' noise. "So anyway, now we're not hanging out." I studied my hands, nervously picking at a hangnail.

"Well, it's his loss and anyway at least six guys asked me for your phone number last night! There are plenty of other fish in the sea. You just need to play the field awhile."

I couldn't help but smile at her, "Any other clichés you want to throw in?"

"Yeah, all study and no play makes Evan a dull girl! I'm going to make it my personal mission to find you a man."

"No, Taylor! Seriously, that's the last thing I need right now." I cringed at the thought of Taylor setting me up on blind dates. She nodded, but the smirk on her face told me she wasn't going to let this go. "I mean it. I'm not ready for that." I grabbed her hand and the imploring expression on my face must have convinced her.

"Fine," she pouted, "I'll drop it...for now anyway."

I supposed that concession was as much as I could hope for.

"So, you ready to go home?" I asked, pitching my yogurt container into the trashcan.

"Home? We haven't even begun shopping for cosmetics or accessories yet!"

———ele———

As we drove home several hours later, I checked my phone. The message light was on. It had been buried at the bottom of my purse all day and I never even heard it ring. Checking the call log, I saw one call from my mom and three from Aaron. Whatever he wanted to tell me sure seemed urgent.

The old Evan would have simply deleted the messages from her phone and Aaron from her mind. The old Evan didn't give second chances or listen to excuses. However, the new Evan felt a little more optimistic. I listened to the voicemail. Mom wished me a happy New Year and wanted me to call her. Aaron's messages were longer, full of apologies and pleas to hear him out.

As we pulled into the parking lot outside Holden Hall, I decided that I would call him back, maybe even arrange a time to meet. The sun was setting and everything had a luminous warm burnt orange glow. We loaded our arms full of shopping bags, anticipating it would take multiple trips to get everything upstairs. As we walked up the lawn towards the front doors, Taylor said, "*Somebody's* anxious to see you."

I looked up to see Aaron waiting on the stoop. He looked nervous...squirrelly. "Hey Taylor," he said. "How's your New Year so far?"

"Great! Sorry, I missed you at the party last night. Thanks for taking care of our girl." Embarrassingly, she bumped my hip with hers.

"Evan...do you have a minute?"

Taylor gave me a knowing glance and started taking the bags from my arms.

"I'll take these...you two kids run along," she said teasingly. I rolled my eyes at her as she disappeared into the building.

"So are you and Taylor like best friends now or something?" he asked. Aaron had heard enough of my criticisms about Taylor's constant partying, revolving string of boyfriends, and stuck-up sorority sisters to know that our hanging out together was quite unusual.

"Are you judging me for having a personal relationship that I wasn't completely upfront about?" I asked sarcastically.

"Touché," he said. "So can we take a little walk?"

"Aaron, I don't think that's a good idea. Classes start tomorrow and I still have a lot to do."

"Come on Evan, just hear me out...please." Damn it! He was giving me those smoldering puppy dog eyes again. I was sure he knew the power those eyes had, and he wasn't afraid to use it.

"Fine...five minutes." I started walking towards the quad.

"Thank you," he said, catching up. "So how are you feeling today? You were in pretty bad shape last night." He was actually smiling about it!

"Are you referring to the alcohol or the betrayal?" I said seriously.

He was quiet then. After a few moments, he sighed and began talking in a very somber and remorseful tone that I had never heard him use.

"Evan, I want you to understand that I never set out to *betray* you. In fact, I never set out to do *anything* with you. I just wanted to be friendly to a girl that seemed lonely over the holidays."

I stopped then. The anger was welling up and burning my cheeks. I turned and faced him. "Wow, thanks so much for taking pity on the poor lonely girl. I can't believe I'm saying this for the second time today, but I'm NO charity case."

I started to head back, but he grabbed my arm and stopped me.

"Will you please let me finish? I didn't mean it the way it sounded."

I shook my arm loose and said, "OK, then...three minutes left." I resumed walking, picking up the pace. Aaron did a little jog to catch up.

"Look, I just meant that I didn't plan to...fall for you." I felt a pang of electricity that took my breath away, but I kept walking. I did not want to give him the satisfaction of seeing the surprise on my face. "I kept telling myself that we were just friends, and there was nothing to feel guilty about, but I began to look forward to our time together more and more. Then, one night you were telling me a story and I was looking into your eyes, and...well, I knew that friends wasn't going to be enough for me." My heart skipped again, but I refused to let him charm me.

"Have you told all of this to Becky?" I asked spitefully.

"She knows some of it. She knows I've been spending a whole lot of time with you and she's not happy about it at all."

He had told her about me? This took me off guard.

"I want to tell her more...how I feel about you, but it's difficult with Becky."

"And how exactly *do* you feel?" As soon as the words were out, I almost clasped a hand over my mouth. I couldn't believe how bold the new Evan was! I never would have asked a question that directly before. I would have been too scared to hear the answer.

Aaron stopped walking, grabbed my arm, and turned me towards him. I couldn't look up at him.

"Well, I know this is going to sound crazy. I mean we've known each other such a short time, but it feels like I've known you for years. There is just some kind of connection between us that I can't explain. I feel....alive when I'm with you, and like I'm waiting to breathe when I'm not. I feel like you understand depths of me that I didn't even know existed. There's something about the way you look at me, with those eyes...those astonishing, luminescent eyes...I dream of those eyes."

I did not know what to say. I was literally speechless. I had no idea that he felt like that or that he could express himself so eloquently. I was astonished. My face burned and I felt his eyes boring into the top of my head, but I still couldn't look up at him. I knew that if I did my resolve would crumble and I would fall into his arms, into his kiss...

What I couldn't tell him was that I felt exactly the same way. Part of the reason I had been so interested in Aaron and his memories was for my 'research', but I also knew there really was a connection between us, in ways I didn't even understand yet.

"So, why are things so... complicated...with Becky, I mean," I said her name in a whisper, still staring at the ground.

He sighed deeply and walked over to a nearby bench. He sat silently, waiting for me to join him. I acquiesced but sat as far away as I possibly could.

"I've known Becky my whole life. Her family moved in next to ours when we were just babies. Our mothers were best friends, so we grew up spending every day together. She doesn't have any brothers or sisters of her own, so she was like the sister we never had. My mom thinks of her as the daughter she always wanted.

"Her dad died before she was born. She never knew him. So, she and her mom were always at our house...barbeques, holidays...they were just part of the family. And that was the way I always thought of her...like a sister...until..." he drifted off. He was kicking at a stone that was wedged in the ground, trying to knock it loose. We both watched the stone instead of each other.

"*Until*..." I finally said, anxious to hear the reason.

"Until she got sick. I remember her first seizure like it was yesterday. I remember it so clearly because it happened at my granddad's funeral...as if the day wasn't already bad enough."

I stopped breathing.

"We thought she was dying that day. Her mother was in shock. The doctors said it was epilepsy and the medications worked for a few years, but as we got older the drugs failed and now her disease has become almost debilitating. When the seizures first started we were only ten, but I took on the role of protector because we were exactly the same age and in the same classes. I felt like it was my job to watch over her. I suppose as the years passed that grew into...more." He knocked the stone out of the ground and started rolling it back and forth between his feet.

"What caused them?" I asked. My voice was trembling and I could barely get the sentence out. I felt sick.

"No one knows. They did all the usual tests and looked for tumors, chemical imbalances, and head injuries, but the results were inconclusive. The assumption was that it was just a genetic thing. Something wired wrong in her brain I guess. Who knows what finally set it off." I swallowed hard and closed my eyes.

"No one on her mom's side has a history of seizures. Her dad died in a car accident, but there was no evidence of epilepsy on his side of the family either. It's really a mystery."

I could feel cold sweat on my face and neck. My hands were trembling and I held them tight in my lap, my fingers laced together. I kept looking down at the stone. Had I done this? Was it possible? I felt insurmountable guilt. This changed everything! My heart raced.

"She wants to be an early-ed teacher. She wanted to come to Harper too, but it was impossible. The seizures got worse, sometimes occurring daily. I told her I would help take care of her here, but she refused. I told her I would just go to school in Houston, but she knew how important tennis was to me and she wouldn't let me throw away my scholarship. When I started school last year, I drove home every weekend. My car was in better shape before I put all those miles on it," he mused.

"Then I began to realize that being here, away from family obligations felt...good. It was freeing not to have to think about meds and treatments and doctor's appointments, just friends and school and tennis. I hadn't been able to do that in so many years. So, my visits home grew fewer and farther between. I even miss holidays, as you know. I blame it on my crappy car, but that's not the only reason." Aaron sounded so self-defeating. Clearly, he had been wrestling with a lot of guilt long before I came along. "Of course, I still call her every day, and she even visits Blythe sometimes, but things have changed, for both of us."

He kicked the rock hard and it sailed over the curb into a parking lot, nearly hitting a car.

"Then you came along. Someone who hadn't known me my entire life, someone who loved to listen to all my boring stories, someone who made me feel excitement and desire. I love Becky and always will but it's different, with you."

He stopped talking and looked at me. I didn't want him to see me cry, so I let my long hair hang down, blocking my face from his view.

"So... do you think I'm a cold bastard now?"

"Of course not," I said. How else was I supposed to reply? I didn't blame him for the way he felt. He had spent many years devoted to Becky, but what was I supposed to do now? Suggest that he dump her to be with me? I already felt tremendous guilt just considering the possibility that I somehow caused her condition. How could I hurt her again by taking Aaron away? There was no way I could be with him now, I thought. In fact, I resolved to do everything I could to make sure she was never hurt because of me again.

"So, what will happen to her now?" I asked.

"Well, they've tried every medication possible to stop the seizures. The concern is that if they get worse she could have a stroke, which could potentially result in paralysis. Plus, there's always the risk that she could severely injure herself if she was unsupervised and had a very violent seizure. So, the next step is to try surgery. They are running all kinds of tests to figure out which part of her brain is triggering them. If they can figure that out, it may be possible to remove the damaged area."

"Remove part of her brain!" I gasped.

"Yeah, pretty scary huh? They have to make sure not to disturb any of the healthy parts. Now you *must* think I'm a cold bastard, huh?" He pulled my hair to the side, trying to see my face.

I wiped my eyes and looked at him. "Aaron, I don't blame you, and I don't think you're a cold bastard. I think you have been incredibly courageous all these years. Most guys would never have lasted, never have stuck by someone like you have. I don't even blame you for not telling me about Becky. I would've done the same thing. But..."

He stopped me then. "Evan, please don't say what I think you're about to say."

I took a deep breath to strengthen my resolve. "*But* I can't be the reason you desert her now." I tried to hold back the tears.

"I would never desert her!" I could see his eyes were watery too.

"So, what do you suggest? We embark on some secret relationship? As you said, I haven't known you very long, but I feel like I understand you well enough to know you couldn't deceive her like that. And I understand myself enough to know that I couldn't let you."

"So, I'll tell her," he said. "I'll just explain my feelings." He was desperate now, grasping at straws.

"You can't do that to her, and you know it. She's going to need you now more than ever with this surgery and all."

He hung his head down. He knew I was right. He sighed and ran his hand through his hair, uncovering the scar. In the light of the sunset, his golden highlights almost shimmered.

"So where does that leave *us*?" He asked, sounding defeated.

"We're friends, aren't we? Nobody said we can't be friends...good friends." I used my most optimistic voice.

"Can we be?" He looked up and gave me a half-hearted Elvis smirk that made my belly tingle. I knew that we *had* to be just friends...or nothing at all.

———ele———

As I returned to our room, Taylor was preparing to go out.

"Hey, you're finally back! Listen, you are going to fill me in on the new developments with Aaron James, but right now I have to dash. Rob called and wants to get together for dinner!"

"The football player from last night?" I asked.

"Yeah. Why don't you come with? You can meet him."

I was fairly sure she was just being polite, and I was in no mood for socializing anyway. "No, you go. Thanks for the offer, but I have to call my mom."

She looked at me skeptically. "Are you OK? Your eyes look kinda puffy."

"I'm fine. I just really need to call my mom back. Plus school starts tomorrow and I have to coordinate all my new outfits!" I managed a weak smile.

Taylor laughed, "OK, I guess I'll let you off the hook for that."

Before I even started to dial, the phone rang in my hand. When I saw Mom's phone number pop up on the screen, I decided that we must be in some kind of mother/daughter telepathic sync. Stranger things had happened, especially in my world, I thought.

"Happy New Year!" Mom announced when I answered.

"Happy New Year, Mom. Any resolutions?" The new Evan still hated small talk.

"Oh, you know the usual...lose weight, exercise more."

"Mom, you don't need to lose any weight." Why do all women constantly think they need to lose weight? I wondered.

"Speaking of weight...how is yours? Are you eating?"

"Of course, I'm eating Mom." Moreover, why do all mothers worry about their kids' diets?

"But are you getting enough vegetables? You know you tend to get anemic, and it *is* cold season. You need to make sure you're getting enough iron, and have you gotten your flu shot yet?"

"Soon, Mom," I said flatly.

"I did make one other resolution," she said, her voice sounding serious now.

"What was it?"

"I resolved to be more forthcoming with you."

"About what Mom? It's not like you've been keeping secrets or something." Not like me, I thought.

"Well, not intentionally anyway. But, I've been thinking a lot about...what we discussed before..." There was a long pause before she continued. "It wasn't my intention to keep anything from you, but I should have discussed *him* more with you. I should have known you would be curious. It's just so hard still...and your father always said there was no point in bringing up painful memories." She sounded so sad.

"You know Mom, I actually think it's the painful ones you *have* to deal with because the deeper down you bury them, the worse they feel when they finally rise to the surface." I didn't know if I was talking about her memories or mine.

"I suppose you're right. Evy, when did you become so wise?" I wanted to laugh because lately, I felt like I didn't know anything. "So Evy, are there any questions you have? Anything else you remembered and wanted to talk about..."

"About Aaron?" I asked, and his name caught in my throat.

"Yes," she said in an artificially upbeat voice.

"Well, actually I was wondering if there had been a funeral for him... and where he was buried." I felt so callous asking, but there was really no other way to find out.

She cleared her throat. I knew it was so hard for her, but I rationalized that maybe it really would help her to get everything out in the open.

"It was difficult to decide what to do. We were so shocked by his..." She couldn't bring herself to say death. "I mean we didn't really understand what happened to him. We had to decide quickly what to do about...the arrangements. I mean, there wasn't any family or hometown to take him to... So uh, we just had a very small service in the Army chapel on base. You were in kindergarten that day. We didn't think you would understand. Maybe that was wrong. Maybe you somehow needed to grieve in your own way."

"Did I even realize he was gone?"

"Yes, you asked for him for months. You cried when we told you he wasn't coming back. We told you that he had just peacefully gone to sleep, but never woken up. You were afraid to sleep by yourself for weeks... afraid you wouldn't wake up either. I didn't mind though. It was comforting to sleep with you in my arms."

Why didn't I remember any of this? What was wrong with me? I strained so hard to remember... anything, but there were no memories, apart from that Christmas morning. I thought of that morning, his little face in the dim light of the bedroom. At least I had that memory of him.

"It makes me sad that he's so far away. I mean I know he's not actually here... on earth... anymore. But still... I wish I could visit his grave." I thought of Aaron's vow to visit Omaha Beach to honor his granddad, and said, "Why don't we go back to Hamburg together one day?"

"That would be nice Evy. I know he wasn't with us long, but sometimes I miss him so much. I wonder what he would have been like now."

I immediately thought of Aaron. "Mom, where did you get his name...Aaron James? It's really lovely."

"Well, your dad and I couldn't think of any boy names we agreed on. Then I remembered that a good friend of mine had named her son Aaron. Their last name was James, and I had always thought those two names sounded nice together."

My heart raced and there was a frog in my throat, but I managed to croak out, "Your friend?" I couldn't believe it! There *was* a connection between Aaron and my brother. My brother had been named after him. I had to find out more.

"Did you stay in touch with her? What is *her* Aaron doing now?" The questions were coming fast. It was hard to sound calm, and I was biting my nails, which I hadn't done since I was a kid.

"No, we grew apart over the years. Guess we just got busy with the business of life, raising kids and all. Then, of course, we were moving all the time. I really should drop her a line..." She drifted off distracted.

I tried to refocus her, "So, did you know her from the Home?"

"Uh...yeah, she was a few years older than me, so she was in the big girls' building."

My mother had been raised in a 'children's home'. She didn't like the term 'orphanage', but that's essentially what it was. Her mother had run off and left her with her dad when she was just a baby, then he died when she was just a few years old. There was no extended family capable of raising her so she was sent to the children's home in Portales, New Mexico. Growing up, I always had this Oliver Twist-like tragic image of her upbringing, but the truth was she never despaired about it. She only ever had fond memories to share about living in the Home.

She said she never missed her parents because she never really knew them, and there were 'house parents' that lived at the Home and supervised all the children. She came to love and think of them as her own parents. She always said that she grew up in a loving home with a set of parents and eighty-five brothers and sisters!

I thought about how Aaron said he was so used to a crowded busy house that he worried he would go crazy if he lived by himself. I imagined that his mom's life, with five kids, reminded her of her own childhood, and wondered if the solitude of life with just me and my dad had been difficult for my mother. I desperately wished my brother had lived, for both our sakes.

Chapter 8

DISTRACTIONS

"**H**ey-hey." Taylor flipped my ponytail and then plopped down in the desk next to mine. "I thought you were going to start leaving it down." She sighed in exasperation.

"Give me a break. I actually put together an outfit *and* put on mascara this morning. All this stuff takes so much extra time! What are you doing here anyway?" I had no idea that Taylor was interested in history. I guessed that maybe the course fulfilled some of her first-year requirements.

"Have you *seen* Dr. Browning's hotness rating on Rate-my-Prof.com?" She asked wide-eyed.

Admittedly, I had not. However, taking a long look around the room, I registered that about ninety percent of the students in the class were female. Suddenly, I understood why the course had filled up so quickly.

"Well, let me fill you in...Ian Browning is *the* hottest professor at Harper. He's only a few years out of grad school, so he's practically our age. And rumor has it that he's not above dating students!" She said it like this was some kind of a good thing.

"Classy," I smirked.

"Oh, get over yourself Miss High and Mighty. As soon as you see him you're going to be praying that rumor is true."

"Taylor, if that rumor were true, he wouldn't even be working here anymore, so *you* can just get over *yourself*," I said, pulling out my notebook and multicolored pens.

"Praying," she said teasingly. "Mark my words."

The one sure thing I quickly realized about Ian Browning was that he liked to make an entrance. First, he was over ten minutes late to class. When he did arrive he threw the door open and dashed in like he had almost forgotten to come at all. Then, despite the rush to get to class, he took his time setting down his papers and taking off his jacket. After which, he silently surveyed the room before casually making his way to the board to write his name, the title of the course, and the course number. By the time he said a damn word we were fifteen minutes into class time.

"Can anyone tell me why we should study history?" his voice echoed through the large lecture hall. He had an accent that I couldn't quite place.

No one said a word.

"Come on, don't be shy." Irish, it was definitely Irish, I thought. Not a heavy brogue like some Irish I had met, but it was distinct, and very out of place in West Texas.

There was still no answer.

After another long silence, I couldn't take it anymore. I had to offer an answer. It was in my nature. I raised my hand.

"Yes, Ms....." he said pointing in my direction.

"Wright...Evan Wright. Because if we don't know the past, we're doomed to repeat it." I offered, very proud of myself.

"Well....I suppose that's the vanilla answer, Evan," he responded.

I heard a few snickers around the room.

Vanilla! What the hell did that mean? I had given the most accurate answer possible. Everyone knows that! I silently shouted at him. I was not used to being wrong or being laughed at in class. I already despised this insolent, grandstanding professor. I slunk down in my chair and pouted. Taylor shot me a sideways glance, which I didn't return.

"Anyone else venture a guess?" he asked the class.

You could have heard a pin drop. No one dared to offer an answer after the way he had shot mine down.

"We have all hour..." he said, sitting on top of his desk and folding his arms.

Finally, the silence was broken by the familiar voice next to me. "How about to understand ourselves better?"

Professor Browning shot up. "Exactly! Ms...."

"Dorsett" she answered.

I swung my head around, nearly giving myself whiplash, and saw Taylor sitting straight up in her chair beaming.

"Class, Ms. Dorsett has hit the nail on the head," he boomed.

This was ridiculous. Upstaged by Taylor in a *class*? I could hardly believe it. I could understand Taylor outshining me in dating or... pilates, but in an actual academic environment? You couldn't be serious. Her answer wasn't even very good.

"Without considering our history we have no context in which to frame our present." Dr. Browning continued. "The blind Czech historian Milan Hubl once said that the first step in liquidating a people is to erase its memory. Destroy its books, its culture, its history, then have somebody write new books, manufacture a new culture, invent a new history. Before long, the nation will begin to forget what it is and what it was. The world around it will forget even faster." He paused for effect.

"This semester we will be discussing some of history's greatest mysteries. I know, crap course title, not my choice." There were a few laughs, but I sat sullen, arms folded. "I will warn you that this will not be a series of bedtime stories told for your entertainment. We will not be discussing the Bermuda Triangle, aliens landing in Roswell, or crop circles.

What we will discuss are important historical events that are not completely understood, either because records of them do not exist or their testimonies were destroyed and/or recreated to someone else's advantage.

The missing portions of these events have been filled in by different people at different times. Your job this semester will be to consider how the different interpretations of these events have shaped the future, or what we now call the present."

Dr. Browning paced back and forth while he spoke, looking way too intense for a Monday morning. He walked straight over to a girl sitting in the front row, grabbed the cell phone she was busily texting on, and turned it off.

"I will give you another warning. This course will be writing *intensive*. If you cannot even compose a coherent paragraph, then I urge you to drop my class *now*, instead of wasting the time it will take you to write your gibberish, and the time it will take me to give you an F." He handed the girl back her phone as she stared up at him, mouth agape.

I wondered how many of these girls would be scared away by his warnings, and how many of them would take the 'F' just to have the pleasure of staring at him for three hours per week. Despite my disdain for him, Taylor hadn't been kidding. He was *incredibly* gorgeous. Not, just attractive or *cute*. No, he was gorgeous in a leading man, rock star, underwear model kind of way. I suspected that he resented being eye candy for a class full of girls and acted tough to counteract his good looks.

His hair was most likely dark brown but it was cropped so short that it was hard to tell the true color. Although the buzz-cut was probably meant to detract from his looks, it had the opposite effect of highlighting his face, which was perfectly chiseled. He had a strong brow, jaw, and chin, which was covered in three-day-old stubble. However, the pièce de résistance was his incredibly piercing brilliant blue eyes. I had never seen anything like them in real life.

Professor Browning was one of those young professors, probably in his late twenties, who didn't yet have tenure. Since he was so young, he had a lot to prove to his peers but he acted like he didn't have to prove anything to anybody. He was wearing worn jeans and a t-shirt, but threw a sports jacket over them to look more formal.

I looked down at his feet and was amused to see that he was wearing, what appeared to be, snakeskin cowboy boots! I wondered if it was a satirical statement on living in Texas, or if he really liked them. He wasn't as tall as Aaron, but the boots gave him an extra few inches. I wondered what his story was...how an Irishman had found himself in Blythe. No doubt, the mystery added to his appeal.

"So class, I am feeling particularly good-humored today, thus I will let *you* pick the topic of your first assignment, as a group. It must be a historical event that is not completely understood. Your job will be to write a thesis, which is at least twenty pages, on how the mysteries surrounding this event have been interpreted and how these interpretations have changed the course of history." There were audible gasps around the room when he said 'twenty-pages'. "Right then, who wants to volunteer a topic?"

One thing was for certain, there was no way I was going to say a word. I didn't want to give him another opportunity to embarrass me, plus I wasn't going to be the one responsible for inflicting a tough topic on the whole class. The process was painful. Everyone was either too shy or too intimidated to speak up. There were a few lame attempts, like 'who built the pyramids or Stonehenge' mostly suggested by the few brave boys in the class, but Dr. Browning quickly dismissed them as fanciful and boring. Finally, after it was obvious that we as a class were completely "inept and lacking in both decisiveness and creativity," Dr. Browning decided he would call on one student who would decide for all of us.

"Ms. Dorsett, as you are the only student who has, as of yet, demonstrated any insight into what this course is about, you will decide on the class's first assignment topic."

I think this was meant to be a compliment; however, it was apparent by the look on Taylor's face that it was in reality a punishment. I was suddenly very glad that he hadn't liked my answer! I could tell by the sudden flash of pink on her cheeks she was embarrassed, and I honestly felt sorry for poor Taylor.

"Well... I suppose that 'who killed JFK' is one of the most famous mysteries in history." Taylor said in almost a whisper. It wasn't the most original idea, but much better than the others that had been suggested, I thought.

I quickly looked from Taylor's to Dr. Browning's face, wondering if he was going to love it or hate it. He didn't say anything for a few beats, just stared at Taylor. Then he rubbed his stubbly chin with what looked to me like exasperation. I thought she was done for. However, after a few moments he looked up at the class and announced, "All right then, the mystery surrounding the death of John Fitzgerald Kennedy will be your first assignment! Thank you, Ms. Dorsett.

"Now, I do not want you to simply watch the film, by Mr. Oliver Stone, and regurgitate the conspiracy theories he laid forth. Your ideas need to be original and thoughtful. Remember, everyone will be working on the same topic, so *you* need to come up with a novel idea. Be creative! Be daring! You will be graded not only on your own work but how your work compares to the rest of the class. This is an event that has been dissected and theorized upon for decades, by countless scholars and lay people alike. *Do not* simply repeat those theories back to me. Tell me what *consequences* they had. How they shaped the world and the times we now know."

As I listened to the tempo of his fervor my mind began shaping a plan.

"You can use any resources at your disposal, just be sure they are grounded in fact. Movies, books, and websites based on fictionalized accounts or unfounded conspiracy theories will not cut it, and you *will* be providing me a list of references you used to compose your papers."

Any resources at my disposal...I repeated his words over in my mind. My plan was crystallizing.

"Yes. You in the back..." Dr. Browning motioned to the brave soul who had raised their hand.

"Um... when is this assignment due?" a girl in the back stammered. I could already tell from her tone and deer-in-the-headlight look, that this was a student who would be dropping the course.

"It's all in the syllabus." He began passing around sheets of paper. "This assignment will be due the day we return from Spring Break. It will compose forty percent of your final grade. Another forty percent will come from a second thesis that will be considered your final. And yes, it will also be twenty pages." Another round of groans spread through the lecture hall.

"The remaining twenty percent will come from short essays and class discussions." Now I joined in the groans. I usually didn't mind class participation points because, unlike many students, I always came to class and was never shy about answering questions. However, I could tell that in this class, things would be very different.

"He seems tough," Taylor said as we walked out of the lecture hall.

"He seems like an ass." I corrected her.

"Come on, did you *see* those eyes? You're just mad because he didn't like your answer."

"So how did things go with the football player last night?" I asked, changing the subject. She had come home late after I was already asleep.

"OK I guess, but I think Dr. Browning has spoiled me for all mortal men now. Speaking of men, you still need to spill the beans about Aaron! You have time for lunch?"

"No, I have to head straight to Psych class then Calculus after that, I won't be done until six." I was happy to have such a full schedule because I was dreading talking to her about Aaron. I still had not decided exactly what to tell her. Plus, I was trying to avoid thinking about him entirely. Trying, but failing.

Now that the big mystery of why he and my brother had the same name had been solved, I should have had a feeling of resolution, yet I felt disappointed. I suppose that a big part of me hoped the connection had been deeper than a random coincidence. Also, with the mystery solved, I had no good excuses to seek him out. Yet he was still on my mind all the time.

Now that classes had started again, I wondered what time his tennis practice started and if any of my classes were close enough in proximity to justify walking by the courts. I wondered if he would ever call me again, or if I should call him after some time had passed. I thought about which spot in the library would give me the best view of the check-out desk. I was wondering too much about Aaron, that was the problem!

~ele~

Things did not get much better as the days turned into weeks and I heard no word from Aaron. He had not made a single attempt to contact me, nor I him. I hadn't been able to stop thinking about him though. During the day, I managed to stay busy with classes and studying, but as I lay in bed at night, my thoughts always fell to Aaron.

I fought the fierce compulsion to travel back to New Year's Eve...and the kiss. I considered that this time I would be sober. I would be fully in control of my actions and I wouldn't push him away. No, instead, I would pull him closer...much, much closer. I reasoned that if I went back, my senses wouldn't be clouded by anger or alcohol and I would be able to fully savor the experience. I knew it was a terrible idea, but sometimes these thoughts consumed me and I worried that as I drifted off to sleep I might unintentionally fall into the memory.

It never happened though and I was always sadly disappointed when I woke up in my bed the next morning, alone. Although I ached for Aaron, *she* was always in the back of my mind. The image of her on the floor in convulsions haunted me and I struggled with the guilt that I was responsible. Therefore, no matter how much I craved to be with him, I didn't seek him out. Still, I subconsciously looked for him everywhere I went...the movies, the coffee shop, walking across campus...I always hoped to see his face in the crowd.

Apart from missing Aaron, I felt pretty good. I knew that the incident with Bret had changed me, but I was still realizing the effects. Thanks to my Psychology class, I had done a lot of self-analysis and now realized how much the incident between Bret and I had shaped my personality. The untrusting, angry, insecure girl I had been was becoming a stranger to me. In her place, I was becoming a confident, fun-loving, self-assured woman. I embraced the new me. Even the way I walked and held myself was different.

I found it amazing how the outcome of one small event could change a person so much. It made me wonder if who we end up becoming is decided by just a few defining moments in our lives, and the rest is just filler. I still felt driven to succeed, my grand plans were unchanged, but I wasn't as rigid and disciplined as I used to be. I still wanted all the things I had wanted before, it was just that now I wanted more. I wanted to know the secrets of the universe, but also wanted friendship, love, and passion. I wanted to experience everything!

I had begun helping Taylor study and she even convinced me to tutor some of the jocks on the football team. It seemed that this was her compromise for not trying to set me up, although I knew she anticipated that all that studying would lead to something more. While I didn't have the slightest interest in the jocks I tutored, the extra money was nice and I welcomed the distractions that Taylor and her friends offered. I had to admit that even McKenna was growing on me now that she had stopped calling me Lane.

The problem with the new me and all the fun I had been having with Taylor was that I just wasn't getting enough work done. I didn't even care about getting the highest grades anymore! I was doing OK in all my classes but I was becoming much more interested in my electives than the classes required for my major. I was obsessed with finding an explanation for what was happening to me.

In Cognition, we learned how emotion can have a powerful effect on memory. Countless studies have shown that memories associated with emotional events were more vivid than others, and tended to be more influential on a person's psyche. I certainly could attest from my experiences with Bret that this was true. We also learned that memories of emotionally neutral stimuli tended to decrease over time, but memories of emotionally arousing stimuli tended to remain the same or become exaggerated. I also did not doubt that this was true considering how vivid and stimulating my memories of Aaron's kisses were.

In my Existentialism class, we were discussing the philosophies of Friedrich Nietzsche. He spent years pondering humanity's struggle with the apparent meaninglessness of life and people's use of diversion to escape from the boredom of their lives. He valued human experience over hard sciences like math and physics, and for these reasons and others, I had never even considered his theories before. Now I was completely captivated by all the theories that attempted to answer the pivotal questions concerning humanity and our journey through life.

Then there was History. Dr. Browning continued to irritate me but admittedly, his class was my favorite. The topics were so interesting and his viewpoints were thoughtful and imaginative. By far, the thing that made the class so interesting was the knowledge that I could travel into the past and discover the answers to the mysteries we discussed...potentially. I still had to test this theory, but I couldn't think of any reason why it wouldn't work.

I already knew I could travel to past events I had never experienced myself. I just had to find out enough about the place and time to picture myself there. Although I had been too scared to attempt time travel after what happened to Becky and the episode with Bret, I was anxious to try again.

I knew I was going to have to be extremely careful. First off, I would be traveling to events that had shaped the course of history. I couldn't change *anything*, not even the tiniest thing. I had already seen how much changing one small thing in my past had changed me...*and* Bret. Imagine if I changed an event that had influenced millions of people. No, I had to only observe. I had to blend in and remain undetected, and there in lay another major problem.

Most of the historical events we were discussing in class happened long ago in foreign lands. I could speak modern-day English, and a little German and Spanish, but beyond that, I was sunk. For example, I couldn't risk going to turn of the century France to witness the beheading of Marie Antoinette, where everyone spoke French and wore elaborate gowns and wigs. How would I blend in, or communicate if I had to?

Also, many of the major mysteries in history occurred amid battle. For example, one of the most fascinating mysteries in the history of our own country surrounded the circumstances under which the American anthem was written. Everyone knows that Francis Scott Key wrote the anthem, supposedly after the defeat of the British in the War of 1812. The thing was, he had never actually made it to the battle, but had to watch from eight miles away.

He had watched the smoke and blasts from the battle all through the night, but in the silence and dark of the very early morning, he couldn't tell who had won. The story goes that he waited in suspense until the first light of dawn when he saw the American flag waving in the breeze. Then he knew the British had been defeated and in a fit of emotion, he took out an old letter from his pocket and began scribbling on it the lines of our national anthem.

However, historians believe that this iconic story is unlikely. First off, other accounts report that the night of the battle and subsequent morning were rainy and foggy. From eight miles away, it is unlikely that Key would have been able to see the flag, especially through all the fog and smoke. Even if it had been raised, they asserted, the rain would have made it a soggy mess, not the majestic banner blowing in the breeze that Key had described. Thus, there is still a controversy about what he actually saw, as opposed to the idyllic image that has so shaped our country.

As we discussed this mystery in class, I considered how amazing it would be to observe this event for myself. Not only to solve the mystery of what Francis Scott Key had seen, but to share the same space and time that gave birth to our country's National anthem! However, as with so many of the mysteries we discussed, traveling to this one carried with it the very real risk of death. There was no way I was going to put myself into the middle of a battle with cannons and guns being fired all around me.

When I excluded the mysteries that involved significant danger, foreign lands, or elaborate wardrobe problems, there weren't very many left. Therefore, I was focusing all my attention and effort on the essay project of JFK's assassination. It was actually kind of perfect. I didn't need to know any different languages or come up with period clothes. Of course, it did involve a shooting, but as long as I stayed out of the motorcade, I would be safe. Plus, Taylor had been right, it was one of the most important and speculated upon historical events ever.

However, I hadn't done much research on the topic yet, and Spring Break was rapidly approaching. I knew I had to buckle down and start getting some serious work done. I needed to find out everything possible about the assassination of JFK. If my plan worked I would not only give Know-it-All Browning the most original paper on a historical event he had ever read, but also solve one of the most notorious puzzles in history!

I needed to find some old newspaper reports of the Kennedy assassination that weren't online. That meant I needed to search the archives in the library, and the library meant Aaron. I had been avoiding the trip, but I couldn't put it off any longer. The thought of seeing Aaron for the first time in months both thrilled and terrified me.

I spent a ridiculous amount of time getting ready, even putting on make-up and blow-drying my hair. It had been slightly chilly that day, which gave me an excuse to wear my new boots and leather jacket. As soon as I put them on, I felt powerful and confident. When I was satisfied that I looked as good as possible, I headed off.

As I walked into the library, my eyes darted to the check-out desk, but my heart sank when I saw that he wasn't there. Instead, it was the stern old librarian, who had chided me for bringing food into the library, sitting behind the desk. I looked down hoping he wouldn't recognize me and focused on the task at hand. I still chose a table that gave me a clear view of the check-out desk, just in case Aaron made an appearance. I retrieved the archived articles that couldn't be checked out and made meticulous notes on their contents. Most of the articles focused on the eyewitness accounts of that day in Dealey Plaza.

I made photocopies of any pictures I could find. Most of the papers had all the same famous pictures I had seen a million times before, especially the one of Jackie standing next to Lyndon Johnson who was taking the oath on Air Force One. Her clothes were blood-stained and her eyes conveyed shock and despair. I stared into her eyes and tried to imagine what she must have been feeling. I wondered how she had told her children that their father was dead.

I paid close attention to the reports from the people who had been there. These were the first accounts, before any home movies and pictures had been analyzed. It was amazing how varied and ambiguous they were. The day had been chaotic with no real understanding of what had happened. I also paid close attention to the other, seemingly irrelevant details...descriptions of the weather, landscape, and ambiance. These were the details I would need to focus on to get there. The other things...like who actually did the shooting, I would learn later.

I had visited Dealey Plaza with my parents when I was twelve. We toured the 'Sixth-Floor Museum' and the 'Grassy Knoll', which was good. I knew I would need every bit of imagery and knowledge to make my plan work.

I was so lost in my planning that I nearly jumped out of my skin when I heard a voice right next to my ear say, "Hi beautiful!"

My heart leaped as I spun around, but instead of Aaron's smiling face, I saw Sam. Sam was one of the football players that I had been tutoring for the last few weeks and he was easily my least favorite pupil. I would have quit tutoring him entirely if he hadn't been the best friend of the guy Taylor was dating. Oh and he wasn't just any football player, he was the Harper Warriors' starting quarterback, which meant that it was imperative to a lot of people that he passed his courses. No pressure.

The problem was that Sam had no interest in learning anything except what I looked like naked. He was known far and wide as the biggest man-slut at Harper. His conquests were legendary and the list of girls he had slept with was almost as big as his head. At first, I found his constant flirting funny. He would say the most clichéd ridiculous lines with these serious expressions that were meant to be alluring. Honestly, I could not believe that so many girls fell for him. Lately, he just annoyed me and I quickly became exhausted trying to redirect his focus from my chest to his textbooks.

"Uh hi Sam," I didn't try to hide my disappointment. I quickly returned to my pages hoping he would get the hint and leave me alone. It was no use though, Sam collapsed in to the chair next to me. He laid his head on the table and looked up at me with a pouting face and protruding lower lip. When I continued to ignore him, he began whining like a puppy.

You cannot be serious; I thought as I rolled my eyes and looked at him. "What is it?" I huffed.

"I'm just so sad that you're not happy to see me." This was followed by another whine and then he began nudging my arm with the top of his head as though I should pet him.

"Ugh!" I pulled away. "What are you doing here anyway? Wait let me guess, you heard the library was a good place to pick up chicks."

"Evan, you can pretend to be mean to me all you want, but I know deep down you want some of this." As soon as I saw his hand headed towards his crotch, I shot up out of my seat.

"Honestly, isn't it time for your narcissists' anonymous meeting?" I grabbed a handful of articles and headed towards the copy room, praying he wouldn't follow. I stood at the machine concentrating on making my copies without damaging the fragile newspapers.

The copy room was empty but there was a machine in the corner that was spewing out hundreds of copies. I found the steady sound of the papers passing through the machine and the smell of printing ink soothing. I was so lost in my daydreams that I didn't even hear him enter the room. He was standing right next to me before he spoke.

"What are you doing with *him*."

I jumped about two feet into the air. "You scared me!" I yelled at him. "Why did you sneak up on me like that?" My heart was racing from both fright and the excitement of having Aaron so close again.

"Why are you here with Sam?" he repeated. His voice sounded angry.

"I tutor him sometimes. Why are you so worried about it?"

"He's a jerk. He's arrogant and he uses people. You don't want to get involved with him." He was jealous and I had to admit it made me happy.

Aaron looked great. He was much tanner than the last time I had seen him and I guessed he must have been playing a lot of tennis. He was wearing a red T-shirt that said 'Geology Rocks'. It was kind of random, but it was quirky and suited him perfectly. He had the usual stylishly unkempt coif, but it was a little shorter. It had been cut, and the golden highlights were even more obvious. I wondered if he still ran his hand through it as much, now that it was shorter.

"So how are you? How's your semester going so far?" I asked, trying to be civil.

"Not great."

"I'm sorry to hear that. Have you been playing a lot of tennis? You look tan." I was trying my hardest to be congenial and friendly, without sounding desperate. The truth was, I was so happy to see him that my heart was bursting.

"Yeah, you look different too." He said, looking me up and down. "So what are you Taylor's little clone now? Have you already pledged to her sorority?" His tone was judgmental and he looked pissed.

"Why are you being so mean?" I demanded.

"I'm not being any way; I'm just making an observation. You used to be different, your own person. Now you're just another wanna-be, shaking your ass for rich jocks like Sam."

The fury rose in me. My face was hot and my eyes watered from the heat. He just stared at me waiting for a response. I knew that he was trying to make me angry and elicit a reaction. I wished I could be strong enough to ignore him, be the better person, and just walk out.

"You're a bastard Aaron, and to think I wanted to try to stay friends with you."

"I can't be friends with you, Evan." His tone was less malicious now and more somber.

Now I *was* going to leave. For some reason, he was trying to hurt me and it was working. I wouldn't let him do it anymore. I calmly took my papers off the copier and walked to the door.

"That's fine, just run to Sam. But let me warn you after he's used you up, it's going to be hard to find another guy who will want you." He spoke to my back, yelling to be heard over the copier.

I tried to just leave, my hand was on the door handle, but the anger took over and I couldn't control myself. I wanted to hurt him.

"So what am I supposed to do, just wait around for your girlfriend to die?" As soon as it came out of my mouth, I knew I had crossed the line. Tears welled up in my eyes and I darted out of the room before I could hear his response. I didn't dare turn to look at his face. I walked back to the table as fast as I could. Mercifully, Sam was gone. I grabbed my notebooks and darted out of the library and into the night, vowing never to speak to Aaron James again.

—ℓℓ—

"I speculate that the great majority of you have not even begun your midterm project. I want to assure you that if that is the situation in which you now find yourself, you should be extremely worried and may want to consider dropping this course." I felt the beads of sweat starting to form on my upper lip.

"For those of you who have used the ten weeks leading up to this moment to your advantage, and are now in the final steps of completing your essay, I encourage you not to hesitate to seek out my help if you need it. I will be on campus throughout Spring Break and will even extend my normal office hours. However, DO NOT come to my office asking for help in forming your hypothesis. You should be well beyond that point."

Dr. Browning dismissed the class, but as everyone else left the lecture hall excitedly discussing their projects, I sat dazed and fixed to my desk. Although I had memorized the pictures, and knew all the details of the events leading up to the shooting, I hadn't attempted to go back. I told myself that I was waiting for Taylor to leave for Spring Break, but deep down I knew that was not the only reason.

All the other times I had traveled to the past, I was either visiting my own memories, or I had imagined I was someone else and visited theirs. I had carefully focused on either what I or they were feeling at the time of the event. I knew that the mood and atmosphere were a big part of it. This time though I was detached, just looking at a snapshot of history from the outside. I had no sense of the emotions connected to it.

I knew what I needed to do. I needed to identify with one of the people there... study their recollections, and learn how they 'felt' the day of the assassination. I needed to *become* someone in that place and time. I just didn't know how to do it and I was very worried that I had been wrong about the whole thing. Now I wasn't even sure it was possible at all. And if it wasn't, how was I going to come up with a thesis *and* write it in the next week? Meanwhile, Taylor had been working diligently on her project for weeks.

Dr. Browning was gathering his things to leave when he noticed me still sitting there.

"Ms. Wright, class was dismissed."

I looked up at him, trying to hide my trepidation. "Yes, I know. I was just wondering...when will you be available next week?"

He looked at me disapprovingly and I was sure that he guessed I was one of the students that had been neglecting my project. "I will be in my office from twelve to four every day."

I wrote the times down in my notebook and started to gather my things.

"Ms. Wright, your work has been articulate and insightful thus far. I am expecting great things from your essay."

"Great," I mumbled under my breath.

—ee—

I hadn't seen Aaron since our altercation in the library, but I couldn't stop thinking about what I'd said to him...and what he had said to me. I was still so raw from the argument, but the searing anger had melted into a constant dull pain. I was sure he would never forgive me for what I said, so imagine my shock to see a bouquet of red roses waiting for me back in our room.

Taylor looked like the cat that had swallowed the canary when she gave them to me. The card was sealed but she knew exactly who they were from. I wasn't as confident, but sure enough, the card read:

Evan, please don't hate me. Love, Aaron.

Love Aaron! I didn't understand him. What was this supposed to mean? He didn't try to contact me for months, and when he finally spoke to me it was to insult me, and now this! I'd had enough.

He was sitting at the check-out desk reading a textbook when I walked in. I headed straight towards him without hesitating. I was sick of playing games. We needed to have this out once and for all! I wasn't going to spend months pining again. I was going to face him head-on. I walked right around the desk, taking him off guard.

"We need to talk," I whispered in his ear.

This time *he* jumped, quite literally right out of his seat. "Evan! Uh...hi."

"Can you take a break?" I hissed.

He was obviously surprised by my directness. Clearly, he had been expecting me to avoid him again.

"Uh...OK...just let me see if Mr. Sawyer can take over here for a...few minutes."

Aaron left, returning with the cranky old librarian. Mr. Sawyer gave me a dirty look. I was sure he recognized me from New Year's Eve. Great, I thought, now he hates me!

"Alright Miss, can you show me which machine your copies are stuck in?" Aaron gave me a look indicating I should play along. I just turned and headed towards the copy room.

Luckily, the room was empty and quiet. As soon as the door closed behind us, I faced him. He was wearing gym shorts and a Harper Warriors sweatshirt. He had probably come straight to work from tennis practice. He looked at me expectantly, but in my hurry to confront him I hadn't really planned out what I was going to say. Now I was all fired up without a clue of what to do. I swallowed and steadied myself.

"First you say that we can stay friends, then you don't call me for months, and next you're yelling at me about Sam and telling me you can *never* be my friend. Now I have a bouquet of flowers sitting in my room. What is going on Aaron? Because to tell you the truth I don't think I can take much more of this."

Aaron looked at the ground. I could tell he was having a hard time deciding what to say to me. He started to talk and then stopped three times before he finally got a sentence out.

"First off, I wasn't the only one who didn't call. My phone wasn't exactly ringing off the hook these past few months. Secondly, the reason I didn't call you was because I wanted to...*try* to forget you. I thought if I just stayed away from you I could stop feeling the way I'm feeling. Of course, that was a stupid idea because it didn't work at all. Then, when I saw you with Sam ...well...I just lost it. I'm sorry I was so vicious. It's just...the way he treats girls...I couldn't stand the thought of him...*touching* you." He stepped closer to me, and his eyes finally met mine. "I still can't."

As he spoke, he reached out to brush a loose strand of hair away from my face. "I've missed you." His hand lingered close to my cheek. I held my breath. "When I saw you with Sam I thought that you had just forgotten all about me."

Although his hand barely brushed against my face when he pushed my hair back, it left a trail of tingles that ran from my cheek, all the way through my body. The effect of that tiny touch was incredible...and dangerous. In the instant our skin touched, it was almost impossible to remember reason or restraint. I knew it would be so easy to lose myself in him. Thankfully, he didn't test my resilience. He stepped back as if he sensed the danger too.

With him a safe distance away, I was able to think more clearly and compose myself.

"Of course, I didn't forget about you. I think about you all the time, but what are we doing here Aaron? Can we be friends or not? Because if we can't, then I think we need to stay away from each other." The words caught in my throat. I hated saying them. "You said that you couldn't be my friend. Was that true?"

"If those are my choices, stay away from each other or be friends...Then I choose friends. I can't stand the thought of you not being in my life. The past few months have been hell."

"I haven't been happy about not seeing you either, but we have to be realistic. If we decide to be friends, there can be no more flowers, jealous rages, or brushing hair away from my face." He smiled at me, realizing the effect of his touch. "I'm serious. What happens if I start seeing somebody? Can we still be friends then?"

"As long as it's not Sam," he said seriously.

"You don't have to worry about that, I promise." The thought of it practically made me gag.

"Then we're good." He held his hand out for me to shake. "Friends?"

"Friends," I said, shaking his hand and trying to stay optimistic about the chances of it working out.

"Can I just say one thing...and I mean this in a friendly way...I didn't mean what I said last night about the way you look now. I think you look amazing. You're not Taylor's clone, she can't hold a torch to you."

I tried to stop myself from blushing. "Thank you, I will take that as a friendly compliment." I felt uncomfortable and changed the subject. "So...with all things considered how has your semester been?"

"Pretty bad, but it's looking much better now." He flashed me an Elvis smirk and my heart melted. I hadn't realized exactly how much I had missed him. I knew it was going to be hard to be around him and remain...platonic...but he was right, it was better than being apart.

"How are your classes?" I asked.

"Same old, same old. How about you? Are you taking any interesting courses this semester?"

I filled him in on my change in curriculum, explaining that I thought I needed to broaden my horizons from the strictly science path.

"You know Evan, it's not just the clothes and hair, you really seem different...softer, more... open-minded, accessible."

"Thanks. It's been an incredibly introspective semester so far."

He looked puzzled, but let it go. "Well, whatever it is, it suits you."

I was so happy to hear him say that. I knew that I had changed a lot in the past few months, but I also knew that I wasn't objective enough to appreciate the extent of those changes.

"So, what are you doing for Spring Break? Do you have any tennis tournaments?" I secretly hoped that he would be stuck in Blythe again.

"Uh...no. I'm leaving Saturday and spending the week at home." He seemed disappointed about this.

"Oh...that's great." I lied. "I guess it will be good to be home and see your family after such a long time."

"Actually, I've been home quite a bit this semester. I got the transmission in my car replaced and it's been much more reliable. It's been good to see the folks...and Jack." We both knew who else it had been good to see.

"It's OK to talk about her you know. If we're going to be friends then we should be able to talk to each other about...things." As I said the words, I tried to convince *myself* of it as well.

"I guess. It just feels weird to discuss Becky with you." I wondered how long it would take before the sound of her name didn't make me cringe.

"No really, it's OK. I can handle it." I said smiling, trying to assure him and myself.

"Well, she's been having a lot of tests. Next week she will be in the hospital for another round. That's why I'm going home for Spring Break. You know, moral support and all." He gave me a weak smile.

"So, do they think...I mean does it seem like they can fix...the problem?" Her face flashed in my mind again, eyes rolled back...

"Well, hopefully, we'll know after next week. They are...I mean *we* are...hopeful."

Before I could respond, the door flung open and Mr. Sawyer walked in.

"Aaron! What's going on? Is the machine fixed or not? I have over two hundred books that need to be cataloged. I can't spend all day sitting at the check-out desk." His face was red and he knew very well there was no copy machine crisis. "Finish up and get back to work, now!" He shot me another dirty look before he stormed out.

"Sorry, I got you in trouble. Is everything going to be all right?" I was mostly referring to the situation with Mr. Sawyer, but from the way he looked at me, I could tell that we both knew the question was far more encompassing.

"Don't worry, he's all bark and no bite. He's just pissed because I'll be gone all next week and he'll have to pick up the slack. I should get back though before he has a minor stroke."

"Of course. I'm happy we got all this sorted out and I hope you have a...good...or well, successful...trip. Will you call me when you get back? Maybe we can get together sometime."

"Absolutely, I promise. I'm looking forward to it." He stepped towards me and then hesitated. There was a brief awkward moment when he tried to decide to go in for a hug or just shake my hand. He ended up giving my arm a brief caress then hurried off to placate Mr. Sawyer.

Chapter 9

FALL OF THE PRINCE

I spent the weekend depressed, moping around campus. I missed Taylor and Aaron. I was so bored I even missed tutoring the jocks, except for Sam of course. Taylor had asked me to come home with her again, and I was so tempted to take her up on the offer. But if I had gone there was no way I would be able to complete my History project. The old Evan would have loved all the time alone, but in the quiet of solitude, I simply found disappointment in myself for neglecting my studies.

Since Taylor had left, I had tried and failed to travel to November 22, 1963, several times, and the more I failed, the more I began to doubt myself. Ever since I had discovered my ability I had felt special, almost superhuman, and I had been sure that I was destined for greatness. After the changes I set into motion by confronting Bret, my hubris had grown even greater, and my physical appearance had changed as well.

I relished my secret. I imagined that this was how Clark Kent and Peter Parker would have felt had they been real. They walked around, appearing to be normal people, but inside they were keeping this miraculous secret that they were different and special and possessed powers that no one else had.

That's how I *had* felt...until Spring Break. However, being alone with my power failing, I doubted everything about myself. The old insecurities were back, with a vengeance. I felt like I was being punished for my vanity, and now I was going to have to suffer the consequences of losing my academic ambition as well.

I was behind in my classes and was very seriously thinking about dropping at least one. I knew that if I did drop a class it should be one of my electives, not one required for my major. The problem was, that I liked the electives better, and it was becoming increasingly difficult to keep up with the others.

Being honest with myself, I realized that all I wanted to do was forget about everything except Aaron, my friends, and my quest to understand my power. I wanted to explore it and test its boundaries. I was scared though. I didn't want to make any mistakes, hurt anyone...else, or change myself anymore.

On Monday I decided to go talk to Dr. Browning. I wasn't especially excited about meeting with him one-on-one, but I needed more insight into the day of the assassination, and I was running out of time.

When I arrived, there was already a student in his office and I had to wait for forty-five minutes before the door finally opened. When it did, out walked Dr. Browning with a girl that I recognized from class. They were obviously discussing her thesis project, but they were also laughing and joking around. I immediately remembered what Taylor had said about Dr. Browning dating students. It immediately made me scrutinize the girl.

She wasn't unattractive, but she had this whole Goth, combat boot, eyebrow-ring thing going on, that detracted from her looks. Her hair was jet-black and styled in a short pixie cut, and in addition to the eyebrow ring, there were several other piercings in her face.

She was petite and had small features that reminded me of an elf. Yes, she looked like a Goth elf, a Gelf. I thought that she could be very pretty if she took the metal rings out of her face and washed all the black crap off her eyes. As she walked out, she told "Ian" that she would "catch him tomorrow." I decided that if Dr. Browning did date students, and she was one of them, I seriously had to question his taste.

As the girl walked off down the hall, Dr. Browning turned and finally noticed me sitting in the chair next to his office.

"Ms. Wright...I didn't see you there. Please come in."

He led me into his cramped dark office. The room hadn't started small, but it was so packed full of stuff, that there was very little room to even move. Crowded bookcases lined three of the four walls, and a desk that was too large for the space was wedged awkwardly at an angle between the two of them. Stacks of books overflowed from the bookcases, covering the desk and most of the floor, and in the spaces between books were piles of papers.

In the corner opposite the desk was an ancient-looking velvet-covered loveseat. The crimson material on the cushions was worn and faded from decades of use. I noticed a heap on the floor at the far end of the couch that looked like a blanket and pillow.

As the office was in the basement of the History building, there were no windows, save for a small slit of a window high up on the far wall, which didn't let in much light. Instead, the room was lit by a small antique-looking lamp with a tasseled fringe, which sat on the desk.

The air was thick and stale and smelled of old books and dust. There were a few pictures on the walls. They were mostly aged black and white photographs of people I didn't know, except for a metal plaque that said "Guinness is Good for You!" The office looked like it belonged to a professor who had been at Harper for dozens of years, rather than that of someone who had been here less than two.

"I heard that they had opened a used bookstore on campus." I said, motioning to the piles. I could tell from the look on his face that my lame attempt at a joke had fallen flat. I tried to break the ice again, "So where in Ireland are you from?"

"Galway," he said in a slightly annoyed tone, which implied that he got this question all the time.

"Oh, the west coast, did you go to the National University then?"

He looked at me with a little more interest. "No, actually I went to university at Trinity College in Dublin."

I was impressed. Trinity was the top university in Ireland, actually one of the best in Europe for that matter. I had toured Trinity with my parents during a visit to Ireland when I was fourteen. It was founded in the 1500s by Queen Elizabeth I. Located right in the middle of Dublin, across from the former Houses of Parliament, it was grand and historic, and very beautiful.

"Trinity seems the appropriate place for a historian." I said, "I mean you got to study in the very same library that houses the Book of Kells." The Book of Kells was a biblical text written by Celtic monks in 800 AD. It was called an 'illuminated manuscript' because the intricate illustrations were drawn mostly in gold and silver and gave the text a glowing effect. I had seen it on display in a glass case in the Trinity library.

"How do you know so much about Ireland?" he asked.

"My dad is in the Army. We lived in Germany and Belgium and traveled all over Europe. Ireland is one of my favorite countries."

He looked at me with a newfound respect. "It's pretty rare to find Americans, especially young ones, who are so well-traveled."

I wanted to laugh at Dr. Browning calling me *young*. He wasn't all that much older than I was! I recognized his sentiment though. Many Europeans felt that Americans were ignorant when it came to world affairs, uncultured, and irrationally arrogant in their national pride.

I thought how frustrating it must be for Dr. Browning to teach history to American kids. We were taught American History and maybe the history of our own state, but all too often that's where it ended. Most college students in the States couldn't tell you about the Crusades, the signing of the Magna Carta, the Battle of Thermopylae, or the rise of Stalin. Most of us learned our world history primarily from the movies.

"So, what's on your mind, Ms. Wright?"

"Evan," I said out of habit.

"So *Evan*, what's on your mind?"

I liked the way he pronounced my name. His accent was subtle, but it occasionally surfaced when he said some words and phrases.

"Well, I've been working on my project, and I'm having some trouble..." I wasn't sure how to put it. "...understanding the...perspectives of the time."

"I'm not sure I follow." He looked perplexed, and I couldn't blame him. I barely understood what I meant.

"I mean that I need some insight into the mood of the times...what people would have been *feeling* the day of the assassination. The people that gathered to watch the motorcade, I mean. I suppose they would have been excited by the anticipation of catching a glimpse of the President and First Lady, but there has to be more...other more subtle undertones of emotion."

The way he stared at me made me realize just how crazy I must have sounded. His brow was furrowed as if he was trying to make some sense of the blathering idiot in front of him. Despite the grimace, his face was so incredibly handsome that I found it almost impossible to retain my train of thought. Instead of focusing on the task at hand, my mind betrayed me and found its way to more... carnal thoughts involving Dr. Browning.

This must be a common problem for girls who came to see him during office hours. I found it incredible that *any* woman could sustain a meaningful conversation with Dr. Browning for very long. He was *too* good-looking, everything about him screamed gratuitous, wanton sex. My face was so hot that I knew it must be beaming like a lighthouse. I was happy that the light in the room was so dim.

"That's a very compelling question, Evan. Most students are worried about getting all the factual details of the event correct. They want to know about dates, names, and places. I'm not sure I've ever come across someone as worried about understanding the *emotions* of the event as you are...its...very interesting."

I couldn't tell by his tone if he thought it was interesting in a good or superfluous way. One thing was for sure. He was intrigued, and this was an accomplishment in itself. Usually, Dr. Browning just seemed bored by the things students had to say. He leaned back in his chair.

"Well, 1963 was one of the most tumultuous years in U.S. history, and I suppose that the mood of the people gathered to watch the motorcade pass that day depended a great deal on the color of their skin."

"How do you mean?" I asked, hoping he would elaborate.

"Well, take Selda Henry for example. She was a sixty-four-year-old black housekeeper from Dallas and a witness to the assassination. She had probably waited patiently for hours that day just to get a spot to stand that would allow her a good view of the president. She was probably one of the millions of African Americans who felt great pride and hope in the man who had earlier that same year made a historic civil rights speech, in which he had demanded that blacks should receive "the kind of equality of treatment that we would want for ourselves." Dr. Browning leaned forward and his voice was somber.

"Remember Evan, this was the same year that four young black girls died in a bombing while attending Sunday school in Birmingham, Alabama. After which, protests ensued and thousands of African Americans, many of them children, were arrested and even had fire hoses and police dogs unleashed on them.

"Martin Luther King, Jr. himself was arrested in one Birmingham protest on the trumped-up charge of 'parading without a permit', and the civil rights leader Medgar Evers was murdered in Jackson, Mississippi. However, 1963 was also the year that Reverend King delivered his *I Have a Dream* speech on the steps of the Lincoln Memorial to an audience of 250,000 people, and the U.S. Supreme Court ruled that everyone, even the poor, had a right to a lawyer. So, for many people, there was a hope and anticipation of the coming change that President Kennedy would help usher in."

I tried to focus on the gravity of his words and their implication on the mood of the day, but the adolescent part of my brain, kept noting how sensually his mouth moved as he spoke.

"However, that wasn't true for everyone. For example, thirty-three-year-old Robert Lee Mason, a white patrolman on duty that day, probably agreed more with Alabama's Governor George Wallace who proclaimed "segregation now, segregation tomorrow, and segregation forever!" in his inaugural speech earlier that year. This same governor also famously stood in the doorway of the University of Alabama to protest against integration, before stepping aside to allow two African Americans to enroll later in '63.

"The patrolman Robert Lee, who was on crowd control duty in Dealey Plaza that day, would be convicted several years later for the beating death of a black man whom he had pulled over for speeding. Unfortunately, as it was the South after all, there were probably several people there that day who very much disagreed with President Kennedy's views and felt that his policies explicitly impinged upon their way of life.

"Despite the dichotomy of the individuals there, I think the overall feeling of the nation at this time was one of hope, pride, and looking towards the future. This was especially true considering that President Kennedy had announced just two years before that America "should commit itself to achieving the goal, before this decade is out, of landing a man on the moon and returning him safely to the earth."

I sat quietly for a moment considering Dr. Browning's impassioned speech. "I find it amazing that you could have so much insight into the sentiments of a nation that isn't your own, at a time before you were even born," I commented.

Dr. Browning smiled. "Thanks for the compliment Evan, but understanding History *is* my job after all. I just hope that I was able to help."

"Oh yes. I think I have a much better grasp of things now. Thank you." I stood up to leave.

"So, Evan...I have never heard your name used in the feminine before. It's quite...nice actually."

The blush flared up from my chest into my cheeks and I had to look down. I wanted to tell him how my parents had been so sure that I would be a boy that they hadn't even thought to pick out a girl's name. They were so attached to the name that they decided to keep it, even though their poor daughter would be mistaken for a boy for the rest of her life. I wanted to tell him, but I was suddenly so flustered that all I managed to mumble was "Thanks."

I was still standing with my hand on the doorknob, poised to leave, when he spoke again.

"Can I ask...you said that Ireland is one of your favorite countries...what was your favorite part?"

It was so odd. If I hadn't known better, I would have thought that Dr. Browning was trying to keep me from leaving, but I couldn't imagine why. I thought carefully before answering his question. I had seen so many amazing things in Ireland, but I definitely had a favorite.

"I would have to say my favorite was Newgrange." I looked at his face to try to judge his impression of my choice. He leaned forward, rested his elbows on the desk, and folded his hands in front of him. He stared at me, eyes squinted and brow furrowed, as if he was confused or trying to make a decision. My eyes flitted about, unable to hold his stare.

"That's an interesting choice. People usually say the Cliffs of Moher or Blarney Castle. Newgrange isn't even on most people's itinerary. What did you like about it?" He scrutinized me, and the pressure was intense. I felt like I was taking an oral exam. I was still standing with my hand on the doorknob, but as I thought hard about how to answer his question, I sat back down in the seat opposite Dr. Browning.

I pictured Newgrange in my head. It was this amazing prehistoric site located in the countryside about an hour outside Dublin. It's an archeological masterpiece *and* a huge mystery. Most people don't realize that Newgrange is the oldest, still-standing, man-made building on the planet.

It is comprised of several large 'burial mounds' that are hundreds of years older than the Pyramids *and* Stonehenge. I remembered that the largest mound covered an entire acre! We got to go inside it by walking down this long narrow tunnel that led us into a cruciform-shaped chamber.

The guide told us that the mounds were probably used as tombs because recesses in the inner chambers held large stone basins in which human remains were discovered. I also remember them saying that the construction of the mounds was a mystery because it would have taken the constant work of several hundred people over thirty years to build. Plus, there are over five hundred large stone slabs that comprise and surround the mounds and it is still not understood where they all came from or how they got there.

Above all though, I thought the biggest mystery surrounding Newgrange was its astronomical significance. The burial mounds were constructed precisely so that only on the shortest day of the year, the Winter Solstice, the light of the rising sun would enter a small window above the entrance to the passage. Then, the beam of light shines all the way down the long passageway and illuminates the central chamber.

On our tour, the guide simulated this process with a flashlight and the effect was spectacular. One minute you were standing in a nearly pitch-black chamber, and then slowly an orange shaft of light begins to travel down the tunnel until it eventually breaks into a bright glow that lights up the entire chamber.

I realized he was waiting for me to answer, so I tried to sum up my feelings about the place. "Well, apart from its beauty, I suppose that I loved the mysteries surrounding Newgrange. There's so much about it that no one completely understands, from the unlikely logistics of its construction to its actual purpose.

"I love that no matter how smart we think we are, or how advanced our technology is, we can still only guess about what those ancient people were up to at Newgrange. I wonder why the place was so important to them that they spent generations of labor on it. I wonder how long it took them to engineer the structure so perfectly that only the light from the sunrise of the Winter Solstice could penetrate the inner chamber, and why that particular day was so important to them. I just love all the unknowns about Newgrange and the possibilities it holds."

His eyes were wide as if he was glued to my every word. Of course, looking into his eyes was mesmerizing and completely made me forget every single thing I was about to say. Not only were they the most amazing blue I had ever seen, but now I realized that his irises were very big in proportion to the rest of his eyes, which made them stand out even more.

He must have realized that I had lost my train of thought because he blinked quickly several times and broke his stare. Surely, he knew the power his eyes had. This must happen to him all the time, I thought. He must be used to girls becoming utterly stupid around him.

"What do you mean by the *possibilities* it holds?"

I was so lost in his gaze that I barely registered that he was speaking, much less understood the question. "Huh?" I eloquently asked.

"You just said that you loved all the unknowns about Newgrange and the *possibilities* it holds. What did you mean by possibilities?" His eyes were probing again and I couldn't figure out where he was going with this.

"Did I say possibilities? Well, I guess I just meant that I love the fact that any number of explanations could be put forth to explain Newgrange...its meaning, people, and purpose."

Dr. Browning was quiet for a moment or two. He seemed to be deep in thought. Then his head suddenly snapped up and he said, "Well, I have something for you then."

He popped up out of his chair and turned to the bookshelf behind him. He scanned the bookcase making little clicking sounds with his tongue.

This was the best way to look at him...with his back turned to me. Not only was the view spectacular, but I could let my eyes linger without the embarrassment of my telltale flushed cheeks.

Dr. Browning normally dressed a little too casually, but since it was Spring Break, all bets were off. He was wearing faded loose-fitting jeans, without his usual brown leather belt, and an old gray t-shirt that was perfectly worn in. It hung off his broad shoulders perfectly and was thin enough that I could see the ridges of the muscles lining his back and shoulder blades.

Dr. Browning finally spotted the book he was looking for on the top-most shelf. When he lifted his left arm to reach it, I could see the faintest outline of that amazing muscle that is only visible on very toned guys...the oblique, I thought it was called. It cut a line in the t-shirt right below his ribs and wound down in a smooth sinewy trail that disappeared under the front of his jeans. Too soon he had the book in hand and was turning around.

I felt like one of those old-time Southern Belles who were always saying 'Oh my' and fanning themselves. I was flushed and literally breathless. The room suddenly seemed very stuffy. I had never been claustrophobic, but I felt like I had to get out very soon.

Dr. Browning walked around the front of the desk until he was standing right by my chair. I stood up to leave, for the second time, and found myself right up against him in the cramped corner by the door. I awkwardly edged back as far as I could and almost fell over the chair. Dr. Browning had to grab my arm to steady me.

"Whoa, are you OK?"

I was so embarrassed that he was having this effect on me, but his proximity was too much. A perfect musky-sweet combination of cologne and sweat filled the air between us. I thought that his scent had to contain about two hundred different kinds of powerful pheromones because my head was swimming from it.

"Uh yeah, I'm fine. Just got a little lightheaded, forgot to eat today I guess." I felt so lame.

"I think you might enjoy this book." He held out an aged leather-bound copy of a book entitled 'Irish Myths and Legends'. "There are several stories involving Newgrange in it. Have a read and tell me what you think."

"Thanks," I said. I grasped the book, but as he released it, his fingers brushed across my wrist. It was a natural motion, especially as we were squeezed into this tight space, but I could have sworn that his fingers lingered a few beats too long. This surprised me and my eyes darted up to his face. He was staring again, and the look in his eyes instantly reminded me of Aaron. My heart began to race and I nearly fell again trying to get out of his office.

I inhaled deeply as soon as I got outside, trying to clear my head of the foggy stupor Dr. Browning had put me in. As I walked across campus, I considered if it was possible that Dr. Browning had just been flirting with me. Although Taylor had said he dated students, I had never seen any evidence of that or even heard the rumor from any other source. Plus, he just didn't seem the type.

I mean, I had hated him at first, and I still thought he was occasionally grandstanding and pompous, but I also thought he was honorable. He didn't seem like someone who would break the rules or take advantage of his students. No, I was pretty sure what I had just experienced was more wishful thinking than anything else, and I was sure I wouldn't be the first or last of Dr. Browning's students to become smitten with him. First Aaron, now Browning...why did I keep falling for men I couldn't have?

***

I tried to block out all my illicit thoughts of Dr. Browning and focused on finishing my midterm assignment. I had been so frustrated by my failed attempts before, that I was determined to get everything right before I tried again. This time I was even dressed more appropriately. I had studied all the pictures I could find of 1963 and spent one whole day scouring the local secondhand clothes shops and Goodwill for the appropriate attire.

I found a beige cotton sheath dress that cinched at the waist and a coordinating brown cardigan in the style of the early sixties. The dress/sweater set was marked 'vintage' in the shop and priced pretty high. I had managed to talk the shop owner down and even though the outfit was a little more than I wanted to spend, it fit almost perfectly and I decided to buy it.

At the Goodwill store, I bought a pair of low-heeled dark brown pumps. They certainly weren't from the sixties, but they were similar enough to the style of the time and low enough that I could walk around comfortably in them. It kind of grossed me out to wear used shoes, but the two-dollar price tag and a good dousing with Lysol helped me get over my squeamishness.

I finished my outfit off with something I had never worn before in my life...pantyhose! They were uncomfortable and I hated the way they looked, but I didn't think it was appropriate to walk around with bare legs in 1963. The hippie movement was only just beginning and the *Summer of Love* and *Woodstock* wouldn't happen for another four years, so I didn't think I should be running around like a bohemian. The objective was to blend in and remain undetected.

I had read all the conspiracy theories and knew that most of them involved some person or persons shooting the President from the grassy knoll. Even polls taken very recently revealed that most people still did not believe that Lee Harvey Oswald had acted alone and that it was very likely others were involved in the actual shooting. The more I read I even had to admit that it seemed very unlikely that one man, located high up in the book depository, could have done such a precise and effective job with such a crappy and imprecise weapon.

Most of the conspiracy theorists believed that the fatal shot was fired by a man or men from behind the fence located at the top of the sloping grassy knoll. This area was on the President's right, on the Northwest side of Elm

Street, as his limo drove by. I remembered how close that area was to the large X painted on the road, indicating the spot where the president had been shot when I visited Dealey Plaza with my parents. It was only about thirty feet from that fence to the X on Elm Street.

The grassy knoll certainly seemed to be a much more accessible area than the book depository, which was also on the North side of Elm Street, but about two hundred feet away and behind the motorcade at the time of the shooting. More than a third of the witnesses who testified indicated that the shots had come from the grassy knoll, which was in front of the President.

Although dozens of people had run up to the fence after the shooting, in an attempt to catch the shooter, no one was found. However, there were no published accounts from people who claimed to have seen the area either immediately before or during the shooting. Behind the fence were several potential hiding places and escape routes including a tool shed, a parking lot, a railroad yard, and several manholes. Many people believed that the hypothetical assassin or assassins could have fled from the knoll without being detected.

My plan was simple. I would travel back to that day and position myself in such a way that I could see behind the fence on the grassy knoll during the shooting. I had studied every picture I could find and watched the famous home-movie shot by Abraham Zapruder several times. I had memorized the sequence of events and locations of everyone who had gone on record.

Right next to the grassy knoll, opposite the fence, was a large white pergola. Zapruder had stood on a short concrete wall that jutted out from that very pergola as he shot the most famous amateur video of all time. If he had only panned over to his right he would have filmed the fence, which was only about twelve feet away from him, and potentially caught whoever may have been there on video. Instead, he had understandably kept the camera fixed on the President's motorcade and filmed the horrible moments of the shooting.

I thought I would try to position myself at the pergola, which would provide an excellent vantage point of the grassy knoll, while affording me cover from several large oak trees, as well as the pergola itself. From the pictures, I could see that there were surprisingly few people in that area, as most had preferred to line the street.

I sat on my bed in the dark, dressed in my new 'old' outfit. I had styled my hair in a ponytail, which was common for girls my age in 1963. Ironically, I realized it was the first time I had done so in months. I focused all my energy on picturing that fateful day. I wasn't trying to *imagine* being there, I was trying to *experience* being there. I thought of Selda Henry. I found a picture of her online with some information about her life. She had stood with the crowd lining Houston Street, which meant the motorcade had passed her before turning onto Elm, just seconds before the assassination.

In the picture, Selda looked so happy. The shot had been taken immediately after the limo passed her. The First Lady had been on the left side of the limo closest to Selda and may have even waved at her. Selda had a huge smile on her face. She was wearing a red and white flowered dress, covered by a black coat. They were probably her best clothes, and this picture had probably captured one of the happiest moments in her life. Sadly, one of the worst moments would occur just seconds later.

I suddenly had an impulsive thought. I jumped out of bed and unlocked my desk drawer where I kept all my 'research' notebooks. I retrieved another item that I had been hiding in my drawer...Aaron's small white rabbit's foot. I had gotten into the habit of carrying it around. I liked the thought of it hidden in my pocket, out of sight. For me, it had come to represent my much bigger secret. It soothed me to reach into my pocket and stroke it. Now I hoped it would bring me luck and comfort me, as if a little piece of Aaron was with me. I climbed back onto my bed, focused, and clutched the foot tightly in my hand.

I remembered everything I had read about the Civil Rights struggle and tried to become Selda in that moment. So proud to see her President, the Prince of Camelot, and his Princess, just a few feet from where she stood. She probably had to miss work that day to be there and would sorely miss the few dollars from the housekeeping job that kept her family afloat, but seeing President Kennedy was worth it. I tried to imagine everything this woman would have witnessed in her life leading up to this point.

Being born at the turn of the century, Selda Henry had witnessed technology like cars, phones, televisions, and planes come into wide use. She had lived through the Great Depression, two world wars, the Korean War and was now enduring the agony of having two grandsons fighting in Vietnam. She had lived before the discovery of antibiotics, and many vaccines, when children died of polio and common bacterial infections. However, by far the greatest struggles of her life had been because of her race.

Selda had been born to a poor family in the South when there was little hope of a black girl like her growing up to have a very bright future. She was only two generations removed from slavery and one hundred years before this date, her own grandfather had fought in the infantry for the Union in the Civil War.

As she stood with the crowd lining that street in Dallas, she might have thought about how another great president had issued the Emancipation Proclamation almost one hundred years before. Now she was about to see the man who she believed would transform the country again, making it a fair and equal land of opportunity.

Opportunity was not a concept Selda knew well. She had spent most of her life enduring segregation under the Jim Crow laws, which meant that she had been forced to attend separate schools, see different doctors, eat at separate restaurants, and use separate facilities, including bathrooms and water fountains, from whites. Theoretically, these laws were supposed to guarantee "separate but equal" status, but everyone knew the facilities assigned to the "colored" were far less than equal, sometimes bordering appalling. By design, these policies were meant to make blacks feel inferior, but Selda had never succumbed to those feelings. She knew that it took incredibly strong people to endure the trials that her ancestors had endured and she was extremely proud of their strength, ingenuity, and grace.

Imagining Selda's life, I became acutely aware of how easy mine had been. I had never felt hatred or the despair of inequality. I had never had to struggle for basic freedoms, in fact, I just took them for granted. I also felt guilty for not having appreciated the struggle that many people like Selda had faced. I wondered how, despite the horrors she had witnessed and the struggles she had endured, she remained steadfast in her faith for her country and her love for this new young President. I let all of her feelings flow into me, the fear and resilience, the despair and hope, and most of all the anticipation and excitement of the coming change and possibility of true freedom. Once I truly appreciated all that she was, I began to feel it.

It started very small, just a faint flutter in my stomach like I was scared or nervous. Although I certainly was nervous about this trip, I knew that this was not the cause of the feeling. I welcomed the coming nausea and let the sensation wash over my body. I continued to think about Selda, letting her emotions and perceptions guide me.

The waves of nausea slowly transformed into tides of pressure that pushed me down in a steady rhythm matching the beat of my heart. With each heartbeat, the mysterious force pushed me harder and further down, as if great invisible hands were performing rhythmic chest compressions. With each push, I gave in more and let my body sink into the abyss of time. Then, all of a sudden, there was a final firm push from the invisible hands and my body abruptly slipped through the metaphoric bottleneck.

I was plunging down and my head swam with the disorientation of falling through darkness. I fell for a long time, longer than ever before, and although my eyes were tightly closed, I thought I saw periodic flashes of light. It was like someone turning on a light when you are sleeping, and despite my curiosity, my natural reaction was to squeeze my eyes shut even more tightly, blocking out the light.

After several moments, my body was jolted as I hit the ground very hard. When I landed I was still sitting, but the force of the fall made me tumble over onto my side, scraping my elbow pretty badly. I heard the noise of a crowd very close, and quickly opened my eyes, frantically looking around. At first, I was confused because it seemed too dark. However, as the disorientation and dizziness dissolved, I slowly began to comprehend what I was seeing and hearing. It was dark because I was in the shadows under the pergola, exactly where I wanted to be. The voices of the crowd gathered at the bottom of the sloped knoll echoed off the concrete walls amplifying the sound. Thankfully, I wasn't close to the crowd, but I wasn't alone either. My heart raced as I heard the footsteps quickly approaching.

"Miss! Are you OK? You really took a fall."

I looked up and saw a young blonde man in a policeman's uniform reaching an arm out to help me up. This wasn't good. I needed to stay undetected, and certainly not attract the attention of the police!

"Uh thanks," I said taking his hand and letting him pull me to my feet. "Yeah, I slipped...very clumsy." I kept my head down as I dusted off and straightened my dress. I didn't want him to get a good look at my face. I knew that in the coming hours, everyone here would be interrogated about everything they observed...everyone they saw. Every detail would be scrutinized, and his description of me needed to be as vague as possible.

"Man...that was weird. It was like you dropped out of the sky! I mean I could have sworn that this area was completely deserted, and then all of a sudden I looked up and saw you take a hard fall. That had to have hurt."

Great...he was definitely going to remember the girl who mysteriously appeared and then ate it in front of his eyes! This was *really* not good. I mumbled that I was fine and not hurt, all the while trying not to meet his eyes. My elbow was killing me and I thought it might be bleeding, but I didn't want to call any more attention to myself.

"OK...well, we're trying to keep everyone down by the street. The motorcade should be here soon, so why don't you come on down with me." He extended his arm as if to guide me. However, luck must have been on my side, because at that exact moment, a loud staticky message came over the policeman's walkie-talkie.

I couldn't understand the voice on the other end, it just sounded like garbled noise to me, but the young man standing in front of me certainly seemed alarmed. He told the person on the other end he would be there "right away." He quickly told me that I should head down to the street, and then took off in a flat-out run. I watched him run down the knoll towards the junction of Elm and Houston. What the emergency was, I couldn't tell.

I collected myself after the way-too-close call and stepped out from the shelter of the pergola. It was like stepping into a dream. An absolutely amazing, unbelievable, impossible dream! I was physically standing in Dallas, Texas and it was 1963...decades before I was even born. I laughed at the ridiculousness and sheer wonder of it.

I looked out over Dealey Plaza. I had looked at a million pictures of this scene, but it was very different actually being here. The pictures were so artificial and dull, everything had that yellow, aged look that old photos always do. I guess I had naïvely expected things to actually look like those old pictures. Instead, everything was so vibrant...the sounds, colors, smells...they were so...real.

This was one of the most important days in history and I was here! I could hear the excitement of the crowd below. I could smell the freshly cut grass and feel the breeze on my skin. It was a beautiful warm sunny day. I remembered reading that forecasters had actually predicted it would be much cooler, so Jackie Kennedy had worn that iconic pink Chanel heavy wool suit. However, when the couple arrived in Dallas they were pleasantly surprised by the unseasonably warm weather. This warm spell had been a terrible twist of fate because it meant that the bubble top had been removed from the limousine, and the bulletproof side windows were rolled down, as President Kennedy preferred to ride on nice days.

I clearly remembered being here before, standing in this exact spot with my parents. Of course, my visit to Dealey Plaza wouldn't occur for several decades. I noticed the trees were a lot smaller now, and of course, there was no big white X painted on the road below.

There was already a large crowd gathered so I thought it must be near noon. As I looked out from my vantage point beside the pergola, I immediately recognized several of the people lining the street from the photos I had researched. I could see the Newman family, Bill, and Gayle with their two children. Bill was standing with his beautiful blonde-haired son on his shoulders. They looked like the picture-perfect family. It greatly saddened me that photos of Bill and Gayle laying flat down on the grassy knoll, shielding their children from bullets with their own bodies, would be broadcast around the world very shortly.

Directly across Elm, I saw Jean Hill in her brilliant long red coat, standing next to her friend Mary Moormon in her contrasting navy blue. Jean and Mary would be the closest witnesses to the assassination, as the President's limousine would be directly in front of them when the fatal shot made contact, and Mary's eight-millimeter film would help the FBI decipher the sequence of events that day. Both of these women would later testify that they had heard shots and saw smoke drifting away from the fence behind the grassy knoll.

I couldn't see Selda from where I stood, but I knew she was only a block away, around the corner on Houston St., proudly standing in her red and white flowery dress excitedly waiting. I looked down Elm towards

Houston Street and saw the red brick book depository building. I counted six floors up and looked over to the last window. I could tell the window was open, but I saw no movement.

It sickened me to know what was lurking in that room at this very instant. I had studied so many pictures of that room and even seen it for myself in its preserved state in the sixth-floor museum. I could picture Oswald sitting in his sniper's nest right now...just waiting. The thought of it made the hair on my arms stand on end. And knowing he was up there, looking down at the crowd, I suddenly felt very exposed. I realized that despite the warm day I was shivering.

I looked directly to my right and realized with amazement that standing only ten feet away from me was Abraham Zapruder! It was beyond bizarre to realize that this man was actually dead...well in my time he was, but here he was unquestionably alive. He was already standing on the concrete retaining wall, camera in hand. He was talking to a young woman standing behind him. Seeing him standing there getting ready to start filming made something snap inside me.

All at once, the reality and gravity of the situation sunk in. This wasn't just a horrible tragedy that had happened a long time ago. This was happening now! Someone was about to die right now, and not just someone...the President of the United States was about to die. Suddenly the thought of it was unfathomable.

I knew it was crazy but I couldn't help thinking that I could stop this horrendous event from happening. My mind reeled as I tried to devise a plan. All I had to do was find a police officer and tell him that someone was about to shoot the President. Of course, they would arrest me, but if I made a big enough scene, they would probably divert his motorcade. Then Lee Harvey Oswald, or whoever actually did this monstrous thing, wouldn't get their chance.

I searched frantically trying to find the closest police officer. As soon as I spotted one, standing on the corner of Houston and Elm, the adrenaline thrust my body forward. I took several steps out of the shadows of the pergola, heading down the embankment. My legs were compelled to sprint forward toward the policeman on the street corner. The struggle between my instinct and emotions and my self-preservation and logic was strong, but logic finally won out and I managed to stop myself.

Although the thoughts of trying to prevent what was about to happen consumed me, I knew it wasn't possible. If I went through with it, I would change history in a billion different ways, each with a billion potential ramifications. Who knows, maybe by preventing President Kennedy's death I would somehow do the world a lot more damage than would be done today.

The thing was, I didn't know what would happen. I *couldn't* know, and it was way too dangerous to try. So, I had to stand idly by and just allow this atrocity to happen. I wouldn't watch it though. I couldn't. I had barely been able to handle watching the blurry Zapruder film. It made me sick. Instead, I would do what I came here to do, which was to try to figure out exactly who killed him.

Calming myself, I stepped back into the shadows under the covered walkway. As soon as I did, I heard a loud rumble coming down the road. I saw Abraham lift his camera and start filming. This was it! I looked to the Northeast and saw two motorcycle police rounding the corner onto Elm. It was all happening too fast! I didn't have time to think. I wasn't ready and I knew I had less than a minute. It was now or never.

I swung around to the right and saw the wooden picket fence behind the grassy knoll, just a few feet beyond where Zapruder was filming. I walked quickly through the pergola until I was standing at the opening. All I had to do was take about ten steps and look over the fence. However, it meant stepping out from the shadows. I would be completely exposed and I suddenly worried about what would happen if I did catch someone standing back there about to shoot. Would they turn their gun on me?

There were loud excited cheers and shouts from the crowd and I could hear the sounds of several car engines. I didn't turn to look, but I knew the President's motorcade had just rounded the corner. I stared at the length of the fence. Surely if there was a shooter back there I would be able to see a gun, the top of a head, or some movement, I reasoned. I didn't have time to mentally debate the situation. Without even making a conscious decision, my legs began to move my body forward.

I walked out into the sunlight and quickly crossed a paved walkway over to the fence. I didn't stop to consider what I was doing. If I had, I never would have reached the fence. My legs trembled and my heart raced. I had never been this scared in my life. The cheers of the crowd below filled my ears. I kept my head low. The fence was only five feet high, and with my tall frame, I felt like a sitting duck for whoever may be back there.

My hands swept across the decrepit splintery wood as I crouched beside the fence. I just had to stand up and look but I was shaking violently, my knees felt like they would buckle and I was frozen with fear. Then I heard a loud crack and thought that I had somehow pushed against the fence too hard and broken a plank. However, it was quickly followed by two more cracks that were much louder than the first. The deafening sound echoed from all the surrounding buildings, and I knew it had happened.

I bolted straight up, adrenaline pumping through my body in bursts, and frantically scanned the area behind the fence. I looked everywhere from directly behind it on the ground to several hundred yards away where the freight trains were parked and saw absolutely no one! The area was completely clear of people. There were no mysterious figures, no guns, no smoke, nothing.

Once I had convinced myself that what my eyes were seeing was true, I turned and ran back under the cover of the pergola. I crouched in the shadows. People were screaming. I looked towards the road and saw the tail end of the midnight-blue limousine disappear under the highway overpass as it sped away. Along the knoll on my side of Elm and the lawn on the other side of the street, people were lying down flat with their arms over their heads.

I quickly glanced over to the book depository, but still saw nothing in the open window. Panning back to the knoll, something caught my eye. Directly across Elm, very close to where Jean and Mary now lay on the ground, I saw a woman. She stood out because, as everyone else near her cowered on the ground, she was standing very calmly taking in the scene.

I scrutinized the woman. She was wearing a black dress, covered by a long baggy beige coat. Her shape seemed odd to me. Her clothes weren't fitted as was the style. Instead, they were loose and gave her an amorphous shape. I couldn't make out her face because her head was covered by a heavy head wrap. Unlike the light silk scarves so popular at the time, this was bulky and looked more designed for concealing than for style.

People were now getting to their feet. Some were yelling and pointing to different areas around Dealey Plaza, others were running in all directions. Some people just stood still with blank looks on their faces or sobbed and hugged the person next to them. However, despite all the activity around me, everything else disappeared as I closely watched this woman.

I marveled that she was incredibly calm. She wasn't hysterical or in shock or frantically looking around trying to figure out what happened. In fact, she was carefully focusing on something in her hands. I strained to see what it was. It looked like she was holding a movie camera, but she seemed to be taking it apart.

I desperately wished that I had a pair of binoculars. I couldn't make out details, but it seemed like she was pulling pieces off a camera and putting them in her purse. I wondered if she was removing the film. It was a possibility. The FBI was going to confiscate all the cameras and film from everybody here. Maybe she realized this and planned to try to sneak the film out. I racked my brain to remember who this woman was. I had read so many of the witness reports and seen so many photos, but I could not recall her!

I tried to stay focused on her, but people were running up the embankment now to the top of the knoll. Many people were running up to the fence. I stayed crouched down in the shadows, praying I would remain unseen. The woman looked at her watch, which seemed to me a very casual gesture considering the circumstances. Then she turned and casually started walking South towards Main Street, opposite Dealey Plaza and the book depository. She had a wide husky gait, and I began to wonder if under all those bulky clothes this really was even a woman! Her behavior was so odd that I wondered how others had not noticed it. Why had I not read about this strange woman...or person before?

The police were starting to round up the people that were running about. I knew that each one of them would have to undergo extensive questioning and I had to get out of here before they found me. I needed to concentrate on getting back, but I was captivated by this person.

She made it all the way across the lawn without being stopped and I watched her step off the curb onto Main. I had to go, but wanted to wait and see if she was rounded up with the others or if she was allowed to leave the scene. I strained my neck to keep her in view without standing up. I could see police officers on either end of Main stopping people and I watched to see which way she would head.

As she crossed the street, a police car passed between her and my line of site. As the car continued down Main, I stared unbelievingly at the spot where the woman should have been, but she was gone! I stood up and frantically searched the whole length of the street. The woman had completely disappeared in the time it took a car to drive past her!

This was unfathomable! What the hell was going on? I looked at all the people in the area around Main Street, but no one seemed to have noticed it. I wondered if she could have bolted across the street and quickly found a hiding place, but there was nowhere directly across Main for her to hide. There was only another large open grassy area. She had completely vanished!

I didn't have time to think about what I had just seen because there was now another policeman running towards me! I knew he had seen me because he pointed right at me. There wasn't much I could do. I couldn't make a run for it. Instead, I crouched back down and scooted back into the shadows under the pergola until I felt my back touch the concrete wall. I only had seconds to get out.

I closed my eyes tightly and focused as though my life depended on it. I could hear voices headed in my direction, but I blocked them out and channeled every ounce of energy into getting home. I completely consumed my thoughts with images of my room. I longed for the warmth and security of my bed with every fiber of being. The feeling didn't slowly emerge as it did getting here, it was a sudden shockwave that felt like a truck hitting me full force. It knocked me off balance and then swept me down the long dark tunnel towards home.

I lay in my bed. The room was completely dark except for the bluish neon glow of the alarm clock. My whole body shook with sobs, fear, and deep sadness. I felt like I had just run a marathon. I was too exhausted to move a muscle. I could barely think. Just holding my eyelids open was way too much to handle. They fluttered closed, and I slipped into oblivion. The rabbit's foot, still clutched in my hand, fell to the floor.

Chapter 10

NEW GIRL AT THE DANCE

"Ladies and Gentlemen, I have graded your theses and will return them at the end of the period." He paused for some time, staring at the pile of papers on his desk. When he finally looked up, he had a very curious look on his face. As he spoke, he looked only at me.

"However, I want to pose a question to you first. You have now spent some time pondering the effects that the different interpretations of John F. Kennedy's death had on history. Considering everything you have learned; I want you now to think about what would happen if you could somehow *know* the answers to these mysteries. What if you could travel to the past and see the events firsthand?"

My breath caught. He was addressing the class, but he was staring straight at me. It was as if he was challenging me, and I was afraid he would see my panic. I couldn't hold his stare. I let my eyes fall and immediately felt like I had just incriminated myself.

Questions filled my mind. Could he know? That was impossible. But somehow, if he *did* know what I had done...why wouldn't he just confront me? Or *was* he confronting me? I couldn't look up at him and I certainly couldn't leave the room, which is what I really wanted to do.

"It wouldn't matter what you saw. No one would believe you anyway. You would be locked up in a mental institution if you tried to tell people the truth." I looked towards the sound of the voice and saw the pierced

Gelf girl. I chanced a quick glance at Dr. Browning and saw that he was now looking at her too.

"Are you saying that there would be no advantage to learning the great mysteries of the past since no one would believe you anyway?" He challenged her.

"I suppose you might get some kind of personal satisfaction out of knowing you possessed the answers that everyone else wanted, but what good is knowledge if you can't share it? You would probably just go crazy in the end." I was impressed with this girl's zeal. Not many students dared to go head-to-head with Ian Browning. I was also a little disheartened by her answer, considering, after all, she *was* talking about *me* going crazy in the end.

"Well, what if you could *prove* you were telling the truth? Let's say you could take a digital camera with you. You could photograph the event, then come back and download the pictures." There were several laughs at Dr. Browning's comment. I wasn't laughing though, in fact, the wheels in my brain were turning a million miles a minute.

"You would be a superstar. The most famous person in the world," the Gelf yelled out.

"You could work the talk show circuit!" Someone else commented.

"You could become rich by taking time-traveling jobs to solve mysteries for people, find their missing relatives and things." Another student in the front said.

At this point, the lecture hall erupted into the excited whispers of several mini conversations all around the room by students who were too shy to voice their comments out loud. I strained to hear them all.

"OK, settle down. I think you're all missing my point. What I'm asking is what would *the world* gain by knowing the answers to the mysteries of the past." He looked at me again. It was as if those crystal blue eyes were penetrating my soul. "What do *you* think Evan?"

The class was hushed now and everyone looked at me waiting for my response. The heat of my blushing face almost brought tears to my eyes. I was sweating and couldn't catch my breath. I was sure that I looked like I was about to have a heart attack or a panic attack at the very least. I was so busted. I considered faking a fainting spell to get me off the hook. Although, the way my heart was racing I thought I might not need to fake it after all. I tried to guess what Dr. Browning *thought* he knew and how.

It had been a week since I turned in my assignment and, granted I had been quite rushed when I wrote it, I certainly didn't think that I had written anything incriminating. I had tried to link the assassination to the temporary decline of the civil rights movement that followed.

I hypothesized in my thesis that the controversy and conspiracy theories that swirled around the murder of JFK particularly affected the African-American population. Many of them believed that the government had masterminded the assassination to intentionally derail the movement, and I postulated that these perceptions would be validated with the assassination of Martin Luther King Jr. a few years later.

I knew that the essay wasn't my best work. I had essentially written the whole thing the day before it was due. I hadn't woken up until 3:00 p.m. the day after my trip to 1963. I had slept almost twenty hours and had woken up disoriented and sore. It had felt like the worst jet lag, combined with the most massive hangover you could imagine. My whole body ached, especially the bits that had crashed against the ground when I landed. I still had a scraped-up elbow from the fall.

The trip affected me in other ways too. I was an emotional wreck for days. I couldn't forgive myself for my inaction. All logic told me that doing nothing had been the best decision, but I felt horrible. I couldn't get over the fact that I had been there and let it happen. Even though I hadn't seen the murder, the sounds of the shots and the screams still gave me nightmares. I wondered if the Gelf was right and the only future I had in all of this was going crazy from guilt, remorse, the helplessness of not being able to change anything, and having everyone think I'm insane if I tell.

Then there was the mysterious disappearing woman... or man... or person. I had spent all of Saturday trying to figure out who she, or it, was. It didn't take long to find the 'Babushka Lady'. She was all over the conspiracy theory websites. I couldn't believe that I hadn't seen her before.

She was called the Babushka Lady because the heavy scarf she wore on her head was similar in style to those worn by Russian grandmothers, who were called babushkas. Her image had been captured by a number of different cameras that day, although none of the pictures were very focused or detailed.

There were several blurry photos of her that showed her arms elevated and most people who had analyzed these pictures supposed she was holding a camera. She also appeared to be holding a large camera bag, which hung from a strap over her shoulder. In these blurry photos, she stood right where I had seen her, on the lawn across Elm, close to Jean Hill and Mary Moorman.

From her location, it was thought that the Babushka Lady had actually filmed the limousine approaching and that her camera could have captured the Book Depository building in the background, and other important information. However, no one would ever know because the Babushka Lady completely vanished after the assassination, and whatever images she had potentially captured on her camera, vanished with her.

The Babushka Lady had caused quite a stir at the time of the assassination and during the extensive ten-month investigation by the Warren Commission the following year. The FBI publicly requested that the woman come forward and give them the footage she shot, and a significant effort was made to figure out who she was, but it was all in vain. None of the witnesses knew her or got a very good look at her, and of course, the photos of her were too vague to use for identification.

I had spent the entire day following my trip trying to learn as much as possible about Babushka Lady. I was certain that somehow, she held important information about the assassination. Either she possessed key evidence, or she was somehow involved herself. However, there was nothing that could explain the way I saw her disappear, and that was what intrigued me most.

I couldn't help but wonder if it was possible that she was also a tourist in 1963. I mean I couldn't really be the only person in the whole world to have this ability...could I? Was it so hard to believe that there were others out there traveling through time as well? After experiencing what I had in the past few months, one thing was for sure...I knew that anything was possible.

"Evan, we're waiting." Dr. Browning's voice startled me as I sat dazed and completely lost in my own thoughts.

"Sorry, what was the question?" I knew everyone was staring at me awaiting my response, but I couldn't even remember why now.

Taylor leaned towards me and whispered under her breath. "Evan...what's wrong with you?"

"Ms. Wright while you've been daydreaming the class has been anxiously waiting to hear what *you* think the world would gain by knowing the answers to the mysteries of the past." His tone was condescending, and he had this incredibly smug look on his face. The heat emanating from me now was not from embarrassment anymore but from anger. I still couldn't guess what he *thought* he knew, but it was obvious that he was trying to intimidate me, and I wasn't going to let him.

"Well Dr. Browning, people like yourself have devoted your lives to *guessing* at what happened in the past, and no matter how much time you spend hypothesizing about these events you'll never have the satisfaction of knowing whether you're even remotely correct.

"You told us on the first day of this class that a famous historian once said that the first step in liquidating a people was to erase their memory.

Destroy their books, their culture, and their history, then have somebody write new books, manufacture a new culture, and invent a new history. So, I suppose that the world would certainly gain a lot more by knowing the *true* answers to the mysteries of the past rather than the conjecture that historians put forth. I mean aren't historians really just inventing their own version of history, and then encouraging people to believe it? In fact, isn't every recorded historical account just an interpretation of what really happened, tainted by all of the personal beliefs, biases, and prejudices of the person writing it?"

I held his stare as I spoke, and I could see venom rising in his eyes. He was not used to students challenging him and here I was criticizing his entire profession. I heard Taylor mumble "Jeez, Evan" under her breath. I continued to hold his stare and this time *I* had the smug look on *my* face.

I could feel the tension in the class. It was so quiet you could hear a pin drop. It reminded me of the staring competitions we used to have in grade school where you would have to stare at your competitor without blinking, trying your best to intimidate them and make them back down. It felt like several minutes passed with the two of us locked in combat before Dr. Browning finally acquiesced.

"Well, Ms. Wright has certainly given us a lot to think about. She seems to find little value in the lifetimes of study that historians devote to understanding just one event in the past because those interpretations will always be susceptible to their personal biases. I suppose there is some truth to her comments, although as we all know there is no alternative to simply *guessing* about the past. It is after all impossible to *know* what really happened. So, for the next class, I would like you to write a ten-page essay on whether it is better to view history through the *tainted* eyes of historians, or not at all."

There were sighs all around the room and I was sure that I had darts flying at the back of my head from all directions, but I didn't look at my classmates. Instead, I kept my eyes fixed on Dr. Browning. I was so pissed at him. He was obviously punishing me for my audacity by giving the whole class extra work, knowing they would blame me. His behavior was in such direct opposition to last week in his office, and I had no idea why he had changed his attitude towards me.

"Before I dismiss you and return your graded midterm papers, we need to discuss the topic of your final exam. The project will be similar to your midterm. You will be required to write a twenty-page thesis on a historical event. However, instead of examining how the interpretations of the mysteries surrounding the events affected history, this time you will become historical detectives. You will research all the material you can find surrounding the event and use all of your own *tainted* perceptions, beliefs, experiences, and prejudices to interpret what you think really happened."

I despised how he kept using my words, mocking them.

Dr. Browning was pacing in front of the class, hands behind his back and head down. "This time, however, *I* will choose the topic of your thesis, and we will compare how each of your different perspectives shaped the conclusions of your theses at the end. So, for your final project this semester you will research and gather historical evidence to support your thesis on how and why the burial mounds of Newgrange in Ireland were built."

Dr. Browning stopped pacing and looked up at me. Despite my anger, I couldn't help but give him a sly smile. It obviously surprised him because he furrowed his brow again, blinked quickly, then looked away. He dismissed the class and asked us to pick up our midterms on the way out. I suspected he wanted to avoid any students who were irate over their grades because he was out of the door in a flash.

Taylor was out of her seat the instant class was over, practically running down the aisle to the front of the room. I could see her with a group of students rifling through the graded essays. I took my time gathering my things, preferring to avoid as many of the others as possible. As I stood up to leave, Taylor was headed back up the aisle with a big smile on her face.

"You must have done well." I guessed.

She flipped around the paper and held it tightly to her chest. There was a big red circle with an A- in it and 'Good Job!' written across the front.

"Wow! That's awesome. You must be thrilled."

"I worked my ass off on that project. You bet I'm thrilled." Taylor put the paper in her notebook and gathered her things. She followed me down the aisle to the now deserted table at the front of the classroom. There was one lone paper left, face down, on the table. I took a deep breath and turned it over, very conscious that Taylor was peering over my shoulder. However, there was no big red encircled letter on my paper. Instead, there was only a message written in red pen that said, "See me."

A terrible feeling of foreboding, strangely mixed with the excitement of anticipation, swept over me.

"Evan, what the hell is going on between you and Browning?" Taylor was also clearly confused by the message written on my paper.

"What do you mean?" I asked innocently.

"*Hellooo*! What was that little episode just now? It's almost like you two were having a lover's quarrel, and now this...how well do you know him, Evan?" She gave my arm a little shove and winked at me.

"Don't be ridiculous. I don't know him at all. I don't know why he's picking on me like this." And it was true. I had no idea what he was up to, but obviously, if I wanted to find out my grade, I was going to have to go see him again.

———ell———

I met up with Taylor for dinner. I had hardly seen her in the week she had been back from Houston. She had been spending a lot of time with Rob, her 'tight-end', as she liked to call him. I was desperately hoping she would mention Aaron. I thought maybe she had seen him around the tennis club over break.

Spring Break had been one of the longest weeks of my life, followed only by the week after. Aaron monopolized my thoughts every waking day and sleepless night. I took comfort in his promise that he would call after returning to Blythe. The day classes resumed I must have checked my phone a hundred times. When he hadn't called by that evening, I phoned him, and it went straight to voicemail. Tuesday was the same story, followed by Wednesday...me anxiously waiting for his call and him not calling. I also made a point to walk by the tennis courts every day on my way back to the dorms, even though they were completely out of my way. I never saw him.

After four days, I felt like such a desperate loser that I stopped. I could not understand it. I had felt sure after our reconciliation in the copy room before Spring Break that we were *both* looking forward to reconnecting and moving forward with our friendship. But now he was blowing me off. I wondered if something bad had happened with Becky and he was still stuck in Houston. It still didn't explain why he hadn't returned my calls unless the news was *really* bad.

Taylor and I had decided to meet at Roscoe's, the burger joint across from campus. The burgers were big, greasy, and delicious, plus the place had the best fried cheese sticks in the state. Even Taylor ditched her diet for their cheese sticks.

Taylor was over twenty minutes late when she finally decided to make an appearance. I was severely disappointed to see she wasn't alone. Rob was following close behind like a faithful puppy. All my plans of girl talk and gossip were dashed. I put on a fake smile and tried to pretend I was happy to see *both* of them.

It wasn't like I hated Rob or anything. He was OK. He just bored the hell out of me, and I hated the way Taylor acted around him. She transformed from a witty, sarcastic, and amusingly bitchy gals-gal, to a giggling idiot. When Rob was around, she didn't have any interests or opinions of her own, she simply deferred to him on everything.

I hated it when women changed their whole personalities to conform to some guy's expectations. It infuriated me and I had to work very hard not to call her on it in front of him. I knew how much she liked him though, and because I loved Taylor, I put up with it. I had however let my true feelings slip a few times when it was just the two of us, and I had a feeling that was one of the reasons she had been so distant lately.

Despite my feelings, I had resolved not to come between the two of them. I didn't want her to feel like she had to choose between us, and honestly, I was afraid that if she did, she wouldn't choose me. I could not risk that. Taylor had become too important to me.

Taylor and Rob sat opposite me in the red vinyl booth. They were so close that she was practically in his lap.

"Should I get a full or half order of fried cheese?" I asked Taylor.

"Oh, none for me. I have to fit into my new dress for the Spring Formal!"

Jeez, who was she kidding? Taylor never refused fried cheese. "OK, a full order then," I said to the server. Taylor shot me a dirty look.

Dinner was painfully long and mostly consisted of Rob and Taylor discussing important topics like upcoming dances and sorority events. I tuned the two of them out and used the time to text my mom.

Just when I was beginning to think the whole evening was a wash, out of nowhere Taylor said, "By the way, Evan, I saw Aaron James at the club over break." *That* got my attention!

"Who's he?" Rob asked.

"Oh, he's just a friend of the family. He used to go school here." Taylor said offhandedly.

"What do you mean *used* to go here?" I demanded.

"Yeah, well that was what I was fixin' to tell you. I saw him one day when Simon and I were at the club. He's back there working with his dad now. He asked about you Evan...wanted to know how you were, what you had been up to, blah, blah, blah..."

I could not believe she was acting so blasé about this. This was the most important information I had received in weeks, and I was getting blah, blah, blah! I could have slapped her.

"Anyway, he said that Becky was going to be having surgery in the next few months and that he felt he needed to be there. So, he dropped his classes for the Spring and hoped he would be able to return after summer."

Taylor started picking at a leftover piece of fried cheese. My whole world was falling apart before my eyes, and she was acting as though she had just told me the weather forecast. Rob was staring up at the flat screen above us, completely oblivious to our conversation.

"But that can't be right. I mean he has the tennis team...his scholarship..." I was grasping at any straw I could find to make it not be true. I looked beseechingly at Taylor. "Did he say anything else?"

She shrugged her shoulders and then looked up at me. When she saw the desperate look in my eyes her face transformed as she finally understood.

"Oh...I'm so sorry Evan. I should have told you sooner. I just...had so much on my mind."

"Yeah, I know...the Spring Formal." I threw a twenty-dollar bill on the table, slammed my chair against the wall as I stood up, and then stormed out of the diner. As I walked out the front door, I heard Rob's irritating voice ask, "What's *her* deal?"

———

I lay in bed tossing and turning trying to get to sleep. I had a big Immunology exam the next morning and knew I should get a good night's rest, but I could not stop thinking. I could hear Taylor snoring softly across the room and although this usually sent me right off to sleep, tonight it was just annoying. I clutched the brown afghan to my chest. It had become my security blanket in more ways than one.

I knew I was not going to be able to sleep, so I got out of bed and slipped on a pair of jeans and sneakers. I threw a light cardigan over my sleep shirt and quietly headed out of the room, trying not to wake Taylor. It was still an hour before curfew so I thought taking a walk might clear my head and make me tired enough to sleep.

There was a full moon, and the campus was bathed in a soft pale-white glow. It was so quiet and peaceful that the only noises I heard were my own footsteps and the occasional far-off car. I came to a set of stone benches at the far end of the quad and sat down, acutely aware that this had been the very spot where Aaron had confessed his feelings about me... and his relationship with Becky.

That felt like years ago, and now he was gone. I had lost him... Despite the sadness I felt, something inside me knew that things were not finished between Aaron and me. There was still too much left unsaid, still too many questions left unanswered. He and I were connected. Our mothers had grown up together. My brother had been named after him! These things were not just coincidences. I felt it with every fiber of my being. I also felt deeply that somehow, some way Aaron would be mine... eventually.

It was as if all these roadblocks between us were transient and just a necessary evil whose purpose would become clear in time. Or maybe it was just wishful thinking. After all, he hadn't even bothered to tell me he wasn't coming back.

I wondered why I had to find out every awful truth about Aaron from Taylor. I was beginning to wonder if I was just some big sap who was very good at inventing one-sided relationships. I had to admit that one reason I hated being around Taylor and Rob was because I was jealous. I envied their relationship. I was tired of being alone. I wanted someone to cherish me.

I left the stone benches and walked for at least half an hour. I hadn't been thinking about where I was going, but when I actually registered my surroundings, I realized that I had somehow made my way to the History building. The building was completely dark save for the one faint light coming from the ground-level slit of a window along the front of the building. My stomach knotted, and I wondered if this could be a sign.

I walked up the stairs to the front double doors of the main entrance. I grasped the large brass handle and tried to pull, but it was locked up tight. Oh well, it was worth a try I thought, and headed back down the stairs. I took one more look towards the faint glow coming from Dr. Browning's office window and noticed that there was a side door, at the back end of the building. I thought that since I was here, I could just give it a quick try.

I walked the length of the building and came to the back entrance, which was set down a level so that I had to descend about five steps to reach it. The door was located next to a large metal grate that must have been attached to some kind of exhaust system because I could hear the gentle whine of an engine and feel warm air blowing out.

I reached the door and gave it a pull. It opened easily and I stepped into a dark stairwell, lit only by the red neon glow of a fire exit sign. I traversed the stairs, carefully descending one flight into the basement. It was odd being in these dark deserted hallways. It was a different place altogether from the bright bustling halls of a school day. It was creepy.

I walked quickly down the hall until I was standing in front of Dr. Browning's office. The door was closed, but I could see light coming from under the door. I listened carefully for noises from inside. I wondered what he could be doing in there at this time of night. What if he was with someone?

I had made up my mind to leave when the door opened abruptly, and I was suddenly standing face to face with Dr. Browning! I literally jumped and let out a little shout, holding my hand to my chest. He was startled too and quickly brought up his clenched fists in a defensive motion. Thankfully, he quickly recognized me and dropped his hands.

"Holy Jaysus, Evan! What are you doing here? I nearly took a swing at you!"

"I'm...sorry...I didn't mean to startle you. I was just passing by and saw your light on. You wrote that you wanted to see me..."

"I meant that you should come see me during office hours, I didn't mean you should come skulking around at..." he glanced at his watch... "11:25 pm."

I felt ridiculous standing here in my nightclothes. I wrapped the cardigan more tightly around myself. "I wasn't skulking. I couldn't sleep so I was taking a walk and just happened to pass by...I'll come back tomorrow." I stepped back and turned to leave.

"Look, since you're here why don't you come in?" He pushed the door open behind him and gestured for me to enter. As I walked into his office, I couldn't help but feel relief in knowing he was alone. "You know, you really shouldn't be walking around campus by yourself at night like this. It's not safe."

"I don't...usually. How about you... Are you always here so late?"

"I just had some research I needed to do."

He glanced over at some papers on the corner of his desk, but before I could see what they were, he covered them with a manila folder.

"So...you wanted to see me then."

"Uh, yeah." He rubbed his eyes and I noticed that he looked very tired. His eyes were bloodshot and his dark hair, which was now growing out from the buzzcut he had at the beginning of the semester, was tousled. For the first time, I realized that his hair was actually so dark brown that it was almost black. The new growth was thick and lush, and I had only seen hair as shiny in commercials. It was almost a crime that he insisted on whacking it all off.

"So, you were pretty harsh in your disregard for historians today." He said, giving me a weak smile.

"I didn't mean to be disrespectful. I guess I just don't like being put on the spot like that. I felt cornered and came out swinging, but I'm sure that I'll have plenty of chances to make amends for my harsh words in the ten-page essay we have to write."

"I guess you will," he said flashing me a devilish smile. That smile was so incredibly gorgeous that it made it impossible to be mad at him. I suspected he knew this and was using it to his advantage.

He was staring at me again in a way I did not understand. It was as if he were studying me, trying to figure something out. It made me feel like a sideshow curiosity. Step right up ladies and gentlemen and see the bearded lady!

When I couldn't stand the scrutiny anymore, I broke the silence. "Was there some problem with my paper? There was no grade on it." I said, stating the obvious.

He sighed and rubbed his face again before he began to speak. "Actually, I am a bit torn about the grade. On the one hand, your observations about the civil rights movement were thoughtful and you impressively weaved different aspects of that struggle into your thesis. Your narrative was insightful and well-written." He paused and seemed to be struggling with what to say next.

"Sounds pretty good so far..." I said, filling the awkward silence.

He looked up at me and tilted his head, giving me an amused but weary look.

"The problem I have is that the assignment was to theorize on how the interpretations of JFK's assassination affected history as we know it. However, you wrote half of the paper on how there could have been others involved in the shooting that were not fully considered by the Warren Commission. You spent pages just discussing the potential significance of this...Babushka Lady. You knew that I did not want conjecture and conspiracy theories. I explicitly warned the class about that."

"But it wasn't conjecture!" I blurted out, immediately regretting it.

"Evan, conjecture is defined as an opinion or conclusion based on guesswork. Are you telling me that you can actually prove the hypotheses you put forth?" His bloodshot eyes gazed into mine.

I remained silent, defiantly holding his stare. He sighed, clearly growing weary of my antics. "Well...are you in possession of some privileged knowledge that has escaped the rest of the population for half a century?"

I was angry but sensible enough to realize I had no right to be. He was right. I had clearly broken the rules. Of course, I wasn't just guessing about the suspicious actions of Babushka Lady, and I *was* convinced that she was somehow involved in the assassination, but it's not like I could explain myself to him. Instead, I just swallowed my pride and apologized for not strictly following the guidelines of the assignment.

"Evan, to be honest, I quite enjoyed your paper, even if it somewhat departed from the assignment. The details of your narrative were quite vivid. The imagery was incredibly accurate, I could almost picture that fateful day through your eyes. You must have spent a very long time examining descriptions and pictures of the event.

"In fact, I became so intrigued by your speculations that I actually spent some time myself researching the accounts of Babushka Lady." Dr. Browning lifted the manila folder on his desk and retrieved the papers that were stashed below it. He held them in his lap, studying them while he spoke. At this point, I was beyond curious about the content of these papers he was 'researching'. However, I had no choice but to be patient and wait for him to let me in on the secret.

"You know, as a historian, I have spent a fair amount of time researching this event over the years. I have seen the photos and home movies a number of times and read all the conspiracy theories. To be honest, I have become a bit bored with it all. Thus, I was not at all happy when the topic was chosen in class and I realized I would have to read hundreds of pages of prattle about it."

He paused and shuffled the pages in his hands. "That was...until I read your paper. As I said, your insight and novel ideas intrigued me. So, I spent some time searching the web. I wanted to refresh my memory about the Babushka Lady, and your observations were accurate. She *was* a very mysterious figure in the crowd that day."

Dr. Browning placed one of the pages he had been holding in front of me on the desk. It was one of the color still frames I had seen a thousand times now. It showed the blurry figure of a husky woman wearing a beige overcoat and a heavy headscarf. My mind instantly flashed to the image of her stepping off the curb to cross the street, right before she disappeared. It still gave me chills. I peered at the page and nodded my head slowly in agreement. I could feel Dr. Browning's eyes on me like a lead weight, watching every movement, every reaction.

"It certainly was odd that this woman was never identified, and it's tantalizing to speculate about the potential images she might have captured. However, now that I go back and study all of those conspiracy theories again, I realize that the even greater peculiarity was the other woman that mysteriously disappeared right after the assassination."

I stopped breathing as Dr. Browning carefully placed another page on the desk in front of me. On this page was another still-frame color photograph. It was taken from the south side of Elm, maybe even by Jean Hill's camera. The very tail end of the President's midnight blue limousine was just visible on the left side of the photo. As the cars driving down Elm were the focus of the photo, the grassy knoll on the opposite side of the street, was mercifully out of focus. However, despite the blur, there was the very obvious figure of a young woman peering over the wooden fence at the top of the knoll.

Similar to the Babushka Lady, this one was also wearing beige, but it was more form-fitting and topped with a dark brown sweater. However, the most distinguishing feature of this woman was the long auburn-colored ponytail that ran from high on her crown down to the middle of her back.

My hand began to rise as I subconsciously started to touch my hair. Then I realized what I was doing and dropped my hand, holding it in my lap. I was absolutely stunned! I could not believe that I was staring at a picture of myself taken in 1963, nor that I had been so completely stupid as to not have anticipated this.

Why had I not thought about the possibility of someone capturing *me* on film? Why had I not even thought to go looking for these pictures after my trip? I had been so consumed by trying to understand the Babushka Lady and complete my assignment that I didn't even think of the possibility that *I* had unintentionally become a new source of conspiracy.

My mind raced to get a grasp on this new development. I pulled my cardigan more tightly around my body to stop the shivers that were racing up and down my arm, then realized with horror that I was wearing the exact same cardigan as in the pictures!

My eyes darted up to Dr. Browning's face and I realized he was studying me more intently than ever. I tried to clear the panic and confusion that I knew must be written all over my face. He was waiting for me to speak, but I couldn't because if I did, the fear and alarm in my voice would do me in. No, I knew my only strategy was to be as calm as possible, try to figure out what Dr. Browning was thinking, then get the hell out!

Finally, after a long intense silence he spoke again, and this time I could hear the bewilderment in *his* voice. "It's just so odd...I mean I have studied this event for years...but now...I just don't remember ever hearing of this person...or do I?"

It was so strange to hear the confusion and doubt in his voice. Dr. Browning was always so composed and confident, but now he was mumbling and befuddled. "You know they call her Bobby-socks on the conspiracy sites because with that ponytail she looks like the type of teenage girl you would see at a high school sock-hop."

Oh God! They had a name for me? I was desperate to get out of there and search the websites myself. I had to know if there were any more pictures or...home movies! Holy crap. I didn't have to wait long, Dr. Browning placed another sheet of paper in front of me. It had three more photos of me on it. Unlike the first, where you could only really see part of my profile, these were taken with me facing forward. They were taken from across the street and were certainly grainy, but there was absolutely no mistaking me.

I had to be sensible though. Of course, *I* knew it was me, but these pictures were taken decades before I was even born, there was no way Dr. Browning could really suspect they were me. He was sitting back in his chair just studying me. He held his clenched fist at his lips and was clearly in deep thought. I decided the best way to handle this was just to face it head-on. I mean was he really going to accuse his eighteen-year-old student of being involved in JFK's assassination? I almost laughed out loud at the thought of it!

I summoned all my confidence, cleared the frog from my throat, and spoke for the first time since he had revealed the pictures. "Yeah, these conspiracies are quite fascinating. It seems like there are so many unexplained people and circumstances surrounding this event. I guess I just got caught up in it all. I'm sorry I veered off track with some of the topics covered in my paper. I will certainly try to stay more focused next time."

I was actually impressed with myself. I thought I sounded nonchalant and self-assured. He didn't say a word though. He just kept staring at me! His expression gave away nothing. I couldn't tell if he was angry or suspicious, it was unnerving.

I wished I knew what was going on inside his head. He was acting so strange and the way he looked at me made me squirm in my seat. I could tell that he was grappling to understand what was happening. Despite every logical explanation running through my brain, I felt that somehow, he *knew*.

After several moments of ridiculously uncomfortable silence, I rose to leave. "Well, it's late and I should get back to my room. Test tomorrow and all..." I turned my back to him and fiddled with the door. Despite my composure, now that I was on my feet trying to make my escape, I felt scattered and was all thumbs.

I didn't even hear him walk up behind me, but as soon as I managed to get the door open, the knob slipped from my hand and the door slammed shut. Dr. Browning's hand was level with my eyes, his palm flat against the door. I spun around and found those piercing blue eyes just inches from my face. I let out a loud gasp, but before I could say a word, he quickly took a step back.

"Sorry, Evan. I didn't mean to scare you. I...I'm just...a little wired tonight I guess."

I tried to remain calm, there flattened against the door, but I was trembling as he studied my face. I was too scared to budge and after what felt like minutes, he said "Your eyes...are just so...*incredible.*"

I stopped breathing and my stomach did a summersault, but then he suddenly dropped his hand and stepped further away from me. "Uh, I was just wondering...have you had a chance to read the book I gave you?"

The book?! Here he was, acting so incredibly strange and scaring the crap out of me, and now he wanted to know about the book? I had to take a moment to compose myself before answering.

"Um...no. Not yet, but I suppose I should start considering the topic for our final exam." He was not inches away anymore, but he was still awkwardly close and, just as before, his proximity made my whole body tingle with excitement.

Then, as suddenly as he had appeared behind me, he turned and walked back around his desk. He collapsed into his chair, rubbing his face roughly. I reached behind my back and turned the knob smoothly this time. "Well, OK...I'm going then."

He looked up suddenly and said, "I should walk you to your dorm. It's late."

"No, no...I'm fine. It's just around the corner."

"Uh...OK," he said distractedly.

As I closed the door, I saw him pick up the pages with my pictures on them again.

———*ele*———

I spent all night on the computer. I searched for every picture, description, witness statement, and theory about the 'Bobby-socks' girl. I had searched these same websites in the days following my trip, and I knew for a fact that none of this information had been there. Whatever was happening...however all this worked, it seemed like it took a while for things to change. It was not instantaneous. It was more like a ripple effect, like a stone thrown into the water, the ripples slowly radiated out. Slowly, the gears were shifting into place and creating a new reality, a new 'present'. I had really screwed up. I was such an idiot!

I recorded all these observations in my journal. I also added a new rule to my list: *9. Never allow myself to be photographed in the past.* I wondered how long it took for everything to settle and if it depended on how far in the past the change occurred. Fortunately, so far it didn't seem like I had altered things too much. However, I couldn't be sure that things had finished 'shifting' either. There was certainly new material on the conspiracy websites, and although I was prominently featured, it seemed like the information about me was just lost in the mix.

The most popular theory about Bobby-socks girl was that she had indeed seen someone behind the fence and was subsequently 'taken care of' by the CIA, never to be heard from again. Similar to Babushka Lady, there had been various people over the years who claimed to be the Bobby-socks girl, but none of their stories had ever really held water. So, I appeared to be off the hook, for the most part. But still, it was clear that I needed to be much, much more careful, and of course there was still the problem of Dr. Browning.

Chapter 11

EAGER ASSISTANT

Weeks went by. The weather was getting warmer with temperatures reaching into the mid-eighties most days. It was incredibly dry, and the hot wind blew out of the west. It blew so hard sometimes that dirt storms colored the sky reddish-brown and reduced visibility to just a few feet.

Walking around campus was miserable. Any exposed skin was pelted by the dirt, blown at over sixty miles per hour. By the end of the day my clothes, hair, and even teeth were coated with grit. My eyes were constantly red and watery, and my sinuses ached. I felt like I was existing in an alternative reality...a hazy dull remnant of the bright vibrant world it had been just a few months ago.

The funk I was in was not just because of the weather. I still missed Aaron. Taylor and I hung out occasionally, but things just weren't the same. Plus, I had completely missed my last Immunology exam after I had stayed up all night researching the Bobby-socks girl. Rather than face Dr. Marshall, I had just dropped the course. I hadn't been doing well anyway, and honestly, I had no motivation for it anymore. I had already dropped Calc II, and I was muddling through the others, certainly not doing my best. I had some fleeting thoughts of using my 'ability' to help me pass my classes, but I was terrified of traveling again after my last big screw-up.

I felt lost, confused and depressed. I did not know who I was anymore. I certainly was not Evan, the type-A perfectionist, who was uncompromisingly driven towards her goal of becoming a Nobel Prize-winning biomedical scientist anymore. Who was I now? Was I the fun and edgy badass adventurer skipping through time in my riding boots and leather jacket? Was I the sexy intellectual co-ed that drove men crazy with my brains *and* bod? I didn't feel like any of these people. I felt like a girl who had no one and knew nothing.

It was hard to believe that the semester would be over in a little more than a month. My grand plan included taking classes over the summer, but now I was considering extending the short ten-day trip I had planned to take to Guam into a three-month trip. I had no desire to be at Harper alone anymore. There was however one thing in my life that had become...interesting in the last few weeks, and that was Dr. Browning.

He had become a strange and constant presence. I saw him everywhere. I saw him in the coffee shop when I stopped to grab a quick drink. He was in the grocery store when I shopped. As I studied in the library, I would look up to see him only a few tables away, reading a book. He never acknowledged my presence verbally, but many times I would catch him staring at me. It was eerie...and exciting.

I got an 'A' on my midterm, and had taken great care to be very complimentary of historians in the short essay he had assigned. In my essay I described historians as important curators of the past, comparing his profession to the Native American storytellers who had the great honor of passing down the chronicles and traditions of their people.

He had given me an 'A' on that paper as well, adding the comment "Thanks Evan," written in red pen. I was intrigued, and although everything else in my life was miserable, I found solace in his bizarre constant presence. I didn't bother overanalyzing it like I did most things. It just felt nice to be noticed. In fact, it was the thought of Dr. Browning's interest in me that kept me from not slipping into total depression when the letter arrived.

It was another horrible, hot, windy day. I had fought against the gusts of dirt to make it back to my dorm after classes were over. I stopped by the front office to pick up my mail as usual, but unlike the typical day, I had something in my mailbox. Little did I know that this was just the first of three letters, I would receive in the next month that would change my life forever and set me on the path to whom I would eventually become.

It was an official-looking envelope from the University. At first, I thought it must be something to do with tuition, or renewing dorm-room assignments. However, once I opened the letter, I realized it was much more serious.

Dear Ms. Wright

It has come to my attention that there has recently been a significant change in your progress toward the completion of your degree plan. As you are well aware, all students on academic scholarships must receive pre-approval from their academic advisor before dropping courses, especially those required for their major.

Furthermore, if a student wishes to change his or her declared major, this action is also subject to the approval of his or her academic advisor. Therefore, after careful review of your progress this semester, I am requesting a formal meeting on Friday, April 10th, at 4:00 p.m. to discuss your plans for continued enrollment at Harper University. Failing to make this meeting will result in automatic academic probation and possible cessation of your scholarship.

Sincerely

Dr. Albert Chaney
Academic Advisor
Student Services, Harper University

I could hardly believe it! This was how far things had disintegrated. How had I let this happen? I spent the evening admonishing myself and trying to think up excuses for my behavior. However, by 4:00 p.m. the next day, as I sat sweating in the lobby of the counselors' office, I was no closer to knowing what I was going to say than before.

I sat staring at the frosted glass on Dr. Chaney's office door, waiting for him to call me in. It was like waiting to go to the gallows. My only strategy was excessive contrition and begging. I had worn my most flattering, low-cut blouse in case I needed to resort to plan 'B', which was flirting.

After an eternity, the door finally opened, and Dr. Chaney's beady little eyes peeked out from around the corner. He was a strange-looking little man, with a bad comb-over and a mustache that made him look a little like Hitler. He perspired excessively and always seemed a little uncomfortable. From my Psych classes I had diagnosed him as antisocial, or at the very least socially awkward, which was crazy considering that he was a counselor.

"Evan we're ready for you." He opened the door more widely and beckoned me in.

We're ready for you. Who were *we*? I slowly got up and tentatively walked towards the office. Dr. Chaney recoiled slightly as I passed, which reminded me that he was also a little weird about his personal space.

I was taken aback as I entered the office and saw Dr. Marshall and Nurse Thorn sitting at a table in the corner of the room. I had been ambushed. It was like some bizarro intervention. My instincts told me to turn around and run, but that was neither a reasonable nor a feasible idea.

Dr. Chaney cleared his throat. "Please have a seat, Evan." He gestured to an empty chair at the head of the oblong table. "Dr. Marshall and Nurse Thorn have been kind enough to join us."

Lucky me, I thought. I pulled out the chair and perched on the very edge, just in case I needed to make a break for it. I went over the prepared speech in my head again. However, I had not expected it to be three against one. Suddenly I didn't think the excuses I had planned to give Dr. Chaney were going to fly with the other two here, especially considering that Nurse Thorn had seen me clearly out of my head the night I almost drowned in my bathtub. I wondered what she had told Dr. Chaney. I mean, weren't those things supposed to be confidential?

"Evan, I have summoned you here because I...well...*we* are concerned about the change in your academic progress this semester." He flipped through a file that apparently contained all my pertinent information. "I see here you have dropped two courses that are required for your major..." He cleared his throat again. "...uhm Calculus II and Immunology II.

"As I'm sure you know, because you are on an academic scholarship, dropping these courses requires pre-approval from an academic advisor." He tapped his pencil on the folder in his lap and looked up at me for the first time. "So, what is your explanation for this?" He was so bad at communicating. I seriously wondered why he was in this line of work.

Sensing the strain and awkwardness, Dr. Marshall jumped in. "Evan, what I think Albert is getting at is that we're all worried about you. You are a gifted student and none of us want to see you fall through the cracks. I have to tell you that I was very upset when you dropped my class. I knew you weren't doing as well as you did last semester, however, I hoped that you would have sought my help or advice before taking such a drastic measure. Evan, it just doesn't seem like you."

I quietly listened and I appreciated that Dr. Marshall was much more personable than *Albert*. He had always been one of my favorite professors.

However, it bewildered me that he knew what 'seemed like me'. *I* didn't even know anymore.

Dr. Marshall continued, "Last semester you were so sure about the course you wanted your life to take...graduate school, PhD, biomedical research...you seemed to have all the steps figured out. Have you changed your mind about your future?"

They were waiting for me to speak. Instead of delivering my prepared speech and telling them what I thought they wanted to hear, I decided to go with the truth...or at least one version of it.

"I appreciate all of your concern, and I'm sorry I broke the rules. I should have spoken to you both before I dropped those courses. Well, the truth is that college has been a little more than I...expected. Yes, I thought I had everything figured out my first semester, however meeting different people and taking different classes has changed my...perceptions...broadened my horizons. I know Dr. Chaney for one always encouraged me to think about things other than just science, and now that I have, I'm not exactly sure what I want to do in the future."

"So you don't want to be a scientist anymore?" Dr. Marshall looked a bit crestfallen.

"I *do* think I still want to be a scientist...of *some* kind."

"Well, the only real way to decide that is to get some research experience. I know you were planning to try to find a lab to work in, have you pursued that?"

"Well, no...not exactly" I answered, ashamed.

"Evan, it's fine that you are taking some time to *find yourself*." Dr. Marshall said compassionately. "In many ways that is what college is for."

Dr. Chaney butted in annoyingly. "Peter, the issue is not about Evan finding herself. The issue is that she is not adhering to the stipulations of her academic scholarship. She *must* maintain a 3.5 GPA, and she cannot drop courses without the approval of an academic advisor!" Dr. Chaney sounded like a petulant two-year-old, as he repeated this fact for at least the third time.

He continued. "Evan, you had the highest SAT score of your entire entering class. You were a National Merit Scholar, and we had extremely high hopes for you here at Harper. However, you have not yet completed your freshman year and already you are falling short of these expectations. Whatever your problems are, we need to nip them in the bud before it's too late. If you fail to abide by the stipulations of your scholarship, you will be placed on academic probation and could have your scholarship revoked."

This was horrible. All my life I had been an over-achiever and a pleaser. I was not used to disappointing people or being in trouble. It felt awful. I dropped my head and fought hard to hold back the tears.

"Let's not get carried away here. Evan has certainly had a bumpy semester, but I think it's a little premature to start talking about academic probation and withdrawing scholarships." Dr. Marshall's sympathetic voice made me feel better instantly. "We're just worried about you Evan. We want to understand what's going on so that we can try to help."

Dr. Chaney made a 'humph' sound, and it was clear that there was a difference of opinion on how I should be handled.

Suddenly I heard Nurse Thorn clear *her* throat. I had almost forgotten she was in the room. "Evan, you can tell us if there are any *personal* issues that are affecting your studies. We may be able to help."

This was a tough one, I thought. She knew that I had had some issues with panic attacks, or at least that was the excuse I had given her for my behavior on Christmas Eve. I had told her that I would make an appointment for counseling, but of course, I never had. I hadn't even returned the blanket she gave me that night because I couldn't face her.

I knew what they were all thinking. Here I was, an eighteen-year-old girl, obviously undergoing some kind of identity crisis because my behavior and even appearance had changed so much in the last few months.

They probably suspected drugs, an eating disorder, or maybe even an abusive boyfriend. I could assure them that none of these were the case, but I didn't know what alternative I could give them that would explain all of the changes. I tried the truth on for size.

Let's see, in the last few months, I've discovered that I can travel through time. So, you can understand how it's been rather distracting. Plus, I've been quite busy researching historical events, like JFK's assassination, so that I can go back and figure out what really happened. Ironically, during one of my trips to the past, I ended up changing one of the decisive events in my own life, and this resulted in a major shift in my personality. This partially explains why I am no longer so fixed on excelling academically. Oh, also there's this boy that I stupidly fell for, but it turns out he has a girlfriend. It's awkward though because she's deathly ill from a seizure disorder that I'm worried my time-traveling could have caused. Any advice?

I quickly decided against telling the truth. Three pairs of eyes were fixed on me. It seemed there was going to be no easy way out of this.

All of the sudden, there was a quick rap on the door. It slowly opened, and there stood Dr. Browning out of breath.

"Sorry, I'm late. I ran straight over after my last class."

Even Dr. Browning knew about this pow-wow? I wondered if *all* my professors had been invited to my roast. I was so embarrassed. Dr. Browning closed the door and made his way over to the table. He sat opposite me at the other end of the table.

"Thank you for joining us, Ian. We were just exploring why Evan dropped Calculus and Immunology this semester," Dr. Chaney focused his beady eyes on me again.

"So Evan, Nurse Thorn asked if there were any personal issues you would like to discuss with us."

"No," was all I could say. I felt defeated and sat with my head slumped down.

"Well, if you aren't having any *personal* issues, are you having time management problems, or did you just lose interest in the subjects?"

I just wanted out of there. I didn't have any answers they would be happy with, and I felt exhausted from agonizing over it.

"I'm sorry, but I have to confess that I think all of this is my fault." The rich intonations of his smooth Irish accent filled the room. I jerked my head up to look at him, completely confused about where he was going with this. The others were staring at him as well, clearly intrigued by this new development.

"*Your* fault?" Dr. Chaney chirped.

"Yes, you see Evan has been such an excellent student in my class this semester. Her observations are so...uniquely insightful. She was just the student I had been looking for to help me finish a special research project that we are hoping to publish soon.

"I approached Evan early in the semester about the possibility of working as my research assistant on this project, and she generously agreed to help. However, I now understand that I have been monopolizing more of her time than I realized. I didn't know that she had dropped these courses, and I suspect that she didn't tell me because she didn't want me to know I was placing unreasonable demands on her. I should have known better."

My mouth was agape. I could not believe what was happening or why Dr. Browning was saying these things. The look on his gorgeous face was of total contrition. I was happy the others were staring at him because if they had seen the expression on my face his charade would have been exposed. Dr. Browning must have realized this too because he looked at me intently and raised one eyebrow. I had no idea why he was helping me like this, but I knew that I needed to get with the program before I got us *both* in trouble.

"You've been doing research for *Ian*?" Dr. Marshall turned to me now. Oddly, his tone verged on anger. Clearly, for some reason, this new development did not please him at all. I quickly reined in my surprise and tried to look nonchalant. I simply nodded my head in agreement, because I didn't trust what I might say.

"As I said, I guess I didn't quite realize how much time she had been spending on the project." I could tell that Dr. Browning was trying to get the attention off me and back on him before I blew it.

"So, what exactly is this *research* project, Ian?" Dr. Marshall's words dripped with hostility. There had to be a story here, I thought.

"Well *Peter*, I'm sure you'll understand that I can't go into much detail, as we are planning a publication on the project, but I can tell you that it is an extension of my post-doctoral studies." Dr. Browning's tone matched the animosity of his colleague.

"Oh, the cave stuff..." Dr. Marshall snipped.

"They are pre-historic burial mounds."

Ah, he was talking about Newgrange, I ascertained. At least I now knew what the research project that I was allegedly working so hard on was about. The two of them were shooting daggers at each other, and it was becoming extremely uncomfortable. I was relieved when Dr. Chaney butted in.

"OK, well. Let us get back to the problem at hand. What are we going to do about Ms. Wright's situation?"

Dr. Marshall tore his eyes away from Dr. Browning and focused on me again. "Well Evan, I really do not want you to drop my class. I would be willing to readmit you and allow you to do some extra credit assignments to make up for the test you missed."

I swallowed the frog that was still in my throat and squeaked out, "Thank you. That would be great."

Dr. Chaney added, "It's probably too late for Calculus as you dropped that course several weeks ago, but you were taking twenty hours, which is quite a full load, especially considering the research you've been involved in. It will be offered again next semester so you can take it then." I nodded my head in agreement.

"Well Evan, you're off the hook this time, but you need to be more forthcoming and transparent in the future. You *must* get approval to drop courses, and you need to make sure your overall GPA stays above 3.5. If you are having any personal or academic difficulties, you need to seek help before things get to this stage." I nodded my head enthusiastically.

"I would also appreciate it if you would keep me abreast of your research. It would look very good for our program to have a published scholarship recipient." I could see the twinkle of excitement in his eyes.

"Yes, I will," I said and looked at Dr. Browning.

Dr. Chaney snapped my file shut and stood up. "OK, this was a very productive meeting. Thank you everyone for joining us."

And just like that, we were dismissed. Everyone rose and Dr. Browning was the first out the door. I desperately wanted to talk to him and quickened my pace to catch up, but as soon as I was out of the administrative office suite Nurse Thorn caught up to me. "Evan, can I have a sec?"

I saw Dr. Browning round the corner headed towards the exit. I didn't want to talk to her, but what was I supposed to say? I stopped and faced her. As we stood in the hallway, Dr. Marshall walked past us and said, "See you in class Evan?"

"Yes, thank you again." He waved his arm back in acknowledgment as he walked down the hall and rounded the corner himself.

I looked at Nurse Thorn expectantly, trying not to convey my annoyance at being stuck there.

"Evan, I just want you to know that I did not tell the others about the incident on Christmas Eve." She put her hand on my forearm.

"I appreciate that," I said in honesty.

"The things that happen or are said in my office stay there. I just want you to know that you can trust me."

"Yes, thank you." I was getting tired of thanking people. She looked at me intently and I could tell that she was disappointed that I was not being more open.

"Were you able to speak with your mother about your panic attacks?" She probed further.

Ah, the phantom panic attacks I thought. "Actually, I just decided to wait it out before I worried her, and luckily it's never happened again." I smiled warmly at her and prayed she would drop it. She still grasped my forearm as if she was afraid I would try to run away.

"And I suppose you didn't ever make an appointment for counseling either?" Her eyes searched my face.

I sighed. I was growing exasperated, but I couldn't be angry with her. Her intentions were nothing but good. "Nurse Thorn, I know that I was...a little...bizarre...that night. It was Christmas, and I was lonely and coming off the stress of a long semester. I thought at the time I might have had a panic attack, but it hasn't happened since. If it does, I promise I will definitely see a doctor."

She released my arm. "As long as you know that there are people who care for you and can help if you need it." Her face was so kind and compassionate and something about her reminded me of my mother.

As I hurried down the hall towards the exit, I yelled back at her, "By the way Nurse Thorn, I still have your blanket. I promise to return it soon." I flung the door open and broke into a run. The wind was fierce and pushed me off balance as I ran. I squinted to keep the dirt from blowing in my eyes. I dashed across campus and headed toward the History Building. I finally saw Dr. Browning in the brown haze and sped up to catch him. By the time I caught up, I was out of breath and covered in dirt.

"Dr. Browning....please...wait..." I practically had to shout for him to hear me over the wind.

"Evan, I have to hurry I'm late for another meeting."

"I just wanted...to say...how much..." He grabbed my arm and pulled me into a nearby covered walkway. Thankfully, we were out of the wind.

I caught my breath and said, "I just wanted to tell you how much I appreciate what you did in there. It has been a crazy semester, and I guess I got myself into a little trouble. I don't know how... or why..."

He interrupted me. "Don't mention it, Evan. However, I have to admit my motives were not completely altruistic. I really do need a research assistant for the project I'm working on, and I guess since I've now implicated us both in this...alibi, we will need to produce something."

"Yes, of course. I would be happy to...well, what exactly am I working on?"

"Listen, Evan, I have to run. Come to my office tonight and we'll discuss it." He headed back out into the dust storm.

"What time?" I yelled after him, but the wind was too loud. He disappeared into a brown cloud.

What had started as one of the most depressing days of my life had taken a very unexpected turn, and now I was feeling more excited and optimistic than I had in a long time. I was going to be Dr. Browning's research assistant! Of course, I still had very little idea what we were going to be researching, but I was excited about the possibility of actually publishing something...and of course by the thought of spending long hours working side-by-side with Ian Browning.

Just the thought of us toiling away night after night in his office sent tingles through my body, but I had to be serious now. I was being given a second chance and I was determined to buckle down and work incredibly hard to prove to everyone that I was worth their efforts.

I dug through the pile of books and papers on my desk and found the small leather-bound book Dr. Browning had given me. I thought maybe it had something to do with the research he was working on. As I flipped through the 'Irish Myths and Legends' book I noticed right away that many of the stories about Newgrange involved fairies.

These stories described the burial mounds as dwelling places for fairies, or fairy hills. In the stories, the long passages were presumed to be portholes to the 'otherworld' and the mysterious carvings on the large 'kerbstones' were taken to be symbols drawn by fairies.

There were dozens of accounts, dating back hundreds of years, from people describing the 'little people' that only surfaced at night around the countryside in County Meath, where Newgrange stands. It was a popular legend that the reason these ancient archeological treasures still stood, after centuries of war and invasion, was because the fairies protected them and that damaging the Neolithic mounds would unleash the anger of the fairies who built them.

The stories were certainly entertaining and fascinating, but I was hoping that Dr. Browning's research did not involve fairies. I couldn't imagine being taken as a serious researcher while investigating the fairy occupation of Newgrange.

I became lost in the Irish legends for the rest of the afternoon and jumped when I glanced out the window and saw the darkening sky. I had not realized how late it was. I threw the book in my backpack with a new spiral notebook for taking notes on our research project. *Our research project*, I grinned at the thought of it.

Just as I was about to leave, I impulsively went into the bathroom and put on some eyeliner, mascara, and lipstick. I brushed my hair out and applied a quick squirt of Taylor's perfume. OK, now I was ready, I thought. But right when I placed my hand on the doorknob, ready to dash out, there was a loud knock from someone on the other side. The shock of it made me jump. I opened the door to find a man in a Fed-ex uniform standing in the hallway.

"Can I help you?"

"I have a registered letter for Ms. Evan Lynn Wright."

I took the large envelope from him. "Don't you usually leave letters and packages downstairs at the front office?"

"This is a registered letter. It requires a signature and can only be delivered to the intended recipient." His tone was quite condescending and made me feel dumb for asking.

"Uh...OK, then. Thanks" I said as I signed. He walked off without saying another word. I had never received a package like this and wondered if I was supposed to tip him. Oh, well he was already halfway down the hall before I even thought of it, and besides I hadn't appreciated his tone anyway...not to mention the fact that I was perpetually broke. I watched him disappear around the corner, and after giving him a short head start, I threw the envelope in my backpack and took off.

This time the History building was unlocked and there were still a few students and staff milling around the halls. Dr. Browning's door was wide open, but the office was empty. Just as I plopped down in the chair outside his office, he walked around the corner carrying a pizza. As soon as the wonderful aroma hit my nose, my tummy started rumbling.

"Hi-ya Evan. Have you eaten?"

"No actually. I'm starving."

"Well, come on in." I stood up and followed him into his office.

Dr. Browning cleared a spot on his cluttered desk and opened the pizza box. "Dig in. Sorry, I don't have any plates or anything," he said, handing me a napkin.

I dropped my backpack on the floor next to his desk and grabbed a slice of pizza. I sat in the chair opposite Dr. Browning. "I just want to thank you again for this afternoon. You really saved my ass...I mean helped me a lot." I blushed at my slip.

He gave me a devilish grin. "It was my pleasure," he said chewing his food. He reached under his desk, and I heard what I assumed to be the door of a small refrigerator open. I heard the clank of bottles and wondered if he had beer in there. He lifted two Cokes onto the desk, passing one over to me.

"Thanks," I said.

"Don't get used to this. I won't be providing dinner every night" he said giving me a wink.

"Every night?" My stomach fluttered as I wondered how much time we were going to be spending together.

"Well not *every* night, but we do need to arrange a relatively rigorous schedule if we're going to get the work done by the end of the semester. You do realize we're looking at only a month here?"

My eyes were wide as I looked at him. The pizza sat forgotten in my lifeless hand as I wondered what I had gotten myself into.

Picking up on my concern, he said "Evan, this is going to be a lot of work and I need someone serious about it. There seemed to be a significant concern today about your ability to handle your course load. I don't want you to commit to this project at the expense of your classes. I would be very upset with myself if that happened, and I know for a fact that Albert and *Peter* would have my head." I heard the venom in his voice when he said 'Peter'.

"Anyway, if you don't think you're up to this challenge I certainly won't hold it against you. I have other students who are chomping at the bit to work on this project. Jill for one has been all over me about it."

I was pretty sure that Jill was the Gelf, and I didn't like the image of her 'all over him' at all. "I don't want you to sacrifice your grades or your personal life to work on this with me." He looked very intently at me when he said, 'personal life' and the inflection in his voice made it seem as if he was almost asking a question.

I put my piece of pizza down on the lid of the cardboard box, took a deep breath, and exhaled. "Dr. Browning, I am very sure I want to work with you on this. All I have ever wanted to do was contribute to a research project. Admittedly, I always thought it would be a science project; however, a lot has changed for me this semester. My horizons have been broadened and one very big reason for that has been your class. You have taught me to think in ways I never have before. My appreciation for history has grown immensely." Mostly because I have experienced it for myself, I thought.

"You have been very inspiring, and I don't know why you chose me to work on this with you, but I am honored and will be very committed. I had a few...distractions earlier this semester, but I am used to working extremely hard and you do not have to worry about my other classes suffering. And as for my personal life or lack thereof...you don't have to worry about that either."

It was Dr. Browning's turn to be embarrassed. He looked down at his pizza as I spoke. When I finished, he finally looked up and said, "Well, that's sorted then."

We sat in silence scarfing down pizza for a few moments, until I spoke up again. "Dr. Browning?" He stopped me immediately.

"Evan, we're going to be spending a lot of time together over the next month. Please call me Ian." I was shocked! I had never called a professor by their first name. I knew it was going to be hard to get used to...but I liked it. "Sorry, please continue..."

"Uh...Ian..." The sound of his name coming from my lips gave me tingles. "I was just wondering...what *is* the project we are going to be working on?"

He leaned back and laughed a big belly laugh. He clearly found my question very amusing. After he had composed himself, he wiped his mouth, wadded up his napkin, and tossed it in the trashcan across the room. He looked at me seriously.

"Evan, are you familiar with the Knights Templar?"

Without missing a beat, I said, "Sure...didn't Leonardo Di Vinci paint clues into all of his paintings that would lead the Priory of Sion, who were descendants of the Knights Templar, to the Holy Grail?" Dr. Browning looked at me stunned.

Before he could start seriously questioning his choice of research assistant, I started to giggle. "Joking! I'm joking."

He let out a sigh of relief. "You had me worried there. That *was* a great book though. So, what do you *really* know?"

"Well, not a lot I suppose. I think the Templars were involved in the Crusades. I know they wore white uniforms with big red crosses on them. I only know that they became very rich and powerful. It seems like all the legends I've ever heard about them have to do with the Holy Grail." I was embarrassed I didn't have any more insight into the topic. I wished I had known he was going to ask me about the Knights Templar. I could have brushed up on the basics.

"You're right; the Templars were involved in the Crusades. They were formed just after Christians had captured the Holy Lands during the first Crusade. You see, there were many Christian pilgrims who wanted to visit Jerusalem, but there were bandits in the outlying areas who kept slaughtering them as they traveled through the countryside. The Templars originated as a small group of poor monk-like ex-crusaders called the *Poor Knights of Christ and the Temple of Solomon* who guarded these pilgrims during their travels."

"What did they have to do with the Temple of Solomon?" I wondered aloud.

"Oh, they were named that because the King of Jerusalem gave them the captured *Al Aqsa* Mosque as a space for their headquarters. The Mosque, which of course you know is an Islamic church, was located on the Temple Mount in Jerusalem. Have you heard of it?"

"Sounds vaguely familiar," I said lamely.

"Well, the Temple Mount was, and still is, one of the most important and contested religious sites in both Judaism and Islam. It is the spot where Jews believe God created the world, including Adam and Eve. To Muslims, it is the site where the prophet Muhammad, who founded Islam, ascended to heaven. The mount has been the site of many mosques, temples, and churches over the centuries and the Al Aqsa Mosque, which the Templars were given, was believed to have been built on the ruins of the Temple of Solomon, thus their original name."

"And why the 'poor' part? I thought they were really rich." I asked.

"They started out meek, impoverished monks, but that didn't last for long. Once the church officially endorsed them, they became a very popular charity in Christendom and acquired several very rich and powerful benefactors. They were given money, land, and titles. They were also granted special favor by the Pope. He decreed that the Templars were exempt from all authority but his. They could go anywhere and do anything. They didn't even have to pay taxes."

"Wow, sounds like a good deal." I was wide-eyed, absorbed in his story.

"Yes, it was. As you can imagine it became very desirable to be a Templar and their ranks grew to over twenty thousand. Ironically, only a small fraction of the Templars were knights who actually fought in the Crusades, the majority organized the financial infrastructure for the Christian theocracy and were the originators of the banking system. They ran businesses, built hundreds of temples and fortresses, and basically became an important network throughout the land."

"Sounds like the mafia...so what happened to them?" I wondered.

"Basically, it was political. The Knights Templar was an official, ordained order for about two hundred years. However, the combination of a new Pope, who was not as enamored with the Order as previous Popes had been, and a King of France who was deeply in debt to them, conspired to accuse the Templar of a series of heresies.

"They plotted so that on one specific day, Friday, October 13, 1307, dozens of French members of the Knights Templar were simultaneously arrested, tortured, and burned at the stake. Some people believe that Friday, October 13, 1307, was the origin of the Friday the 13th superstition."

"So all of their *assets* went back to the Church then?" I was thinking of the famous stories that implied the Templars knew the whereabouts of the Holy Grail.

"I suppose you're referring to the religious artifacts that the Templars were supposed to be in possession of?"

I nodded.

"Scholars agree that most of those stories were false. The stories originated because the Templars had occupied the Temple Mount. Many people felt that they *must* have excavated the area during their occupation and speculation abounded, even in their own time, about the relics they might have found there, but no one really knows the extent of their possessions or what became of all their assets."

I pondered the possibilities, but I could not figure out what it all had to do with Newgrange. I wondered what I was missing. "So the research project involves the Knights Templar?" He nodded in agreement. "And Newgrange..." He raised an eyebrow and looked and me, obviously waiting for me to make some connection. I hated to disappoint him, but I was completely lost. "Umm...I guess I don't see how they're related."

"Did you read the book I gave you?" His blue eyes probed my face.

"Well, some of it. Mostly I just read stories about fairies." Ugh, I hated not having the right answers. I should have read that book cover to cover. That's what Jill, the super Gelf, would have done.

"I take it you missed the story describing the Knights Templar's occupation of Newgrange." I looked away from him to hide my shame at not finding this, and fumbled with my backpack, pulling the book out. I flipped through as he spoke.

"It's well documented that the Templars came to Ireland during their rule. As in many countries, they were revered and given various properties throughout Ireland. Their principal house was a large spread in Clontarf, near Dublin. However, the Templars were always searching for more...mystic places, and although Newgrange was not 'rediscovered' until

1699, some believe that the Templars actually found Newgrange during their time in Ireland.

"Some of the Templar documents still in existence provide cryptic references to ancient mounds in Inis Fail or the Island of Stone, one of Ireland's ancient names. Therefore, it was thought that the Templars used Newgrange for their furtive meetings and secret ceremonies. Furthermore, it was speculated that they eventually used Newgrange as a hiding place for their...assets when the order was disbanded."

"When you say assets, do you mean the religious artifacts they possessed?" I was enthralled.

"Maybe" was all he said. He smiled and I could tell he was enjoying unfolding this mystery before me.

"Wait a minute, are you saying that the *Holy Grail* is hidden in Newgrange?" I felt like my eyes would pop out of their sockets.

He leaned back and let out a great big belly laugh again. I really loved hearing his laugh, despite the fact that it was at my expense.

"Sorry, I'm really not laughing *at* you, Evan." He wiped his eyes and tried to compose himself. "It's just when you hear it out loud..." This statement started him on a new round of laughter.

"There's no evidence that the Templars had the Holy Grail or the Arc of the Covenant in their possession. Scholars widely agree that these are probably just legends." He paused and I admit I was a little disappointed.

"However," he continued, "there was one...item...for which several accounts do exist." I looked up excitedly. "There is some evidence that the Knights possessed a golden statue or idol. The accounts differ as to the exact identity of the statue, but most call it Baphomet." I had never heard that name before.

"Granted, most accounts for the existence of this idol were the confessions of the Templars, given under torture. Thus, many doubt their accuracy. The thing is..." he leaned forward staring intently into my eyes.

"Many of the Templars independently gave the exact same description of it." His intensity gave me chills.

"If it were only for these confessional accounts the story would probably have fallen into disbelief pretty quickly. However, there are half a dozen other accounts from witnesses in different times and places about the item the Templars possessed. Many described it as their greatest treasure."

"None of the accounts ever described what it looked like?" I asked.

"There are a few inconsistent descriptions, nothing reliable. The name Baphomet came to have different meanings in the centuries following the Templars. However, several modern scholars believe that the name is a bastardization of the French name Mahomet, which means Muhammad. The implication was that the Templars must have incorporated Islam into their Christian beliefs, during their lengthy occupation of the Holy Lands. Obviously, their inquisitors would have seen this as heresy."

"So, the Templars worshipped a golden statue of Muhammad?"

"Well, who knows if they worshiped it. That allegation was probably just part of the trumped-up charges. However, such a relic, if it really does exist, would be extremely rare. You see, there are very few depictions of Muhammad throughout Islam. It is very unusual to see his image in paintings or sculptures. The Templars did occupy the Temple Mount after all. I mean this was the very spot where Muhammad allegedly ascended to heaven, so if such an artifact did exist, this is certainly where it would have been found."

"And you think it's at Newgrange?"

"Oh, even if it *was* there, it's extremely unlikely it still would be. The place is a national heritage site; it has been extensively excavated. No, *if* it actually existed, and was ever there, it probably disappeared between 1307 and 1699."

"Between the fall of the Templars and the discovery of Newgrange?"

"Exactly." He said smiling.

"And where do you think it went?" I suspected this was the topic of our research project.

He leaned back in his chair again, looking very thoughtful. "Well, that's very difficult to say considering we don't even know *if* the Templars were ever at Newgrange, or what exactly they did if they were. However, I think the most likely scenario is that the Templar's artifacts if there actually were any, were removed when Newgrange was 'rediscovered' in 1699."

"Is this the subject of the research project then?" I was quite excited about the prospect.

"Yes. This is a theory I have been intrigued by for several years. It was even the subject of my postdoctoral studies. However, since then there has been a very exciting development. Recently, a series of manuscripts has been discovered in Ireland. The matriarch of a prominent Dublin family passed away and her children came across nearly three dozen bound volumes, containing many accounts of contemporary Irish events in the seventeenth and eighteenth centuries."

"You mean you actually have these books?"

"No, no. The family endowed them to Trinity College; however, I have a few connections." He winked at me, and my pulse raced. "We have hundreds of pages of photocopies." He pulled out a pile of papers and set them in front of me, and I noticed several boxes full of copies in the corner of the room. "We're looking for any references to Newgrange or a discovery of artifacts. Mark anything that seems remotely connected." He handed me a highlighter.

We sat silently reading the pages for what felt like hours. Every now and then Dr. Browning made a 'hmmm' sound or said 'interesting', but other than that the rest of the evening was devoid of conversation. I had not found anything very interesting in my pile of papers. Most of the writings were summaries of different political events of the time, but there were also news reports, property surveys, and census data.

It was pretty dry material, and the Old English was very difficult to read, especially considering it was all handwritten script, presumably originally written by ink and quill. Plus, there were many places, names, and phrases written in Gaelic that I couldn't understand. Eventually, my eyelids began to droop, and I couldn't suppress the yawns that kept escaping my mouth.

"OK, why don't we call it an evening?" Dr. Browning's voice shocked me out of my tired stupor. "Tomorrow is Saturday, we can get back to it then."

I nodded in agreement. I handed him my stack of photocopies and started packing my things to leave when I spotted the large FedEx envelope in my backpack. I had completely forgotten about it! I pulled it out and ripped open the tab at the top. I pulled out a letter and immediately noticed that it looked very official. My eyes widened with sheer disbelief as I scanned down the page.

Lloyd Goldschmidt & Williams

3601 PALO ALTO

SANTA FE, NEW MEXICO 87501

ATTORNEYS AT LAW

(P) 505-378-0087 (F) 505-3780088

Evan Lynn Wright

323 Holden Hall

Harper University

Blythe, Texas 79430

Re: Transfer of Evelyn Grace Lambert Estate

Dear Ms. Wright

Firstly, we here at Lloyd, Goldschmidt, and Williams

would like to express our greatest sorrow and warmest regards for you and your family during this time. Our firm represented Evelyn and managed her estate for over two decades. She was not only a valued client but also a wonderful, warm friend whom we were privileged to know.

As executor of Evelyn's estate, it is my responsibility to notify all beneficiaries of the manner in which she wished her holdings to be distributed. Please phone me at your earliest convenience to arrange a time that you may visit our office to complete the necessary paperwork. We sincerely hope that we will have the opportunity to serve your legal needs as we did your grandmother for so many years.

Sincerely,

Kendrick Williams
Senior Partner

Chapter 12

ROAD TRIP

My first reaction was skepticism. I was sure it had to be fake. I read the letter over and over, squinting my eyes and inspecting every detail. Finally, Dr. Browning noticed my strange behavior.

"What do you have there?"

"Well, I don't really know," I said handing him the letter. I studied his face while he read, waiting for a reaction. As he got to the end his brow furrowed and his eyes flashed up to my face.

"Evan, I'm so sorry for your loss." His eyes were full of worry.

"No, no...please don't be. It's no loss really. I didn't even know her." Dr. Browning looked confused. "She ran off when my mother was very little. She was never in our lives. In fact, I didn't even know she was still alive. I guess I thought she died years ago. I wonder if she's been living in Santa Fe all this time..." I drifted off into my own thoughts.

"Well, nonetheless I am sorry."

"Thanks" I managed. I didn't know how to feel about this. "Dr. Brown... I mean Ian... sorry... do you actually think this is real? I mean could it be some kind of scam?"

He examined the letter more closely. "This isn't exactly an email from a Nigerian Prince asking you to send him all your personal information so he can issue you a check for a million dollars."

I laughed and he added, "Also, I don't think scammers typically operate using certified mail, but let's check it out." He started typing on his computer and I realized he was searching for info on the law firm.

"Here's their website... Lloyd, Goldschmidt, and Williams... Santa Fe." He tilted the screen so I could see better. "They look pretty legit to me. Maybe you're an heiress, Evan." He smiled at me.

"Yeah right." I rolled my eyes at him.

"Well, if I were you, I would contact them soon. You should really have someone go with you to the meeting. Do you think your parents will be able to fly in for this?"

This was a problem. I would have to talk to my mom, but it seemed unlikely she would be able to get a flight at this short notice, and honestly, I really didn't even know if she would want to. I mean she never talked about her mother, but I had always assumed that she hated her. I would have if I were in her shoes. Plus, what would be the point of them coming all the way from Guam for this anyway? What would Evelyn Lambert's estate really consist of?

Still, I didn't want to go alone. For one thing, I didn't have a car and Santa Fe was hundreds of miles away. I supposed I could ask Taylor, but things just weren't great between us at the moment, and she was always so busy with Rob. He would probably end up coming with us, and that would be unbearable.

My silent deliberation must have clued Dr. Browning into my predicament because he cleared his throat and said, "Evan, I certainly don't want to be too forward but if you need someone to go with you, I would be happy to do it. My knowledge of legal matters is certainly lacking, but I can help you with any... arrangements."

God, the word 'arrangements' made me think of coffins, burial plots, and funerals. I flashed on a vision of Frank's service. Surely, I wouldn't be expected to write a eulogy for someone I'd never met.

"That's incredibly nice of you. I may take you up on that offer." Suddenly my pulse quickened at the thought of a road trip, alone in a car for hours with Dr... Ian.

"I guess I just need to talk to my parents and find out what they think I should do."

"Yes, yes, of course. Just let me know if you need assistance," he said handing me back the letter.

——ele——

I called as soon as I got back to my room.

"Evan? Is everything OK there? It must be..."

"It's just after midnight, Mom."

"Are you OK?" she sounded worried.

"Yes, I'm fine. But Mom, I've had some news. I got a letter today..." I paused giving her time to speak up if she somehow already knew. I thought that maybe she had received a letter too.

"What kind of letter, hun?"

"Um Mom, when was the last time you heard from your mother?"

"My mother? Why would you ask that? Evan, what is going on!" Her voice was stern, verging on angry. It was uncharacteristic.

I read her the letter, listening carefully for a reaction. I really had no idea what to expect. She was completely silent, and I hated the miles between us. I needed to see her face and look into her eyes. I needed to know if she was sad, shocked, or indifferent. I finished reading and there was only silence. "Mom?" I finally said.

"So, she's dead."

I couldn't quite place the tone of her voice. She didn't sound sad, shocked, or indifferent. She sounded... vaguely curious.

"Are you OK?" I asked trying to get more of a reaction from her. Then she totally surprised me... she started laughing! It wasn't the kind of big belly laugh that I had heard from Ian earlier, it was more of a sarcastic, half-hysterical laugh that you might hear before someone started to cry. But she didn't start to cry, she just kept laughing in that odd way. She was starting to scare me. "Mom! Are you OK?"

"Yes," I heard her say through the laughs.

"Why are you laughing?" I was becoming impatient and wondered if my dad was around in case she needed help. Finally, the laughs subsided.

"Sorry, Evan. It's just... I have wondered for so many years about her... if she was alive or dead... if I would ever see her again. I guess knowing that the wondering is over is... a relief."

"So, you hadn't heard from her...?"

"No. She left when I was young. I hardly remember her. Then..." she paused.

"Then what? Did you ever see her again?"

"Only once. I was a teenager. She showed up at the children's home one day, out of the blue. She told the staff she was my aunt, but I knew... I knew it was her. She never admitted to being my mother but looking into her eyes... I knew those eyes from pictures I had seen of her. They were large, almond-shaped, and differently colored...one brilliant green and the other hazel."

"Like mine" I gasped.

"Exactly like yours. In fact, you look very much like her Evy."

"What did she want? What happened?" I wondered why she had never told me this before.

"She didn't want anything. Here she was my mother, who had not seen me since I was a baby, and she didn't ask me anything. She didn't ask if I liked school, or what I wanted to be when I grew up. She didn't ask if I had a boyfriend or if I had ever broken a bone. She just didn't care..." Now her voice *was* sad, and I could feel her pain over the miles.

"So, she came to see you and didn't say *anything*?"

"Nothing sane. Evan, I really believe my mother was crazy. Maybe she had been her whole life. She did speak to me that day, but she was secretive and spoke in hushed tones. There was only one thing she asked me and then she was on her way. I never saw her again."

"What... what did she ask you?"

"The only thing she asked was if I had *the power*." She started laughing again.

I could barely contain myself. It was all I could do to keep from bursting with excitement. I kept myself busy during the next two weeks. I had several tests, which were actually blessings because they forced me to study and intermittently took my mind off my grandmother.

I was convinced this strange woman held the key to the mystery of what I could do. She had asked Mom if she had 'the power'. That had to mean what I thought it did, and even though she had not kept in touch with my mother, she somehow knew I existed. I was determined to find out what else she knew.

My mother had given me her blessing to meet with Evelyn's lawyers, although she expressed no desire to go herself. She had not received a letter, which I think was a final slap in the face from the woman who had thrown her away. The way Evelyn had treated my mother gave me a sick feeling down in the pit of my stomach, but I still needed to know...about her...about myself.

Ian had agreed to take me to Santa Fe, in fact, he seemed eager. His only condition was that we work on the way. The firm had agreed to arrange for a Saturday meeting so I wouldn't have to miss school. I briefly considered asking Taylor to drive me to Santa Fe, but the meeting was scheduled for the same day as her Spring Formal, so I knew it would be out of the question. She and Rob had been planning that damn dance for months.

They were both representing their respective sorority and fraternity on the planning committee.

Waiting the two weeks had been hell. Thankfully, my work with Ian kept my anticipation at bay. Although we had not found any references to Newgrange in the volumes of documents yet, I was enjoying spending time with him. Ian was charming and witty, and when he was excited or happy, the gleam in those sea-blue eyes was blinding. He was the kind of guy that was always the life of the party. Rooms were brighter when he walked in. If there was a crowd, he was its pulse.

I carefully watched the way he interacted with the steady stream of students and faculty that stopped by his office. His opinion was sought after and respected by people even twice his age. He seemed to know everything about everything. From discussing Middle Eastern politics with Dr. Ali, the Iraqi political science professor, to pop-culture events with the freshmen girls who flocked around him, he was knowledgeable, articulate, and engaging.

I thought he could probably sit on a stage and read the phone book for two hours, and the crowd would be completely enthralled. He really should have been an actor I thought. His amazing looks, mesmerizing accent, and easy way made him irresistible.

There was also another side to Ian that I began to notice after spending so much time with him. Sometimes his mood turned darker. Not angry or mean, just extremely intense. The lightness would fade, and I would catch him staring at me intently. It wasn't a menacing stare, but it was penetrating and made me feel uncomfortable. It was as though he was trying to look into my soul. During these times, usually late in the evening, he seemed to just drift off into his own thoughts. It was as if he just checked out and I felt completely insignificant.

Spending time with Ian was so different from being around Aaron. Aaron was an open book, always happy, warm, and friendly. Ian was much more complex and mercurial. There was a much bigger spectrum to his highs and lows. He very rarely talked about himself and kept his past completely closed to me.

Having a conversation with Ian was not as effortless as it was with Aaron. I felt tongue-tied and worried I would sound dumb. I caught myself fidgeting and playing with my hair...doing all the silly things I hated to see girls do. Despite this, I loved working with him.

Everyone knew I had become Ian's assistant. The professors that stopped by his office all knew my name, and the Gelf was so jealous she shot daggers at me every time she saw me. Even Taylor made time to ask how our research was going. It was fun being recognized for something, and *this* research I could actually tell people about. But mostly I loved the way my whole body came alive when I was around him.

It was true he made me feel on edge, nervous, and self-conscious, but in a good way. When I was near him the hairs on my body stood on end, and every nerve was alert and ready. It was so unlike being around Aaron who made me feel warm and safe, like home. If Aaron was home, Ian was the French Riviera- exotic, beautiful, enticing, and I could not wait to be alone with him for twenty-four glorious hours.

We left Blythe on Friday afternoon after Ian's last class. He picked me up off campus. We decided that we should probably keep our little road trip a secret. It probably wouldn't look good for a professor to be taking one of his students on an overnight trip. I had debated about what to tell Taylor. I honestly was not even sure she would notice me missing, but I ended up telling her some vague story about visiting a friend of my Mom's in Amarillo.

As I stood on the corner waiting, overnight bag in hand, I realized that I had never seen Ian's car. I wondered what kind of car suited his personality best. I decided that a motorcycle was probably the best fit. Not a loud ostentatious Harley, but maybe a slick, statelier vintage BMW. I knew this was not the case though, because there was no way we were driving five hours to Santa Fe on a motorcycle. When he rounded the corner and pulled up beside me, I instantly changed my mind about the motorcycle and decided that the automobile he was driving was definitely more him.

"Wow, nice wheels! What exactly are we driving?" I asked, as I climbed inside the odd, left-sided passenger side and threw my bag into the tiny back seat. I had never seen a car quite like it.

"It's a 1961 Aston Martin DB4," he said clearly pleased with himself. "I had it shipped over from Ireland when I moved here. I rebuilt this baby while I was a graduate student. It's beautiful, eh?"

Almost as beautiful as its owner, I thought.

Ian told me how he worked in his father's garage when he was a kid. His dad had found the Aston for him. It had belonged to a client who didn't want to bother with the expensive repairs it needed. Ian had spent weekends and holidays at home from University working on the car. He said after all that work, he wasn't going to leave it to rot in Ireland.

Since I knew precious few details about Ian's personal life, I used the opportunity to ask about his parents. He said his dad owned a motor garage, which I took to mean he repaired cars. Apparently, Ian had helped his dad run the business, even when he was quite young. He didn't mention his mother, but I did pick up on the name Avril, which I took to be his sister.

We were already thirty miles out of Blythe when I realized that this was the first time I had left town since I started school at Harper! It was exhilarating. The flat boring landscape whizzed by, and the loud hum of the motor filled my ears. After gleaning the scant details I could about Ian's family, I finally asked him one of the questions I had been dying to know.

"Ian, what are you doing here? In Blythe, I mean? I'm not trying to be rude, but it just seems to me you could've gone anywhere."

"I could ask the same of you Evan." I smiled at the compliment. "Actually I did have a few other job offers. There was a position at Georgetown and another in Edinburgh."

"And you came to Blythe, Texas!"

He laughed his big belly laugh. "I know. I wonder the same thing sometimes. But look at all this..." He gestured out the window to the flat, desolate landscape.

I waited patiently for a real answer. Then his face became serious, almost reverent, and when he spoke it was in a low whisper. "I can't exactly explain it. I guess I was *compelled* to come here. When I saw Harper, I just knew that it was my...destiny." He looked at me and flashed his charming smile, becoming himself again. I realized that there were goosebumps running up my arms.

"And don't you miss your family? I mean, being so far away and all?"

"Sometimes, but I stay busy." He turned on the radio and started scanning through stations, signaling he was done with the conversation.

I decided I should get some work done, and even though reading in the car made me feel a bit nauseous, I owed it to Ian for coming with me on this trip. The sun was setting, and I strained against the dim light to read the documents. It was a struggle to keep my eyes on the paper. They kept drifting over to gaze at Ian's strong hand gripping the stick shift. I kept my head down pretending to read, but he was so distracting... his scent, the little movements of his legs, his soft coughs and sighs.

I kept wondering what he was thinking, or if he was looking at me. I daydreamed. A thousand scenarios ran through my mind...Ian slowly moving his hand from the gearshift to my knee. Ian gently pushing my hair to the side and caressing my neck...and of course my favorite...Ian pulling the car over and us passionately making out on the hood, under the stars.

I had gotten used to working side-by-side with Ian in his office, but this new locale offered a whole new series of fantasies that tantalized me. Of course, he had never been anything but professional, and it would be completely out of line for my professor to... well *do* anything with me. But at least the fantasies kept me from thinking about Aaron, and that was good. I snapped out of my trance realizing that I had spent twenty minutes reading one page. I hoped Ian hadn't noticed.

I rolled down the window and breathed in the cool air of the desert rushing by. After my head was clear, I renewed my effort to concentrate. I read the pages carefully, quickly banishing my lustful thoughts as soon as they seeped into my mind. The hours crept by and finally, it was completely dark.

I thought I would have to stop reading altogether, but Ian turned on the interior light, which I took as a cue to continue. After more than one hundred pages, I came across something promising. We had been searching for weeks for this. My eyes widened and I read the passage three times to be sure before I told Ian.

"I think I've found something!"

"Read it!" he said excitedly.

I read the whole page aloud to him. This entry of the chronicle was dated September 16th, 1699, and was written by a member of the Irish Cultural Society. It described the discovery of an interesting "ancient monument" in "Miss Nancy's Moat" on the farm of Charles Campbell. It said that authorities had been notified "a fortnight" after workers from the farm were carting rocks and found a huge intricately cut stone by an entrance "into the earth." It went on to explain that the monument was going to be investigated by the Welsh Naturalist Edward Lhuyd.

We were just entering a small town and Ian quickly turned into the parking lot of a diner. He parked the car and grabbed the page from my hands. He sat quietly reading the page. As he came to the bottom of the page a huge smile broke across his face, and he said, "Time to eat!"

Obviously, the last thing on Ian's mind was eating. In fact, it seemed to me that looking at the menu, conversing with the waitress, and even eating his burger and fries was just an annoyance. He read the page I had found, as well as the next several over and over, excitedly making comments now and then.

I, on the other hand, was famished. I quickly ate my food, and then hungrily eyed the remnants of Ian's fries wondering if it would be too unlady-like to ask if he was going to finish them. I was immensely pleased with myself. I had found something that excited Ian, and I finally felt like I had lived up to his expectations.

"So do you think it's important?" I asked him.

"Absolutely! It's brilliant." He didn't take his eyes off the page as he answered.

"But does it give you any new information?" I was happy I had found a reference to Newgrange, but I didn't understand the significance of the entry or what exactly he was so excited about. He looked a little annoyed to have to put down the papers and address my questions.

He rubbed the scruff on his chin and leaned forward eyeing me seriously.

"So, we know that the mounds at Newgrange were discovered by Charles Campbell's farm hands. Campbell had been using stones from the mounds to build walls on his property for years. We also know that Edward Lhuyd was called in to excavate the ruins. What has been unclear is the timeline of those events. It was assumed that Campbell immediately contacted the authorities after the discovery, and then they sent for Lhuyd. However, this document clearly states that the discovery was made a fortnight before anyone was notified!" He looked at me excitedly waiting for me to make the connection. I stared at him blankly.

"So, this is new?"

"Yes! Don't you see? Campbell and his crew had two weeks before any officials were on the property!"

"And you think they found something during that two weeks?" Now I realized where he was going.

"I think it's certainly possible, and this is the first account I've read that describes this inconsistency in the timeline." He smiled a devilish grin.

"I take it that 'Miss Nancy's Moat' was the area around Newgrange."

He laughed. "Yes, it's a rarely used term referring to the Brú na Bóinne, or the riverside area of County Meath where Newgrange stands. No one actually knows the origin of the name, but it confirms the date of this document because the term was only used around the 16th and 17th centuries. Evan, this is exactly the break we've been looking for." His smile was broad, gleaming, and irresistible.

I loved seeing Ian excited like this. Even on a bad day, he was beyond gorgeous, but when he was in this kind of mood, he was radiant. He was like a huge magnet that attracted every ray of light in the room, and every bit of female attention as well. Our waitress must have come over ten times to check on us, and even though I don't think Ian ever looked her in the face, she lingered like a puppy a few feet away from our table. I sat up straighter and combed through my hair with my fingers, trying to appear worthy of sitting with him.

When we got back in the car, I grabbed the next dozen or so pages and placed them in my lap. Ian put his hand on the pages and said, "Forget these for tonight. You've worked enough." He picked up the papers and placed them on the backseat. "We've still another hour or so. Talk to me about yourself."

I had not expected this. I knew he was in a good mood, but he hadn't asked me any real questions about myself since we first started working together. "What do you want to know?" I asked a little hesitantly.

"Well, why are *you* here? In Blythe, I mean."

I laughed. I told him about my scholarship, which he already knew, and how I too could have gone to other, more prestigious, schools.

"And don't you miss your family? I mean being so far away and all?" It was dark, but I could tell he was smirking.

"Can't you think of any *original* questions?" I smiled, hoping he wouldn't begrudge my bravado.

He laughed. "OK then, why don't you have a boyfriend?"

I was completely blindsided by this question. I was glad he couldn't see my blushing face in the dark. "Well...I guess I just haven't found the right person or at least not the right *unattached* person." I tried not to sound as flustered as I felt.

"Hmmm, sounds like there's a story there. Care to elaborate?"

"Uh...no," I said smiling. I desperately wanted to pose the same question to him, but before I could gather my nerve, he shot another question at me.

"You said that you're an only child and don't really know your extended family." It was a statement, but he posed it to me as a question.

"Uh-huh." I wondered why he was suddenly so interested in my personal life.

"So, why do you think your grandmother singled you out as a beneficiary?" He kept his eyes trained on the road.

"Uh, well... I guess I don't really know. I don't know a single thing about her other than she was cruel enough to leave her family. I had always thought that she left for some personal crisis that we just didn't understand. I assumed that she believed her daughter was in the safe and loving hands of her father, and didn't realize he had died or that my mom had been sent to an orphanage. But now I know that's not true. She knew my mom was there. She even came to see her, and was cruel beyond belief." I felt tears well up in my eyes at the thought of what my mom went through.

"She came to see her? What did she say?" Ian sounded fascinated by the story.

"Uh...not much. She pretended she was an aunt, but my mom knew."

"That's horrible," he said.

Ian continued asking me questions until we arrived in Santa Fe. He wanted to know when and where I was born, about all the places we had lived, and everything I knew about my parent's ancestry. By the time we drove into town, I still knew precious little about him.

We pulled into the parking lot of the hotel, and I stayed in the car while Ian went to check in. He looked distressed as he walked out. He walked over to my side of the car, and I rolled down the window.

"What's up?" I asked.

"Apparently it is 'Indian Market' weekend at the Plaza." He looked uncomfortable.

"Are they full?" I knew I should have reserved the rooms ahead of time!

"Uh...they said they have one room available." He quickly added, "I told them that we definitely need two, but they assured me it would be unlikely to find another vacant room in town." Now he looked *extremely* uncomfortable.

So, we were going to have to share a room, I thought. My reaction was somewhere between elation and panic. I suddenly wished I owned sexier pajamas, like Taylor's. The sweatpants and old t-shirt stuffed into my overnight bag were just embarrassing.

"Look, I think the best idea is if you take the room and I sleep in the car."

"Don't be ridiculous. You are the one taking the time out of your busy schedule to help me. I won't have you sleeping in your car!"

It took a lot of arguing to get him to stay in the room. In the end, it was the weather that finally convinced him. The unseasonably cold temperatures in Santa Fe were in the low forties. Once we had both unpacked and discussed the logistics of the next morning's meeting, the atmosphere turned very awkward. We were both acutely aware of how taboo the situation was. In fact, it was very possible that Ian could lose his job if someone found out about this little escapade.

He made sure to keep as much distance as possible between us in the room. Luckily, there was a small couch in the sitting area that Ian made into his bed. He spent a very short time in the bathroom, then climbed under his blanket and turned off the lamp next to the couch. I noticed that he was still wearing his clothes, which made me guess that he had not brought pajamas. I wondered what he normally wore to sleep...or if he wore anything at all.

I took my overnight bag into the bathroom, turned on the light, and stared at myself in the mirror. Under the luminescent lights, I almost didn't recognize myself. What was I doing here? I was in a hotel room in a strange city and the most brilliant, amazingly spectacular man I had ever seen was in the next room. Oh and by the way, he was my professor!

Tomorrow I would learn about a grandmother I had never known, who had left me who knows what, and who also may have had my same 'power'. This was the most strange and mind-blowing feeling I had ever had, and considering the last few months, that was saying a lot. Despite myself, a huge smile spread across my face, and I took a moment to savor the thrill and anticipation.

I pulled my hair back. I looked tired and road-weary. I decided I would shower so that Ian could have more time in the bathroom the next morning. The meeting with my grandmother's lawyers was set for 8:00 a.m., so there would not be much time with both of us jockeying for the bathroom.

I stood still and let the hot water run over my body. My muscles immediately relaxed, and I felt sleepy. As I washed my hair, I let my mind wander and play. I imagined hearing the door creak open. I thought about the way I might react if that happened. Would I be embarrassed and grab a towel to cover myself? No, I knew I wouldn't.

I wasn't sure how long I let the fantasies play in my mind, but by the time I turned off the water and climbed out of the shower the room was completely steamy and my fingers were all pruned up. Why couldn't I project myself into fantasies instead of the past, I mused as I put on my shabby pajamas and brushed my teeth.

I tried to calm my raging hormones, as I quietly got into bed and turned out my light. I wondered if Ian was asleep yet. In the dimly lit room, I could see him on the couch. He was completely covered by his blanket and all that was visible was a bit of hair on his pillow.

My pulse quickened as I noticed a heap of clothes, lying by the couch, and realized that under that blanket he was now wearing very little. I knew it was wrong to have these thoughts about my professor, but honestly, it was impossible not to.

I tossed and turned for hours. I was tired but I couldn't stop thinking. I thought about what tomorrow held and all the events of the last few months that had led me to this point. I thought about Aaron and Becky and wondered if she had already had her surgery and how Aaron was handling it. I felt a pang of guilt about my desire for Ian when I thought about Aaron. But, it wasn't like I had anything *real* to feel guilty about, plus Aaron had Becky.

I tried counting sheep. I tried not thinking at all, but the anticipation was too much. My ears pricked at every noise Ian made. Every time I heard him move, I strained my eyes in the dark to see him. At one point he turned and flung the blanket partially off. For a few moments, I could see half of his bare chest in the moonlight, and any possibility of sleep quickly fled.

He was exquisite, and just as my mind began drifting off into another fantasy, which began with me crawling under his blanket, he pulled the covers back over himself, destroying my view. Most of the time he seemed too quiet, and I wondered if he was also having a hard time sleeping. A few times I almost said, "Ian are you asleep?" but I lost my nerve. Finally, absolute exhaustion took over and I began drifting off to sleep.

I felt like I had just gotten to sleep when the sunlight pouring into the room woke me up. I jumped out of bed when I realized it was already 7:00 a.m.! Ian was still asleep on the couch, and I used the opportunity to get into the bathroom and get dressed. I quickly washed up and got dressed in a cream-colored silk blouse and tweed skirt that Taylor had bought me. Now I was glad that she had forced me to buy a skirt. I finished the outfit off with a pair of dressy patent leather brown pumps on which she had also insisted. I applied makeup and tied my hair up in a loose French twist, pulling a few long tendrils out to frame my face, just as Taylor had taught me to do.

I looked in the mirror and was more than satisfied. Despite the lack of sleep, I really did look great, and I had to thank Taylor when I got home for her wonderful taste in clothes. I emerged from the bathroom to find Ian sitting on the couch scrolling on his phone. He was in the same clothes he had worn the day before and his hair was a mess. I suppressed a giggle.

"Wow, you look amazing!" He said looking up at me. "I guess I should try to pull myself together too." He stood up, ran his hands through his hair, and walked towards the bathroom. "I just couldn't get to sleep last night," he murmured.

—ℓℓ—

We drove to the downtown offices of Lloyd, Goldschmidt, and Williams. There was quite a bit of traffic as we neared 'The Plaza', which was Santa Fe's pueblo-style, old-town city center, where the 'Indian Market' was being held. I could see blocks of brown adobe buildings lined with stalls full of pottery, turquoise jewelry, art, and brightly-colored blankets.

Despite the early hour, hundreds of people already filled the streets. At the end of one narrow street, I could see a beautiful Gothic Revival-style cathedral, complete with spires, buttresses, and stained-glass windows. I wished we weren't here purely on business, because I would have loved to spend some time exploring the square. However, the plan was to head back to Blythe right after the meeting.

We walked through a grand foyer that had a fountain and dozens of exotic plants, including a large magnolia tree that must have been fifteen feet tall. There was no one sitting at the receptionist's desk, presumably since it was Saturday, but a tall, distinguished-looking man in an expensive suit walked into the lobby as soon as he heard us. He was very tan and had salt-and-pepper hair. He extended his hand and said, "Miss Wright I presume. I'm Ken Williams. It's very nice to finally meet you."

Hmmm, Ken, I thought. I wondered if there was a Barbie at home. I shook his hand with the firmest grip I could muster. "It's nice to meet you as well. Please let me introduce Dr. Ian Browning. Dr. Browning is one of my professors at Harper."

"One of your professors?"

"Yes, and my research mentor as well. Since my parents couldn't be here, he kindly agreed to come...for moral support." They shook hands and I noticed Ken eying Ian very intently.

"So, you didn't bring representation?" Ken asked.

"No, I didn't realize I needed to."

"No, no, of course you don't. As I mentioned in my letter, we here at the firm would be happy to take care of all the necessary details." He smiled a dazzling, too-white smile and I realized that I had just given them my business.

"Please, let's go into my office."

As we entered the lavishly decorated room, Ken offered us coffee and French pastries, which Ian and I were both extremely happy to accept.

"I'm sorry it took so long to arrange for a Saturday meeting. I had several out-of-town commitments, and I wanted to be here for this. I've asked my colleague Ms. Fox to join us and transcribe the details of the meeting." He gestured to the door, and as I turned around, mouth full of pastry, I saw a woman standing in the doorway, notepad in hand. However, this was no ordinary secretary.

First of all, she was dressed in a very flatteringly-fitted pencil skirt, blouse, and blazer. I suspected they were not only designer but maybe even custom-made, based on the fit. She was slender, statuesque, and striking. She had high, pronounced cheekbones, and long legs. However, by far her most distinguishing feature was her long silver hair, which she had pulled back in a low ponytail. She was obviously completely gray, but her hair was not dull gray by any means. It was completely and magnificently silvery white.

I wondered how old she was. I was very bad at guessing peoples' ages, but I supposed she had to be at least forty. Was it possible to be completely gray by forty? I had no idea, but if she was older than that she was incredibly well-preserved. She gracefully crossed the room and introduced herself.

Ian was standing taller and straighter than I had ever seen him stand, and I thought he seemed much too eager to make her acquaintance. She sat in a leather armchair on Ken's side of the desk, opposite Ian and me. Her whole presence, every movement, every word sang of elegance and dignity. It almost felt like we were in the presence of royalty.

"Evan, as I mentioned before, I am happy we could finally meet, although I regret it has to be under such somber circumstances, again I'm so sorry for your loss. I knew Evelyn for years and was very fond of her." Ken's hands were folded on the desk, and he smiled serenely at me.

"Thank you, Mr. Williams, but please, there's no need to be sorry. I never even met my grandmother. In fact, I didn't know she was still been alive until I received your letter." Ken's face suddenly changed, and he appeared completely confused. He shot a glance in Ms. Fox's direction, but she kept her head down taking notes.

I felt like I needed to explain. I told them how my grandmother had left my mother when she was a baby, and how my mother had ended up in an orphanage after her father died. I tried to stifle the revulsion I felt towards Evelyn and make my voice sound neutral. After all, Ken had been *fond* of her. However, the more I explained, the more confused Ken looked. I was beginning to wonder if this was some big mistake, maybe this dead woman had not been my grandmother at all. Maybe they had the wrong person.

"I guess...well, I guess I was confused about the status of your relationship. I always assumed by the way Evelyn talked about you, that you knew each other. I'm sorry."

She talked about me?! I desperately wanted to know what she had said, but before I could ask, Ken was speaking again.

"Well, nonetheless, she did designate you as *the only* beneficiary of her estate."

I looked at Ian and he raised an eyebrow.

"Her estate?" I repeated.

"Yes, Evan your grandmother was a substantially wealthy woman. I supposed you knew. As I said, I obviously did not understand the circumstances of your...relationship. I think it would be a good idea for you to enlist some financial advisors. Our firm would be happy to put you in touch with the right people."

"Uh...what exactly do you mean when you say estate?" I asked.

Ken opened his desk drawer and pulled out a pile of papers. On top was a sealed envelope. "Evelyn's will was very clear. She requested that I read this letter to you before the will is read." He tore open the envelope and pulled out a letter. I could see that it was hand-written. Ken cleared his throat and began to read.

"Dearest Evan, as I'm sure you have begun to realize, this universe has many secrets waiting to be revealed. You are now on your path and your ability will allow you to reveal some of those secrets." I saw out of the corner of my eye that Ian had turned to face me. I could feel him staring.

"I envy your youth and wish I too was just beginning my journey. I searched many lifetimes for someone like you...like myself. It was appropriate that your mother named you after me. Evan Lynn, my advice to you, before we meet again, is to never trust anyone, guard your talent and be extremely careful who you decide to love. Although it may feel like this will last forever, there are only a limited number of lifetimes, affectionately, Evelyn." Ken folded the paper and handed it to me.

It felt like the room was spinning. I could not figure out why on earth Evelyn had requested this letter to be read aloud. If she was advising me to guard my power, why would she blatantly refer to it in front of others? I could still feel Ian still staring at me.

"My mother did say she believed Evelyn was crazy. I think she may have been right." I shook my head feigning bewilderment.

"It's so odd," Ken said. "She always seemed so grounded, smart, and calculating, but now that you tell me the history of your family and considering this strange letter, I wonder..."

I glanced at Ms. Fox and realized she too was giving me the most penetrating stare. She immediately cast her strange gray eyes down, looking at her notepad again.

"Well then, shall we continue?" Ken held up the next set of papers and began to read. "I, Evelyn Grace Lambert, do hereby make, publish, and declare this to be my Last Will and Testament, hereby expressly revoking all previous wills and codicils heretofore made by me. I direct my Executor to pay my judicially enforceable debts, funeral expenses, and the administrative expenses of my estate as soon after my death as practical." Ken looked up and said, "This just means that she has given us the right to deduct the costs of her arrangements from her estate holdings." He gave me a condescending smile like he was explaining simple addition to a five-year-old.

"Got it," I said. He continued reading a lot of legal jargon that explained how provisions would be made for property and estate taxes, and then he got to the meat of the Will. I held my breath.

"Article two. I do give and bequeath to my granddaughter Evan Lynn Wright, all my personal effects and all my tangible personal property, including residences, automobiles owned by me and held for my personal use at the time of my death, and cash on hand in the bank accounts and securities held in my own name."

Ken picked up another paper, took a deep breath, and began to speak again. "These belongings include the land, dwelling, and effects located at 7 Vista del Oro, Cerrillos, New Mexico, the balance of one checking and one savings account at the Santa Fe Commerce bank, and the contents of safe deposit box #172, in said bank." He looked up at me, setting down the paper.

I waited patiently for him to continue, but he just sat looking at me with a faint smile. I looked over at Ian and he gave me a slight nod of his head. Ms. Fox still sat with her head down, busily writing on her notepad. I guessed it was my turn to speak.

"So, I own a house now?" Was the only thing I could think of to say, other than 'How much money did she leave me,' which I decided would be too crass.

"The Hacienda Doña Maria de Santa Fe is a little more than a house!" Ken exclaimed. "It is a six-thousand square-foot estate that sits on over fifty acres of mountain-side land. I think you will be quite impressed."

My eyes were bulging. "So, I own a hacienda now?"

"Yes, Ms. Wright. In addition to the estimated value of Evelyn's home, personal belongings, and bank accounts..." he cleared his throat, "...you are inheriting a little more than 7.2 million dollars." He tapped the stack of papers together to straighten them and placed them neatly on the desk.

Chapter 13

HACIENDA DOÑA MARIA DE SANTA FE

I didn't scream. I didn't faint. I was numb. Nothing felt real. The next hour was a blur of activity. It felt like I was having a near-death experience, floating above my body watching everyone dash around me. It was like they were all on fast-forward and I was on pause. I went through the motions, barely comprehending a thing. For me, everything had stopped when Ken said 7.2 million dollars. I could not get past that moment, could not wrap my mind around it.

Everyone imagines winning the lottery or having Ed McMahon arrive at your doorstep with a giant check and a bunch of balloons. The people in those commercials are always so coherent. They jump around, yell for relatives...immediately make plans for what they're going to do with the money. That was not my reaction at all. I went from feeling numb to doubting the reality of it to sheer fear. I knew it was ridiculous, I should have been dancing around the room, but in all honesty, it was too much.

Eight months ago, I had come to Blythe, Texas as a scholarship student, who felt a million degrees of separation from most of the other kids at Harper. Then, everything I thought I knew was turned upside down during one final exam. The *power* had been a miracle, it had transformed my life, and I was not even close to understanding it. Now, I was being faced with another life-transforming miracle.

I was well aware that most people would slap me silly for my tepid emotional response to this inheritance, but I honestly didn't know if I could handle it. My ability had certainly been a shock, but it was my secret. My life didn't have to change, and I didn't have to live up to anyone's expectations. But this...this was different. People would know. Things were definitely going to change...and I wondered if I really wanted them to.

Ian stood close, steadying me as I signed what felt like a hundred documents. I could have been signing my life away for all I knew. Although Ken tried to explain the significance of each piece of paper, I was beyond frazzled. It comforted me to look at Ian's determined expression, intently scrutinizing each form before I signed it. I knew he had my best interests at heart and would not stand for any funny business.

After an eternity, Ken and Ms. Fox left the office to make copies of all the documents. I collapsed into a big leather chair and breathed in deeply.

"Are you alright? I know it's a lot to take in." Ian said, sitting in the chair next to me.

His comment was perfect. It *was* a lot. I was so happy he didn't congratulate me.

"You're going to think I'm crazy." I closed my eyes and put my face in my hands.

"Try me."

I almost jumped when I felt Ian gently take my hand, pull it away from my face, and hold it in his. This was the most intimate gesture he had ever made and the surprise of it caught me off guard. I looked into his eyes and was overwhelmed by the tenderness and concern in them. It was so nice to know in this moment of upheaval and uncertainty that someone was there who genuinely cared about me. I squeezed his hand tightly.

"Well, we never really had much money while I was growing up, but my parents made do, and I always had the necessities. I never felt deprived, and it never stopped us from spending time together and traveling, which was what I loved most." He was listening carefully, concentrating on my every word.

"But since I've been at Harper, it seems like everyone I know who has a lot of money, has more problems than they know what to do with. I guess I just feel like money...especially this much money can destroy your life." I prayed Ian would not think I was being ungrateful.

"Evan, this is one of the things I love about you. You are so...unexpected. Most people would have had a completely different reaction to just inheriting millions of dollars."

I silently gasped. Had he really just said it was one of the things he *loved* about me? Before I could even begin to start overanalyzing what he meant, Ken and Ms. Fox were back. I cursed their timing!

"So that completes everything on our side. To save your time, and prevent you from having to make another trip, we have arranged with Mr. Thompson, from the bank, to meet with you this morning. It would also be a good idea to make an inventory of the house while you're here too." He held out a set of keys.

"The house?" A new wave of apprehension washed over me as I took the keys from him.

"Well yes. I mean it is yours now...and everything in it. You should at least make a quick visit...while you are here. If you want to sell it, we can always arrange for liquidation. Many people in your situation decide they are just too busy to deal with the estate. Typically, we schedule an auction of the land, dwelling, belongings...everything. Then the revenue from the sale is simply transferred into your account."

"No, no. I definitely want to see it." I needed to find out who my grandmother was. My eyes flashed to Ian.

"Sure. We have plenty of time," he said.

"OK then, why don't you two follow us over to the bank."

As Ian drove, I called my parents. I filled in Mom and Dad, who was listening on a second phone, on everything that had happened. I almost could not get the words '7.2 million dollars' out of my mouth. It still didn't seem real, and I don't think they believed me at first. For several seconds there was just complete silence. The most my mom had hoped for was a small insurance policy that would cover the cost of my trip home this summer. However, after I assured them five times that I was not joking, had not misunderstood, and definitely was not imagining things, the situation finally started to sink in.

I was a little embarrassed when I had to hold the phone away from my ear so that my mother's screams wouldn't pierce my eardrum. Her voice filled the car. Ian just smiled. Clearly, she had a very different reaction to the news than I did. I answered as many of their questions as I could, then almost had to hang up to get them off the phone, because we had arrived at the bank, and Ken and Ms. Fox were patiently waiting beside our parked car.

There was another seemingly endless pile of papers to sign inside the bank, which essentially transferred all of Grandmother's money into my bank account. I was just glad I had one! I had only opened it when I moved to Blythe to hold the paltry amount of spending money Mom and Dad sent me. Then, I barely had the two-hundred and fifty dollars required to start the account!

I wondered what the people at my bank would think when this transfer came in or if everything was handled by computers and no actual human beings ever knew. No, I felt certain that this amount of money would raise some flags. The manager of the bank, Mr. Thompson, seemed a little peeved to be losing my grandmother's business, but this was just a local bank with no other branches. It hardly made sense to keep it there. Considering the number of forms I had to fill out, I almost thought he was intentionally making things more difficult. I just wanted to be done. I was tired of signing forms and talking to these 'suits'.

I was especially ready to get away from Ms. Fox. The way she was scrutinizing me made me feel very uncomfortable. I could feel her stare and strain to hear every word I said. Every time I returned her gaze, her eyes darted down to her notepad. It was almost like she was pretending to take notes. Something about her felt almost...sinister. I wondered if she really had an alternative agenda or if the money was making me paranoid already.

Finally, the last form was completed, and although I was desperate to get out of there, Mr. Thompson reminded me of something I had completely forgotten about.

"Lastly, Ms. Wright, are the contents of safe deposit box #172. Would you like to claim them now?"

Mr. Thompson escorted me down a long hallway and into a square room. He handed me a key and walked out, shutting the door behind him. There was a high table and stool in the middle of the room. Hundreds of safe deposit boxes lined each of the four walls. They varied in size and when I located #172, I was happy to see it was one of the smaller boxes. I didn't know what I expected...maybe some jewelry, passports, or security bonds. Those seemed like the usual types of things found in safe deposit boxes, not that I had ever actually seen one before.

I turned the key and pulled out the long box. I brought it over to the table and sat on the stool. Taking a deep breath, I readied myself for Grandmother's next surprise, but no amount of oxygen in my lungs prepared me for what I saw when I turned the key and lifted the lid.

Sitting on top of the red velvet lining in the box was a sterling silver compact case elaborately etched with rose vines. I noticed that my hands were trembling as I held my breath, picked it up, and flipped it over. The inscription read, 'Love, E.L.' When I bought this compact for Taylor, I had mused how E.L., could've stood for Evan Lynn, but now I realized it really stood for Evelyn Lambert.

My mind reeled as I tried to figure out how and why this compact case was here, but no matter how much I thought, I could not come up with any explanations. I needed to get to her house...see her things. If there were answers to be had, I was sure they were there. Hand trembling, I carefully put the compact case into my purse and started to put the box away when I realized there was one more item in it, way at the back.

I reached in and pulled out a large iron skeleton key. I didn't think that keys like it actually existed. It looked like the type of key that opened a medieval dungeon in a movie. It felt cold and heavy in my hand. The thought of what secrets it unlocked frightened me. The last thing I needed was more secrets and mysteries.

Four sets of eyes were glued to me as I walked into the bank lobby. I could tell that everyone was desperate to know what had been in the box. I knew I didn't *have* to tell them, but their scrutiny was unbearable.

"It was just a key," I said, holding up the skeleton key. Ms. Fox's eyes gleamed and I swear she started to take a step forward but stopped herself.

"Hmmm, I've never seen a key like that one. I wonder what it opens." Ken said.

I was disappointed that he didn't know. It meant that I was going to have to try and figure it out, along with every other mystery that crowded my mind.

Ken offered to escort us to Grandmother's house, but I politely declined. The last thing I wanted was to spend multiple more hours with the suits. Although she did not say a word, I thought Ms. Fox looked especially thwarted by my rejection of their offer.

As we stood on the curb outside the bank, Ken offered his hand again. "Ms. Wright it has been a pleasure. I will be in touch soon. Please call if you need any assistance at the house."

Ian opened my door and walked around to his side of the car. As I started to climb into the passenger seat, a thought occurred to me. I left the car door standing open and ran down the sidewalk until I caught up with Ken. Ms. Fox was already in their car but quickly got out when she saw me coming. I resented that she insisted on recording my every word.

"Mr. Williams, there is one more thing I need to know... How did my grandmother die?" I could not believe that I had only now thought to ask.

"Oh, I'm sorry I should have explained the details of her passing before. She died peacefully, in her sleep. Her heart just stopped."

"So, it was natural causes then..." I mumbled more to myself than him. "How old was she?"

"I believe she was 92 years old."

"Was she buried? Was there a funeral?" I couldn't imagine who would have attended. I wondered if she had ever had another family. I supposed that if she had, they wouldn't be too happy with the details of her will.

"She had very specific instructions concerning her...*arrangements*. Her instructions were to be cremated. There were no services, and her remains were placed in an urn and now...well, actually it belongs to you, along with everything else she owned. You will find it in the house."

"Everything all right?" Ian asked as I got back in the car.

"Uh...yeah sure."

Ian had gotten directions to the Hacienda Doña Maria from Ken. Apparently, it was a forty-minute drive into the mountains that surrounded Santa Fe. As we drove, I heard Ian commenting every now and then on the beauty of the scenery, but I never saw a thing. I kept my head down, reading Grandmother's letter over and over.

I searched many lifetimes trying to find someone like you...like myself. It was appropriate that your mother named you after me. Evan Lynn, my advice to you, before we meet again, is to trust no one, guard your talent and be extremely careful who you decide to love. Although it may feel like this will last forever, there are only a limited number of lifetimes.

No matter how many times I read it, it did not make any sense. What did she mean by "lifetimes?" It couldn't possibly be literal...could it? And what did she mean "before we meet again?" Had I met her before and not known it? She did have my, well Taylor's, compact case. I tried to think back to every old woman I had met since I had been in Blythe, or at least since I bought it. Of course, I didn't even know what she looked like. It couldn't be the same compact case. Could it? And what did she mean by meet again? Like in Heaven?

One thing I was sure of was that she had the *power* too. There was no doubt about that. Could she have visited me when I was younger? Could she have observed me without my knowing it? I knew she could have... Hadn't I observed Aaron? The thought of it made me feel angry and paranoid. Could this woman, who I hated for treating my mother so badly, have been *spying* on my life?

The harsh rumble of the car broke my trance, and I looked up to see that we had turned onto a bumpy dirt road.

"Could use some grading, huh?" Ian said, noticing that I had finally looked up.

"Uh...wow, I'm sorry about this. Do you think it will damage your car?"

"No, should be fine. I'm taking it slow."

The road wound up a relatively steep hill until we came to a large iron gate that blocked the road. I briefly wondered if this was what the skeleton key opened, but Ian pulled out what looked like a garage door opener and pressed a button.

"From Ken," he said.

The gate slowly swung open, and we drove on, ascending a few hundred more yards. As we neared the crest of the hill, the house came into view. Before I could even register a reaction, I heard Ian laugh.

"Brilliant!" He finally managed over the low chuckles. He stopped the car and we both climbed out.

It is difficult to express what I felt the moment I first saw the Hacienda Doña Maria de Santa Fe. I suppose it could be called wonder or amazement, but that would be a significant underestimation of the emotions that welled up inside me. There was a deep feeling of belonging, sadness, and joy all wrapped together. It was like coming home after a long journey. It was like seeing a newborn's face. It was as if *I* was reborn.

The scene was nothing short of spectacular. We were standing on a high vista overlooking a majestic valley. There were mountains in the far distance, across the valley, but it felt like we were much higher than them. And standing proudly like a sentinel, emerging from the side of the mountain, was the hacienda.

It was a large two-story building in the traditional Santa Fe adobe style. The sun-dried clay gave the hacienda a rich red color. There were several flat roofs at different levels, supported by a network of long wooden beams whose ends protruded through the outer facades. The soft, rounded contours of the hacienda conveyed an intimate hominess, despite its massive size.

Tears welled in my eyes as the full depth of the emotions I was feeling sunk in, and I finally understood what they were. It was more than awe and amazement. It was more than appreciation for the sheer perfection and beauty of this place. It was reminiscence, and I knew with every fiber of my being that I had been here before.

"Evan, come on. Let's go inside!" Ian was waving me over from near the front door. The sight of him, so happy and excited, standing in front of this place that I knew I loved deeply, made me happy beyond measure, and I knew already that I never wanted to leave.

I walked through a circular courtyard surrounded by a low adobe wall. In the center was a tiered fountain that was not running. There were several large terracotta planters lining the tiled paths of the courtyard. They contained everything from small trees to large leafy plants and beautifully colored, exotic flowers. All of them looked wilted and in need of watering. A large arched portico loomed high over the eight-foot-tall ornate wooden doors, where Ian patiently waited for me.

"A bit shell-shocked, are you?" Ian took the keys from my hand and began unlocking the doors.

"You could say that," I replied in a dreamy, dazed voice.

As soon as we stepped into the foyer, Ian turned to a wall panel and began punching in a code of numbers.

"Alarm system?" I asked.

"Ken gave me the code." He said, peering at a small scrap of paper. I was glad one of us was on top of things.

I walked through the front entryway into an expansive living area. It was a large open space, broken up into several intimate seating nooks. Unlike most houses, you entered on the top floor. The hacienda essentially hugged the side of the mountain. On the far side was a wrought iron balcony broken by several arched walls.

I walked to the balcony and looked down on the first floor, at least twenty feet below. A massive, tiered iron chandelier hung in the open space beyond the balcony, and a gently curving staircase ran from the far right of the room to the floor below. However, the most striking feature of the room was the vista of mountains and valleys afforded by the glass-paned wall opposite where I stood.

"My god, it takes your breath away, doesn't it?" Ian had come to stand beside me. "Yes," I said in a whisper. We both stood there for some time, completely silent.

The kitchen, formal dining area, and library were on the top floor. On the bottom floor was a small casual dining area, the main living area, and bedrooms. The soft earth tones of the adobe walls gradually shifted from room to room, from burnt oranges to clay red and mud brown. The atmosphere of each room was warm and inviting and combined traditional Southwest/Native American décor with contemporary art.

The centerpiece of the lower floor's main living space was a massive fireplace in the middle of the room. The chimney column rose all the way up past the wrought iron balcony on the top floor to the top of the high cathedral ceiling. I would later learn it was called a 'kiva' and is a main feature of Pueblo-style homes. It was circular and at least six feet wide with iron grates on opposite sides in order to view the fire from either side of the room. The kiva was encircled by a small ledge for seating and an upper mantle where a few vases and pieces of sculpture sat.

It wasn't until after I had been in the house for several hours, that I realized one of those vases on the mantle wasn't actually a vase at all. It was my grandmother! It was beyond bizarre knowing that all that was left of her was in that urn. I stared at it waiting to register some emotion, but honestly, I felt nothing. It was like looking at any of the vases sitting next to it.

There were several large bedrooms on the first floor. Each was decorated differently, but they all maintained the same overall Southwestern theme. Some were two-story with loft areas and several had their own bathrooms. The very last bedroom I found was obviously my grandmother's. It was the only one that looked lived in, and the décor was strikingly different. Instead of the soft earth tones of the pueblo walls in all the other rooms of the house, this room, which was the largest of all the bedrooms, was painted in bold reds and golds.

The room wasn't cluttered, but it was certainly quite full of very expensive-looking, antique furniture. It was like being in a museum. It reminded me of visiting Windsor Castle. It was that same kind of opulence. It was not just a bedroom, it was a *boudoir*. There was a large four-poster bed draped in sheer lace curtains. Several brightly colored crystal perfume bottles, with big bulbs and tassels, sat on a large vanity table. Beautiful armchairs, covered in rich fabrics, sat around the room, and a massive, intricately carved wardrobe rested against the far wall.

I opened the wardrobe door and looked through the clothes hanging on the rail. It looked like a costume shop. There were furs, gowns, blouses, and pants in styles that seemed to span centuries. Immediately, I thought about the dress I had bought to 'fit in' in 1963 and realized that I had already started my own collection of 'period' clothes. Clearly, Grandmother had been at this a long time.

I spent some time searching Grandmother's bedroom and bathroom. There were plenty of 'personal effects', things like toiletries and clothes, but nothing that really told me much about her. I thought about the stack of notebooks and journals, locked in my dorm room that detailed my experiences over the past few months. I guess I had been hoping to find something like that...a journal or diary that would explain everything. Sadly, I had no such luck.

Ian was nowhere in sight as I opened the French doors and wandered out onto the veranda that opened off the main living area on the first floor. It was much larger than a balcony. The first several yards were covered by the overhanging top floor of the house, which was the glass-paneled wall that revealed the spectacular view. However, as I stepped out into the bright, midday sun that bathed the rest of the large expanse, a vivid memory stopped me in my tracks.

I was riding a bicycle around and around the perimeter of this very veranda, laughing, dashing between columns, dodging planters. A feeling of pure joy filled me. It was only a scrap of a memory, just a snapshot or two, but it was vivid and powerful.

I walked to the edge of the patio and peered out over the adobe wall. A fall off here would be severe, at least thirty feet down a steep hill. I could see tall white clouds rolling in from the west. To the east, there was nothing but crystal blue sky as far as the eye could see. I just stood there taking it all in, letting my hair blow in the soft warm breeze.

"This place is absolutely and utterly amazing! Evan, you can never sell it!" Ian's voice broke the silence, and I looked back to see him striding across the veranda with a huge smile on his face.

"That's exactly what I was thinking."

He stood beside me, and we both quietly looked out to the horizon.

"Evan, you know, you don't *have* to let the money change your life or who you are."

"You don't think there will be...expectations?" I asked, turning to look at him.

"Why would there be? Just live your life, Evan. Live it for yourself, not anyone else. The money just gives you freedom, to live it the way *you* want."

I didn't say anything. I wasn't sure what to say. A million different scenarios were playing out in my mind. After a few moments, he spoke again.

"You know, there are a lot of very noble things you can do with that kind of money. Charities, endowments...many ways you can help people. What's more, I don't even know why anyone would have to know about your inheritance if you didn't want them to."

I liked that thought. Of course, my parents could have any amount of the money they wanted, and I wondered what they would do with it. Would my father retire? They could move back to the States...maybe even move into this house. My speculation was cut short when Ian broke the silence again.

"OK, now you have to come see the library!" He excitedly grabbed my hand and pulled me back into the house. We climbed the stairs and made our way down a long hallway. I had not even explored this part of the house yet, but as with all the other rooms, as soon as we entered the library, everything seemed familiar.

It wasn't dark, dusty, and cramped like Ian's office. It was bright and airy with a high vaulted ceiling. Sun poured in through the skylights and mixed with the soft pastels of the walls to bathe the room in a warm glow. Bookcases lined most of the walls and reached high to the ceiling. There was a long ladder on wheels to access the top shelves.

"Many of these are first editions...Joyce, Hemingway, Dickens. Can you believe it? The value of these books alone considerably increases your inheritance, Evan." Ian was walking along the perimeter of the room, letting his fingers graze the books on the shelves. He stopped and gently pulled out one of the leather-bound volumes and sat down at the large mahogany desk in the center of the room.

"Evan, listen to this. This is a first edition of James Joyce's Ulysses. There is an inscription on the front page. It reads, 'Eve, thanks for the Guinness, sorry about your dress. J.J., Oct. 25'...' He looked up at me, eyes full of wonder. "Eve...wasn't your Grandmother named Evelyn...you don't think..."

I quickly did the math. "No, I don't think that's possible." I forced a half-hearted laugh.

"No, no I guess not. Amazing though..."

Ian was like a kid in a candy store as we explored the library. He kept gasping and calling me over to show me this or that book. Grandmother's collection was extensive and quite eclectic. However, I noticed right away that she had a particular fondness for sci-fi and fantasy novels. Everything ever written by Orwell, Huxley, Vonnegut and Asimov was on the shelves. In addition, there were also many non-fiction books by theoretical physicists like Stephen Hawking. I completely understood her fascination.

"Oh my god, Evan...look!"

I spun around and saw Ian, still sitting at the desk, now flipping through a large, red, leather-bound album. I dashed over and as I got closer; I could see that it was full of photographs. I stood behind him, leaning over to see.

"This must be your grandmother. Jaysus, she looks just like you. In fact, if your hair was shorter and a little darker you could be twins." He looked up at me as I hovered over his shoulder.

The photo was a large black and white print, yellowed with age. In it, a young woman was standing in front of what looked like a giant bullet. She was smiling coyly and had one hand on her hip. It was a funny pose and almost looked like she was flirting with the camera.

She was wearing a dress that was low-cut and fitted at the top, while the knee-high skirt flared out. The shoulders were padded and square. Her hair was dark, shoulder-length, and styled in large stiff rolls. She reminded me of Greta Garbo or those pictures of the World War II pin-up girls. And Ian was right...she looked exactly like me.

"Same nose and high cheekbones... and look, it's hard to see in black and white but I swear her eyes could be differently colored like yours!" He was tracing her face in the photo lightly with his fingers. "...she was beautiful..." I blushed and wished he was stroking my face. I leaned in closer until my stomach pressed against his shoulder, and the heat from that connection traveled up into my chest and neck, taking my breath away.

"Do you realize what this is?"

Reluctantly, I focused on the photo again. He was pointing at the object that she was standing in front of. "A big bullet?" I asked.

He snickered. "Your grandmother is standing in front of the West-inghouse time capsule!" He looked up at me again.

"The what?" I was intrigued.

"The Westinghouse time capsule...this photo must have been taken at the 1939 World's Fair in New York. They put dozens of everyday items like fountain pens, magazines, dolls, cigarettes, and money in the time capsule. They had a big ceremony and buried it at the fair that year. It is supposed to be opened in five thousand years. Isn't it amazing that she was there to see it?"

"Uh, yeah." I wondered what other events she had 'been there to see'.

"So, let's see...how old do you think she is in this photo?"

"Mmm, I don't... my age maybe, or a bit older?" I was horrible at guessing ages, but I thought she looked pretty young.

"Well, that would make her..." he did some quick calculations in his head... "...about ninety or so when she died. That's a pretty long life, and it certainly looks like she had fun!"

Ian turned his attention back to the album and continued to flip through. Most of the photos were old black and whites. There were lots of people and places I did not recognize. Then, as he turned to the last page his whole body stiffened and froze.

"What the..."

A small photo was centered on black matting on the last page of the album. I was no historian, but even I realized that it was extremely old. It was a formal picture of a young man and woman. He had a mustache, and short, clean-cut dark hair. He was seated and wearing a suit. The woman standing behind him, with her hand resting on his shoulder, was wearing a beautiful, elaborately decorated, full, floor-length dress that was tight at the bodice. Her dark hair was parted in the middle and pulled back. In this photo, she reminded me of Scarlet O'Hara in 'Gone with the Wind'. She looked exactly like she did in the 1939 photo, just in a different costume.

"It's a tintype. I would guess it's circa 1860..." He was tracing the edges of this photo with his fingers now. "I guess she...she must be...a relation." His voice sounded strange. "Maybe your great-grandmother?" He carefully lifted the photo from the border that held it in place. He flipped it over to reveal a handwritten note on the back. It read 'Thomas and me before the war'.

"But how..." Ian sounded agitated.

"What? What's wrong?" I asked. His tone made me anxious.

"It's written in ballpoint pen." He said flatly.

"So." Stupidly, I still did not get it.

"Evan, ballpoint pens weren't in use until the 1940s."

Thankfully, my phone rang right at that moment. It was about the third time that Mom had called since we had been at the house. I had ignored all the other calls, but this time I used it as an excuse to extract myself from the room, and any other mysteries Ian happened to come across.

"Hi, Mom."

"Evan, why have you not answered my calls? We're going crazy here. Tell me what's happening!"

I filled her in on the last few hours...the bank, the house.

"There was only a key in the safe deposit box?" Mom asked.

"Yeah, and it's a really weird one. It's a big iron skeleton key. I'm worried there's a dungeon somewhere around here that it opens." I didn't tell her about the compact case, or my memories of being here, but I tried to describe as many details as possible about the hacienda. I wanted to convey the majesty and beauty of the place. I needed her to appreciate my fondness for her mother's house so that she would understand why I didn't want to sell it.

"Evy, it sounds amazing. I wish I was there with you right now. Daddy has a work thing he needs to take care of early next week, and then we are going to get on the first flight out there. We need to be there to help you deal with all of this."

"I'm doing fine Mom. Ian has been a great help. He was amazing today with the lawyers and all."

"Ian?" My mother's tone was cynical.

"I mean uh, Dr. Browning."

She made a humph sound and I could tell she did not appreciate the familiarity between us.

"Evy, this man is your *professor*. What is he doing there with you anyway?"

"Mom, he's just trying to help. He knew you and Dad couldn't be here and he cares about me."

She made that humph sound again. "Well, I don't like it, Evy. It just doesn't seem right. How old did you say he was?"

"Ugh Mom, there's *nothing* going on." Although, I certainly wished there was. "He's just a nice guy trying to help, and he's never been anything but professional with me." I thought about today...Ian holding my hand and saying 'what he *loved* about me'.

"Well, when are you heading back to Blythe?"

I hadn't actually thought about that. I was certainly in no hurry, there was still so much to learn here, and Ian didn't seem to be pressed to get back either. "In a few hours." I lied.

"OK, well...why don't you call me before you leave, so I can know you're on your way?"

"Fine Mom." I knew this was not going to end well.

—·ℓℓ—

I didn't return to the library right away. While on the phone with my mother it occurred to me that Ian and I hadn't had anything to eat since the pastries in Ken's office at 8:00 am! The pangs and growls coming from my stomach were becoming painful and urgent. I headed to the kitchen, stopping briefly to admire the view.

The sun was starting to set, and the colors of the sky were incredible. There were shades of pink, purple, and orange that I did not think I had ever seen in the sky before. There were more tall cumulonimbus clouds gathering, and it looked like there was a storm over the mountains to the north. I wondered when Ian would want to head back to Blythe.

Since it would be dark soon, and there was weather rolling in, I contemplated suggesting to him that we stay the night at the hacienda. I suspected that getting him out of the library wouldn't be easy in the first place, much less getting him back to Blythe. I smiled at the thought of the two of us stuck here, playing house.

There wasn't much in the refrigerator and what was there looked a little sketchy. However, the pantry was stocked, and I started some water boiling on the stove to make spaghetti. I wished we had some fresh bread or vegetables to make a salad, but at this stage, I was so hungry that anything would work.

"I take it we're staying for dinner?"

Ian appeared in the doorway of the kitchen. He must have heard me rattling around in the cupboards. I tried to gauge his mood from the expression on his face. I hadn't a clue what, if anything else, he had come across after I left the library.

"Uh, yes. There isn't much, but I thought I would make some spaghetti." I held up the package of noodles.

"Sounds like a great idea." He said smiling.

"While I was on the phone with my mom, I realized how absolutely famished I am."

"And how are your parents? Has all of this sunk in yet?" He sat down across from me on one of the high counter stools.

"I don't think all this has even sunk in with me yet, and I'm actually here seeing it. No, I think they are just ridiculously anxious to be here with me. She said they were going to try to get a flight next week." I put a handful of noodles into the boiling water and poured the spaghetti sauce into another pot.

"Sounds appropriate," Ian said, getting up and opening a few cabinets.

"What are you looking for?" I asked.

"Just trying to find some glasses."

"All I could find were these," I said, opening a cabinet full of wine glasses.

"Ah, now that I think about it...Ken mentioned a wine cellar. He said that Evelyn had quite an impressive collection of vino. I'll be back..."

Ian dashed out of the room on his next quest. I didn't even want to think about what would happen if I tried to drink wine on an empty stomach. The thought of how miserable I felt on New Year's Day almost made me gag.

I was absolutely not going to get drunk and sick in front of Ian. I took out one of the wine glasses and filled it with water. I had to make sure to stay hydrated and fill my stomach with spaghetti, before taking a sip of wine. I put another handful of noodles into the pot on the stove.

Ian returned just as I was dishing out the food. He had a bottle of wine in his hand.

"Mission successful, I see."

"Pinot Grigio, in honor of our Italian feast," he said smiling. "After dinner, you have to go see the wine cellar. It is incredible! There must be two hundred bottles down there. I don't know much about wine, but some are certainly quite old." He was turning the corkscrew, and pulled the cork out with a little 'pop'.

He grabbed my, now-empty, glass and filled it with white wine. "You are twenty-one right?" He gave me a wry little smirk, and I just rolled my eyes. "You know that is something I've never understood about this country. You are old enough to go fight and die in war, but not old enough to drink a beer or glass of wine. It's just silly."

"Yeah, silly" I agreed.

Ian held up his glass and cleared his throat. "To Evelyn... She lived a long full life. May she rest in peace." I smiled and clinked my glass to his.

It was all I could do to eat slowly and politely. Ian was clearly famished too because neither of us hardly said a word. Ian did stop eating once though to refill our glasses. He had already finished his wine, while I had barely taken a few sips of mine. I wanted to pour it out and get another glass of water, but I didn't want to be rude. By the time we were done eating, Ian was on his third glass, and it was clear that we would not be heading back to Blythe, or anywhere else tonight.

I felt so much better with a full stomach. Ian leaned back in his chair, clearly content as well. Outside I could hear the rumble of thunder. I was excited about the prospect of rain. It hadn't rained in Blythe for months...just endless days of dry wind and blowing dirt. I wondered if I even remembered what rain looked like.

"By the way, I think I might have found the lock that matches that key your grandmother gave you."

I bolted straight up in my chair. "Where?!" I could not believe he had preceded that sentence with 'by the way' as if it were just an afterthought! I had been looking all over for a clue as to what the important key unlocked.

"Down in the wine cellar. There's a small door. I couldn't open it, but the lock looks like the same shape."

I was out of my chair before he even finished his sentence. I ran from room to room trying to remember where I had left my backpack. I finally found it in the library, sitting right where I had left it after my mom called. I fished around for the key and felt the cold metal in the bottom of the abyss. I grabbed it and turned to Ian who had followed me into the library. "Which way?"

Ian led me down to the casual dining area on the first floor. There was a short set of stone steps in the corner of the room. "Down here," he said leading us through a cramped and dark passageway into a small narrow room with a low ceiling. Long, multi-leveled oak racks, holding bottles of wine, lined the length of the room.

The floor, walls, and ceiling were stone and the air was damp and musty. The room was lit by a string of light bulbs hanging from the ceiling. They were the big glass type you might see on patios.

"This way," Ian beckoned, walking to the far side of the cellar. He disappeared into a dark recess. I walked over to meet him, steadying myself while my eyes adjusted to the dim light. As my pupils dilated allowing in the light, I saw a small, arched, wooden door.

"How did you find this? It's not even visible from over by the wine racks." He didn't answer my question but pointed to the iron lock instead.

He was right. It looked like a perfect match! I pushed the key into the lock and although it fit perfectly, I couldn't turn it.

"Here, let me try," Ian said, maneuvering in the cramped space to position himself in front of the lock. "Wow, it's really stiff," he said straining to turn the key. I was standing right up against him and could feel the muscles in his arms and back tense and flex until finally the key turned and there was a loud clunk.

Ian pushed the small, thick door open, and its hinges creaked loudly. There was nothing but complete darkness on the other side, and I felt a little panic as I wondered if this really was a dungeon. I ducked through the doorway and gingerly felt with my foot until it touched the ground. Ian helped steady me as I reached into the darkness to feel around for a light switch. Finally, I felt the small switch on the cold, stone wall, and flipped it on.

It took my eyes a few seconds to adjust to the bright light and focus on the objects in the room, but when they had, I knew that I was going to have some explaining to do. Once Ian registered what he was seeing, he almost shoved me down in his urgency to get inside.

It was a chamber about the same size and arrangement as the wine cellar, but it was not wine bottles that lined the multi-leveled shelves and tables in this room. Instead of dim patio lights, this room had fluorescent track lighting, and the light impressively gleamed off the vast array of items.

I let out a loud gasp as I walked into the room and saw bejeweled goblets, golden platters, bronze busts, crystal bowls, and sculptures. I saw an entire small table covered with necklaces, rings, and even tiaras adorned with every color jewel imaginable. There was one whole wall that held dozens of masks, from ones that looked like African tribesmen to Mardi Gras-style carnival masks.

Ian was standing in front of another large counter that I could see held documents of some kind. He held out his hand to touch one, then pulled it back. I walked up behind him and stood on my tiptoes to peer over his shoulder.

"This is in French." He pointed to a yellowed piece of paper written in a script I couldn't read. "I believe it's a letter written in 1818...by Napoleon Bonaparte while he was exiled on the island of Saint Helena." I gasped, and he pointed to another. "This one is signed...by Abraham Lincoln. I think it is a draft of the Emancipation Proclamation."

Ian gripped the edges of the wooden counter and doubled over as if he were in danger of collapsing. "These I can't read, but I know they're in Latin, and appear to be parchment." His head dropped and he spoke in a whisper. "But how... If these are genuine, they should be in a museum...under glass, in a temperature-controlled room... They can't be..." He shook his head slowly from side to side. I knew he was struggling hard to make sense of it.

"What has she done?" I said in a whisper.

He abruptly turned to me and grabbed my arms, squeezing too hard. "Evan, what the hell is this? What is going on here?" His face was urgent, conflicted, and pleading. "You know something you're not telling me. Please..."

Suddenly I couldn't breathe, I felt like the room was closing in. I gasped in big gulps of air but still felt like I was suffocating.

"Evan?" Ian shook me slightly. "Evan! What's wrong?"

I had to get out. I needed air. I broke free of his grasp and ran out of the room, through the wine cellar, and up the steps. I sprinted across the living room, past the kiva, and threw open the Veranda doors. I ran out into the night air, into the storm that was now directly over us. The rain felt cool on my skin. I let fresh air fill my nose and lungs as I breathed in deeply. I lifted my face to the sky and let the rain wash over it.

Chapter 14

Coming Clean

The rain drenched me. It felt cleansing. I wanted the rain to wash away all the guilt and doubt, all the secrecy and lies. I wanted it to wash away the past, so I could move forward into my future. I wanted to be reborn, baptized in it. This rain washing over me was more than fitting because I knew it was time to come clean.

Deep down I had known this would happen ever since I had asked Ian to come with me. I had known there was a good chance that we would find something here that would require an explanation, and the truth was, I wanted to explain...wanted him to know...all of it.

I was tired of carrying the burden of this secret...tired of trying to solve the puzzles of the universe all by myself. I remembered what the Gelf had said in class that day. "What good is knowledge if you can't share it?" I needed to tell someone and if that person couldn't be Aaron, I wanted it to be Ian. As the rain bathed me, I felt all my doubt, worry, insecurities, and inhibitions wash away.

Ian ran out after me. I was just standing in the rain, face to the sky. The wind swirled around us. I started laughing from the relief of making my decision. I knew I was a spectacle, but I didn't care.

"Evan, what's happening to you? Are you OK?" He was shouting over the storm.

"I'm great! I am wonderful. Ian, it's raining!" I knew I sounded like a lunatic.

"Evan, please come in. It's cold, and you're soaked." He was gently pulling my arm as if trying to coax a two-year-old.

"Ian, I *want* to tell you. I am *going* to tell you! *Everything.*" I pulled against him.

He looked into my eyes, and I could see that he was truly worried about me. First, I was hyperventilating and now I was acting like a crazy person. I was sure he thought I had gone mad.

"Evan, please...please just come inside."

Just then a loud clap of thunder startled me, and I jumped. Lightning flashed at the same time, and I realized that it was probably not very safe to be standing this exposed, high on the side of a mountain, in the middle of a lightning storm. I stopped resisting and let Ian pull me inside.

I stood dripping as Ian ran to grab some towels. I realized that I had most likely ruined another of the outfits Taylor bought me. When Ian returned, I saw that he was drenched too.

"I'm sorry," I said.

"Don't be, it's fine. I'm just...worried about you." He handed me a big terrycloth towel and I dabbed at my hair and clothes.

"I'm fine, really. I guess there is just a lot...that's been building up." I stood there, now shivering.

"Evan, why don't you go change? You're freezing. I'll build a fire, and we can talk."

I grabbed my overnight bag and headed to Grandmother's room. I started the shower and took off my wet clothes, throwing them on the bathroom floor in a heap. The hot water felt great and quickly warmed me up. I used the expensive soaps and shampoos that had been my grandmother's. They were flowery and fragrant, and although they wouldn't have been my first choice, the shower still felt amazingly refreshing.

Digging through my overnight bag, I realized that I had no clean clothes to put on. The only dry things were the clothes I had worn yesterday on the drive and the sweats I had slept in the night before. Why hadn't I packed extras, just in case?

I went to Grandmother's bureau and searched for something I could wear. From what I had seen earlier in her wardrobe, I thought the possibility of finding a pair of jeans and a T-shirt was slim. Then I found a drawer full of fancy negligees. They were not the Fredrick's of Hollywood type. After all, these had belonged to an old woman. They were more in the Old Hollywood, 1930s-style that almost looked like long, fitted dresses. They were beautiful. I chose a white satin one that had a matching sheer silk robe.

I admired the perfect fit in front of a long, full-length, mirror. It looked like the kind of outfit you would wear on your wedding night. I spun around like a little girl playing dress-up. My hair was still up the way I had fixed it in preparation for meeting the lawyers, but now it was wet, and more long tendrils had fallen out of the French Twist. I released it from the clips and let it fall over my shoulders and down my back. I then hung my wet clothes up on the shower rod and headed out to see Ian.

He was sitting on the hearth stoking the fire as I entered the room. The fire in the huge kiva was magnificent. It lit the room in a beautiful glow and even from a distance I could feel its warmth. I stood there just admiring Ian in the firelight. I wanted to stay in this moment forever, or at least freeze this image in my mind. However, as soon as he saw me, he dropped the stoker and jumped to his feet.

"Jaysus Evan, what are you wearing?" He actually seemed to be blushing! I was pleased with the effect.

"I found it in my grandmother's things. There are dozens of them! Isn't it great? It reminds me of 'Casablanca' or 'An Affair to Remember'. I think Grandma must have been quite a romantic."

"Uh yeah. Didn't she have anything less...seductive?" He looked down at his feet as he said the words.

"Nope," I said simply, as I strode across the room, joining him by the hearth. I noticed there was a new unopened bottle of wine, sitting next to the first, which was now almost empty. I was glad to see it there. I suspected we would need it. I filled my glass and drank the wine down in three big gulps. I was ready!

"Whoa there. Don't get carried away." Ian took the glass from me and sat it down on a nearby table. "We need to talk...right?" It seemed he was nervous and trying to avoid looking at me.

"Yes, we do." I casually filled his wine glass and handed it to him. "And I think you're going to need this after you hear what I'm going to say." I handed him the glass and he mechanically brought it up to his lips and sipped.

I sat on a large white overstuffed couch by the fire. I could see intermittent flashes of lightning out the French doors and through the glass-paned wall high above us. Ian remained perched on the hearth, and I wondered if he was intentionally trying to keep a distance between us. I tried to decide where to begin.

"It all started right before Christmas Break. I was sitting in Immunology taking my final exam..." I told him, in as much detail as I could remember, about the first time I traveled back...the nausea, the dizziness and disorientation, how I thought I was crazy or had a brain tumor. I carefully watched his expression as I spoke and wondered what he was thinking, but besides the wide-eyed curiosity, I couldn't tell what he made of my story.

I continued, telling him about the incident in the tub. It still gave me the chills to remember the details of that night...the feeling of drowning. I had been terrified. I told him about the memory of that Christmas morning in Hamburg, the dollhouse, the baby.

As I told him about my bloody feet, how hysterical I had been, and how the nurse had thought that I had been assaulted, the look in his eyes became one of pity. I wondered if he was beginning to feel sorry for the clearly delusional girl in front of him. I finished by describing the details of the conversation with my mother, of how the baby that I had seen in the memory had been my brother.

I sat quietly looking at him and waiting for some kind of response. Sensing that I had finished my story, he took a big swig of wine and finally spoke.

"So, you think that these incidents you experienced were repressed memories?"

Ah, logical Ian. He was having the same reaction that I had had to all of this. I laughed out loud, and then he *did* look at me like I was insane. I stood up and walked over to where he sat by the fire.

"Ian, I can assure you that I did not experience the surfacing of some repressed memories." I told him about all the research I had done on the subject and how I had rearranged my whole curriculum to try to better understand the human psyche and how these things worked. I explained how I had experienced all the same skepticism he was feeling now, and more. "But now I know it's not just *my* memories I can travel to, or memories at all. I can travel to anywhere in the past I want, as long as I know enough about it." I took a deep breath and felt a huge relief now that the words were out of my mouth.

Ian stood up now too and started pacing back and forth. "Evan, what you're saying is…"

"Impossible." I finished.

He looked at me, and his eyes were wild and searching. "Yes…impossible. It goes against every rule of physics we know. It's been said that the simplest answer is the most probable answer, and while I appreciate the sincerity of your story, and believe that *you* truly believe what you are saying, the most simple and therefore most probable answer is that you are experiencing…" I could see that he was trying to be delicate… "some mental…abnormalities."

I laughed again. This was exactly why I had never attempted to tell anyone about my experiences. Now *I* tried to be delicate with *him*. "Ian, I understand that it seems like the only explanation is that I must be crazy. Trust me, it took a while for *me* to believe I wasn't crazy. I know what people say about probability, but Aristotle said, '*It is likely that unlikely things should happen*', and as my grandmother said in her letter to me I have in fact realized that '*this universe has many secrets waiting to be revealed*'.

His brow was furrowed, and he scrutinized me. "Are you saying that you think your grandmother also could...I mean...had this...*ability*?"

"Yes, I am. I'm sure she did."

"And the photos in the album...were of her?"

"Yes. All of them."

"And the items in the cellar?"

"Taken from the past," I said.

Ian collapsed onto the couch and sat silently with his face in his hands. I gently sat down next to him and quietly waited for everything to sink in. When he did not speak for quite some time I said, "Honestly, I really thought that somehow, someway you already suspected this."

"What?" He looked up at me with a tired, puzzled expression.

"After I turned in my essay on the JFK assassination, you seemed to be so suspicious of me, confronting me in class and all. Ian, you even asked the class 'what if we could travel to the past and see events first hand', for God's sake! Then you found those pictures of me on the grassy knoll online. I really thought you had figured it all out. It even seemed like you were following me. I saw you everywhere." I let out a little laugh to try to break the tension.

His reaction was unexpected. He started edging away from me, as if I was radioactive. The look on his face was something between horror and disgust. Then, he was on his feet backing away from the couch.

"Ian? Ian, wait...please let me explain..."

"Are you *actually* telling me that you time traveled to 1963 to witness the Kennedy assassination?" His voice was too loud and accusatory. I hated the way he was looking at me! I was beginning to regret telling him the truth.

"Well...yes," I mumbled.

He stopped and put his hand on the mantle of the fireplace, right next to Grandma. He was steadying himself and he looked pale, like he was going to be sick.

"Ian...are you OK?" I stood up and took a few tentative steps towards him. "Ian?" After a couple of moments I heard him whisper something that I couldn't understand. "Ian? Did you say something?"

He repeated himself, whispering a little louder this time. "He was right."

"What?" I wanted to be sure of what I had just heard.

He looked up at me. The disgust was gone, and now his expression was more resigned, but his eyes were watery as if he was on the verge of tears. "He was right."

"What? Who was right?"

"Max." He started pacing again. I could tell he was anxious, and I tried to be delicate and not push him.

"Who is Max?"

The look in Ian's eyes was conflicted and I knew there was a struggle between his logic and gut.

"Wait...you *actually* traveled to Dealey Plaza in 1963?" He repeated himself.

"Ian, you saw me...in the pictures. You know, 'Bobby-socks girl."

"It just...it *can't* be possible."

I slowly reached out my hand, hoping he wouldn't recoil from me. I gently touched his arm. "Ian please, who is Max?" He stopped pacing and allowed my hand to remain. He looked harried and roughly mussed his hair.

"Max...Max Koehler. He was my postdoctoral mentor at Trinity. He was a famed, but very eccentric historian. He had a million wild stories. We all knew he had lived a long time and seen many things, and most people just humored him because he was such a character. Among his many tales, he loved to babble on about how throughout history there had always been these people...*Custodies aetas*." He whispered the last words. His eyes were far off...remembering.

"I don't understand. What is that? What does it mean?"

He refocused on me. "*Custodies aetas*...it's Latin. It means custodians or guardians...of time. He called them 'The Guardians'. Max said they were an ancient and noble group intent on guarding the past. Supposedly they could *move* through history." Ian let out a small nervous, slightly maniacal laugh.

I was flabbergasted! There had always been time travelers, and this man knew about them!

"Guarding the past from what?" I nearly shouted at him.

"I...I don't know." He rubbed his hand roughly through his thick hair again. "I can't remember." He must have noticed the beseeching look on my face. "Evan, you have to realize that these stories were so fantastic that it never occurred to me to actually pay much attention or take notes! We all just thought that crazy Max was ranting.

"But you *have* to remember! If there are these...Guardians...they have to be protecting the past from *something*."

He took a deep breath then spoke in a low voice. "I think that Max believed there were other people, malicious ones that these Guardians had been fighting for centuries... you know, the classic story of good and evil. We used to tease him; tell him that he should write a novel."

I struggled to stay calm, but this wasn't a story. It was reality...my reality, and if this man was right, there was so much more to this reality than I had ever imagined. "Did the others have a name?" I squeaked out.

"I think...he called them *Peregrinus*. It's also Latin. It means wanderer or crusader."

"Wanderers?"

"Yes, I suppose."

"That doesn't sound malicious. Can you remember anything else about his stories?"

Ian sat back down on the hearth. I could tell he was concentrating, racking his brain. I sat down beside him and patiently waited.

"I'm sorry that's all I can remember."

"Then we'll call him. Ian, I *have* to know what *he* knows!"

"Evan, we can't call him. He died over a year ago."

No! The one person that could potentially explain all of this was dead! Now I was the one up pacing. I mumbled to myself, thinking out loud. "So, there *must* be more like me...maybe even *many* more. If Max knew about them then others must know too. Guardians..."

"How...does it work?" Ian's voice interrupted my thoughts.

I gazed down at him sitting on the hearth. He looked dazed, shell-shocked. I tried to put myself in his place. I knew this was a lot to take in. It had taken me months to get used to all of this, and here I was expecting him to understand in just a few minutes. I sat down next to him again.

"Well, I don't really know how it works. I just have to focus all my concentration on a specific event. I have to picture all of the details. All the sensory information must be accurate...visual, auditory and emotional. I have to *become* someone in that specific place in time."

"Then what happens?" He was looking down and I wished I could see his face.

"It's a pulling sensation. It starts like a tickle in my stomach, and then it radiates out and becomes stronger. Eventually, it feels like all of my body is being pulled down into a long, dark tunnel. I feel like I'm falling...falling through time." He was quiet so I continued. "When I...arrive...I'm just me, I mean how I am now."

"And you can interact with people in the past?" His eyes stayed glued to the floor.

"Yes, just like I am with you now."

"Can you change the past?"

"Yes," I said, feeling a little guilty.

"My god. It can't be true..." He bent over and dropped his head into his hands. I wanted to touch him again, caress his back, but I decided against it. I needed to be patient and let this sink in slowly. So instead, I got up and poured myself another glass of wine. I sat sipping it slowly, staring into the fire. I would wait until he was ready...

With the exception of thunder and the crackle of the fire, the house was completely quiet. I watched Ian struggle with his logic, and finally, after what seemed to be an eternity, he sat straight up and looked at me. I couldn't read his expression. He stared into my eyes, and I held his gaze. Finally, his eyes narrowed into a squint and he said, "Show me."

—ele—

"What? What do you mean?" I felt a little panicky.

"Show me. I want to see you do it!"

It was like he was asking the lunatic who just said they could fly to jump off the ledge. He was asking me to prove that what I was claiming was true. Part of me resented his demand, but as I tried to put myself in his place again, I realized that I would have done the exact same thing.

"So, you're testing me?"

"I just need to see it...for myself."

I wondered what he thought he would see. "Ian, I understand why you're asking me to do this, but even if I did...make a trip right now, I don't think you would actually *see* anything. I think that all you would see is me just sitting here with my eyes closed. I know that when I travel to the past, no time passes in the present. So, I don't think it would actually prove anything." I knew this made my story sound even more ridiculous and I was sure he was thinking 'How convenient', but it was the truth.

"You mean if you spend an hour or even a year in the past, no time would pass here?" His beautiful eyes were wide and I couldn't tell if he was in awe or just mocking me.

"That's right...at least, I think. I mean the most time I've ever spent in the past is a few hours." I thought of that night in the barn at Aaron's summer camp.

Ian countered immediately and I could tell that he had put some thought into this. "Well, even if I don't actually see you...physically...doing anything, you can still prove that what you're saying is true."

"How do you mean?"

"When I was fourteen I went on a field trip to Newgrange. It was the first time I ever saw it and the reason that I'm a historian today."

"OK..." I couldn't tell where he was going with this.

"Something happened that day that captured my imagination and made me fall in love with the place." His eyes sparkled and he was absolutely captivating. Now I understood what he wanted.

"You want me to tell you what it was?"

"Yes."

Again, part of me resented the idea of this silly 'test', but the other part knew that if I didn't somehow 'prove' myself to Ian, he would never believe me, and I desperately needed him to. "OK," I said resigning myself to the task.

He got up and joined me on the couch. "So what happens now?" He was excited.

"Well, you have to tell me as much detail as you can about your trip. I need to know everything you can remember, especially how you *felt*."

"How I felt?" He was puzzled.

"Yes, in order to get there, I have to *become* you on that day," I told him about Selda Henry, and how the trip back to 1963 only worked when I truly understood her perceptions of the time and how she must have felt that day. I told him how I had to put myself in her shoes. I could have told him how I first realized this particular requirement by trying to get into the memory of Aaron's bike accident, but I didn't want to discuss that with Ian. It would be telling Aaron's story, which felt like a betrayal.

Ian filled his glass and sunk back into the couch. I curled my legs up next to my body and got more comfortable. Between all the wine and the fire a few feet away, my body felt warm inside and out. Ian took a big drink of wine and started his story.

"It was the summer before I turned fifteen. I wasn't so into school back then, I had resigned myself to the fact that I would become a car mechanic like my dad and work in his shop when I grew up. Therefore, I really did not put much effort into my studies. I was also a bit of a knacker.

"A knacker?" I had never heard the term.

"Yeah, you know a ruffian, getting into trouble and whatnot."

"Really?"

"Ah yeah, I was the scourge of the neighborhood when I was younger. Never got into any serious trouble, but I was still a bit of a hooligan." He smiled warmly, and suddenly I couldn't wait to see the fourteen-year-old Ian. "Anyway, I never would have considered wasting my whole Saturday on a school trip if it wasn't for Mary Hanlon." He smiled a little devilish grin.

"Mary Hanlon?" Why did there always have to be a damn girl! I swear, if he told me that he had been hopelessly devoted to her his entire life and she was anxiously awaiting his return to Ireland, I would scream!

"Mary Hanlon was the fantasy of every boy at the school. Of course, none of us ever had a chance with her. She never gave us the time of day. She only dated high school boys. But the thought of spending a daylong bus ride with Mary Hanlon was what convinced me to go.

"Our history teacher, Mr. O'Conner spent the entire four-hour drive telling us stories about the myths and legends of Newgrange. At first, I ignored him and tried to chat up Mary, but after being shot down several times, I was so frustrated and bored that I actually started to listen. And once I did, I found them fascinating.

"He told us several of the same stories that were in the book I gave you...stories about fairies and spirits, and the mythological origins of New-grange. By the time we got there, my head was so full of romantic legends I couldn't wait to see it.

"As you know, when you first arrive at Newgrange you're supposed to spend some time at the museum and visitor's center before they drive you to the burial mounds." I nodded my head. I knew exactly what he was talking about and pictured it in my mind.

"I hated that part. I just wanted to get to the ruins. By the time the class had finally finished milling around the museum, it was already dusk. We took the last bus out to the site. As we traveled up the gravelly road and I saw the mounds come into sight, I was astounded. I had never seen anything like them, and as we stepped off the bus it was like stepping into history." He looked at me knowingly, and I smiled.

"The guide showed us the markings on the kerbstones and described all the mysteries and lore surrounding their existence. I was enthralled, but could hardly wait to actually go inside the mound. Finally, we stepped inside the dark passageway and the guide led us down the tunnel into the chamber. It was magical!

"As we stood crowded into the small space, we could only speculate at what had occurred in that very spot, thousands of years before. The guide gave us all small flashlights so we could examine the walls and ceilings of the mound. Of course, we extinguished our lights when they showed us how the chamber would have looked on the solstice, as the long narrow beam of the rising sun illuminates the chamber." As he spoke, I remembered back to my own similar experience there but tried to picture it through his eyes.

"However, all too soon Mr. O'Connor announced that we had very little time and that the last bus would be heading back to the visitor's center soon. I was so angry that we had driven all day to spend only a few minutes inside the mounds! Plus, it had been so crowded that I hadn't even been able to get a look inside the recesses.

"I wanted to get a better look at the etchings and see where the human remains had been found. So, as the class was filing back to the bus, I broke away from the others and hid. It was already dark by this time. As I watched the bus pull away, I made my way back inside the tunnel."

I was captivated by his story, hanging on every word, but he didn't say anymore. "Wait...so that's it?"

"I'm waiting for you to tell me what happened next." He looked at me, raising one eyebrow.

Ah, so the gauntlet had been thrown down. I sat quietly considering the challenge. Basically, I needed to travel back to that spot and be inside the chamber when Ian came back in. I needed to see whatever it was that happened to him. It didn't seem that difficult. I had been there before; I could picture it perfectly. His story had not been as detailed as the ones Aaron had told me, but it didn't need to be since I could picture everything already.

The tough part, as always, would be to remain undetected. But how would I do that in a small chamber? Especially given that Ian's whole mission there would be to explore every nook and cranny of it. No, I would have to find some way to observe him from afar.

Of course, I didn't actually know where this mysterious event happened. It could have been outside the mound. I reasoned that even if I did not see exactly what he was referring to, I could provide some other details that would convince him. I just had to try. I would improvise when I got there.

"OK, then," I said looking at him smugly.

As I sat concentrating, I knew it was a bad idea. I hadn't thought it through completely, and I was a little tipsy. But this whole day had been a fairytale so far, why stop now? Plus, I desperately wanted him to believe me. However, it was extremely hard to focus knowing he was there. I could hear him breathing and feel the warmth of his body next to me. After at least ten minutes, I heard him whisper, "Evan?"

I opened one eye and looked at him.

"Did anything happen?" He asked tentatively.

"No!" I snapped. "It's too distracting with you here. I've never done this for an audience before!"

He sighed and I knew whatever small inkling of belief he might have had in me was quickly dissolving.

"I need quiet and dark. I'll be back." I stood up to leave.

"Where are you going?" Ian stood up too.

"Just into my grandmother's bedroom. Don't worry, it won't take long...for you anyway."

I went into the bedroom and turned off all the lights. I tried to relax and pretend I was sitting on my own bed in my dark dorm room. It was so hard to focus under this kind of pressure. I considered the absurdity of my clothes. I had slipped on some shoes, but other than that, I was in no way prepared for the trip.

I decided at the last minute that some kind of light might be beneficial. I didn't want to take the time to try to find a flashlight, but I did see a long lighter used for lighting candles on Grandmother's bureau. As I gripped it, I wished I had Aaron's rabbit's foot with me. I needed some luck.

I sat on the bed and pushed all the thoughts of Grandmother, the will, Max Koehler, and everything else out of my mind, focusing only on Newgrange. I was a fourteen-year-old Ian, full of wonder and recklessness. I tried to picture Newgrange at night and feel the thrill of sneaking off from my class and having the mounds all to myself. Goosebumps rose on my arm as I felt the anticipation of discovery and the exhilaration of being alone in that ancient place that was rumored to be haunted by mythological creatures.

As before, I felt out of control as I fell. But this time I was elated, rather than worried. I was just so happy that I had been able to do it! My biggest fear had been that my ability would fail me and Ian wouldn't believe me. But now I was falling and knew I would see him soon.

Thankfully, the landing was softer than my last one. I smelled wet earth all around me. In the milliseconds before I opened my eyes, I was convinced I was inside the chamber but as soon as my eyes fluttered open, I saw trees, their branches swaying gently in the cool evening's breeze.

I was sitting on the ground just inside a wooded area. There was a clearing to my right and I could see the mounds of Newgrange bathed in the bright silvery moonlight. I could see the entrance to the large burial mound and across from it the road leading down to the visitor's center.

I stood completely still and listened. The wind was blowing, but not very hard. The ground was wet and it smelled like it had rained recently. It wasn't very cold, but I really wished I was wearing something more than a negligee and thin robe. I stood watching the clearing for several minutes and didn't see a single thing move. I wondered how late it was and if maybe my timing had been wrong. Maybe Ian had come and gone already, or maybe it wasn't even the right night at all. All my senses were alert, listening for the slightest noise and looking for even the faintest shadow. Then suddenly I heard a snap behind me!

I spun around, expecting to see someone emerging from the woods. I clamped my hands over my mouth to stop a scream from escaping and as my eyes dilated and focused, I saw something moving across the ground. My heart rate slowed as a big tabby cat walked boldly up to me and began rubbing against my leg. I squatted down to stroke its fur.

"You scared the crap out of me," I whispered. "Are you a fairy of Newgrange in disguise?"

The cat purred and vigorously rubbed against me. "You didn't see a teenage boy come through here, did you?"

I stood up and looked over at the clearing again. There was still no movement. I wondered how long I should wait before...before what? Should I make my way to the mound and risk Ian seeing me? That didn't seem like a very good idea, but was I supposed to just stay here all night and not see anything?

I didn't have to mentally debate it for long because right at that moment I *did* see something. I saw a light erratically moving on the ground outside the mound entrance. I squatted down again and the cat tried to climb into my lap. I gently pushed it away. It was purring so loudly that it sounded like a car motor.

"Shhhh..." I cooed at it.

Then I saw a figure emerge from the entrance to the tunnel. I squinted to see him better in the moonlight. He stood momentarily by the large kerbstone that was by the entrance, then took off in a flat run towards the road. I couldn't make out any of his features, but the figure certainly did seem to be the right size for a fourteen-year-old boy.

It had to be Ian, but within an instant, he had already disappeared down the road! So that was it? I looked frantically around. He was gone and it was just a quiet night. What was the big mystery? What had happened to him in there?

I waited several minutes for something amazing to happen...a UFO landing, lightning to strike...but there was nothing but the quiet and still of night, and of course the overly affectionate cat at my feet. I considered going back, but I hadn't learned anything here. I couldn't go back empty-handed! I stared, contemplating the mounds, and finally decided that if I couldn't bring back the correct answer to Ian, I would bring back something more tangible.

I had been to Newgrange and knew that in addition to the large elaborately engraved kerbstones around the mound, there were smaller carvings on the walls inside. I was going to have to find some way to take one of them to him, to prove that I had been here.

I thought maybe I could chip it away from the rest of the wall. I knew it would take some time, and Ian would be furious at me for defacing this ancient place, but it had withstood way worse than me over the centuries. I would just explain to him that I had only seen him leaving...missed whatever life-changing event had happened and that I *had* to do what I did.

I gave the cat one last pat and stepped softly away from the tree line. It reminded me of how exposed I had felt stepping away from the pergola in Dealey Plaza. I ran as fast as I could across the clearing to the entry of the tunnel. I could not believe I was about to do this! I checked to make sure the lighter worked and then took a deep breath and stepped lightly into the darkness.

I decided I would make my way to the inner chamber and just see if there was any evidence Ian had been there. I knew it was a long shot, but maybe it would be like when Aaron dropped his rabbit's foot. Wouldn't it be convenient if Ian had accidentally left a baseball cap or wallet behind? I almost laughed at the thought of it...and because my nerves were on end and I was scared out of my wits!

I couldn't see much in the light of the small flame. My fingers gripped the wall of the narrow passageway, and I walked slowly and carefully, being as surefooted as possible. Despite my care, about halfway down the tunnel, my foot caught on something and I tripped. Instinctively, my arms splayed out and my hands hit the rocky ground hard as I fell. Seconds later, I heard the familiar purr and felt a furry head rubbing against my face.

"Hey kitty, are you trying to kill me?"

Now I was groping around trying to find the lighter. I felt like a blind baby mole lost in its underground tunnel. The cat walked around me, as I crouched on all fours, weaving its way between my arms and legs.

I finally found the lighter, but just as I started to light it I heard something! It was the indubitable sound of footsteps, near the mouth of the tunnel. I froze, afraid to make a sound, but as the steps grew louder, I saw a spot of light bouncing off the walls of the passageway. Adrenaline rushed through me as I scrambled to my feet. I had no time and nowhere to run. The inner chamber was a dead end. I was trapped!

I closed my eyes tight and thought 'back, back, back'. I could hear the footsteps just feet away now, but I blocked them out and focused completely on the trip back. Everything happened simultaneously. I felt the pull and heard the whoosh sweeping me away, but at the same time I saw a bright light shining through my clenched eyelids.

Automatically, my eyes flew open and as I fell, I saw the beam of a flashlight bearing down on me. At the same time I heard a young male voice yell "Holy Jaysus!" and as the light disappeared into the darkness of time, I heard him yell one more word... "Wait!" The voice grew fainter and fainter until there was only silence.

I half expected Ian to be standing in the bedroom, but it was dark and quiet. I stumbled out into the living room and saw him sitting on the couch by the hearth, just where I had left him. He was staring into the fire, unaware of my presence.

I remembered speculating, after my trip back to Bret, that who we become was determined by just a few decisive events in our lives. I could only imagine how decisive seeing a mysterious woman disappear in front of his eyes in the burial mound at Newgrange had been in Ian's life.

I walked over to him not knowing what to expect. He looked up at me and somehow his eyes looked different. They were just as beautiful as always, but the expression in them was changed. His whole expression was transformed. He was looking at me with a childlike awe.

"You saw me," I said softly, searching his eyes, trying to read his thoughts.

He rose slowly until he stood directly in front of me, then without warning he put his hands on the sides of my face and tilted my chin up. He looked at me and all I could see were those big blue piercing eyes, and suddenly the look in them sharpened and manifested a new emotion. The intensity of his gaze almost frightened me and I wondered if he was angry, but as we stood there staring at each other I began to realize that it wasn't anger he was feeling...it was longing.

Even though things probably had not finished shifting, I knew that what I had done had changed him, but I didn't care. In that moment I only cared about one thing...being as close to Ian as possible. His eyes stayed fixed on mine, but his face was slowly moving closer. His lips were less than an inch away and I tried to meet them, tried to kiss him, but he held my head tight.

He touched my lips softly with his, but instead of kissing me, he just brushed them across mine, back and forth. I felt his warm breath on my mouth and his scent filled the air around me, making me feel almost dizzy. I could hear the crackle of the fire and the rain hitting the windows, but I focused on his breathing. It was slow and deliberate, while mine was irregular and coming in bursts.

His lips were smooth and hot and I wanted to taste them. I couldn't handle his gentle teasing anymore. My hands were limp at my sides, but I brought them up and clamped them around the back of his head, forcefully pressing his lips to mine. Simultaneously our lips parted and I felt his breathing speed up, matching my frenzied pace. He released my head and his hands moved down to my waist, forcefully pulling me against him.

The pent-up desire from all those months of fantasizing about Ian manifested itself as a ravenous hunger that I could not satisfy fast enough! I gripped the back of his neck with one hand, kissing him hard and deep. With the other hand, I clumsily pulled at his shirt. I was beyond feverish. No more was it a matter of *wanting* him, I *needed* him. However, just as my hand touched the bare skin of his chest, I felt his body stiffen beneath it and he started to pull away.

No! I screamed in my head. I gripped him tighter, but he lifted his lips from mine and spoke.

"Evan...wait." His voice was raspy and he was trying to slow his breathing.

"No..." I tried to pull him back to me, but he resisted.

"I... we can't." He barely managed.

The words pained me almost as much as the conflicted look in his eyes. I felt a knot tighten in my gut.

"Yes, you can," I replied feebly, but I knew from the look on his face he had made a decision. I made a desperate attempt to pull him back, but he stepped away and sat back down on the couch.

Adrenaline coursed through my body, making me tremble all over and I wasn't sure whether it was from lust, frustration, or both. I took a deep, shaky breath and slumped down beside him.

"I'm sorry," he said, quickly caressing my cheek. I didn't know if he was apologizing for starting or stopping. "It's just when I saw you... I mean I have spent half my life fantasizing about the otherworldly creature I saw in the mounds of Newgrange and suddenly she was standing there in front of me...incarnate. It was the most intense experience of my life. I couldn't...control myself." His eyes were watery with raw emotion. "But this is wrong. Evan, I'm still your professor."

Even though I wanted him more in that moment than I'd ever wanted anything in my life, the anguish on Ian's beautiful face told me that it *was* wrong, but not for the same reason.

"What do you remember?" I asked, forcing myself to calm down.

"Well, I know that when I was fourteen years old I snuck away from my class on a field trip. It was dark and I was scared but also excited to be alone in the burial mounds. Then I saw the most beautiful and mysterious creature imaginable. She was only there for a second, but I was captivated. Even though I doubted what I saw at many points in my life, I always knew deep down she was real. She was the reason I fell in love with Newgrange. She was the reason I became a historian." He caressed my cheek again.

"You were...are so beautiful, Evan. And you can't begin to imagine what seeing you that night did to my teenage libido!" He flashed me one of those devilish smiles. "I mean there I was a fourteen-year-old boy just starting to discover girls and think about sex. Then I see you...in that!" He motioned to my negligee. "It basically ruined me for all mortal women. No one could ever live up to the fantasies I had about the nymph I saw in the mound."

I wanted to take him in my arms again, but I felt too guilty. I felt like a big fraud, as if I had tricked him into wanting me. I spoke slowly. "Ian, you fell in love with Newgrange before you saw me, before I made the trip back. Whatever happened that made you become a historian, it wasn't me...not originally anyway."

Ian thought a moment, and then said, "Well, seeing you...*that's* what I remember. It's so strange, it's like I had forgotten it all, and then suddenly...all the memories came flooding back."

"But Ian, you have to realize that those weren't memories flooding *back*. They never existed before. They were new memories flooding *in*." I felt so ashamed. First, I had played around in Aaron's past, and now I was using my power to manipulate Ian.

I felt drained. The emotional strain of the day, and the exhaustion from traveling into the past, had caught up with me. Although I fought them, tears welled up in my eyes.

Ian lifted my chin and looked seriously into my eyes. "It doesn't matter. It doesn't change what I saw and it doesn't change what you are to me." He looked at me with pure devotion. He began to lean in closer and I thought he was going to kiss me again, but he snapped back, as if pulling himself out of a trance, and said, "But none of this changes the fact that I'm your professor."

I exhaled loudly, conveying my disappointment.

"I won't be for much longer though," Ian said, with a sly smile. "Now tell me what you remember." He demanded. "I want to hear it all...the whole experience."

I shared every detail I could remember with him. When I mentioned how the cat made me fall in the tunnel he started laughing.

"What?" I asked.

"When I saw you...after you disappeared...there was the cat. I thought you had shape-shifted or something. You wouldn't believe how many books I've read over the years on Native American shape-shifters!"

Ian lay down next to me on the couch, cradling me in his arms. Next to kissing him, I thought this was probably the best feeling in the world, and I instantly felt myself drifting off to sleep.

"Evan, how on earth can this be real?" I heard him ask.

"I wish I knew." I managed to whisper.

"Well, we'll just have to find out together then," was the last thing I heard him say before a huge wave of relief swept me off into a deep sleep.

Chapter 15

BACK TO REALITY?

I n the moments before waking, on the border between consciousness and dreaming, a panic built in me. My eyes flew open and I frantically looked around. As soon as I registered where I was, and realized that it *hadn't* all been a dream, my panic abated. Bright sunlight was streaming in through the windows. I was still lying on the couch by the kiva, now covered by a comforter that I knew belonged on one of the guestroom beds.

I wondered what time it was because I was still so tired. I was just drifting off to sleep again when I heard the front door open. Turning over and opening my eyes, I saw Ian high above me peering over the balcony.

"Hey down there! You awake?"

"Barely..." I groaned and covered my head with the blanket.

"Thought we could use some coffee and food," Ian said, making his way down to me. "I had to drive twenty miles into town to find a Starbucks." He sat down next to me and pulled two big muffins out of a paper bag. I had to admit the coffee smelled awesome.

I lifted the covers off my head and peered at him, instantly running through the previous evening's events in my head. I didn't even realize I was smiling until Ian said, "You look happy this morning." I quickly tried to cool the blush I knew alit my face. Even though Ian had stopped things from going too far between us, and even though I still felt a planet of guilt from interfering with his past, I could not stop the elation bubbling up inside me.

"Thank you," I said.

"For what?" He asked, gently stroking my cheek again.

"For believing me. For helping me. For last night." I smiled coyly.

"Jaysus! I can't believe I almost slept with my eighteen-year-old *student*. I'm going to hell! Or at least to the unemployment line." Ian said, rubbing his hands over his head, mussing his hair.

"Actually nineteen, it's almost my birthday."

"Ah, well, I guess it's all fine then." He laughed.

I did not want to leave. I loved my grandmother's place and I wanted to stay there playing house with Ian forever. But Ian hadn't changed in that he was still incredibly practical and logical. He convinced me that we *had* to go back. We both had class the next day, and although I couldn't care less about school at the moment, he assured me that I would. He explained what I already knew...that there were people and obligations in our lives that we couldn't just ignore. So, although I couldn't even imagine going back to the real world, I knew we had to.

The one comfort I had was that Ian and I made a plan to come back after classes were over and deal with the house, or more accurately the cellar full of relics. He had spent hours down there while I was sleeping taking inventory. He had some good ideas about how I could anonymously donate the items to different museums.

I could not understand why my grandmother had collected all those things. It wasn't like they could be sold, at least not without raising a million red flags. I guessed that maybe they all held some kind of sentimental value for her. I also was coming to the realization that I might never know. After all, she was dead and I wasn't sure if I would ever be able to answer the myriad of questions I had about this enigmatic woman.

Now I just wanted to focus on my future. I couldn't wait to show my parents this place and I hadn't even begun to consider what all I could do with the money I now had. And then there was Ian. The possibilities of a future with him in some form were now slowly consuming my thoughts. Mostly, I could not wait for the moment I was no longer his student.

When I finally forced myself to check my phone, I saw there were numerous messages from Mom and even a few from Taylor. I called my mom right away and explained how the battery on my phone had died so I had had to wait until I was back in Blythe to call her. I explained that I had been so exhausted after the long drive that I had just collapsed in bed. I hated lying to her, but I certainly could not tell her that I was still in Santa Fe, having spent another night with Ian.

I apologized profusely and after she yelled at me for a while, she said that she and my dad were finalizing their travel arrangements and would be in Blythe in less than two weeks! My heart sank when I realized that this was the exact time Ian and I had planned our return trip. I didn't know how I was going to deal with this problem. I certainly couldn't let them see what was in the cellar! Plus, although I wanted to see my parents, I wanted to be alone with Ian more.

I listened to Taylor's messages next.

"Evan, it's me...why aren't you picking up? I thought you were coming back on Saturday! It is now 2:00 a.m. Sunday morning. I just got back from the Spring Formal and you're still not here...call me!"

"Evan...where the hell are you? I just woke up and you are still not home. If you don't call me, I'm calling the police! Or at least the RA!"

Shit! I quickly dialed her number and she answered on the first ring.

"Evan!...why didn't you answer my calls?"

"Taylor calm down...I'm fine, and I am answering...this is me answering your calls!"

"Where are you?"

"Listen, I'm fine but I can't talk now. I'll be home tonight and I'll explain it all then. You didn't call the police did you?"

"No, but I was going to... When will you be home? I have something important to tell you!"

"Uh, I don't know probably late..."

"I'll wait up."

Great, I thought. "See you then." I hung up as Ian was coming down the stairs. He was showered and ready to go. I hadn't even started getting ready. I was intentionally dragging my feet and he knew it.

"Hey, you know what's weird?" He asked.

"Umm, absolutely everything that's happened in the last four months?"

"OK, do you know what *else* is weird?"

"Do I want to know?" I asked him. I didn't think I could handle any more weirdness in my life.

"When I was in town this morning I ran into that woman from the law office."

"The Silver Fox...I mean Ms. Fox?" I suddenly felt like I had a bowling ball in my stomach.

"The Silver Fox?" He chuckled and I shrugged my shoulders. "Well yeah, she was at the coffee shop."

This news made me very uneasy for some reason. Maybe it was because of the malicious vibes she had given me. "What did she say?"

"Not much, she asked how things were going up here. She just wanted to know how we were getting on."

"That's it?" I asked, skeptically.

"Basically. She also asked when we were going back and if I thought you would be selling the house."

"What did you tell her?" I demanded a little too sternly.

"Nothing, calm down. I told her we would be back in a few weeks, and that you definitely would not be selling. Why are you so upset?"

I shook my head. "Sorry, I don't know...there's just something about her..."

I showered, lingering in the hot water for a ridiculously long time, and then reluctantly got dressed in the clothes I had worn on the trip up. I threw my few belongings back into my overnight bag and took one last look around. I walked from room to room, reassuring myself that I would be back soon... just a few weeks.

In the library, I flipped through Grandmother's photo album again. I stared into her eyes... so like mine and wondered about all the things she had seen during her life. My initial disdain for her was rapidly fading and now I just wished she was still here. I needed her to explain all of this, to advise me. Then I thought about what she had written in her letter 'before we meet again', and wondered if somehow it was possible. I stuffed the bulky album into my overnight bag.

I wandered out to the living room and saw that Ian had discovered one last surprise.

He was dangling a pair of car keys. "You know, there's a car in the garage. You could drive it back and then you would have a car to use in Blythe. You do have a driver's license don't you?"

I had totally forgotten that Ken mentioned a car. Although I would certainly miss driving back with Ian, I had to admit it could be useful to have my own car in Blythe, especially when my parents arrived.

"What kind of car is it?" I hoped it wasn't a Rolls Royce or anything too ostentatious. I really wanted to try to keep this whole inheritance thing under wraps.

"Oh, I think you need to come see for yourself." He chuckled.

Great, I thought, it's probably a Lamborghini.

I started laughing as soon as Ian flipped on the garage light. The old Land Rover looked like something you would see rolling over the dunes in Morocco or splashing through a riverbank in Honduras.

"Well, I'm sure it was very practical for getting up and down that hill." Ian gestured to the dirt road outside and I thought about how hard it had been on his little Aston Martin.

"I guess Grandmother was very sensible." I smiled at him.

The Land Rover was not the smoothest ride. I felt every bump, but it certainly handled the rough terrain. I had to wait several minutes for Ian to catch up as we left the hacienda. I felt like crying as I took one last look at our majestic mountain hideaway in the rearview mirror. I already missed it and could not wait to return.

—ele—

We ate lunch at a little Mexican food joint in town and then hit the road. It was already getting dark by the time we crossed the Texas state line. I hadn't driven in a long time and it felt freeing. I noticed that there were over 150,000 miles on the odometer and wondered if this car was really in good enough shape to be driving it so far. I kept my eyes focused on the taillights of Ian's car ahead of me. I wished I was sitting next to him, but I realized that we probably both needed some alone time to reflect on the last forty-eight hours.

When we passed the road signs for Portales, I thought about how my mom would feel coming here. She now knew more about her mother than ever before, but actually seeing the hacienda for herself... I suspected it would be quite difficult for her. I thought maybe we could also visit the children's home where she grew up. I wanted to see it and strongly suspected that it held some pieces to the puzzle. I decided I would ask her to take me there. I wanted to know more about her childhood...with Aaron's mother.

What I had with Aaron was beginning to feel so distant now. The longing and heartache I had felt for him over the last months was transforming into something different. It felt more like the deep fondness you have for a childhood friend who knows you completely. There was no question that I still loved him. I knew that he held some integral piece to the puzzle of my life but now, the searing fire burning in my chest was because of someone else.

I wondered what life in Blythe would be like now, considering all that had happened. Images flashed in my head...kissing, caressing, the way Ian looked in the moonlight. My face became hot and my breathing heavy just thinking about it. How could I possibly sit in one of his lectures without giving myself away? Taylor would absolutely die if she knew!

I also thought a lot about Max Koehler. I wondered if it was possible Ian remembered more now than he had before. I reasoned that if seeing me had opened his mind to the existence of 'otherworldly creatures', then maybe he had been more receptive to Max's 'crazy rants'. So many questions filled my mind as we finally pulled into the dorm parking lot at Harper.

I glanced up at my window and saw the light was still on. To my disappointment, I realized that Taylor really had waited up. Although it was late and the place was deserted, I looked nervously around before jumping out of my car and into Ian's. I had spent most of the drive back thinking of Ian and I suddenly worried that he had spent the hours regretting what had happened between us at the hacienda. My tension melted when he grabbed my hand and tenderly kissed it. He swept his lips across the back of my hand, back and forth, peering up at me intently. My willpower was melting with each sweep of his lips, and I was very close to climbing right over the gearshift and into his lap.

"That was a *really* long drive." He said in the same raspy, wanton tone I had heard the night before.

"Feel like going back?" I proposed.

"*You* have class tomorrow young lady." He said, releasing my hand.

"It's all right. I have an in with the Professor." He laughed, but I could see that I wasn't going to win this one.

"Ian, I do want to ask you something...seriously. I was just wondering...about Max Koehler...did you happen to remember anything else that he might have said about the ones...like me?" Right away, I could tell by the change in his expression that he did.

"Yes...you know actually now that I think about it, I do remember some more details. That's so odd, I don't know why I didn't tell you them before..."

Because they didn't exist before, I thought.

"I remember Max saying that this ability...it was hereditary. But I think we could have guessed that." I nodded. "Yes hereditary...but only on the maternal side."

"What? You mean these travelers, or wanderers, or whatever...they're only women?"

"Yes, I remember him saying that if boys inherited it they died young."

"Aaron..." I whispered.

"What?"

"My brother...the one I saw in my memory. He died as a baby. What else? Can you remember anything else Max said?"

"No Evan, but he kept journals. Hundreds of them, he was always writing in his journals." I thought of the journals in my own desk drawer. "I'm sure that he would have documented whatever he knew."

"Where do you think they are now?" I was desperate to get my hands on them.

"Probably with his widow. She still lives in Dublin, I speak to her occasionally."

"Do you think she would send them to you?"

"I doubt it, and I would feel strange asking."

Feel strange! "Ian, the answers to everything I need to know could be written in those journals!"

"I know, I know. Calm down. We'll just go there! After classes are finished and we've sorted out the house. We'll go. If she still has them, and I couldn't imagine that she wouldn't, I'm sure she'll let us read them."

"Go to Dublin?"

"Yes."

"You and me?"

"Yes! My father has been bugging me to visit anyway. It will be perfect."

I smiled and flew into his arms, the parking brake jabbing into my side. "Oh Ian, I can't wait!"

"Well, you'll have to...just a few weeks."

—————

I bounded up to my room in a wonderful mood, but it was dashed as soon as I saw Taylor's angry face.

"Where have you been? Do you know how worried I was?"

"Jeez Mom, I didn't realize I broke curfew." I plopped my bag down on the bed.

"It's not funny, Evan. You could have at least answered your phone."

"Look I'm sorry, I lost track of time. So how was the dance?"

"Stop trying to change the subject and tell me what happened!"

"Fine." I'd had a five-hour drive to formulate the lie. "The truth is...my grandmother died."

"Oh my god, Evan...I'm so sorry." She came and sat by me on my bed.

"No, no it's fine. I didn't know her at all. She wasn't in my life. But I had to go take care of her things...arrangements and whatnot."

"Why didn't you tell me? I would have come with you, helped you."

"I knew how much you were looking forward to the dance. You guys worked so hard on it. I didn't want to make you miss it." I thought about how dramatically different the weekend would have been if Taylor had gone with me instead of Ian, and I was suddenly Rob's biggest fan.

"You're so ridiculous. So is everything OK? Did she leave you millions?" Taylor teased. I thought I would choke! Instead, I swallowed hard and put on my most sincere face.

"I wish... No, just a few bucks to cover her arrangements and a car."

"A car! She left you a car? What kind?"

I pulled her over to the window and pointed to the beat-up beige Land Rover in the parking lot.

"Hmmm...nice Evan."

I smiled at her sarcasm. "It's great!" I said enthusiastically.

"Sure it is. OK, now my news..."

She didn't even bother to ask where exactly I'd been or how I had gotten there and that was just fine with me. I feigned interest in her big news despite the fact that I really had to pee and was exhausted.

"What...what is it?"

"Ready?"

"Sure."

"After the dance, Rob...well...Rob, asked me to marry him!!" Her eyes were wide and bright and she looked at me expectantly.

I tried desperately to suppress my true reaction and act happy for her, but I was aghast and it showed. "And what did you say?"

"Evan...I said yes, of course. We're getting married this summer...July!"

"Uh-huh." I was bewildered. I had absolutely no idea what to say to her and I couldn't bring myself to pretend I was happy about this.

"Evan?" She clearly was expecting more from me. I thought of all those chick flicks where the girls scream and jump up and down, dancing around the room. Was that what I was supposed to do?

"I have to pee." I walked into the bathroom and left her standing there stunned. When I came back out, she was glaring at me like she wished I was dead.

"So *what* is your problem?" Taylor snipped.

"I just don't understand the hurry. I mean you are only eighteen years old! You've only known him for a few months. This is crazy! Why not just live with him for a while and try it out?"

"I can't believe you just said that! I hate to even justify it with an answer, but Rob's traditional." *Oh please*! I thought about all the mornings Taylor had rolled in at the crack of dawn after shacking up with Rob! "Plus, if we know we want to be together anyway, why wait?" This was so stupid. I could not believe I was having this conversation with her. I was tired and annoyed and she was being ridiculous.

"And to think...I wanted *you* to be my maid of honor, even though McKenna would have been devastated. I have been out of my mind with worry about you and this is how you treat me! First, you disappear, and then you won't answer my calls..." She had walked into the bathroom and I could hear the loud clank of toiletries being banged around as she ranted. "Then that woman shows up looking for you and I thought you were dead or something..."

I was on my feet in a flash. "What did you say? What woman?" I cornered her in the bathroom.

"I don't know...she was tall, with long gray...well silver hair. Very pretty I guess, in an unusual way." She was still seething at me.

"What did she say?"

"I don't know," she shrugged at my reflection in the mirror above the sink.

I grabbed her arms tightly, yanking her around to face me. "Taylor please, this is really important! What did she say?" My intensity must have scared her because she dropped the hostility and sarcasm.

"She just wanted to know when you were coming back." Her voice was small and unsure.

"When?"

"She came by this morning, around 10:00. She was only here a minute or two. When I said that I didn't know where you were or when you'd be back she left."

I dropped her arms, walked out of the bathroom, and sat down on my bed. I had to think...what did this mean? She could not have been here this morning if Ian had seen her in Santa Fe.

"Why are you so freaked out?" Taylor squirted toothpaste onto her toothbrush.

"Just never mind...I don't know. Taylor, I'm sorry about before. I may not completely understand, but if you're happy, then I'm happy for you. OK?" She shrugged and resumed brushing her teeth. When she finally emerged from the bathroom, I had one more question for her.

"Hey Taylor, one more thing... Whatever happened to that compact case I gave you?" Her face flushed.

"Uh yeah, I was hoping you wouldn't ask about that. I uh...actually lost it about a month ago. I always kept it right here on the dresser, but it just disappeared."

I took the compact case out of my purse and tossed it over to her.

"Where did you find this? She exclaimed, clearly happy to have it back.

I gave her a noncommittal shrug and crawled under my covers. My bed felt great compared to the couch I had slept on the night before. I pulled the brown afghan up and closed my eyes.

"Hey, what's this? You left me little a note?"

My eyes flashed to Taylor. She was lying in her bed playing with the compact case.

"What?" I asked, straining to see what she was looking at.

"The note inside it... Are you leaving me secret messages now?" Then I saw she was unfolding a piece of paper.

I nearly flew across the room, landing right on top of Taylor and grabbed the paper from her hands.

"Hey, what the hell...get off me!"

"Sorry." I stood up taking the note with me. I finished unfolding the heavy card stock paper and read the words scribbled on it.

Do __not__ believe her!

"What is it?" Taylor asked.

I kept my back turned to her and struggled to keep my voice flat. "Uh, it's nothing, just a receipt." My hands trembled as I struggled to refold it. I was glad Taylor couldn't see the look I knew must have been plastered on my face as I tried to comprehend why this mysterious message was written in *my* handwriting.

⎯ℓℓ⎯

I was a complete basket case by the time I caught Ian alone after class the next day. I semi-hysterically blurted out all the details about the note and visit from Ms. Fox. I had assumed that my grandmother had traveled into my past before she died and stolen the compact, as she had stolen so many other things. However, I couldn't wrap my mind around the fact that it contained a note *I* had written. How had it gotten there and who was I supposed to be warning myself about?

I felt certain it was the Silver Fox that I shouldn't trust, nothing else made sense. Ian held me tight and assured me that there was nothing we could do other than what we were already planning...find Max's journals and figure out who these people were. So, as the days went by I was guarded, but resumed life as usual...sort of.

Classes were excruciating. I counted the seconds until I could be alone with Ian, but even that was frustrating. He had become irrationally paranoid about 'being discovered' and refused to touch me, even when we were locked in his office late at night. He reasoned that I would not be his student very much longer, and then things would be different. He worked like mad. He was doing all of his lectures and preparing for finals, trying to finish the Newgrange paper and researching the long list of relics we had found in my grandmother's cellar.

I studied for finals. It was hard to muster the motivation when all I could think about was the end of the semester and going to Europe with Ian. I made a million plans and was already booking flights. Our trip to Dublin had now expanded to include Germany, Italy, and Greece.

I decided that I needed to go back to Hamburg and visit my brother's grave. The other places Ian chose for one reason or another. Most of his interests had to do with the different objects we had found in the cellar. He was obsessed with discovering their origins. Some, he said, were items that had famously gone missing and some had never even been described in the history books at all. Ian said we needed to figure out where they had come from before we could decide exactly what to do with them.

I told myself over and over again, that all I had to do was just get through the next few days...finish my finals, and then we would be free. I wasn't sure if I would ever return to school, especially not at Harper, but I had promised Ian that I wouldn't just blow off the semester. I especially felt indebted to Dr. Marshall who had believed in me so completely. So I studied extra hard for his Immunology final and thought I had pretty much aced it.

In those last weeks of the semester, Dr. Marshall had occasionally asked me how my research with *Ian* was going, and his sarcastic tone always reminded me to ask Ian what the deal was between the two of them, but I still hadn't brought it up.

My Mom called daily with the latest details about their trip. They were scheduled to arrive the day after finals. I planned to drive them to Santa Fe, and then stop at the children's home, in Portales, on the way back. I just hoped they weren't as enamored with the hacienda as I had been because I wanted the trip to be as brief as possible.

I wasn't sure how long they planned to stay, but the sooner they left the sooner Ian and I could start our adventure together. I had been devising a plan that loosely consisted of telling my parents that I was spending the summer abroad for a history class. I was going to suggest that maybe they go on a cruise, depending on how much time Dad had off from work.

Taylor was already knee-deep in wedding plans, and although the important job of maid-of-honor had thankfully ended up going to McKenna, I was still expected to be a bridesmaid. I couldn't face telling Taylor that I might not be around *at all* during the summer. I didn't know if she would ever forgive me for missing her wedding, but honestly, I was hoping she would come to her senses and back out of the whole thing before it came to that.

And then there was the mystery of the Silver Fox. She hadn't returned to the dorms after the night she spoke with Taylor, but I was constantly looking over my shoulder. There was only one thing I could think of that explained how she was in a coffee shop in Santa Fe and here in Blythe a few minutes later. If she could travel through time too, it would explain why she was so interested in me, but how could she know about my power? And what did she want with me? My gut told me she was dangerous, and my note assured me I shouldn't trust her.

As theories and plans filled my head, I watched Ian lecture. I realized with a little sadness that this would be the last formal lecture I would ever see him give...at least as his student. We were supposed to turn in our final essays after class, and despite my protests, Ian had actually made me complete the assignment! He said that he had already betrayed the student/professor compact once and did not want to do it again by giving me preferential treatment when it came to assignments!

I reluctantly wrote it, but my narrative took a slightly different turn than he had probably intended. The assignment had been to theorize on how and why the burial mounds of Newgrange were built. I proposed that the mounds of Newgrange were not used for burials at all, but instead, they were ancient bordellos where nubile nymphs danced at night, bewitching young men and stealing their virginity. Admittedly, I had written it as an inside joke between the two of us, and I especially tried to make my imagery of the copulations as vivid as possible. I figured he deserved it for making me complete the assignment.

I waited until the lecture hall was empty to make my way down the aisle. I could see that Ian was lingering as well, spending way too much time gathering up the class's essays.

"Here you go. Enjoy." I said handing him my paper.

"I look forward to reading your insights, Ms. Wright." A devious grin spread across his face, but then I noticed his eyes flicker up to the back of the room. I turned and saw the super Gelf still sitting in her seat, watching us.

I dropped my voice to a whisper when I spoke. "Should I come by your office tonight?"

"Uh no, actually I'm going to be swamped reading these essays. I only have a few days to get final grades submitted."

I jutted out my bottom lip, exaggerating a pout.

"How about I make it up to you?" He offered.

I lifted my eyebrows in consideration. "I'm listening."

"Tomorrow night, my place."

"Your place!" I tried to keep my excited voice low. "You have a place? I just assumed you lived in your office." I said sarcastically.

"My place, tomorrow night. I'll cook. We still have to celebrate your birthday...and the fact that I'm not your teacher anymore." He rushed out the last few words because the Gelf was making her way down the aisle.

I looked down as she joined us. I knew my face was flushed, and I cursed her timing.

"Uh OK then...Dr. Browning...I will...uh...finish reading those documents," I babbled, referring to nothing. Glancing up quickly I saw the confusion on both of their faces before I awkwardly and abruptly turned to leave. *Smooth*, I thought to myself as I skulked out of the lecture hall.

A few hours later, a huge weight fell from my shoulders as I handed in my last final exam and walked out of my Existentialism class. Despite all the drama and mystery in my life, I was ecstatic! A feeling of freedom consumed me as I strode across campus.

Nearing the dorms, I noticed the bustle of students packing their cars. I thought about the last time I had witnessed this scene, just before Christmas break. It seemed like a lifetime ago. I had been a different person then. It was shocking to think about how much had changed. Just five months ago I didn't even know Ian or Aaron, and barely knew Taylor. I had just discovered my *ability,* and I didn't even realize it was, in fact, an ability.

Taylor was packing when I walked in. This too was a scene I had witnessed several times during the past year. Taylor happily packing her designer suitcases, heading off somewhere, while I stood still...stuck in Blythe. Things were going to be so different now. Now *I* would be headed off on a romantic adventure, the likes of which I had never imagined!

"Hey Evan! How'd your finals go?"

"OK... and you?"

"I think I squeaked through. So look, I've been thinking, why don't you come down to Houston after your parents leave? With McKenna stuck here taking summer classes, I'm going to be swamped with wedding planning...flowers, caterers, dress fittings...I could really use your help."

"Can't Rob help?"

"Come on, you know guys are no good at that stuff. Plus, my dad has a full schedule of hunting, tennis, and golf that will keep him busy. The fact is, if I don't have someone there on my side, my mom will completely take over everything. She's already invited all of her friends to the ceremony and I haven't even booked a church yet! Plus, she's already arranging to have my reception at the club!"

The Club...*Aaron.* I felt a pang in my chest at the thought of him. Was it sadness, guilt, or a combination of both?

"Come on, it will be great. You have a...*car* now." She snickered when she said car. "You can stay with us. Oh, and after the first summer term is over we are all going to Austin. McKenna's throwing me a bachelorette party on Sixth Street!" She looked up from her packing excitedly.

"Taylor, you guys aren't even old enough to drink."

The excitement drained from her face. "So, we can still go dancing. Evan, don't be such a buzz kill." She went back to her packing, obviously missing the deeper point of my comment.

"Sorry...I'm sure it will be fun. Uh, I'll try to make it, but I can't make any promises."

I helped Taylor pack up the rest of her things and load her car. It was bittersweet and hammered home the reality that Taylor would not be coming back to our room. When she returned in the fall, she and Rob would be married and they would find a little love nest off campus.

I cringed at the thought and wondered if she would even finish college after completing her M.r.s. degree. I couldn't criticize her too much though, since I was debating whether I would return as well. I had arranged to keep my dorm room over the summer though. It was much easier than trying to deal with all my stuff, especially when I had no idea what would happen or where I would be after summer vacation was over.

Conveniently, Rob arrived just after we had carried down the last of her boxes.

"Hi, Rob!" I forced myself to sound congenial.

"Hey, what's up?" As usual, he spoke to me in an indifferent tone without meeting my eyes.

"Well, take good care of our girl, OK?" I felt tears welling up in my eyes as I hugged Taylor goodbye. I heard him mumble 'Uh huh."

"Hey you're not going to cry are you?" Taylor looked at me cautiously.

"No, don't be silly," I said roughly sweeping my hand across my eyes. I could not believe I was suddenly feeling so emotional.

"I'll see you soon right?" I could tell from her voice that the emotion was mutual.

"Yeah, yeah of course." The truth was I had absolutely no idea what the future held.

I stood waving as she pulled away, following Rob's pickup truck. Just before she pulled out of the dorm parking lot, she rolled down the window and yelled.

"Evan please think about coming to Houston, OK?"

I nodded vigorously and then waved as she drove out of sight.

Chapter 16

Best Laid Plans

"Hi, Mom. I just finished helping Taylor load her things into her car. I can't believe that all that stuff actually fit in our tiny room! I am exhausted, but you should see all the closet space now! Anyway, how are you getting on? Are you guys all packed?"

"Evy honey, I have some bad news." The tone in her voice immediately concerned me.

"Mom, what's wrong? Are you OK?"

"I'm fine, but Daddy's not feeling so well."

"What do you mean?"

"Well, he's been under the weather for about a month now. You know, just tired and whatnot. But he's had this nasty cough that he couldn't shake."

"A month!" Why was I just hearing about this?

"We didn't want to worry you, but I forced him to go to the doctor yesterday...you know how your father is. Well, it seems he has pneumonia."

"Pneumonia!" I was flabbergasted. My father had never been sick a day in his life!

"Yeah, we were surprised too. He'll be fine. He's on some very strong antibiotics, but the doctor doesn't think he should travel until the infection clears." Her voice seemed artificially cheery and I wondered exactly how worried I should be.

"I'm so sorry Evy. You know how much we were looking forward to this visit." I seethed at myself for the feelings of relief and even happiness that were surfacing. I was a horrible daughter!

"Mom please, it's fine. Obviously, the priority is getting Dad better! Is he there? Can I talk to him?"

"He's sleeping, but I'm sure he'll want to talk to you when he wakes up. He feels terrible about the situation. I'm sure he'll be fine in a couple of weeks and we'll be on our way."

I thought about the flight reservations I had already made for Ian and me. "Yeah, sure...a few weeks." I wondered if we could intercept them by making a pit stop in Guam at some point during our excursion. We wouldn't exactly be in the neighborhood, but I was going to have to placate them, and of course, make sure my dad was OK.

"Mom, do you guys need anything? Anything at all?" I desperately wanted to do *something* to help...and alleviate my guilt about being a horrible daughter.

"Evy, you've already done so much." She was referring to the sizable deposit I had made in their bank account after we got back from Santa Fe.

"Mom, that doesn't count. It didn't really take a lot of effort."

"Well, it was very generous nonetheless."

⁓ℯℓℯ⁓

Ian agreed to move up our departure date after I told him the news about my parents. The plan was now that I would stay at his place and we would leave for Santa Fe early the next morning. I had booked flights for us from Albuquerque to Dublin for the following Wednesday. That gave us four days to deal with my grandmother's *collection*.

There was so much to do and not much time at all to do it. I spent the day running all over town buying new luggage that actually matched and travel-sized everything...shampoo, conditioner, lotion, toothpaste, and even shaving cream for Ian. I was obsessed with the cute little miniature packaging. I even bought us snacks for the following day's road trip.

Four nights alone with Ian in the hacienda... I could not stop my mind from running wild. I was such a wound-up ball of nervous excitement that it was all I could do to keep from giggling out loud. I even made a stop at Victoria's Secret, deciding that I was going to seduce Ian in my own, rather than my granny's nighties, which when you thought about it was kind of gross.

By the time I got back to my dorm, it was nearly time to meet Ian for dinner. I packed as quickly as possible, making sure to grab the essentials-passport, itinerary, and wallet. I threw all my clothes, including the newly purchased intimate apparel, haphazardly in my new suitcases and quickly swooped up my toiletries into a small shaving kit.

I figured that if I forgot anything I could always just buy it on the trip. That feeling of being able to just buy anything I wanted, anytime I wanted was going to take some getting used to. On my way out, I quickly checked my mailbox. I was so anxious to get over to Ian's that it took me at least a full minute to comprehend what I was holding. I held my breath as I opened the letter and began to read.

Dear Evan,

Sorry it has taken me so long to get in touch, but I didn't know how to tell you that I am planning to stay in Houston for a while. When I knew I wouldn't be back, I really wanted to tell you in person. I felt weird just calling or emailing you. So here it is, a good old-fashioned letter. I am mailing this today because I saw Taylor at the club and whatever happens I don't want you to hear it from her first.

I spent most of the last week at the hospital with Becky. She's had every test you can imagine and they finally think they have found the source of her problem. The doctors think that she has a lesion on her temporal lobe that is causing the seizures. The good news is that they think they can fix the problem with surgery. The bad news is that the surgery, called a temporal resection, involves removing part of the brain responsible for memory and emotions, so many people experience speech and memory problems afterward.

They say the best-case scenario is that Becky will be normal and seizure-free after the surgery and a few months of speech therapy. However, although they didn't actually tell us this, I know from the internet, that the worst-case scenario is that she would end up with no memory at all and the speech of a two-year-old. Even though she knows the risks, she is willing to go through with it, because her seizures have become so frequent and unbearable, that she can't lead any kind of normal life. Anyway, the surgery is scheduled for next week.

Evan, please understand that I need to be here for her...through the surgery and rehabilitation. I have talked to my coach and he's willing to hold my place on the team and my scholarship. They even worked it out so that when I come back in the Fall, I can have my same dorm room. My roommate is ecstatic because it means he gets the room to himself for a while. Here's the thing though. I've decided that no matter what happens, I'm breaking up with Becky after she recovers from the surgery. Too many things have changed between us and it is just not fair to her or me.

Evan, I have no right to ask you this, especially in a letter, but I just thought that maybe you would consider...giving me another chance. We both know there is something special between us. We could be great together. I haven't been able to stop thinking about you every moment of every day, and I'm tired of feeling guilty and hating myself for it. I just want to be with you. Anyway, that's what I've been up to.

I miss you.
Aaron

The letter was postmarked March 17th. Aaron had mailed it months ago, during Spring Break! Before I had traveled back to 1963, before my grandmother died, before...Ian. He hadn't just forgotten about me, hadn't blown me off. He had asked me to wait for him. Why had I only received it now? Damn the U.S. postal service.

I drove over to Ian's in a daze. I couldn't imagine what Aaron thought of me now after never receiving a response. I couldn't stop thinking about what things would be like if I had received this letter when I was meant to. I wondered where Aaron was now and what had happened to Becky.

I sat outside Ian's apartment complex reading the letter over and over. I knew that this should be one of the happiest nights of my life. Classes were finished, and tomorrow I was headed off on my great adventure. I had more money than I knew what to do with, and I was about to spend the night with the most incredibly gorgeous man I had ever seen in the flesh. Yet, now all I could think about was Aaron, and all I felt was...regret.

Finally, I folded up the letter and stashed it in my purse. I couldn't think about this anymore now. I grabbed my small overnight bag and left the rest of my things in the car. There was no use bringing everything up to Ian's, just to turn around and bring them back down in the morning.

Ian opened the door before I could even knock. He looked as anxious to see me, as I had been to see him.

"Make yourself at home. Dinner is almost ready," he said, carrying my bag to a back room. His apartment was a larger-scale version of his office. Unpacked boxes were sitting in the corners of every room, relatively nothing on the walls, and books everywhere. The décor, or more actually, the lack thereof, gave me no insight into Ian's personality other than that he procrastinated at unpacking and really loved books.

"Uh...nice place."

"Yeah I know, it's in a pretty sad state, but honestly I just never have time. Plus, I'm not here much. Nor do I have the first inkling about interior design."

"No, really?" I said, sarcastically.

He smirked at me. "So I'm making Italian. I guess it's a tradition now."

"I hope it's better than the stale spaghetti I made."

"That was the best spaghetti I ever had," he said, walking over and taking me in his arms. He slowly lifted my chin and my pulse quickened as he moved in to kiss me, but just as our lips met, a loud buzzer went off in the kitchen.

"Oops, hold that thought...dinner's ready!" He smiled as he backed away.

As we ate, Ian excitedly talked a mile a minute about all the things around Dublin he wanted to show me. He filled me in on the research he had done on the artifacts and showed me Eurorail map routes he thought we should take. Once dinner was over and we had covered all the trip details he looked at me seriously.

"Now, more importantly, how did you do on your finals?"

I suddenly felt like I was in the counselor's office again. "Uh, I managed."

"Managed?" Ian said scrutinizing me.

"I think they went well," I assured him.

"Well, you certainly seemed to have done well in my class. Anthony said your essay on Newgrange was the best he read."

"Anthony?"

"Anthony, you know, my graduate assistant. When we moved up our departure date, I realized I was never going to get through all the papers before we left, so I gave some to Anthony to read. Plus, I figured it was best if I wasn't the one to grade yours, more objective you know."

My face grew hot thinking about the things I had written in that essay.

"Anyway, congrats for getting an 'A' in my course."

"Uh... thanks," I mumbled.

"So that just leaves us with the research paper to complete."

I had completely forgotten about that. I mean, I knew Ian had been working on it, but wasn't sure if he had finished.

"Oh, so how is it going? Do you think there's enough new material from the documents we reviewed to publish something?" I knew that for both of our sakes, Ian would have to come up with something to show Dr. Chaney for all our 'research efforts' this semester.

"Well, that's what I want to talk to you about, but first I have a surprise. Come on."

He handed me a glass and grabbed the wine bottle in his other hand. He led me down a short hallway, and into a dark room illuminated by the light of at least a dozen candles. The first thing I noticed was his bed, and in the middle of it was a birthday cake.

"Time to celebrate," he said, raising one eyebrow.

My heart raced as he led me to the bed and lit the three candles on the cake.

"I think you're a few short. I'm not *that* young."

"Just make a wish and blow them out." He said grinning, obviously very pleased with himself.

"What on earth could I possibly wish for? I already have everything I could want."

"Fine, then I'll wish!" And before I could protest he exhaled, extinguishing the flames.

"Hey! You can't steal my wish."

"Well, I just did and now you have to grant it." Ian's expression turned from playful to deadly serious as he pulled me to him. Every single thought of Aaron was wiped from my mind when Ian's lips touched mine.

All the anticipation of this moment resulted in an urgency I had never felt. All the frustration of not being able to touch each other over the last weeks erupted into a frenzied mêlée. It was like being driven wild with hunger only to taste something so intensely delicious that you nearly faint from your desire to devour it. Then there was the cake, which ended up in places that shouldn't be mentioned.

Within seconds we were on the bed and Ian was hovering above me, chest heaving with quick breaths. He was absolutely and magnificently enticing. I ran my hands across his chest and down to his obliques, those amazing muscles I had so admired that first day in his office. He closed his eyes and his ragged breathing quickened, but before I could thoroughly explore, he pressed his weight on top of me, pushed my head to the side, and started kissing my neck.

I thought how all the fantasies I'd had of Ian doing this exact thing paled in comparison as his mouth traveled slowly over my body. He was intoxicating and I was dizzy with desire. I pulled him to me as hard as I could. His mouth was near my ear and as I gave my body over to him completely I heard him murmur something. It was faint and breathy, but I thought he said,

"I've waited so many years to do this with you."

———

Several hours later, I stood wrapped in a towel watching Ian climb out of the shower. As I admired the exquisiteness of his body, I realized that it was only a few weeks before when I had fantasized about almost this exact same scene in a Santa Fe hotel. Only then, I never actually believed that the fantasy would come true. Now that it was reality, I just hoped it would never end.

"Did I get it all off?" Ian asked.

"Uh yeah, thanks." Ian had made it his personal mission to wash the frosting off me. "It's a shame we didn't get a chance to taste it."

"Oh it tasted alright," Ian said, giving me a sly grin.

My face heated up again. "So are you even packed yet?" I glanced around the bedroom as I slipped on my jeans. I didn't see any suitcases.

"Plenty of time." He winked as he pulled on his shirt.

I started pulling the sheets, that were now covered in cake and frosting, off the bed. I hoped he owned another set. "Hey, didn't you say you wanted to talk to me about something?"

"Yeah, I did. Give me those." Ian took the sheets from me and threw them in the corner. "Have a seat." He sat on the bed and patted the spot next to him.

Something about his expression worried me. "Shoot," I said hesitantly.

"I've been thinking...and I think that all of this...everything that's happened in my life...it's not just random chance." He took my hand in his. "I mean, first I saw you at Newgrange when I was young, and then years later I ended up having Max as my mentor! I mean the one person who knows about people like you. Then the way I was drawn, no compelled, to come to Blythe. It's not just a coincidence... Evan, I think it's destiny."

"Destiny?" I started to speak up and mention again that seeing me at Newgrange wasn't meant to be, it was just a mistake, but he was so impassioned and his eyes so intense. I couldn't contradict him.

"Don't you see...all of this was meant to be. Evan, you and I were meant for each other...I mean come on, you are a time traveler and I'm a historian. Think of the things we could do! Everything I have devoted my life to... It's just been meaningless... until now. You were right when you said that people like me just spend their lives guessing about what happened in the past. However, I don't have to guess anymore! You and I can solve all the mysteries of the past...together.

"Together?" Now his intensity was scaring me.

"Just keep an open mind for a minute, OK?"

"I'll try." I had the feeling that I was not going to like what he was about to say.

"So, you say that when you travel back you're just as you are here...wearing the same clothes, carrying whatever you had in the present?"

"Yeah..."

Ian squeezed my hand, took a deep breath, and said, "So what if you were holding...say...me?"

"Excuse me?"

"I said holding me." I could tell by the look in his eyes that he was very pleased with himself, as though he had just discovered the cure for cancer. He playfully pulled me on top of him, and we both fell back onto the bed.

"Ian, don't." I pushed off him and sat back up. I could not believe what he had just said! Of course, I had *thought* about the possibility of bringing another person into the past with me, but I had never for a moment actually considered trying it. He lay beside me lightly running his fingers up and down my arm. "I can't," I whispered.

His hand froze on my arm, and then he pulled it away. "Why not?" He asked, propping himself up on his elbow. His eyes were fixed on me.

"I don't want to hurt you." The thought of Becky's convulsing body flashed in my mind.

"Come here." He pulled me back down again. I rested my head on his chest and curled my body into his. "How could you possibly hurt me?" He ran his fingers through my hair.

"Once when I traveled back...there was a girl...she had a seizure and almost died." I hated thinking about it.

"And you think it was because of you?"

"I...I don't know...maybe."

"Did it ever happen again?"

"Well no, but that girl...I know she had permanent damage...to her brain."

His voice was gentle and I could tell he was trying to be understanding. "Evan, there's no reason to believe that what happened to that girl was because of you. I mean if it was somehow your fault why didn't it ever happen again? I mean *I've* witnessed you... time travel... and look at me, I'm fine."

"OK, even if what happened to her wasn't my fault, we have no idea what would happen to you if I actually could pull you through. I mean, didn't Max say that only women had this ability? There may be a very good reason for that. Maybe there's something in the male physiology that prevents them from traveling."

"That doesn't seem likely."

I snapped my head up and looked him in the eye. "Doesn't seem likely! What about any of this is likely? Ian, I can't risk hurting you!" Tears welled in my eyes.

"Evan, please calm down. I'm sorry." He was stroking my hair again and his voice was gentle and calming.

"Why? Why would you even want me to consider such a thing?"

"Well, I think the information we found in the Trinity documents is important. I mean it proves for the first time that Campbell and his crew had plenty of time to pillage the mounds before the authorities were notified, but it doesn't prove they actually did."

"So what... you want *us* to go back and see?" I laughed aloud as I said it.

His silence was damning. "Oh my god... you do. You want me to take you back to Newgrange in 1699!"

I edged away from him and stood up. I walked back into the living room and started pacing. I could not believe what he was asking me to do! Ian followed me and sat down on the couch. After a few moments, he spoke.

"Evan. This is a lot for me too and I hate asking you to do something that frightens you like this, but I wasn't joking when I said that I thought this was our destiny. I believe that you and I are going to do amazing things."

"So what if you did find out... what if we *did* travel back and we saw that nothing happened, or something happened... what then? Obviously, you could never tell anyone... what would it really accomplish?"

"This isn't about publishing a paper or fame or anything like that. This is about discovering the truth of something I have studied and researched for years. You cannot imagine what it is like to wonder about one question for so long and so hard that it becomes your obsession, and then find out that the answer is completely within reach. I mean I never thought I could actually know if my hypotheses were correct, but now..." His voice drifted off and I realized that Ian would never give up on this.

"Then I will go alone. I'll go and tell you about everything I see. You will have the answers you seek and not risk...getting hurt," or worse, I thought.

"I need to be there Evan. Apart from anything, you don't know Gaelic and wouldn't be able to understand anyone you might encounter." I opened my mouth to protest, but Ian thundered on. "And there are likely to be things that only someone who has spent years studying the time and place will be able to fully understand." The look on Ian's face was imploring and completely determined.

"You know, I thought that when you finally found out about all of this...about what I could do, I thought you would disapprove...tell me that I had a moral obligation to preserve the sanctity of the past or something. I never imagined in a million years that you would want to..."

"What... see for myself? Wouldn't you? Evan, I'm a historian... It's my love, my passion."

"And I'm just the gateway..."

He walked over and took my face between his palms. He traced my lips with his thumb, looking deep into my eyes. "Evan, you mean more to me than *anyone* ever has. You are my past, present, and future. You are not *just* an anything. You are the most beautiful, amazing, insightful, sensual creature I have ever known and we are sealed, you and me." I leaned my face against his chest and held him tight. "I love you," he said in a whisper and my heart thudded hard in my chest. I was stunned, dumbstruck. His words had touched my soul and at the moment I would have given him anything.

"You won't hurt me." He whispered in my ear.

----- *ele* -----

Why do we do things we know are dangerous? Smoke cigarettes, drive too fast, bungee jump... Is it the addiction, the adrenaline rush? I knew exactly why I did what I did. It was because I loved him. I wanted to make him happy, make him continue to love me back. I wanted us to be partners in all of this and I was caught up in his romantic vision of the adventures we would have.

So, I ignored every cell in my body that was screaming 'this is a terrible idea!' In all honesty, I really didn't believe it would work. I thought I would give it a half-hearted try, and he would be disappointed but content that I had at least made the attempt. How could I have known that the repercussions of this one decision would reverberate through time and affect multitudes of people? I was stupid and cavalier and never considered the aftermath.

Ian had obviously anticipated my lack of resolve because he was ready. He had flashlights and dark clothes for both of us.

"Do you really think it's a good idea to take flashlights to 1699? I mean what if we lost one or something? What do you think the scientists of the time would think considering the light bulb wouldn't be invented for..."

"Another two hundred years, give or take a decade." Ian finished.

"Yeah, I guess you're right. But how will we see if it's dark?"

"Well, my strategy has always been to blend in. I guess we use what they did at the time." I was absolutely not looking forward to this!

"Well, I'm fresh out of peat-moss torches, so I guess a broom handle, wrapped in an old t-shirt, doused with lighter fluid will have to do."

"And *when* exactly are we going back to? I mean, we don't even know precisely when the mounds were discovered. Are we just going to hang around the countryside for a week or two?" I thought that surely he would realize just how ridiculous this plan was.

"No, actually I've found some new entries in the Trinity papers that narrow down the time frame. I am pretty sure that the discovery was made on September 1st, 1699, give or take a few days. But does the exact date really matter?" I looked at him curiously. "I mean you said that you had to try to become someone in that time and place. You had to identify with their emotions and perceptions."

"Exactly," now he would realize how impossible this all was, I thought.

"So I'll tell you everything I know about Charles Campbell and Ireland at that time. You can envision being him at the moment he saw the opening to the passage." He smiled at me, and for the first time I realized it could actually work, and I was petrified.

Ian slipped on a dark gray sweatshirt and a pair of black jeans.

"Not exactly period clothing." I mused.

"Well, period clothing would be a bit tricky. I would need a waistcoat, tights, and buckle shoes...think pilgrim-style. Oh, and probably either a wig or white powder for my hair, which by the way, would be way too short for the fashion. I suppose I might be able to pass for a peasant, but the hair..." Ian ran his fingers through his short hair. "I would probably be taken for a prisoner!"

"A prisoner?"

"Well, the only reason a man of 1699 would have hair as short as mine would be because he had recently been in prison. You see, they shaved the inmate's hair to prevent the spread of lice."

"Ah. And what about me? Surely I don't look like a proper lady of the time." I looked down at my clothes, which were very similar to Ian's.

Ian suppressed a laugh. "Uh, I'm not sure *what* you would be taken for. I think it would be quite shocking to see a woman in pants."

I thought about the collection of gowns in Grandmother's wardrobe. "So, don't you think we should try to dress more appropriately?"

"Evan, we're going to a remote area in the country. Apart from Campbell's farm, there is no one for miles. It should be easy to avoid the few farmhands that may be around. If we do see anyone, we'll just get out of there. You can get out quickly right?"

The question was rhetorical, he had *seen* me do it, but I had no idea what would happen if he was with me. I blocked it out of my mind and focused on Ian's clothes again.

"So what's up with the cowboy boots?" He had pulled the first on and was tugging at the second.

"I figure they'll be good for trudging through Miss Nancy's moat." He winked at me and his excitement was palpable.

"OK, but why do you wear them every day?"

"They're sexy, no?" He laughed. "They were a gift from a friend when I first moved to Blythe. I liked the way they looked, rugged you know, and it was my way of embracing my new West Texas home."

"So, have you ever been on a horse?" I asked.

He rolled his eyes at me. "A pony when I was five, I think. Are you implying I'm a fraud?"

"Absolutely not!" I said sarcastically.

"Well, maybe next time we can go back to the Old West. Oh, I know! We'll go to Fort Sumner, New Mexico, on July 14th, 1881!" He looked at me expectantly.

I shrugged my shoulders having absolutely no idea to what event he was referring.

"Ugh, Evan. You really need to take some more History courses! That was the day Billy the Kid was shot. It's still not known what really happened...if Pat Garrett shot him in the back or not, or if he was even killed at all!"

"OK, now I remember, Emilio Estevez, Young Guns." I smiled at him. Ian let out an exasperated sigh and walked out of the room. "Oh come on, you know that was a good movie," I said, following him.

Ian sat on the couch of his sparsely furnished living room. "So, let's get started." He said moving over to make room for me.

"Uh, what time is it?" I futilely looked around the room for a clock. I knew it had been dark for a long time.

"Five after ten," Ian said, looking at his watch.

"You know it's already really late, and we have to get an early start tomorrow. Maybe we should wait and try this after we get to Santa Fe." I was stalling, but the thought of us at the hacienda again made me feel warm all over. For some reason, I knew that once we got back there, I would feel safe.

"It's not late; you're just making excuses." Ian's face turned hard. "Plus, according to your descriptions of how this all works, no matter how much time we spend in the past no time will pass here right?"

"OK maybe I am making excuses, but if this actually works then I will be exhausted afterward. It will make getting up tomorrow very difficult."

"So you'll sleep in the car." Ian patted the spot on the couch next to him. He was not going to take no for an answer. Reluctantly, I sat down next to him.

"OK, let's talk about Charles Campbell." I let out a deep sigh, which Ian chose to ignore. "How much do you know about Ireland in the 17th and 18th centuries?"

I shrugged. "Not much." The truth was I knew absolutely nothing. Apart from the dry 'Trinity documents', which consisted mostly of land surveys and census data, I hadn't read much about that period of Irish history.

"Well, Ireland at the turn of the 17th century was very much like the rest of Irish history, fraught with conflict and upheaval. Ever since Christianity came to Ireland in the 600's the country had remained overwhelmingly Catholic. Most people at that time would have been peasants or lower-class agriculturalists, and spoke Gaelic."

I felt like I was in another of Ian's lectures and should be taking notes. "Protestants from England and Scotland had taken possession of large regions of Ireland during the 1500s and 1600s. Although there were several rebellions, including a large one in 1641 that lasted for nine years, the Irish were ultimately defeated, and the English would control most of the land, church, and government until the early 1900s.

"Of course, there is very little known about Charles Campbell himself, but we know that he came from a long line of Catholic Irish traditionalists who had owned the land around the River Boyne for several hundred years. This is important because in the 1700s, although Catholics made up 70% of the population, they only owned 5% of the land.

"In fact, Catholics at that time were not legally allowed to vote, marry a Protestant, join the armed forces, or own arms. Therefore, we can assume that Campbell, like most other Irish, deeply resented the presence of the English. Furthermore, he would have taken great pride in the discovery of an important historical monument on his property. You can imagine that he would have undoubtedly surveyed the site himself before allowing the Protestant authorities to come in and confiscate whatever historical treasures may have been there."

I closed my eyes as Ian described the culture, landscape, and politics of turn of the century Ireland. I tried to see it. I concentrated on all the details. I was hypnotized by the steady cadence of his speech, coupled with his accent. I could have listened to him all night and I marveled at how incredibly lucky someone in my situation was to have found a brilliant historian. I didn't even dare to think where I would have been had I not taken *Histories Greatest Mysteries* this semester.

"So...do you think you can get us there?" The abrupt change in Ian's tone, as he ended his story, startled me from my meditation.

"Well, I think I have a good feel for the time." A huge smile broke across his face. "I'm not promising anything. I still think that getting us both there is a major long shot." I didn't want him to get his hopes up and I was still terrified of what might happen to him.

"I have faith in you." He said, caressing my cheek.

Our plan was simple. If we did make it back, we would wait until the mounds were deserted and take one quick peek. Ian promised that all he wanted to know was whether Campbell and his crew had removed anything from the chamber. So, even though I had a million reservations, Ian and I lay down on his bed and embraced.

"You know, I can think of something else I would much rather do right now." I pressed my lips to his.

"We will have plenty of time for that," he said, pulling away. "I'll see you in 1699." He smiled radiantly and I took one last look into those deep seas of magnificent blue before I closed my eyes tight and focused.

I knew Campbell was the key. I had to plug into his emotional state the first time he saw the entry to the Newgrange mound. His workmen would have come to tell him they found something unusual that he should see. He would have been amazed. Nothing like it had ever been found anywhere, ever. I mean he was laying eyes on the oldest, still-standing structure ever created by man. Of course, he wouldn't have known that, but he was an educated man, and he would've guessed it was special.

I guessed that the kerbstone in front of the main entrance was the first thing he would have seen. He would have marveled at the megalithic art carved into the stone, just as millions have since. He would have wondered who carved these spirals, arcs, and serpentine shapes and what they were trying to convey. I pictured the stones and tried to imagine what they would have looked like over three hundred years ago, half buried.

Ian's body was warm and strong beside me. My arms were tight around his waist and moved in a steady rhythm as he breathed. I felt his breath on my face, and his every movement distracted me from my focus.

After a few moments, I opened my eyes and was startled to see him staring at me.

"Ian!" I pushed him away.

"What? Don't stop, come here!" He pulled me close again.

"I can't do it! I just can't focus with you here, especially not with you staring at me!"

"Look, you just have to relax. Pretend I'm not here."

"How on Earth am I supposed to do that? Every single thing about you distracts me! My whole body reacts when yours is near." He squeezed me tighter and smiled.

"OK, then let's try a different approach." I looked at him, intrigued. "If we're going to be partners in this, then let's do it together."

"What do you mean?"

"Close your eyes." I sighed but humored him.

"It's a beautiful summer day, especially for Ireland. You are sitting on your porch enjoying the warm fragrant breeze that carries the smell of heather on it, and the more subtle hint of the evening rain that will come. As you drowsily survey the spread beyond the farmhouse, you see a man run up the path. Something about his pace and the way he's waving, no beckoning, alarms you and you immediately stand and quickly walk to meet him.

Ian's voice was as smooth as velvet. He spoke softly, soothingly. His words wove a fascinating story about a man who made an amazing discovery on a warm summer's day in Ireland. This man was proud, traditional, and God-fearing. He envisioned how this discovery, this miraculous gift from God, would lead to an enduring family legacy. However, this man had grown bitter from the years of persecution he had faced in his own country. He was secretive and wary of anyone in positions of government. He would have guarded his property, and his legacy, fiercely.

I had always been mesmerized by Ian's voice and this was no exception. As had happened earlier this same evening, in this same bed, our bodies moved as one, rising and falling with breath. He described in perfect detail what I, as Charles Campbell would have seen, heard, and felt that day over three hundred years ago, and I completely forgot that I was listening to a story. I drifted off, half-dreaming, lost in his imagery, and I became Campbell...

The first tingles woke me from my trance. I was so surprised that I almost opened my eyes and sat straight up, but I managed to keep my focus and remain still. The tingles turned into a slight tug in the middle of my stomach and I knew without a doubt that it was happening! I wanted to open my eyes and see if Ian had felt anything, but I knew that if I did I would break the fragile cord that was pulling me down. I heard Ian's steady intonations. He was still whispering in my ear. I let myself sink, encouraging my body to descend further and faster.

Then, Ian's words started to fade and I didn't know if it was because he had stopped speaking or because I was being pulled away from him. I struggled against my instinct to open my eyes and look for him. I tightened my grasp around his waist, but my hands were starting to slip. I held on as tight as possible, but I was losing him. Abruptly, I felt my body jerk and I was free-falling. I heard the loud whoosh and felt wind rushing past. My arms were empty.

Chapter 17

LOST AND FOUND

I heard water...the gurgle of a stream. My head throbbed and I saw stars although my eyelids were clenched. I rolled over so that I was on all fours. As I struggled to rise up, the pain in my head was unbearable, and the white stars became splotches, and the splotches began to bleed out. Everything was going white as unconsciousness approached.

I struggled against it and forced myself to crawl forward. The water was close and my hands were sinking in cold wet mud. I fumbled and groped until my hands touched water, then I plunged them in, bringing up handfuls to splash on my face.

Gradually the sickness subsided, and the white splotches shrunk back to stars, then pinpricks that were finally encompassed by blackness. But the black wasn't black. As the stabbing pain in my head retreated, my eyes were bathed in red that throbbed and pulsed as blood coursed through my veins. Slowly I came to realize that I was all right, and as my eyes fluttered open, and I saw the bright sun above, panic seized me. *Ian!*

I held my head as I struggled to my feet. As I rose, it felt like someone was pushing an ice pick into my brain. I pressed down on my temples trying to block the pain out. My balance was off, and I kept having to steady myself. I squinted in the bright sunlight.

"Ian!" I tried to yell, but what came out was a squeak. I saw the river running gently and peacefully by. I saw tall grass, trees, and an incredibly blue sky. It was quiet except for the sounds of running water and the cheerful chirping of nearby birds. The whole of my peaceful surroundings were in complete opposition to the pain I felt.

"*Ian!*" I croaked again and stumbled forward. I scanned the riverbank and searched for any indentations in the grass. I couldn't see him anywhere! I remembered the feeling of him slipping away and realized that it hadn't worked. He wasn't here. The experiment had been short-lived, and although I was disappointed for Ian, I was comforted by the thought of him safe, home in bed.

My relief was quickly extinguished when I heard the deep moan. I spun around trying to pinpoint its source. I ran up the embankment and as I reached the crest, I saw Ian lying splayed out on the ground. I ran to him, tripping through the underbrush.

"Ian!" I fell on top of him and pressed my hands to his cheeks. He was perfectly still. I stared at his chest and felt a huge wave of relief when I saw it rise and fall. "Ian, please...open your eyes!" Another low groan escaped, and my heart raced. "Ian, please..." Tears welled in my eyes as fear took over. "Ian..." I pressed my lips to his and said a silent prayer. If he was hurt...if he was... Then I felt his lips move under mine. He wasn't kissing me, he was... I jerked my head up and looked at him. He was...grinning!

"Are you OK?" I knew he was, but I needed to hear him speak.

He tilted his head, looking from side to side, and then focused back on my face hovering above him. "We're here aren't we?"

"Yes, I think so, but *are* you OK?"

He pushed up onto his forearms and I sat beside him. "Well, I appear to be in one piece, but that was one crazy ride!" He looked at me seriously, but couldn't suppress the thrill in his eyes. "Are you OK?" He grabbed my hand.

"Yeah, I just have one killer headache. I was just...worried...well terrified when I couldn't find you."

"I'm fine," he said squeezing my hand. "Can you believe it? We are here! We are actually here! You are incredible!" He struggled to his feet, and I could see that he was a little wobbly.

"Hey be careful. Take it slow!" but my words fell on deaf ears. He sprinted off towards the river and I scrambled to catch up with him. Ian took a running jump right into the river! It was like he was possessed. He jumped around, splashed, and kicked at the water, which was shallow around his legs. I laughed at the sight of him.

"Evan! We're here. Look!" He motioned around him, and I just laughed. "Come here, you incredible woman!" He held his arms out for me to join him, and caught up in his contagious exhilaration, I did just that. We splashed and frolicked like two kids playing on a hot summer's day. The aching in my head dissipated and I basked in the satisfaction that I had brought Ian such joy.

After the initial delirium subsided, we lounged on the riverbank enjoying the warmth of the day and drying our wet clothes. I rested my head on his lap, and he stroked my hair.

"What time do you think it is?" I gazed up at him.

He looked at the sky, considering the position of the sun. "Maybe two or three?"

"Do you think we should get up and explore? I mean, I wonder if we're even close to Newgrange." In reality, I didn't want to move a muscle but felt like I should at least suggest it.

"It's right over that ridge." He gestured to the area over the embankment, where I had found him.

"How do you know? Did you see it earlier?"

"Evan, I've spent years studying every aspect of this place. I know exactly where we are. We have plenty of time to do what we need to do."

I sighed and closed my eyes. The soothing sensation of Ian's fingers running through my hair, the low gurgle of the river, the warmth of the sun on my face, and the smell of heather... I felt that this was what heaven must be like...or at least should be like. I had almost drifted off to sleep when I heard Ian speak.

"You know, I think you should change your major to History. It only makes sense." I dreamily looked up at him and smiled. "Just think of it, you'll already have a publication in the field. With your abilities, and of course, with me as your mentor, you could be the most famous historian that ever lived."

"I think we need to take care of our mission here before we think about publications and fame." I sleepily closed my eyes again.

"Of course, but when we publish the most important paper on New-grange ever, Peter will be mad with envy!" He laughed.

That reminded me... "Hey, I've been meaning to ask you, what *is* the deal between you and Dr. Marshall anyway?"

"Ha! You picked up on that did you?"

"How could I miss it? He seems almost...hostile when I mention your name."

He laughed again. "He is hostile when it comes to me, but I can tell you that his anger is completely misplaced."

"Do tell," I said, now fully awake and completely intrigued.

"Well, it was my first week at Harper. God, I can't believe I'm telling you this..."

"What? Now you *have* to tell me!"

"OK, OK. So, the Dean had a reception at his house. You know like a meet and greet for the new faculty. Well, everything was fine, people were nice, blah, blah, blah... But towards the end this woman started chatting me up. She was clearly very tipsy, and I was polite but kept my distance. However, when I was leaving, I saw her fumbling to unlock her car. She was about to drive home!

I knew there was no way she should be driving, so of course I offered her a ride." I raised my eyebrows, a little worried about where this was going. "I know what you're thinking but I can assure you my motives were completely innocent. I mean she was attractive for an older woman, but there was a...desperation about her that really turned me off. So anyway, she agrees to let me drive her, but then won't tell me where she lives! I mean we're just driving around aimlessly!"

"She just wanted to drive around with you?" I looked at him skeptically.

"Well, not exactly." He gave me a sheepish smile. "She uh...wanted me to take her to my place."

I sat up stiffly. "Do I really want to hear this story?"

"Of course, I didn't do anything with her! I just drove around until finally it was so late, and I was so pissed by her antics that I just parked the car."

"Did you kick her out...make her walk?" I hoped.

"No, she finally gave in and told me where she lived. But as I dropped her at the curb in front of her house, I noticed a man's face looking out the window and realized she was married, which of course she hadn't mentioned!"

"Dr. Marshall!" I gasped.

"Yep."

"No wonder he hates you!"

"Oh, that's not the end..." My eyes were wide in disbelief. "After that night she started calling me, writing me letters, even sitting in on my lectures. I made it very clear to her that I wasn't interested, but she was persistent."

"Dr. Marshall's wife was stalking you?"

"Unrelentingly."

"So, what did you do?" I already hated this woman and felt deeply sorry for Dr. Marshall.

"I didn't have to do anything, because after about two months of it Peter caught on. Apparently, he found letters and pictures she had taken of me." I gasped again. "It wasn't pretty. He accused me of seducing her. There were scenes in front of other faculty. He even went to the Dean. He made up lies, said I was sleeping with my students!" I thought about the rumors Taylor had told me.

"Of course, there was no proof that I had done a thing with any of my students. And I *hadn't*! Well...until now, anyway." He smiled sheepishly. "But he certainly made my life at Harper hell that first year."

Although the memories of it had faded, I knew that once, in another life, something similar had happened to me. Someone I trusted had told vicious lies about me and it had been devastating. "I'm so sorry Ian."

"It's all right. I managed and if nothing else, it taught me to be cautious and guard myself. Since then, there have been a few students that have developed somewhat of a...crush on me, I guess."

A few! I thought about the lecture hall full of girls and the dozens of sleazy comments that many of the female, and even some of the male students, had written on 'rate-your-professor.com' about Ian. I would have been surprised if he didn't have at least half a dozen students stalking him at any given time!

"Anyway, I make sure to never encourage them, and I always save notes they send and record phone calls, you know in case I need evidence later."

"So, whatever happened to Dr. Marshall's wife?"

"Well, it turned out that I wasn't the first person she had become fixated on. There had been others...faculty, even one of Peter's graduate students. But this broke him, they divorced, and she moved out of the state."

We were both silent for a long while. I felt terrible about what Ian had been through, but I felt worse for Dr. Marshall. I mean he had obviously over-reacted and treated Ian very badly, but he was a good man who didn't deserve what she had done to him.

—ele—

Although I could have stayed there with Ian forever, there was work to be done. I followed him up the embankment and through the wooded area that bordered the Newgrange mounds. However, nothing looked familiar to me. I had been here twice in my life and seen many pictures, but the scene wasn't right.

"Where's the clearing?"

"Shhh! Ian grabbed my arm and pulled me to the ground. He pointed to an area directly in front of us and I saw a man about a hundred yards away. He was pushing a wheelbarrow. He disappeared behind some trees and then reappeared a few moments later. Soon another man joined him, then a third.

"Is that them?" I whispered to Ian.

"Yeah, look." He pointed again to the area by the men. I strained to see what he was indicating. There were so many trees and dense undergrowth, it was difficult to see, but eventually I spotted it...a kerbstone! It was *the* kerbstone, the largest one that stands sentinel by the entrance to the main mound. Then I realized that this was it, Newgrange, but it looked nothing like when I had been here before.

There was no clearing, no paths. In fact, there weren't even mounds, just indistinct hills, camouflaged by the growth of the forest. Why had I expected anything else? These monuments had remained undetected for hundreds of years, and thousands before that, they certainly weren't going to be obvious.

In total, we saw twelve men working to clear the passages. They would disappear into the earth, and then come out pushing wheelbarrows full of dirt and stones. I marveled at their clothes. Here they were, simple workmen in the middle of the country. There was no one else around for miles and still they were wearing long flowy white shirts, tight short waist-coats, trousers that went to the knee and some sort of tights below that.

I couldn't imagine trying to do manual labor in get-ups like that! And Ian was right about their hair. Although all of them wore large, brimmed hats, I could see long ponytails hanging down their backs.

After about fifteen minutes of watching them, I was bored, but Ian was transfixed and he stared with an intensity I had never seen. He watched their every movement and never moved a muscle himself. I on the other hand was miserable in my crouched position. I kept shifting to alleviate the cramps in my legs and each time Ian would 'shush' me and shoot me a stern look.

Finally, I managed to plop my butt down on the ground and stretch my legs out a bit. I knew we were waiting for the men to leave but I hadn't a clue how long that could take. What I really wanted to do was go back to the riverbank and lay with my head in Ian's lap again.

Hours passed. Ian barely moved. I had given up watching the men long ago and trusted that Ian was watching closely enough for the both of us. Instead, I stared up into the sky and daydreamed. I watched the large billowy clouds move slowly across the sky. I watched squirrels scamper through the trees. I watched Ian's face concentrating on the history that was unfolding before him. Then, my stomach started to growl.

It was so quiet, and my stomach was so loud! Ian shot me a look and I shrugged my shoulders, smiling at him. Why hadn't I thought to bring a snack? A granola bar...even a piece of gum! We didn't even have water to drink! I wondered if it would be safe to drink the river water. Then I remembered that thousands of people in Ireland had died of dysentery around this time, and that cured my thirst and hunger.

Finally, the sun started to set, and I thought that surely the men would have to leave soon. Wasn't it dinner time? Didn't they have wives at home who would be waiting for them? Once the sun disappeared, the temperature dropped sharply. I maneuvered as quietly as possible to put on the sweatshirt that I had tied around my waist earlier. Ian's eyes were as sharp as ever, watching everything. I desperately wanted to stand up and stretch.

The dark continued to roll in and with it a strange mist began to envelop us. The fog seemed to come from out of nowhere and the temperature continued to plummet. Soon after, I couldn't see the men anymore. They were swallowed in the cold mist.

This wasn't good. I wondered what we were going to do now that we couldn't even see what the workers were doing. Then suddenly we heard a loud yell. I jumped and Ian spun his head around to me, shushing me again. It came from the direction of the workers. Then I heard it twice again. Someone was shouting the same phrase over again. I looked at Ian and he smiled, calming my nerves immediately. He leaned in closely and whispered.

"They are saying cóisir dinnéir. It's Gaelic, they're saying it's dinner time."

"Think they'd mind two more?" I whispered back rubbing my belly.

We waited another fifteen minutes and then started making our way towards the mounds. The visibility was poor, but not impossible. We could see maybe fifty feet, but it was getting darker by the minute. Finally, we saw the workers' discarded tools leaning haphazardly against the kerbstone. I saw the expression on Ian's face and was suddenly very glad that I hadn't had to follow through with my plan to deface the mounds. I'm pretty sure that would have been unforgivable in his eyes. The place was deserted. I started to walk to the entrance.

"Wait!" Ian grabbed my arm and pulled me back.

"What? They're gone and it's getting dark." Although Ian had the idea of making our own torches, we hadn't ended up bringing them. And we both knew that without the moonlight it was going to be impossible to see a thing very soon.

"Just wait. I thought I heard something," he said. My heart started to beat faster, and my ears pricked listening for even the slightest sound.

"Ian let's go back. We can try again later." I was suddenly very afraid.

"No, it has to be now. Don't worry, it was probably just an animal." I stayed frozen in place, clinging to Ian. "Listen, you stay here. I'll just go have a quick look." He pulled at my hands trying to break free of my vice-like grip.

"No! I'm staying with you." I wasn't going to let him out of arm's reach, because I knew that if something happened and we needed to get out, I had to have him close.

"OK, OK..." he soothed, sensing my panic. "Let's just take it slow." We edged forward and I was glued to him, but after a few steps he stopped and his body went rigid.

"What?" I hissed, heart racing.

"Look..." he whispered, and my eyes scanned the area searching.

"What? I don't see anything." I was frantically searching the woods, certain that one of the men had returned.

"No, inside." Ian pointed to the entrance of the mound.

I tried to see what he was talking about, and then...I saw it...a golden glow coming from the entrance!

"What is it?"

"A torch, I think. Someone's inside!"

"Ian, let's go." I desperately wanted to leave. I tugged at his sleeve.

"No, wait." He insisted.

"Ian, we can't do anything if someone's in there!"

"Just wait." He stared at the entrance.

"Ian, this doesn't feel right. Something's not right!" My panic was building.

"We'll wait until they leave then."

"But Ian, it will be completely dark soon." The fog was already so thick that our visibility had been halved in the last half hour. It was damp and cold and...something felt very wrong. "And who's in there anyway Ian? We've been watching, but no one was even around. Why didn't we see anyone go in there?"

He looked at me curiously, as if I had just revealed the answer to a riddle. Before I could ask another question, we heard the most piercing, shrill, horrifying sound imaginable. Both of us turned towards the mounds. It sounded like a cry, the horrific cry of a wounded baby. It was the kind of blood-curdling cry that made every hair stand on end, the kind that horror movies tried to reproduce, but always fall short, the kind that signaled imminent and unimaginable danger.

Before I could even think or react Ian had slipped from my hands and was running towards the entrance to the mound. I screamed his name, but my voice didn't even come close to rising above the cries. I ran after him. The cries grew louder, and I tried to keep my balance as I ran through the mist, but the ground was covered with undergrowth and wet slippery stones. I tripped and fell to my knees. I saw Ian reach the mouth of the mound and enter without even looking back. I screamed his name again as I struggled to my feet.

I ran forward as fast as my legs allowed and finally reached the entrance. The cries were unbearable and chilled me to the core. I could see shadows bouncing off the walls of the passageway. It went against every instinct in my body to force myself to step inside. I walked carefully through the narrow corridor that was alight with the red-orange glow of flames.

Between the piercing cries, I heard voices. I stopped in the shadows of the passageway, just short of the chamber. I could see Ian straight ahead. He was holding out his hands in a defensive posture that alarmed me even more, but I couldn't see the rest of the chamber or who was in front of him.

The cries became louder and more urgent, and then without warning they suddenly stopped. At the same time, I saw Ian flinch as if something or someone had hit him. He turned slightly and, in the torchlight, I saw that blood was splattered across his face!

My hands flew up, cupping my mouth to suppress my screams. Terror seized me and I nearly lunged forward, but then Ian brought his hand up and wiped at his face, smearing the blood. Although it looked grisly, he didn't appear hurt. Then a booming voice echoed off the walls of the small chamber.

"Cé tá triúr díobh ann!" I didn't understand the meaning, but I knew it was Gaelic. The voice repeated the phrase twice sounding more and more angry.

Then Ian spoke. "Cara, cara!" his hands were out again, this time in a pleading posture.

Oh God! My head spun trying to think what to do. Ian wasn't very far away, just a few feet. Maybe I could focus on getting us back, and then grab him at the last moment. Or maybe we could make a run for it. He was close to the passageway, if only he would turn around, I could signal him to run with me. The voice repeated the same thing over and over, and Ian was repeating the same response. Then a new voice rose above the two of them. It was higher and female.

"*Peregrinus!*"

This word I recognized. *Wanderer.*

"Evan, get out." Ian didn't turn when he said it, and it was no more than a whisper, but I heard him clearly.

Tears welled in my eyes. He wanted me to leave him! No, I wouldn't even consider it.

The voice screamed again "*Peregrinus!,*" and a dark figure swooped in front of Ian. He struggled as someone else behind him, who I couldn't see, forced his arms back. Then I saw the glint of metal in the torchlight. The shrouded figure brought up a large blade and held it to Ian's throat!

"Stop!" I screamed as I stepped into the chamber. Six figures, all cloaked in dark hooded robes, turned to face me. Ian glanced at me, and his face was the embodiment of sorrow. He let out a deep sigh and dropped his head. He didn't look at me again, but I heard him whisper, "I'm so sorry, Evan."

I looked frantically around the chamber, trying to find an escape. I couldn't make out the faces of the dark figures that stood around the perimeter of the room, they were hidden in shadows. But I could see the shadowed face of the woman holding the knife to Ian, and it was cold, hard and menacing.

She didn't make a sound, none of them did. She stared at me, and I back at her. Then, without warning she came at me with the knife. I fell back against the wall of the tunnel, narrowly avoiding the blade.

"*Peregrinus!*" She screamed at me, inches from my face. Ian struggled to break free from the dark figure holding him.

"No!" He screamed at the woman. "She's not what you think!"

She turned momentarily to look at Ian and I sprung at her, shoving her with all my weight. The blade sliced across my wrist, as she lost her balance and fell back onto the ground in front of Ian. The knife flew from her hand, landing in the tunnel behind me.

Ian lunged forward, breaking free of his captor and tackling the woman at his feet. I turned and scanned for the knife in the dark. I spotted the shiny blade a few feet away, but as soon as I took my first step, I heard the woman's voice again, muffled and strained as Ian pressed her down.

"Amach!"

I grabbed the knife and spun around, darting back into the chamber...but just like that...they were gone. I was completely alone.

"Ian!" I screamed and my voice echoed in the small space. "Ian!" I dropped to my knees. I sobbed. I was powerless. He was gone.

The only torch that remained in the chamber was lying on the ground and growing dimmer by the second. I crawled over to it and as soon as I lifted it upright the flame swelled. I saw a large kerbstone in the center of the room, and on top of it, lying limply was a lamb.

Its throat had been cut and blood ran down the altar in streams, winding its way through the spiral carvings in the stone. It was grotesque and the smell of blood made me unsteady. It wasn't just the lamb's blood. Dark ooze dripped from my fingertips and onto the ground leaving a trail of perfect crimson beads in the dirt.

The chamber hadn't even been fully dug out yet. The floor was rough and uneven. There were no wooden beams to secure the ceiling and only one of the recesses off the main chamber was visible. But this large kerbstone in the middle, it was strikingly different, and certainly not in the modern-day chamber. But I didn't care. I didn't care about anything but Ian. The smell of the dead animal was stifling. I stumbled out of the chamber, through the passageway and out into the night.

I breathed deeply. The fog was a pitch-black curtain, but now I could hear voices of people quickly coming towards me from across the field. They were not the menacing voices of the cloaked figures in the chamber. I suspected it was the farmhands. I had to get back.

Ian would be there, lying in my arms. He had to be! I collapsed onto the ground and clutched my wrist to my chest. I still held the knife with my other hand. I thought of Ian's bed...of us together, embracing.

—ele—

I could feel him all around me, smell him, see his things. But he was gone! My head spun trying to make sense of it. How could I be here without him? Where was he? What had I done?

I'm not sure how much time passed, hours maybe. I had no sense of time. My arm and sweatshirt were caked with dried blood. I lay in Ian's bed concentrating harder than I ever had before. I thought of Charles Campbell again. I tried to remember all the details Ian had recounted in his story.

When that didn't work, I thought of the moment, earlier that evening, when Ian had first asked me to take him back to Newgrange. When that didn't work, I focused on our time at the hacienda. I tried a dozen different memories of Ian that were seared into my mind. When none of them worked. I tried to travel back to the moment I first registered for Ian's class, but no matter what I thought about, nothing happened. After each of my attempts failed, I sobbed.

I was exhausted, but I fought sleep. I held his shirt to my face inhaling his scent. My mind spun...where was he? Why couldn't I go back to him? I was terrified it had something to do with Ian himself, that every memory attached to him was somehow blocked to me. I didn't know why that would happen, and I was petrified to even speculate.

Then it dawned on me, and I knew what I had to do. I had to find the one person who could help me. Pure adrenaline propelled me out of Ian's bed, down the hall, across the living room and out into the night. I drove fast through the deserted streets. I clutched the knife.

I don't even remember parking the car or how I got up to my room. My hands trembled violently, but I managed to fit the key in to the lock and pull open my desk drawer. I tossed my journals aside and pulled out my grandmother's red leather-bound album. I had to find her.

I flipped through the pictures. I looked at the tintype of her standing by the man in her beautiful gown. I looked into her almond-shaped eyes, so like mine, but possessing a wisdom that mine lacked. *Please help me*, I silently begged her.

There had to be some way to get back to her, but all the people and places in the photos were a mystery to me. I looked at the photo of my grandmother standing in front of the time capsule. Hadn't Ian said that this was taken at a World's Fair? Where did he say it was? What year? I racked my brain, but I couldn't remember.

There had to be another way! I knew she had visited my mother at the children's home, but I had never been there so I couldn't get a sense of what it had been like. I needed details, something specific. Then it hit me. The hacienda...the memory, *my* memory.

I knew I had been there before. I had been riding a bike around the verandah, the day was bright and sunny. I remembered the joy and delirium... and something else. There had been someone else there that day!

I remembered the feeling of love and companionship. The memory was distant and I knew it had happened a really long time ago, but maybe she was there. It was a long shot, but I was beyond desperate.

I must have been very young, but the essence of the memory was there. If I could just tap into the emotions that lingered, I could put myself there again. My head throbbed and I was so very tired, but I ignored the pain and exhaustion and tried to focus.

I curled up in a fetal position on the bed and concentrated. The hacienda, the blue sky, the exquisite vistas...I could see them as if I was there. The feeling of wind whooshing past me, flying past the terra cotta planters, around the columns...I could see it, see the landscape whiz by. The joy, the feeling of belonging, and the warmth of a loved one beaming down at me. I tried to feel it and connect to the emotions, but I was completely incapable of feeling joy. Although I could visualize the scene completely, I couldn't feel it. Ian was gone and my soul was a void.

I thought I had failed again...but then...then I heard it. The sound I had been waiting for. The familiar whoosh that I knew would carry me away. I heard it, but I didn't feel it...no pull...no falling.

My eyes were nearly swollen shut from crying and exhaustion, but as they opened, I saw a blurry figure standing in the dim light. Ian! I jumped up in bed and rubbed my eyes, trying to clear my vision. The silvery white hair was the first thing that came into focus.

"Eve, what the hell is going on?" Her angry voice pierced through the silence. "What is wrong with you? Where is the historian?"

"Do you mean Ian?" I jumped to my feet, tears spilling down my cheeks.

"Of course I do!"

I didn't trust her, but if there was any way she could help find Ian I had to try. "Look, I need help. I lost him. There were people... terrible, cloaked people and he disappeared with them."

"What?! For fuck's sake Eve, you were just supposed to find the historian and get the information. Now they have him, and you know what they will do with him!" She was now agitated and wild-eyed.

"Who are THEY?!" I yelled, "And what will they do?"

She took several quick steps towards me.

"Stay away from me or I'll scream!" I still had the dagger from the mound and I thrust it forward feebly. I knew I was too weak for a fight, but as soon as her eyes flashed on the knife, she stepped back.

"Eve listen, I don't understand what's happened to you." Her arms were out, palms facing me. "I just assumed everything was going as planned until I saw you in Santa Fe. You seemed so confused. I suspected you had lost time, but not this..."

"Why are you calling me Eve? You know my name is Evan! Who are you? I *know* you don't work for my grandmother's law firm!"

"Grandmother? Jesus Christ Eve, exactly how long have you been here? Who do you think you are?" Her eyes were wide, and she stared at me with complete disbelief.

"Why don't *you* tell me exactly who you are!" I shouted at her, my voice weak and hoarse.

"Eve, for God's sake, you don't have a damn grandmother. It was all just a ruse for the benefit of the historian! *You're* the one who planned it all. You even told me exactly what to write in that bogus inheritance letter." Her eyes were wide and searching my face.

"I knew something was wrong when I saw you with him, but I thought that as soon as you were in your own house, with your own things you would snap out of whatever this is!" She was becoming more and more agitated; her voice becoming angrier.

"My house...my things? Who *are* you!" I yelled at her, tears still flowing down my cheeks.

She stopped and looked penetratingly at me. She took a deep breath and when she spoke, her voice was softer and sympathetic. "I am Fox and you are Eve and we have...*collaborated*...for over...one hundred years."

Suddenly, the loud sound of banging filled my ears as my mind raced to try to comprehend what she had just said.

"Evan!" I heard a male voice yelling from the hallway. "Evan, open the door!"

Ms. Fox spun around nervously and looked from the door to me and back again.

I couldn't move. I couldn't speak. I felt like I was outside my body, and had no control over it.

"Evan, if you don't open the door, I swear I'll break it down!"

"Eve, you have to come back with me. You have set things into motion... we are in imminent danger! They have the historian, and they will kill him once they find out what he knows! This could mean the end of everything." She took two quick steps and extended her hand to me.

Do not believe her. I saw the words, written in my own hand, and recoiled from her.

Crash! The sound of something large hitting my door echoed off the walls. Ms. Fox jumped.

"Kill him? Ian!" I wanted to scream. I wanted to beg her. I wanted to tell her to take me instead.

"Eve, please. I will help if I can, but you're the only one who can save him! You have to snap out of this!"

She closed her eyes and I knew she was about to disappear. I flew at her, my arms reaching out to grab her arm. I couldn't let her leave without me!

Crash! The door flew open and Aaron fell into the room. I felt the tips of my fingers graze her clothing, and then Ms. Fox was gone.

Aaron struggled to his feet holding his shoulder.

"Evan!" He tripped over to where I now lay beside the bed. Sobs ripped through my body, but there were no tears. There were none left.

I scrambled to my hands and knees and groped around for the album. I tore at the pages, scattering the pictures over the floor.

"Evan, please. What's wrong, what are you looking for? My god, is that blood?"

I yanked the tintype out and flipped it over. I gasped sharply when I saw what I had completely overlooked before. 'Thomas and me before the war', written in my own hand.

My body jerked in spasms of dry heaves, and I collapsed onto the floor in a fetal position, clasping the picture to my chest.

"Evan, talk to me. Are you hurt?" Aaron knelt on the floor cradling my head. "I'm so sorry I left you, but I'm here now and I'm not going anywhere. Tell me, please tell me what I can do." He was smoothing my wet, matted hair away from my face. I opened my mouth to speak but the dryness of my throat stopped the words from coming out. I swallowed hard despite the pain and finally managed to croak, "How...did you know...to come?"

A look of confusion darkened his worried face. "Evan you just texted me, not even fifteen minutes ago. You said you needed help...that someone was..." He inhaled deeply and the anguish was apparent. "...that someone was trying to *kill* you!"

I closed my eyes and tried to stop the sobs. "I mean thank God I was here, I only just got into town. Shhhh...just calm down."

His soothing voice and gentle hand, stroking my hair, calmed me and I finally stopped crying. I looked up into his big, brown, imploring eyes.

"Please Evan, tell me what I can do. I'll do anything. I just want to help you."

I knew the blackness of unconsciousness would take me soon, willing or not. I summoned up all the energy I had left to answer him.

"Do you have a passport?"

Chapter 18

THE JOURNEY BEGINS

I jumped, knocking over the half-full plastic cup on my tray table, and jostling the seat of the woman in front of me. I fought to hold in a scream, as my mind recoiled from the dream. I was bathed in sweat. The woman gave me a brief dirty look between the seats and then turned back around. I tried to calm myself by focusing on the low, steady hum of the engines.

The dream slowly began to fade as I forced it back into the recesses of my mind. It was the same one I had dreamed of every night since I lost Ian...the shrill screams of the eviscerated lamb, the fog, the cloaked figures. It was also the reason I shunned sleep and was perpetually exhausted. I fastened my tray table up and dabbed at the ginger ale on the thin red blanket covering me. I kicked the plastic cup under the seat in front of me and tried uselessly to find a comfortable position for my legs. Money buys a lot, but it doesn't add extra first-class seats to an already overly-booked flight.

The cabin was dark, save for a very few reading lights here and there and the dim floor illumination. Only the occasional cough, baby's cry, or closing of the lavatory door could be heard above the sound of the engines. Most people were in a state of restless slumber; where you are so bored and tired that you close your eyes determined to sleep, but find it impossible to get comfortable enough to actually fall any deeper than a half-awake dreamy doze. That is, except for the person snoring softly in the seat next to me.

I gazed over at Aaron, who was completely crashed. His head was tilted back, resting half against his headrest and half against the closed window shutter, mouth widely agape. The sight of him was almost funny enough to bring a smile to my face...almost.

I subconsciously picked at the scabbed-over gash on my wrist where the dagger had cut me. The painful remnant of that night in the mounds was nearly healed. The knife had cut quite deep and Aaron had desperately wanted to take me to the emergency room. Luckily, it was mending just fine without stitches. I knew he suspected I had done it to myself and was seriously worried about my mental health.

I stared at Aaron in the dim light and once again felt the incredibly painful pang of guilt that had tortured me for the past ten days. It was so stupid and dangerous to include him in all of this, and I knew I was being selfish, but I was scared and he made me feel safe...somewhat. Still, the reality was that I had already lost Ian because of my recklessness, and if anything happened to Aaron... Well, I would be so devastated that there would be no coming back.

I had tried to keep him out of it. I had fought him for days, and once even driven out of town without him. But in the end, my selfishness won out, and I returned. Although I finally, reluctantly agreed that he could come along, I vowed to keep him as ignorant as possible. He didn't know much, and I was going to keep it that way.

From the little I *had* told him, he had pieced together a vague story that basically consisted of me inheriting a lot of money from a long-lost grandmother that I had never known. He believed that some of her disgruntled relatives were out to get me and that I was on a mission to figure out exactly who she had been. I neither confirmed nor denied his assumptions. In fact, I hadn't said much of anything to Aaron or anyone else.

I was pretty sure that Aaron thought I had lost it, considering the state he found me in that night. At first, he had wanted to call the cops. He was sure I had been attacked, and maybe worse. But after I went completely psycho on him, screaming and begging him not to tell anyone, he changed his mind. After I swore to him that I had not been attacked or violated and that I had not cut my own wrist, he never pressed me for details about what happened again.

I was semi-catatonic on the drive to Santa Fe the next day. For five hours I sat, immobile, staring at the photo album in my lap while Aaron drove. Every once in a while he tried to make conversation, and although I could hear his voice, I didn't even try to make out the meaning of the words. At one point it occurred to me how cosmically cruel it was that Aaron had traded his sick girlfriend for a crazy, catatonic psychopath. The thought of it made me sink deeper into my despair, and although I wanted to ask him about Becky, I couldn't muster the effort.

A million thoughts circled in the whirlpool of my mind as I stared at the photos in the album that day. I tried like hell to register a memory, a recollection, even a flicker of familiarity in the places and people in those pictures, but there was nothing. I stared into Evelyn's...Eve's eyes. Was it possible that I really was this woman? How could I have lived for years...even a century before, and not remember any of it? I had heeded my own warning, 'do not believe her', and I didn't. But even though I didn't trust Ms. Fox something in me knew she wasn't lying...not about this.

One-hundred years. She had said...one-hundred years! I struggled to wrap my mind around it. Assuming it was true, how could it be possible? I mean I knew that when I traveled into the past, no time seemed to elapse in the present. So, I supposed, in theory, I could spend years in the past, only to return to the present at the same instant I had left it, and thus no older. But one-hundred years?

It would be like being immortal. Except I *could* die, I thought, as I absentmindedly touched the cut on my wrist. And if it was possible, had

I just given up my whole life, everything I knew, everyone I loved to live in the past? Why would I have done that? For eternal youth, glory, adventure? I gazed into the face of the man in the picture named Thomas. Had I loved him?

Ms. Fox said I had come back to Harper to find Ian. Why would I have been looking for him in the first place, and why on earth couldn't I remember? Was it possible that everything I had experienced in the last six months was just another trip into my past? It was beyond comprehension.

We holed up in a nice hotel in Santa Fe's old town while we waited for Aaron's expedited passport to arrive, but despite his adamant and sometimes angry protests, I spent most days on my own. On the opening of business Monday, my first trip was to the law offices of Lloyd, Goldschmidt, and Williams. I caused a bit of a scene when, despite the secretary's insistence that I couldn't see Ken Williams without an appointment, I barged into his office. The man I saw sitting behind the desk was young, probably early thirties, and looked nothing like the 'lawyer' I had met before. After a few half-hearted apologies to him and the client he was meeting with, I sulked out before the security guards could be called.

A quick stakeout of the bank assured me that the banker I had dealt with was genuine, and I contemplated pumping him for information, but I decided he was probably just a chump like me. Ms. Fox and Ken must have fooled him too and I worried that if I came in making claims about imposters, he might somehow withdraw my 'inheritance,' and if that happened I would be in even worse shape than I was now.

For our remaining time in Santa Fe, I left Aaron to his own devices and spent my days at the hacienda. There was no way I could bring him there. It just felt wrong. If there was any doubt left in my mind that I was Evelyn Lambert, it quickly dissipated when I stepped back inside my house. Just as with the first time I had seen it, I was bombarded by strong emotions, and the very distinct feeling of 'coming home'.

I went straight to the urn sitting on the mantle of the kiva. I carried it out to the veranda and poured out the contents. Granted, I have never actually seen cremated remains before, but I highly doubted they looked like the pile of sand that sat before me.

I practically tore the house apart looking for something, anything that would help explain things or remind me of who I had been. The bedroom, the library, the cellar...I went through the contents of each room racking my brain, trying to remember...anything. But no matter how many possessions I studied, no matter how many of the period clothes I put on, which of course all fit me perfectly, no matter how hard I tried to remember the past, I couldn't. The only things I could remember, with heart-aching clarity were the two days Ian and I had spent at the hacienda.

I sobbed, cried out for him, and at least twice every day tried to travel into our past. I even willed Ms. Fox to come back. Even if she was dangerous and couldn't be trusted, she knew more than I did.

Eventually, Aaron's passport arrived.

"Ma'am, do you need anything?"

I jumped at the flight attendant's voice. "Uh, no...I'm fine thanks."

"We'll be landing soon. You may want to wake your friend."

My friend. I gazed back at Aaron. He slept so soundly, oblivious to everything around him. He looked so peaceful; I couldn't wake him. I envied his peaceful sleep. I hadn't really slept in weeks. Every night, the dreams came...the terrible dreams. I knew they plagued me because of my guilt.

I had no idea where Ian was or what was happening to him, but I did know that it was all my fault. I vowed to do everything in my power to find him. I just hoped I could keep Aaron safe in the process.

"Ladies and Gentlemen, in preparation for landing the captain has put on the seatbelt sign. We ask that you please return to your seats, put your seats and tray tables in their upright positions, and stow your belongings. We will be landing in Dublin shortly.

Continue your journey through time by reading *Double Vision*, the second book in the *FOCUS* series, available now.

ABOUT THE AUTHOR

 Kendra Rumbaugh, Ph.D. is a world-renowned microbiologist and medical school professor who runs a research laboratory in West Texas. When not in science mode, she enjoys letting her imagination run wild writing science fiction. She is the author of the Vision time-travel series, which includes *Focus, Double Vision and Foresight*. She is also a sunset connoisseur, yoga enthusiast and travel junkie.

Reach out and say hello on my socials and find out more on my website.

Facebook: Kendra Rumbaugh
Twitter (X): @KendraRumbaugh
Instagram: @kprumbaugh
LinkedIn: kendra-rumbaugh-060b5829
Bluesky: @kendraRumbaugh
Threads: @kprumbaugh
BookBub: @KRumbaugh
Goodreads: Kendra_P_Rumbaugh

www.ingramcontent.com/pod-product-compliance
Lightning Source LLC
Chambersburg PA
CBHW051228260626
47162CB00002B/323